PRAISE F

"*Trust No One: A Jack West Novel is* a fast-paced thriller that flows effortlessly. It is impossible to put this book down once started. This thriller just works so fantastically well. There is no indication of deceleration to King's limitless supply of ideas or more extraordinarily, her striking characters. She truly is a runaway train on course to strike the mainstream literary world."

~R. Hill. Manager of Half Price Books, Waco, Texas

"Detective Jack West's reputation for solving crimes has him stepping outside of the Houston P.D. and into an inside D.E.A. criminal operation. Will this bring him closer to finding the person responsible for his unsolved triple homicide? Ever resourceful and tenacious, he will use his skills, partnering with brilliant and competent women in his professional and personal life. Join this bulldog of a detective as he solves the crime and drags men into the world of gender equality and mutual respect."

~Genevieve West, Owner of A Wicked Read Book Store, Canton, Texas

"*Trust No One* by Deanna King is the fourth installment in her Jack West series, and it does not disappoint. This is a high-octane thriller that will have readers up until well after bedtime. Strong characterization, a cracking plot, and a fast-paced easy-to-read style, that will more than satisfy existing fans and win over some new ones. I recommend *Trust No One* to all lovers of the detective genre."

~Robert E. Kearns, Award-winning Author of *Ossuary*

"Deanna King once again brings the reader into the world of Detective Jack West, this time with a host of new characters to shake up the Houston Police Department and the D.E.A. Fans will recognize the older characters from previous novels, as all have a role in helping to solve the latest round of homicide cases, involving drugs, human trafficking, deep deceit, and betrayal. *Trust No One* will keep you guessing till the end!"

~Lisa Petrocelli, Author of *The Gloves Come Off*

ALSO BY DEANNA KING

JACK WEST NOVELS

Twist of Fate

Lethal Liaisons

Vicious Vendetta

Saving a Sioux Legacy

Gracie's Stories

TRUST NO ONE

A JACK WEST NOVEL

DEANNA KING

ISBN: 979-8-9856982-4-4

Book Cover by Chandra Fry
https://stainedglasspublis.wixsite.com/bookpublisher/ppromoting

Edited by Lisa Petrocelli

Formatted by Staci Olsen

Published by Deanna King Writing

deannakingwriting.com

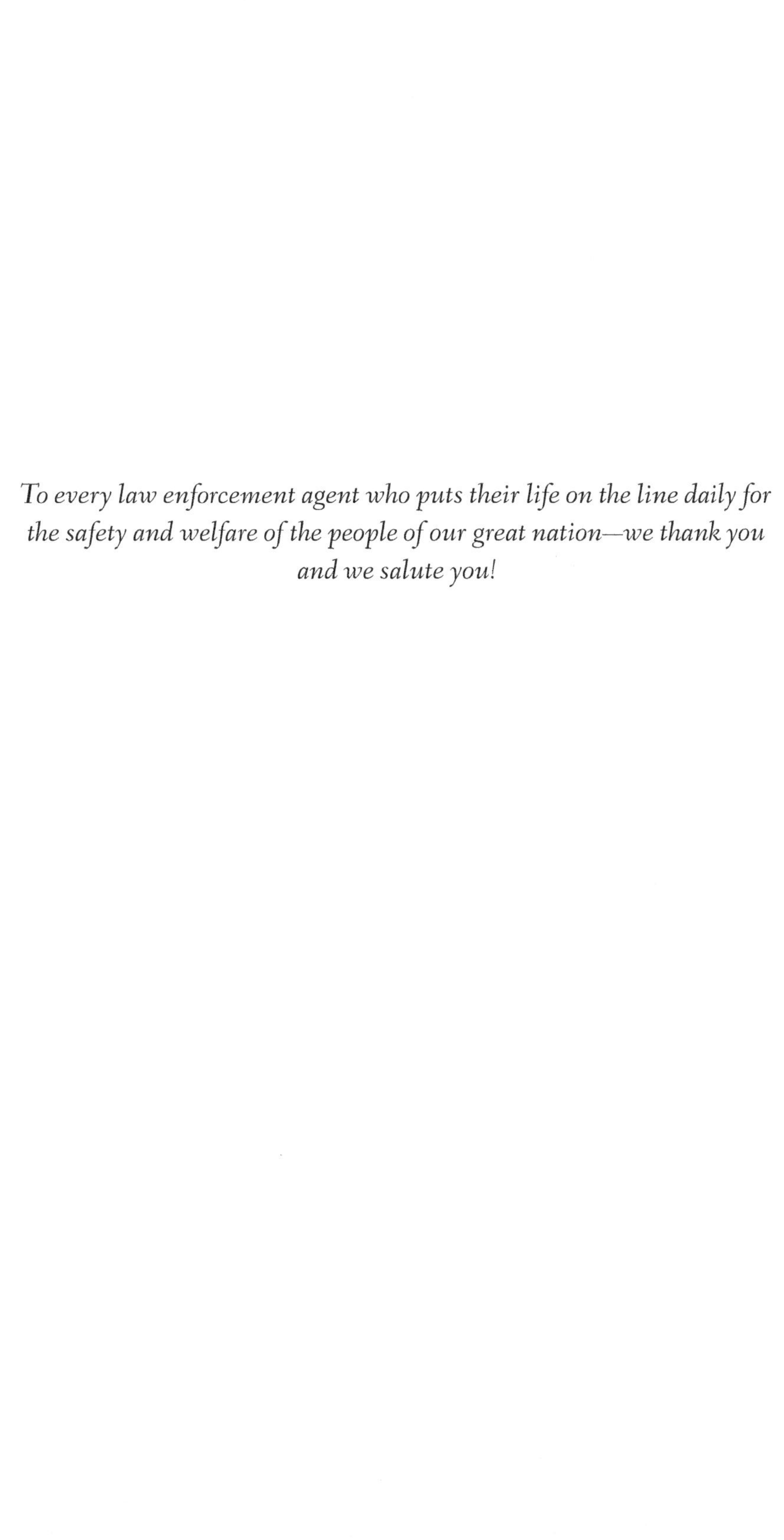

To every law enforcement agent who puts their life on the line daily for the safety and welfare of the people of our great nation—we thank you and we salute you!

PROLOGUE

The Attorney General's Office—Houston, Texas

"Janet, what we discuss goes no further than this room, understood?"

"Of course, sir, I understand."

He explained her assignment and watched her eyes fill with anger.

"Janet, you feel they passed you over because you're a woman, but believe me when I tell you I wanted them to assign this fucking job to you. They asked for Bebchuk and Cleef. I have to adhere to my orders. Damn it!" Deputy Director of Field Operations Remy Walsh slammed his fist on the desk, his face screwed up and jaw muscles flexed.

Janet did not flinch. She didn't have to like it, and she damn sure didn't.

"This comes directly from the Inspector General, Gavin Kemper, at the OIG office." Walsh was adhering to orders from his boss, Senior Director of Field Ops Carmichael McKay, who got his orders from Deputy Assistant Attorney General Kelli Slater. Everyone followed orders from a chain of command, which began at the top with the Inspector General.

"Yeah, and Inspector General Gavin Kemper is a man. I'm the only female under your direct command since the last three female agents asked to be reassigned, and we know why. Look, sir, God knows I've taken flak from men who can't take a piss standing on their own two feet without peeing on their shoes. I love living in Houston. I don't wish to transfer, but this is for shit." Janet shook her head in disgust. She was running a race with the agency because she was a woman. The problem was one foot was always nailed down as she ran in circles.

Walsh sat back and exhaled. "Spears, take the assignment. I'm sorry if what they've asked seems like a one-and-done order with no other involvement. They asked for you directly, which should make you feel good."

"Uh-huh, it should, but it doesn't. Let me get this straight. My assignment is to head over to the Houston Homicide Division and order them to stand down on their newest case involving a triple homicide. Afterward, the DEA sends me an agent to work with. It's my job to send that agent to pick up all the documents and murder books. We keep the police in the dark, pissing them off. Is this correct?"

"That sounds right. Agent Spears, is there an issue with your orders?" Walsh's ire was rising. Janet was a hell of an OAG agent and deserved a fairer shake. Politics concerning genders incensed the female employees daily. Remi Walsh believed in equality and he would've put her in charge if he had the choice. But he wasn't in charge, the Inspector General was. The HPD was ordered to stand down because there were bigger issues. Once he got brought deeper into the loop, he'd learn more. He knew as much as Spears. As the Deputy Director of Field Ops, it pissed him off not to be brought into the need-to-know.

"Yeah, fucking-A, there's a problem. Once I'm done, I'm fucking done. Agents Bebchuk and Cleef, those assholes in the DEA office, take over the assignment. Me? Well, I get to hang out in the office, twiddling my thumbs. Oh, then maybe one day you a-holes will give me a real job. Begging your pardon, sir, but you feel just like those two chauvinistic pigs, don't you? Us weak womenfolk should be at home, safe and sound, right?" Janet's face hardened, as her anger became near palpable. The volcano inside her was about to erupt, and she didn't care if he reprimanded her or put her on notice for insubordination, because she was tired of being placated. Perhaps she should scream at the Inspector General in person; however, it would do nothing but cause her embarrassment—and embarrassment to the OAG office. This would not help further her career.

Remi Walsh squinted, his brow furrowed. The woman was ballsy and tough. Janet Spears was a formidable agent and could hold her own against any male agent, but right now he'd keep these thoughts to himself and follow orders.

"Sir, why not let the DEA issue the order to stand down? Why have me as a middle man?"

"Spears." Walsh looked down, breaking the intense stare between them. "Go to HPD, have them stand down. Let me also add that somehow you need to convey to the lead detective, without saying it, that he should continue to investigate the case on his own. I don't have the clearance to share more."

"Convey to him to work his case. And I do this without speaking? Are you joking, or serious? These days I can't tell the difference, sir."

"I'm serious, Spears."

"How am I going to manage that? Pass a note? Use telepathy, what?"

"A look, hell, in code, but don't say it directly. I want you to call Craig Bower afterward. IG Kemper asked him to assign Agent Sophia Medina to you, and that is all Bower knows. You can't tell Craig anything. Send Agent Medina over for the case files and murder books. Tell her the same thing. Without saying it, communicate to Detective West somehow to keep working his homicide on the side. From what I've heard about this man Jack, he's smart and will read between the lines."

"Remy, why all of this TV movie kind of secrecy? I'd like to understand why the Inspector General is asking us to order the Houston Police to stand down on a case, then send a DEA to pick up files. And somehow I am to give the detective working the case a telepathic message to continue his investigation, even after we've just ordered him to stand down. Then you give the damn case to DEA agents, not Sophia, but Bebchuk and Cleef, and they take over. Why? Help me understand. "

"All I can tell you is this goes a lot deeper. The rest of your assignment is for you and Medina to take HPD's triple murder case, tear it apart, compare notes, and then wait. I've been informed that you'll get new orders later."

"Tell the higher-ups thanks for the fluff assignment. Yeah, just wait. It's the story of my professional life. I can sum up my career for you. Agent Janet Spears was a good agent who *waited—for nothing*. Anyway, if I bitch and moan, it just makes the men happier. Two-thirds of our agents believe males are the only type of agent any organization needs." Janet clenched her teeth, balling her fist and digging her nails into her palm. It made her furious, but she kept from shrieking.

"You'll get your shot, and it won't be because you're a woman. It'll be because you're a devoted agent with a strong sense of right and wrong, without all the bureaucratic bullshit."

Janet Spears, straight-faced, stared into Remi Walsh's eyes. She watched his body language. His resolute expression said volumes.

"So, are you in or not?"

Janet Spears' face was a blank page. As she crossed one pant-covered leg over the other, folding her arms, she raised her shoulders, inhaling and releasing the air from her lungs. She looked at him with determination in her eyes.

"Hell, yes, I'm in. I guarantee you, once you put me out front, you, the Inspector General, or the Attorney General will never regret it."

Walsh knew she could go the distance and her loyalties were in place. Janet Spears wouldn't be pulled over to the dark side. He wished he could say the same for a specific DEA field agent. Something was off with that one and he just couldn't pinpoint it.

WRITTEN at the top of the file was *Medina, Sophia*. Her parents, father Caucasian, mother Columbian. She spoke fluent Spanish, and she'd blend in with the locals without a problem. Janet snagged her phone and called her assistant.

"Shelly, get Craig Bower over at the DEA office on the phone for me, please?"

She tapped her nails, waiting.

"Craig, how are you?"

"Good, I guess, just snowed under like everyone else these days. What can I do for you, Spears?"

"I'm told you know about sending Agent Sophia Medina to meet with me. Can you send her over next Wednesday, 10:30 sharp?"

"What is Medina's assignment?" Craig wondered how much she knew, and if she'd been apprised. He sure the hell hadn't been.

"It's on a need-to-know basis, sorry, Craig."

"Right, got it, so the higher powers believe I don't need to know. Sure, I'll send her. Oh, yeah, tell Roger I said hi, will ya?"

"Yeah, I'll tell him." She hung up. Roger, a creep in Records, one man she didn't see often or care for, but if she saw him she'd pass along a hello from Craig at the DEA. Somebody always wanted you to tell someone else hello. Tell Joe Shmoe I said hey, howdy, or hello; it was how 75 percent of her conversations ended these days. Networking and brownnosing are what it boiled down to.

Three Days Later—Wednesday—Janet Spears' Office

A KNOCK SOUNDED. Spears looked at her watch. 10:20. Medina was punctual.

"Come in," she called out, getting off her chair and extending her hand.

"Agent Spears, thank you for this opportunity," Sophia started.

"Call me Janet, and don't thank me yet, not until you've heard the details. "

Janet went into the details as given to her by Deputy Director Walsh two days after her initial meeting. It wasn't much. However, it was more than she had from her first meeting with him.

"This is sort of vague, isn't it, ma'am?"

"Medina, I'm working with what they've given me and yeah, it's not much. Your job is to find intel we can follow up on. And yep, it sounds easy, but I doubt it will be. I created you a cover legend. You're a magazine columnist doing a piece about that area of Mexico. Nobody will question your inquiries as long as you are careful in how you ask. Act like a tourist of sorts; don't throw up red flags. Also, don't let on you speak fluent Spanish. This way they'll talk in front of you, thinking you won't understand."

"That's it? A secretary could do this job. I figured I would—"

"Fly under the radar, gather intel. It's what you'll do, Medina. Should I get another agent?" She read Sophia's face. The woman's personnel jacket indicated she was a bold and stubborn agent. Janet noticed a spark of determination in this woman's expression, seeing herself.

"You go in blazing with your girl balls to the wall, Sophia, and your death is on my head. Do you understand me?"

"I hear you loud and clear." Sophia paused for half a beat. "I'm headed, alone, to a poorer part of Mexico, where 96 percent of the residents are not your upstanding, honest citizens."

Agent Spears stared across the desk at Sophia, frowning and her head bobbing. "You're correct, I'll get another agent. I'll make a call to—"

Medina cut in, "No, I can do this assignment. It's what I'm trained for. I'm stating facts, not complaining or wussing out. Brass won't shoot me down this time. They've jerked the rug out from under me for the umpteenth time. Reassigning it to a man because they thought it was dangerous for me. No, I want this assignment; it's time I get the chance to prove myself, Agent Spears."

Janet let out a vast sigh. "First, call me Janet, and I'll call you Sophia. You and I will spend a helluva lot of time together looking over files and information. Unless I tell you that you're ready to leave, you aren't going, understood?"

"Yes, Agent...I mean, Janet, understood."

"Yesterday I ordered the Houston Police Department to stop working their homicide. Their case intersects with what we're working on, and we can't have them interfering. We'll go through their files with a fine-tooth comb. Listen, I tried to impart a silent message to the detective to keep working the case even though he was ordered to stand down. When you go to retrieve his case files, talk to him and just him. Convey the same idea, Medina. Send an unspoken message for him to keep working on this case. If the man read me right yesterday, he's copied the files."

"Why not ask him to work it with us? Why so hush-hush?"

"The case has been going on for three years. I'll be briefing you later."

"With him working the investigation, isn't that compromising it? How does this help your office or the DEA?"

"This keeps our agents off the streets. DEA agents scare the bejesus out of those people. He's also familiar with the area and the residents. We'll call him once we need him and not any sooner. This detective is a bulldog. Once he gets started on a case, the Deputy Director said—"

A grin popped up on Sophia's pretty face.

"You find this humorous, Agent Medina?"

"No, Janet, *ma'am,* I was wondering why someone hasn't offered this supercop a job with the agency."

A grin spread on Janet Spears' face, her white teeth glistened in contrast to her brown-sugar skin tone. "Funny you should mention it because we just might do that."

Sophia's mouth dropped open. "You're offering him a job?"

"I might. He might enjoy working for us. I'd never turn my back on a talented prospect."

"Well, he better be a crackerjack detective, because I won't work with any loose cannon. My life could depend on this man. I'd like to see his personnel jacket so I can learn about him. Wouldn't you, if you were me?" Sophia crossed her arms. Several detectives had exceptional abilities, however, not all did. DEA agents had better extensive training, and she wouldn't have time to babysit.

Janet Spears stared at Medina, humor dancing across her face. "It's funny you say he needs to be a *crackerjack* detective."

"Oh yeah, why's that?"

"Well, Medina, his name is Jack, Detective Jack West."

1

Three Months Later

"Whew, it's humid, worse than Houston." Sophia's voice was flat as she tugged at the T-shirt under her Kevlar, lifting it off her skin. Alone in a land time had forgotten, she was, she guessed, three miles from her starting point. For the previous four days, she'd been hunting, catching nothing except insect bites.

"Freaking blood-sucking mosquitoes." She swatted at them. This morning she'd slathered on insect repellant in gobs, but this hadn't worked out as planned. She wished she had brought the can with her. A knapsack with bottles of water and nonperishable foods was heavy enough, adding to her body armor. She might go faster if she had a team. For now, she was alone.

Closer to the base of the mountain, she sidestepped a narrow wet patch, but shifted and her right foot sunk into a small trench, throwing her off balance. Sophia pulled her foot up and squinted, looking down at where she slipped. The weeds and overgrowth weren't odd. What was odd was the mound of dead weeds. Who would pile dead weeds out here? With a loose limb, she moved the heap in hopes it wasn't an animal's nest, and prayed he wasn't home!

She uncovered a gap big enough for a man. Sophia dropped onto her knees with a small flashlight. She peered down. The hole was too steep and had no ladder. Her flashlight pointed into the darkened cavern and she saw what she needed—notches for going in or coming out. It had been dumb luck to find the entrance. She stood, slipped off her backpack, grabbed a bottle of water, and chugged it. She looked around for a place to stash the backpack. Under weeded overgrowth next to a tree three yards away, she dropped the knapsack, covering it with loose tree limbs. With her gun unholstered, she chambered a round and checked her belt for extra magazines. She bent to inspect her backup piece on the inside of her left ankle and the knife she had strapped to the outside on her right. Since she was right-handed, she had the flexibility to move into a sweeping toe-touch, and in fewer than five seconds, she'd have her backup piece.

Sophia rolled her shoulders, then dropped hands to her side. She flexed her fingers and shook her arms, inhaled and exhaled. "Not the wisest decision you've ever made." Her voice was low as she slid in on her belly, feet first, grabbing a notch to begin her descent.

Fifty yards of support poles were in place with droplights strung out in uneven increments. *Damn long extension cord*, she thought to herself, thankful beams were in place as paltry amounts of earth sprinkled on top of her head. "Lord, don't let this cave in while I'm in here," she prayed under her breath.

She stopped to work out the kinks from her shoulders rubbing the perspiration off her upper lip with her shirtsleeve, wishing she'd brought a bottle of water. Darkness loomed ahead. "Shit. They ran out of droplights," she groused and took the flashlight off her belt.

Whoever dug the tunnel placed double and triple beams, which narrowed the passage in a few spots. As she walked down the passageway, a thought occurred. If she were to encounter someone, what would she do? She was alone with no backup. Chances were an

AR-15 or AK-47 assault rifle would greet her the minute her head popped out of the hole.

Duh, Sophie, you gotta gun and you're wearing Kevlar. You're a DEA agent, act like it. She shook her head silently scolding herself.

Further down she came to a curve, which was odd. Most tunnels were a straight shot. Not this one, though. More droplights hung above, and she switched off the flashlight. She veered right. The walls were further apart, with the beams set closer together.

Further down on her right, she passed four beams. In a line, but not straight, they created a small nook. As she passed each beam, the area widened, and she saw a shadow...something...a shape, and every nerve in her body tingled. Her gun in hand, she took slow deliberate steps, closing in on a body lying in the dirt.

He wasn't moving, he was lying in an awkward position, and she knew there was no need for her gun. Sophia holstered her weapon, stepped closer, and peered down. Dried blood matted the man's greasy, stringy hair that stuck to his right cheek. One bullet entry wound in his forehead meant he had faced his killer. Out of habit, she stopped to feel for a pulse. No pulse. She raked her palm over his face to close his eyes.

With her phone she clicked two close-ups and one full body shot of the dead man, then several of the area where he lay. Her plan was to get someone to run this through facial recognition. She gnawed her top lip in thought. However, who could she count on? Not one person, and absolutely none of the assholes in her department. She had zero faith in any of them, except for Janet, and she was feeling iffy about whether she should depend on her. For now, she would wait. She had the photos, and she would decide what to do with them later.

The faint sound of voices came from further ahead. Sophia froze. She was not alone, yet she *was* all alone. With a steady hand, she pulled her gun from her holster, wiping the sweat off her forehead. Her heartbeat kicked into overdrive and she heard it beating in her ears, hoping the thudding was not a thousand decibels loud. The voices were too close, too clear, and two separate voices. Only two voices. That didn't mean it was just two men. Who knew how many she would face?

Careful with smaller steps, she crept with her back against the wall, keeping her eyes front, until she came to the first bend she had rounded. There wasn't time to get out. She had to hide. Sweat rolled between her breasts, and panic rose in her throat. The nook she had seen was the sole place to hide. The recessed area was narrow but the crevasse deep enough to conceal her, buying so much time. She squeezed in sideways, sucking in her middle, feeling like a piece of sandwich meat between two slices of bread. She had to get out before they found her and killed her. She shuddered.

Two men walked up. There were speaking in Spanish, discussing how they should get rid of the corpse. One suggested burning it, while the other wanted to drop him into the river with cinder blocks tied to his ankles and let the fish, snakes, and turtles do the job. They argued the benefits of each disposal—one method left bones while the other method erased the dead guy as if he never existed. They decided to burn his body to ash.

"Sin un cadáver no hay asesinato," the one man said to the other.

Sophia grimaced. Damn. *Without a body, there is no murder.* A few minutes passed, and she heard them dragging the corpse as the sounds of his feet scraping along the dirt gave way to silence. She wanted to see their faces, but she would not chance being seen, so she waited a full fifteen minutes before peering out to check. No dead guy and no other men. Sophia walked backward, her gun up, until she felt safe enough to turn. She needed a better plan, and not going it alone was a great plan, so she hightailed it to the other end of the tunnel.

It was tepid water, but it was water. It washed off the grime and sweat accumulated from being a tunnel rat. The semi-hot water refreshed as she stood underneath the ancient pipes. Toweled off and dressed, the stifling humidity would make her sweaty again.

The building was once a hacienda, owned by a couple who ran an avocado-growing business. The structure was built over fifty years ago. Left to crumble, new owners converted the place for travelers to stay, installing a few stand-up showers, cheap sinks, and toilets. All they'd done was add a few walls here and there to create separate rooms, installing substandard flooring and cheap door hardware. They had painted the walls with what was likely lead-based paint and plastered bathroom walls with horrid wallpaper. A bed in each room was covered with bargain bedding, sheets, and thin cotton bedspreads, all of which needed a wash. One area was converted into a dining room, however, there was no free Continental breakfast included. If you wanted to eat, the resident cook could throw together tacos, burritos, breakfast or not—pozole, mole sauce, and tamales.

Travelers visiting here, indeed! More likely people running away or outlaws in hiding. Two old geezers were the only boarders besides her. This was their slow season, maybe similar to Catskills with seasonal vacationers. This made her laugh.

The owner trucked in supplies biweekly, but the amount trucked in exceeded his needs, which threw up a red flag. The place boomed in the late 60s. It was rumored that it went from avocados to marijuana. The place was abandoned again later on. Places like this thrived later as the drug trade took an upswing and cartels moved in. People conducting unsavory business needed these hideaways. All-in-all she doubted it was a place for mountain and hiking enthusiasts.

She removed her knapsack from under the loose floorboards beneath the uncomfortable twin bed. Sophia pulled the laptop out of her computer bag and activated the system. After inserting her thumb drive, she filled in her daily log report, and then pulled out three thick files, flipping through them again for the millionth time. She wanted fewer questions, questions without answers, which kept her bogged down and going nowhere.

Today was her closest call. Damn, she was unhappy with working it single-handedly. It was time they sent her a team or at least one more person. The war they fought was with people who had zero respect for human life. She needed one person she could trust to have her back.

Her eyes closed, she leaned back recounting the day the slob, who'd tried to best her in a drinking contest, told her about the tunnels of white powder.

THREE WEEKS EARLIER, Agent Medina sat in the run-down shithole with one bartender/owner, a server, and a cook. One place to socialize and search for intel. Tonight the place was jumping with six customers—four men and two women.

"You drink good, for a woman, maybe." He spoke with broken English, revealing cracked, chipped, and decaying yellow teeth. Sophia eyeballed the sweaty, grungy man. Nobody in this bar would pass as a model citizen. Fat Man was not the exception. She'd seen the gun tucked in his waistband.

The fellow drained his third large mug of beer before looking at her. "*Pero no te emparejas con un Mexicano cómo yo.*"

Yeah, Sophia understood, but still looked at him as if he had two chicken heads attached to his ears.

"You no *bueno* drinker like Mexican"—his English stilled—"man, as me."

Hell, nothing exciting had happened since she'd arrived and she was sick of the mundane, so why not?

"See if he wants to have a tequila-drinking contest," she communicated to the bartender in English, enunciating each word.

The bartender conveyed her message and the Mexican man nodded, again displaying his rotten, ugly teeth. "*Si*, senorita."

He was in for a surprise. Sophia came from a family of drinkers. Accustomed to cheap rotgut alcohol, whether it was tequila, whiskey, or rum, she could best him in drinking. After getting a glimpse of his gun, she'd make damn certain he was dead drunk first.

The bartender set down a bottle with two shot glasses. Onlookers gathered around to watch. Shot after shot, they drank head to head. She poured her seventh shot, lifted her glass, swallowed in one gulp, her eyes never leaving his, then upturned her glass.

The man sighed, taking hold of the bottle, and pouring his next shot. A woman kicking his tequila-drinking ass crushed his pride. In Spanish, he began bragging about how valuable he was, and one day he would meet the grand jefe. He smirked when he spoke of knowing about the passageways and the dealings of the cartel. Not a single person flinched at words Sophia feigned to understand.

"*Debajo* means under, uh, like underground, a tunnel?" She looked at the bartender.

"*Si*, underground perhaps is a *sustantivo túnel*, how you say, uh, tunnel." He shrugged.

Well, now she was getting somewhere. She poured her ninth shot and threw it back, upturning her glass with a thud. She wiped her mouth with the back of her hand.

"Eh, uh, a *sustantivo túnel*?" she asked, sounding oblivious and keeping the excitement out of her voice. Agent Medina stared at him, reclining and relaxed while her facial expression invoked a challenge, saying, *it's your turn—do it.*

The slob took his shot glass and filled it. His lips broke apart in a nasty grin revealing yellow tobacco-stained, rotted teeth. "*Si, niña, los túneles del polvo Blanco.*" (Yes, girl, the tunnels of the white powder.) The words slurred, he tossed the shot back, and Sophia figured the next few shots should have him sliding off his chair to the floor and underneath the table. As he set the glass down, his hands, not working well, caused it to wobble. A smirk flitted across his unshaven face.

Agent Medina threw him a blank expression of indifference, then poured out her tenth shot, examined the liquid for a minute before throwing it back, and with a firm *kerplunk*, upended her glass. Her performance could win her an EGOT.

It was his turn again. His hold on the tequila was unstable, and he overfilled his glass, sloshing tequila everywhere before setting the bottle down with an unsteady hand. The container rocked before it stilled, settling in place. His hand slipped when he reached for the glass, overturning it. Tequila spilled out across the tabletop as he slithered off his chair onto the floor, lying faceup. Nobody moved to help him. Sophia picked up the bottle of tequila, pressed it to her lips, emptied it, and then set it down beside her stack of shot glasses. The woman tourist, Sophia, produced 500 pesos, dropping it next to the pyramid of glasses, leaving them all slack-jawed and silent.

THE RESIDENTS WHO LIVED HERE, 150 miles on the outskirts of Ocampo, Tamaulipas, Mexico, knew very little about Agent Medina. She did not speak Spanish, and they considered her an American-born Mexican showoff tossing pesos around in sizeable amounts. Oh, they would tolerate her if she kept tossing pesos and dollars their way.

With a populace of 87 residents, if you counted the number of chickens roaming free-range, you might get to 100. These poor people inhabited a toilet bowl town with no law office, no medical facilities, no schools, and unpaved roads 118 kilometers away from a real town. Americans might call this worse than living out in the sticks. Agent Medina landed in a town time had forgotten—a small dirty town—a place for criminals to hide. She blended into the shadows, conducted illegal business under the radar of the Mexican Federales, and did business with the crooked Mexican Federales.

Sophia Medina was there to research the northwest regions of Mexico for the magazine, *Realms of Discovery*. Her assignment was to write about the land and people in the mountain areas. Attempting to interview the locals was nothing short of a disaster, since the language barrier became an issue, even though it was a ruse. They thought the Americans were stupid for sending a person who did not speak their language. She used the bartender as her interpreter, because he spoke enough English to assist her with what she needed.

They had pegged her as *Una estúpida Media Blanca Criada,* a stupid white mixed race and *estúpida* (stupid female). They called her the *Chicana,* a Mexican-born American, unsure of who she was. Sophia wondered how they'd react to finding out the truth, especially about how fluent she was in Spanish. To her, this was funny; to them, if they knew the truth, probably not.

Her crossed leg bounced as she jiggled her foot in a nervous gesture, sitting on the rim of the bed, flipping through the files. Sophia's adrenaline still pumped after finding the entrance. She was itching to get back out. This was, however, a short-lived victory; it was no longer safe going it alone. She required a team; she needed dependable people, and she wanted them yesterday. Making a call to her office had been a mistake. Clive Bebchuk, what a prick, along with his scummy sidekick, Stan Cleef.

"Wait it out, Medina, we don't have the agents to spare, and if you call again bellyaching I'll pull you and put someone else on, got it?" Bebchuk warned her, his whiney voice irritating her last nerve. Yeah, she got it. Clive Bebchuk, senior agent or not, hated women in the Department. He wanted her to give in and quit, then use it against the other women. She'd overheard him saying females did not have the physical stamina to be field agents. Men were the more superior, smarter, stronger agents. They were detached, not letting emotions play into the job. The agency should keep men in charge and women at their desks. What a jerk-wad.

The entrance to a probable tunnel was a phenomenal find. Cartel leaders hid underground like the rats they were, and if she were discovered, a bomb would explode. Then she'd end up a wisp of smoke in never-never land. Not a soul would be the wiser. They'd sent her here alone to work. Okay, fine, then; she'd take care of getting help on her own too. Disappearing without a trace was not an option. Sophia typed out her text: *Janet, I need your advice and your help—go to chat room 005564. We need to talk. I'll get online in half an hour.*

Sophia reopened her laptop and began preparing the security parameters and the many steps it took in this godforsaken cesspool of a town to get secured Wi-Fi. She keyed in the code name of the special website, entered her username and password, and in seconds, another screen appeared at which point she completed the security steps.

The screen went blank, blinking back on three seconds later to a new screen. Agent Medina was transported to another world. Government seals rolled across the upper half of the page, and a coded list populated the screen. Clicking on a link called "Symposiums," numbers populated the page in rapid succession before the speed slowed and the page stopped. Sophia depressed the alt and control keys and a box appeared. She typed in numbers 005564—another window opened and a curser flickered. Now set to chat with Agent Spears on a secure site, she waited.

Hope you are well. The words typed across the screen. *What's up?* Janet began the conversation.

Sophia: *I'm fine, but I need your help. Will you make the call for me?*

Janet: *I'll do what I can, within my scope of power.*

Sophia: *This has to be in your scope of power, Janet. I'm winging it here on my own—not enough agents to cover every fucking bad thing in our world. Janet, make the call, the one we discussed months ago.*

Janet: *You imagine he'll help you after waiting this long to contact him? Crap, I'm not sure if he is still in law enforcement. I stopped checking on his status a while back.*

Sophia: *Yeah, he's back at work. He got back almost eight months ago. I have people who have kept me informed. Are you gonna call him?*

Janet Spears' hands hovered over her keyboard for a nanosecond before she began typing. *Yes, I'll call, and get him briefed on your situation—however, I can't guarantee what his answer will be. You understand, right?*

Sophia: *Oh, he'll be onboard. This is an excellent diversion for him. The man's been through hell.*

Janet: *What makes you think he'll even want to help? He was expecting you to contact him fourteen months ago, and you never did. I'm guessing he'll tell you to fuck off. I would if I were him.*

She had a valid point, but Sophia felt she understood the guy better than Janet did.

Sophia: *He won't. His case is still open and he'll come back for this reason alone. He will want to close his case.*

U.S. Attorney General's Office Agent Janet Spears grinned as she typed. Yet she worried too.

Janet: *We will talk day after tomorrow, at 7 pm, chat room 295561. Give you his answer, but until then, be cautious. I've been monitoring your reports. Jesus, Sophia, the shithole you are in, the lowlife scum you've had to deal with, you amaze me every day.*

Sophia: *Copy that. I'm talking about the shithole part, that is. Read my next report and you will understand why I'm asking for one more agent. Hell, my effing office has no one to spare in the field, and I sure as fuck do not want any pantywaist DEA copyboy sent out to help get me killed. Gonna sign off now.*

Sophia hit the key to click off the secured chat room, shut her laptop, and then she stored it and her satchel back under the floorboards, pulling her duffel bag over the boards for extra concealment. She hoped she was right about him.

Janet Spears slipped the tattered business card out from her blotter. This card had remained on her desk ever since the day she'd ordered the detectives to stop investigating their murder case. With the shabby card in hand, she dialed his cell number. She listened to it ringing and counted four rings before he picked up.

"Jack West."

2

Fourteen Months Before the OAG Called Him Back

Jack walked through the well-kept cemetery once again, his boots scraping over loose gravel roads, taking one turn after the other until he saw the spot where Gretchen lay interred. The mound of fresh dirt had yet to settle and wire stands still held now-withering wreaths of flowers next to her headstone. There was no bench like when he visited his big brother's grave, and Jack made himself a promise to remedy the situation. He'd work on getting a nice bench installed here for her visitors, one with flowers, hearts, and angels. And he would have it engraved, *For my Angel, Gretchen, Love, Jack.* Simple and heartfelt.

"Gretch, I have to fly home to Texas." His voice caught in his throat. "Thank you for loving me for the two years we had together. I realize I can't drop by anytime I want, but I promise I'll do my best to get back and visit you and see your family." Jack bent down to touch her headstone, intending to keep this promise for as long as he could.

Life moved on following the aftermath of Gretchen Benson's murder, but not for ex-Detective Jack West, and it never again would for Gretchen. His resignation had been the turning point, and without his badge, gun, and purpose, he shut himself off from the world. He never left his home, except for the occasional run to the liquor store or to check his mail. Each day was the same. He got up and dressed in sweatpants and a T-shirt, not caring if they were clean or dirty.

This morning he'd eyed himself in the bathroom mirror after brushing his teeth. His beard scraggly with no desire to shave, he grabbed a ball cap and plunked it on. Why did he need to comb his hair? He wasn't going anywhere. He needed a haircut, but the ball cap worked fine.

His phone rang and rang and rang. Much to the caller's disappointment, Jack never picked up. No one, he wanted no one in his life—not Dawson Luck, Xi, or Jace. Lucky had been persistent until Jack texted him to leave him the fuck alone. If he wanted to talk, he would call him. He hated to be an ass, hoping his partner understood and forgave him one day.

Five months in, he took out the boxes he'd stored filled with copies of his homicide case wondering if DEA Agent Sophia Medina was still running the investigation. Saying he was still pissed at the US Attorney General Agent Janet Spears for ordering them to stand down was putting it mildly. He should have started a bonfire and burned the copies to ash.

"You guys, you bureaucratic asswipes never called me, you pack of freaking liars." He flipped the lid off the carton of files with vigor. Had they closed the investigation and now things were hunky-dory? Was HPD's triple murder now a new unsolved case? Yeah, right, no call from the supreme rulers of law, because they didn't need him. He had a news flash for both the OAG and DEA—he didn't need them either.

Jack was mad because his case was still open and unsolved, and the OAG and DEA didn't give a rat's ass. They had what they needed. Those assholes would let it stay open and unsolved. Shit. A triple murder was not important; it was small potatoes to them. Neither the murdered men nor their families would ever get justice. Jack, the ex-homicide detective, knew it didn't matter if it was a crooked drug-dealing lowlife. Every murder victim deserved justice.

"Why do I have these copies?" Muttering, he stuck his hand in the box and pulled out a binder. He'd duplicated the files. Janet Spears and Sophia Medina had both conveyed to him a message he felt he'd read correctly. However, neither woman had verbalized, "Hey, Jack, make yourself a copy of the file, you will need them." His gut said make copies; now he wanted his gut to explain why. He wanted a phone call from Spears or Medina, but if they needed him, they would've already called. Damn those bastards.

Jack propped his feet on the coffee table, took two more files out of the box, sat back, and opened them. He scoured his written notes, looking for something, and only found more questions. An exhale of frustration escaped his lips, and he shut his eyes, leaning his head back, wondering what he'd missed.

Alright, Jack, what do you have? he thought as he mentally sorted through the information, creating a pseudo-folder in his head, taking the bits and pieces he had before getting yanked off the investigation. His Irish friend, Owen McCready, flat out disappeared; Pham Trong flew off to Vietnam; and Boyce Carter, driver for a bus company, father to a dead boy—was he involved? What piece was missing? Mentally he listed the timeline of events:

- Three killed
- Smokin' Hot looted
- Altercation with Cazalla, Carter, Trong, and McCready.
- McCready gets a beating
- Trong leaves the country
- McCready disappears into the wind

None of it made sense. A closed-mouth laugh escaped him. An Irish man, Vietnamese man, bus driver, and a cartel soldier walk into a bar, and the bartender says what? Just what would his punchline be to this joke?

Over six months into his I-am-no-longer-a-detective life, Jack refused to take his position back. Chief of Detectives Davis Yao pressed him hard but never got past the front door. Jack sent him packing after a one-minute speech telling him thanks but no thanks, and good-bye.

Today would be different. Yao felt confident as he raised his fist and rapped on the doorframe. The knock was a hard, straightforward two-knock, bang-bang.

No energy to handle this crap. Jack got off his couch, walked to the radio, turned the volume lower, and called out, "Just a minute," his tone flat. He knew who it was. Davis Yao, the single fellow ballsy enough to not quit. In a group text, Jack typed: *Fuck off, I don't want to see anyone, and if you persist, I will consider it harassment and will take action. Don't make me go there.* Then everyone left him alone.

Jack frowned after pulling the door open. "Davis, you're not gonna give up, are you? Come in. My neighbors are nosy." His shoulders sagged as he stepped back to let Davis Yao pass.

Past the front door, this was progress. He and Jack might have a full-fledged conversation after all. His confidence grew.

After a short, "how are you, how's your family" chat, Chief of Detectives Yao jumped right into the deep end.

"Our city needs its best detectives working for them, and Jack, it's time to become part of the world again."

"Nothing is the same, Davis. It will never be the same. Not for me."

Davis drew in a sharp breath and exhaled in frustration. "Jack, shit happens. Besides, it's not your first incident. You've—"

"Look, killing Cyrus Shelton was not the way I wished to end things, Davis, but damn it, it made me feel good even though I'd rather have had the fucking bastard fry with the entire world watching."

Davis was on the verge of speaking when Jack stopped him with a headshake.

"No, I'm not finished. Shelton would have stayed on death row for years, even decades, before his death became a reality, filing appeals, pulling every legal trick he could to reduce his sentence to life without parole. When he tossed his knife, the bastard gave me the excuse I needed to squeeze off two rounds and drop his ass. I don't feel any remorse, Davis, none, not an ounce."

Jack knew one certainty, one he would keep buried for life. His plan was to shoot Shelton, no matter what. Most cops would feel shooting Shelton was a justifiable homicide, without a second thought. Everyone in Houston would agree shooting the son of a bitch to purge the city of a monstrous bastard was acceptable. Even better, Jack was damn glad the monster helped him make it a clean shoot to keep his conscience clean.

Davis Yao looked at Jack with his lips set in a straight line, and he nodded. "I understand you, Jack. Hell, most cops in Homicide feel the same way you do. Swifter justice should prevail in every case. I feel the same and I'd rather drop and bury 'em than have to pay out dollars to keep them fed, housed, and clothed cuz them bastards don't deserve it. You realize you would've—"

Jack butted in again, knowing where he was going with this conversation.

"Yeah, yeah, OIS would have been able to clear me. They would have deemed this a clean shoot. They would have suspended me with pay and I'd be back. But I...me"—he pointed to his chest—"screwed myself. Punching Brooks, knocking him flat on his face was the hole I dug for myself, but by God he deserved it."

"Jack." Yao's brows wrinkled. "Brooks got two things. A punch in his snout, which he deserved, but I cannot admit I agreed with your actions. But you granted him his other wish by quitting. I overheard him bragging that it was worth the busted nose to get you gone. Shit, Jack, I even concocted a vague bullshit story. I told IA he grabbed your shoulder when you were not expecting it and at a time you were under great stress. You just saw the raped, beaten body of a girl you loved. Afterward, you had to kill the man responsible in self-defense.

"Under duress and trauma, you jumped and came around, swinging. I argued with IA. It was Brooks' fault; he did not handle the situation as he should have. Christ. Those bastards in IA should understand the strain it puts on a man. Cop or not."

"Well, from what I got wind of, *Inside Assholes*, our beloved IA Department, couldn't find one person who would admit to seeing what happened, not even one member of Brooks' Butt-Kisser's club. Plus, they say since no one came to Brooks' defense, he's more of a prick than usual." Jack disliked his ex-captain before and now he loathed him.

"Yeah, Brooks was so pissed off at what he calls the jag-off witnesses who left him high and dry. No one, not even his boys, would admit to having seen the truth, as he calls it."

Davis made no move to interject his opinion or thoughts on the matter. He was silent.

"You want a cup of coffee, Davis?"

"Yes, please, straight up and strong."

"Coffee—straight up just like the sludge you're used to at the station." Jack handed him a cup. "Let's go out back."

Coffee cups in hand, they walked to his back patio. There was a cool breeze. Rain loomed overhead and the humidity was not as thick as usual. They sat in silence, sipping coffee, staring into Jack's small but neat backyard.

"You have a nice place, Jack. It suits you," Davis remarked, setting his cup down.

His words reminded Jack of a time long ago. When he'd said something similar to Gretchen about her house, the house her grandmother left her. "*It's a nice house, Gretch, fits you.*" Words spoken, he felt, a lifetime ago. Jack did a face shrug, whispering, "Yeah, I like it."

"Jack..." Yao began.

"I understand, Davis. Also, I appreciate why you're here, and I'm aware you want an answer and you want the answer *you* want to hear." His palm lifted to stop the captain from speaking when Yao twisted in his chair to stare at him, his mouth on the cusp of opening to speak.

"You're right, Davis, I bleed blue. I'm a homicide cop, not a security guard or a gumshoe, but a bonafide cop. Crap, the Department is gonna make me go through hell. I'll have to make an appointment with the division's psychiatrist and they'll try to figure out if my head is on straight. It's enough to keep a cop from wanting to stay in. Not to mention Brooks, the asshole." His last few words dripped with malice, and his fist hit the small iron patio table with a thud. Yao did not flinch, jump, or blink at Jack's anger. It was, he thought, a deserved reaction.

"Brooks is my concern, Jack. He's not your worry, he's mine." Davis Yao did not go into detail, and Jack didn't give a damn where Brooks was or what he was doing. Jack did not utter a word for a full six minutes.

"Ahem, uh, Jack," Yao's voice pulled him to the present.

"Yeah, Davis, I need to go back to what I love doing—serving the people of Houston. Just gotta do the steps. Gonna be a little rough, but I'll manage."

"You will, Jack. You're more determined than anyone I've ever met. I mean, for Christ's sake, you still work on Cole's case. Hell, it's been over twenty-five years. You never quit or give up."

Three weeks later, a clean-shaven Jack fulfilled his anger management courses, passed his psychiatric evaluation, and his review with the internal investigative boards. He re-qualified on the shooting range. They re-issued him his service weapon, and he clipped on his badge ready to be who he was, the fellow he'd been before these tragedies—Jack West, Homicide Detective, seeking justice for the dead.

Jack tapped in the inside doorjamb. "Chief, you needed to see me?" He poked his head in the doorframe.

"Yeah, Jack, come in. How'd it go on the firing range?"

"No issues, I made—" Jack stopped short, his exhilarated mood slipped away when he saw an unfamiliar woman in the chair against the far wall. *Well, shit,* he thought, the last time Yao summoned him to his office, he met OAG Agent Janet Spears. The day he and Dawson Luck were told to halt their investigation of a triple murder. What was the freaking deal now? He had just gone back to work.

Davis Yao suppressed a grin. Jack had not been told Homicide's newest leader was a woman.

"Jack, meet Captain Veronica Justice, our newest member at HPD, and your new Captain."

"It's a pleasure to meet you, Detective West. I've heard a lot about you." She rose, outstretched her palm, and he accepted it. Her handshake was solid and firm. Jack looked at their clasped hands, then back at her.

"You've heard a bunch of things, I know. Now, you wanna hear my side?" His eyes bore into hers, trying to get a read on her.

Captain Veronica Justice nodded, pulling her hand from his, and taking her seat.

"Jack, can I call you Jack or do you prefer plain old West?"

His forehead lifted in amusement. Someone had filled her in on Brooks' habit of never once calling him Jack, just *West.* Brooks had never been affable, not with him. First name recognition was for Brooks' boot-lickers.

"Jack is fine, ma'am, uh, Captain Justice."

"I've already heard both sides. I came to my own conclusions. Don't call me ma'am, Jack, I'm Roni, or Cap. I'm not big on titles. Titles such as Chief or Captain or Mayor or beat cop, it doesn't matter. You do the job you're qualified to do and give it 100 percent. It's all I expect. For example, I'm gonna call you Jack, unless I'm introducing you, then I'll call you Detective West. You and I both get it. Your job is to find the killers. Nobody has to remind you that you are a detective. Get me?"

Jack liked this woman. "Yes, I do. Just like you're my Captain, responsible for keeping Homicide running the way it should run. It's your business to set standards for our department and lead us in the right direction. I get it right, Roni?"

The woman's pearly whites glistened against her almond-colored skin, and she let out an honest-to-God belly laugh.

"Uh-huh, Jack, and you're the first person to use my own words to remind me of what my job is. I like it, I like it a lot." She looked over at Davis Yao. "Davis, you were right. He's quick."

"Yeah, he is, and he'll always be a straight shooter too." Yao was glad to have his friend and valued detective back at work.

"Jack, I realize you and Luck were partners before this, uh, let's call it hullabaloo, happened. I've teamed Luck and Webb up and I'm leaving them together, for a handful of reasons. You and Luck will partner in the future. That's a given."

Skip Webb, a Brody Brooks fan. Poor Lucky was not so lucky anymore. Who was his new sidekick? Hoping not to have the same luck as his unlucky partner and draw a shorter than short straw. Captain Roni Justice took Jack's silence to mean he understood.

"When I assign you to a call, you'll work with Reed; until then, I have a specific task for you two." She paused for a second. "You have a question, Jack?"

"Yes, Roni, I do. Any breakthrough on the triple homicide, is the DEA still working their case?"

"Jack, keep your nose to the Department's grindstone, don't go poking it where you shouldn't. We're at the bottom of the ladder without permission to climb. I hope I make myself clear." She angled her head to watch him full-on, meeting his eyes with her own.

"Hmm, yeah, I get it. My case ain't never gonna get solved and we continue to be in the goddamn dark, pardon me, but it pisses me off, Cap."

Roni Justice and Jack locked eyes, wordless, reading each other. It showed in his eyes. Unless she fired him, he would not stop looking into this triple murder, and she wouldn't be able to stop him. "Jack, believe me, I understand more than you can imagine." She stood to leave and turned to Jack.

"Welcome back, Jack. I believe we will get along fine."

Austin Reed swiveled his chair when the door squeaked open.

"Jack, it's great to see you."

"Good to be back, Austin."

This was his normal, at his desk, in this room talking to another detective. Davis Yao had stated a definitive truth. Jack bled blue, and being a cop ran through his veins. Police work was much more than that. It was embedded in his soul and made him Jack West.

He and Reed partnered for the next few months. The Homicide Department experienced a lull in cases for a brief period, not the norm for this city. Heavy rains came in late spring, rocking his fair city with sporadic flooding in multiple areas, and chaos followed. Businesses were hit hard by looters, people forced out of their homes. Some were fortunate to have the means to live while they rebuilt. Others weren't as lucky. In lower rent areas, the renters and older folks who owned their small homes were forced out by the rising waters with nowhere to go. Most lived on fixed incomes or worked minimum wage jobs. Shelters filled with no more room to spare increasing the homeless population, which increased the crime rate. Houston's crime wave became a crime tsunami. It took everyone in law enforcement to do his or her job and go beyond the call of duty to power through this ordeal, to keep the city from imploding.

The Robbery unit had its hands full with several thefts in a high-end neighborhood after the flooding chaos became more manageable. The thieves were getting bolder. When robbery detectives found two bodies, Homicide was called. Jack felt alive again. It was strange, even morbid; death and murder made him feel alive.

3

At home, with his feet resting on top of the coffee table, Jack opened his beer and took a long pull as he flipped back to the crime scene pictures. One man was dead, the other two transported to Ben Taub where they had died making it a triple homicide, still an open, unsolved case. Something in the way his new commander, Veronica Justice, acted gave him a gut feeling. If he worked on this case, she wouldn't fire him. The expression he'd seen on her face conveyed something opposite to her orders.

Jack headed to the kitchen, grabbed another bottle of Miller High Life, hot salsa, and a bag of tortilla chips off the counter. He reached for the folder labeled *Owen McCready*. Beer in hand, he took a hefty swig, reading reports he'd read more than a dozen times and would keep reading until he figured it out.

McCready had disappeared. Searching for him had zip to do with the triple murder. Jack was searching for a missing person. It might be a waste of time; however, this was his time to waste. Before he took back his badge, he'd done nothing but stare at four walls, so he had lost time to make up for.

From Agent Spears to Agent Medina trickling downward to his

new captain, Veronica Justice, each woman conveyed to him it was still his case to work, albeit under the radar. No one said it aloud, but the word was clear—"*Jack, investigate, we won't stop you.*" Was he reading what he wanted to read into this? If, and it was one huge if, he found something breaking the investigation wide open, and it blew whatever Sophia Medina was working on, then what?

He downed the beer then moved to the chips and salsa, and continued reading. Nothing new, but he was missing something. The salsa had bite, and he wanted another beer, so he closed the folder, moseyed to the fridge, grabbed a bottle, and drained half of it. Loads of investigating loomed ahead of him, and he knew there was much more to the unsolved triple homicide.

Before daybreak, in the early morning hours still covered by darkness, Jack was at his desk, away from prying eyes. He could trust his compadres, but dragging them in meant more people working on a case that was not his. If it became necessary, he knew whom he could count on.

Jack switched on the small desk lamp and logged onto his computer. His search for Owen McCready had garnished nil. McCready was not listed in the Department of Motor Vehicles, in any state, as having a driver's license. Jack found it odd. Did he even own a car?

It had taken major cajoling and promised favors, but one nurse at Ben Taub who had cared for McCready came through giving him a social security number, name, and phone number of a friend listed as McCready's emergency contact.

The dilemma was the phone number McCready had given the hospital was missing one number at the end. Or was it the first number? It was a Boston area code. Why had McCready listed an old friend from Boston as a contact? Why not someone from here in Houston? Boston was over 1800 miles away. No next of kin listed either. Another oddity. Jack's extensive list of anomalies was growing.

Jack made several trips to the address on file, but McCready was never home. Jack drove by the house again a month ago and nothing had changed—no signs of activity.

The cigarette shop, Smokin' Hot, had been a bust. Closed up, full of inventory, the doors padlocked, and the place still for sale. His next move would be to find an address associated with the post office box. What he got was zip. No one was paying for the mailbox any longer.

Jack pulled up the Social Security Administration's employee-only website. His fingers hovered over the keyboard. No official authorization, no signed warrant—this was chancy. He inhaled and exhaled, then keyed in the social security number. The screen stayed blank before it flickered and searched. Data popped up. He shook his head, leaning back in his chair staring at the screen, not the least bit surprised. The owner belonged to one Mary N. Habith, age 98, or she would have been 98 on her next birthday. She'd been dead eleven years.

Jack tapped his fingers on his desk wondering who Owen McCready was, because the guy he met was flesh and blood but didn't exist on paper. The DMV had been a bust. He had a bogus SS number. He thought this gave him a reason to keep searching for the man. HPD had implemented a new program, Trace-Tracker, so he logged in and got what he expected—zilch.

He didn't want to pull anyone else in, but it was necessary. Jack had to have somebody with some expertise at digging. The person needed to be a bit of a nerd. But they had to understand catfishing, dark web crap, and how to cover up a technical footprint. Art Walsworth, a tech supervisor, was his first choice. Art would be an exceptional asset; however, he was too much of a straight shooter. Art was a by-the-book kinda employee. Assignments not sanctioned by the higher-ups would be off-limits. Better to keep Art out of it, find someone else.

His monitor populated with an employee roster. Jack scrolled through faces. A mix of technical nerds, young kids, and he hadn't worked with many of them. Homicide used the Tech Department less than any other division. Lifting his fingers from his mouse, Jack stopped on a name and something clicked in his brain. This was his recruit. He had to depend on the guy. Jack changed his current going-nowhere research into researching a prospective partner.

Jack opened the door into a dim hallway on the second floor. He tiptoed down the hall to the end office on the corner. Entering an office he had no business being in, he switched on the light as his booted feet made no noise on the worn carpet. At the filing cabinet, he hesitated for a millisecond before sliding the drawer open. Somewhere down the pike he'd learned Clarissa Joyner, who headed up the Technical Department's Human Resources, was a file pack rat. Clarissa kept impeccable records, and thorough. Each file cabinet drawer housed a list of employees by year, and by status—active or non-active. He searched the active files and found what he was looking for: Bergman, Kasper, active status, hired on four years ago. Jack leaned against the wall to read:

Father retired from his last station at the US Army Department in Arden Hills, Minnesota. He moved his family to New Germany, Minnesota, with a population of less than 400.

"A military brat, perfect," he mused, and kept reading.

Kasper had grown up living in many places—the United Kingdom, Guam, Italy, Bahrain, and even a short stint in Turkey. Bergman came to Houston on a full-ride scholarship to Rice University and studied Computer Science. The kid graduated top 10 in his class with a major in computer analysis, and submajor in cybersecurity with a notation in his file and a passion for computer forensics.

Jack recalled the first time he'd met the kid. Art had him working on cell phone triangulations for a case he and Luck were working, and the kid hit on an issue no one had bothered to check.

The primary suspect in that case was her ex-boyfriend, Calvin Jones. They had a love-hate-love-again-hate-forever relationship. Calvin and the victim had previous altercations documented in police reports. The suspect and victim ran into each other at a bar they frequented on Thanksgiving eve. The victim's new male partner got sloshed, and it went downhill. Witnesses verified the victim and Jones argued, him threatening to end her sorry life. No one called the cops, and the bouncer tossed them out of the club.

Four days later, Sunday evening, a friend found her dead. Calvin Jones became the prime suspect. The medical examiner's office estimated the time of death between 5:00 and 6:00 Friday night. No one missed her because it had been a holiday weekend and her friends thought she had gone to Conroe, Texas, on Thursday morning to surprise her sister since Thanksgiving was also her sister's birthday.

Jones told police he was shopping alone at the Galleria Mall; however, no one they questioned recalled seeing him. Friday being the biggest shopping day of the year, the mall was full of wall-to-wall shoppers, who were using cell phones, which overburdened the cell towers. The overburdened towers were transmitting cell phone calls to the closest tower, creating a domino effect. A continuous cycle throughout the day until the towers were less burdened. That happened when the callers stopped crowding the air as the mall emptied at closing time.

Calvin Jones called his mom and his aunt while shopping and Tech traced his phone to a neighborhood ten miles from the mall. It was a strange coincidence that his phone bounced off a cell tower near the victim's apartment complex. His story about shopping at the mall without one purchase to back it up never changed.

Kasper had a gut instinct, and he led with it, tracking the phone records back as far as he could, and not once had the ex-boyfriend's phone ever pinged or triangulated near the victim's neighborhood.

Not even close. The victim lived in her apartment sixteen months. Jones had never been to her residence. Nobody went anywhere without their cell phones. If he were in the area, he would've had his phone with him.

Kasper proved Jones was at the mall by pulling phone records from a couple of store clerks who had worked on Friday. Jones' cell pinged in the same places as mall employees' cells; therefore, law enforcement could not discount this.

Evidence found at her autopsy proved the victim's new male friend had murdered her, sealing the case. The argument she had with Calvin Jones led to an argument between her and the new boyfriend, who thought she still wanted Calvin Jones. In a drunken rage, he strangled her. It was a funny thing, the smallest granule, or tiniest hair proving DNA by far outweighed cell phone triangulation evidence. The DNA was the cake—the cell phone info was the cherry on top.

Kasper's tenacious assertiveness impressed Jack. Bergman had a gut feeling, and he went with it. Intuition, Jack liked it. Bergman listened to his inner voice; so few did. He skimmed through the man's employment jacket, his interview paperwork, his resume, and his application paperwork. Something in the back of the file caught his eye. A questionnaire: a growth plan, where they wished to be year-to-year and how they planned to achieve their goals. He'd forgotten she had her special questionnaire. If Clarissa knew their future goals, it prompted her on how to manage the employee to get the best out of them. Growth meant losing her staff to better things, but she got your best before you moved on.

Bergman, Kasper: 3-year plan: advance to assistant supervisor- 5-year- supervisor for cyber tech and surveillance—then after 2 years, apply for a job with the FBI.

Impressive plans, Jack thought closing Bergman's jacket. If Bergman was in, he'd get experience in risk-taking and undercover work. If the kid said no, he'd swear him to secrecy and pray he was trustworthy and stayed quiet.

He left Clarissa Joyner's pristine office the same way he found it and headed back to his desk. This was progress. Now he had a plan.

Reed left the squad room. It was the perfect time to call Kasper Bergman. Jack would ask to meet him. He wanted to be off the phone before Reed returned.

"Hello, Detective I, uh, you want me to do something for you?" Kasper rushed his words. Jack intimidated him and his request to speak with him scared the crap outta him.

"Kasper, meet me at Quinn's Pub tonight; you familiar with the place?"

"Uh-huh, and uh, well, I don't drink, not much, and uh, I, uh—" Nervous, Kasper couldn't seem to complete a sentence.

"Look, kid, all you hafta do is listen, you don't hafta drink. And for Christ's sake, I ain't gonna bite you or shoot you. Stop being so jittery, got it?"

"Sure, Detective I...sir...fine, see you tonight, is 6:30 okay with you, sir, because I could meet you later?" Kasper knew he was rambling, and his hands were sweating.

"I'll be there at 6:30, kid, unless I get a case, then I'll text you. Give me your cell number." Jack wrote the number down and disconnected the call, aware of one thing after talking to the kid. If Kasper Bergman agreed or not, his lips would stay sealed because the poor kid acted scared shitless. Jack made one last call, this time to retired Lieutenant Colonel Melvin Bergman.

4

Visiting the Lone Star Saloon to toss back a cold one was not possible. Memories of Gretchen flooded back, so he couldn't go. Perhaps one day he could. But it was still too soon, so Quinn's Pub became his new place.

After closing one night, Jack hung around, the owner locked the doors, and they had a few shots of Irish whiskey and a couple pints of dark Guinness. Jack needed a friend not part of the HPD. Grady Quinn fit the bill, and as a bartender, was a much-needed listener. Jack spilled his story. Quinn listened without judgment. Little by little, Jack let go. Talking to a stranger had been a therapeutic release, someone who had no cause to judge him. Jack got to know the old man.

Grady Quinn bought the pub when he was 46 and was today in his early 70s. He'd been on a destructive path, choosing crime and the wrong people to consort with. He said he got wise, because if he hadn't gotten out when he did, instead of owning this pub he would either be behind bars in federal prison or dead. Grady had a past. Jack would not open a can of historical worms. He liked the old man.

"You want another, Jack?" Grady gathered empty mugs left by the last patrons, wiping off the bar.

"Yeah, make it a boilermaker this time—Jim Beam and Heineken."

"Rough day, Jack?" Quinn poured a shot of whiskey, sitting an icy bottle of Heineken next to it.

"Nope, just want to clear the cobwebs. I thought I'd burn 'em out."

Jack shot the whiskey then took a healthy swig of his beer.

"Well, if ya need more, just shout."

"Yep, I will."

In the mirror behind the bar, he saw Kasper. Jack swiveled his barstool and waved.

"Detective West, sir..." Kasper reached out to shake hands. "Nice to see you again."

"Call me Jack, Kasper, and I won't bite you, I swear. We're gonna need privacy to talk. Pick us a table at the back. Whatcha drinking, kid?"

"I'll have a—uh—Bud Light." Kasper drank little, practically never. However, he'd man up and have one with the detective.

Jack waved at Grady. "A tall boy, Bud Light, and would'ja bring me another boilermaker?"

"Yep, coming right up."

"Come on, kid, let's grab a seat, and while we're waiting on our drinks, tell me a little about yourself."

An hour later and two tall boys down, Kasper, the lightweight drinker, was clearheaded, not drunk, but relaxed; even his mannerisms relaxed.

"That's a heap of places to live, kid. Too bad you weren't mature enough to enjoy Italy and the UK."

"Yeah, bummer, but hey, got pictures to prove I was there." Kasper shrugged with a lopsided grin. "Detective West, you didn't invite me here to make a new friend, so I'm curious why you did." He pushed his empty mug away. Jack eyed the glass.

"You want—" he started, but Kasper stopped him in mid-question.

"Two tall boys are sufficient for me. You can say I'm a bit of a lightweight. You've been asking a lot of questions about my past, schools, college life, and a few odd questions concerning my job. I hafta say this has given me the impression you've been vetting me. Am I right?"

The boy was smart, even astute enough to know his drinking limits. This meant Kasper did not stretch himself beyond his capabilities.

"You're smart, kid, and I admire a couple of things about you. One, you know your limits, and not drinking another beer means you aren't trying to impress me. Two, you follow your gut instincts, like you did on the Black Friday murder case. Your idea to research how the phones transmitted from cell towers was impressive."

"The DNA evidence convicted the killer, Jack. It wasn't what I did with the phones." Kasper was being modest.

"Take the credit, kid, you deserve it. What you did with the cell phone triangulation and the towers solidified the case."

"Uh, Jack, will you do me a favor, please?"

"Sure, what's on your mind, kid?"

Kasper Bergman's face flushed pink, and he cleared his throat. "Can you call me Kasper and stop calling me kid? I mean, I know I'm younger, but I'm not a kid."

With a straight face, Jack stared him in the eye, and Kasper's nerves kicked in.

"I'm sorry, if you wanna call me—"

Jack cut him off shaking his head with a tiny chuckle. "Sorry, ki... uh, Kasper, it's a habit I have with younger people. It rubbed off on me from my first partner; he called me kid a lot. Kasper it is."

"I appreciate it, Jack. You've got me here for a reason, you wanna clue me in?"

Jack dove into the story.

"So you're telling me you need someone to dig deeper, as in the dark web deeper? Plus cover our footprints?"

"Yep, and listen, keep this classified. No one, and I mean no one, can find out what you're doing. I don't want you to risk your job and if you're not in, I'll understand."

"Jack, I'm in, I mean, geesh, nothing exciting happens in my world and I'd never get this experience otherwise."

He clapped him on the shoulder. "Kasper, welcome aboard the Jack West train. It's gonna be a scary bumpy ride, and you could lose your job, so hold on tight, got it?"

Kasper Bergman saluted with the army callout, "Hooah."

"Army all the way, Bergman, no oorah, or aye-aye captain for you?"

"The Army was for my dad. I respected that, but the military is not for me. My plan is to one day flip out a badge and say, 'I'm FBI Agent Kasper Bergman'." He looked Jack in the eye and grinned. " But you already knew this, didn't you?"

This kid was smart. Extremely smart.

5

At 8:30 p.m., Jack parked across the street and got comfortable, all set to observe. He had checked the schedule. Two buses were expected to arrive within two hours of each other, and two were expected to depart. This would be a long night. The object of this stakeout would be Boyce Carter.

The initial bus let off a load of older couples who were entertaining to watch and laughed aloud once or twice.

A second one pulled into the terminal merely minutes behind the first. He looked at the schedule, watching as the vehicle sat, idling, no one disembarking, nothing for twenty minutes. His interest peaked when he saw two guys walking toward the vehicles. Neither were drivers, vacationers, nor mechanics. Jack snapped a few pictures.

Jack watched the man haul out two large crates from the luggage cargo. He sat them at the curb, and then knocked on the side to signal the driver to pull up. Ten people disembarked—four men and six women—all Hispanic under age 30, nowhere near a full load. A third bus pulled in fifteen minutes later. It was on time. Jack glanced at the schedule again. The first and last buses were due. So, where did the second one, with a mere ten passengers, fit in? Were they transporting illegals? Would someone be so blatant about it?

A guy spoke to the passengers as he was herding them toward the station waiting area, and he disappeared inside behind them. The dude in the darker shirt got on, stuck his arm out, hit the side, and waved the last bus to move forward as he and the driver took off heading to the bus barn.

Jack missed seeing who grabbed them, but when he looked back the two large cases were no longer at the curb, and the third bus pulled forward, cutting off his view.

The entire setup was bizarre. Sea Star Coaches was not an ordinary touring company. Normal tours traveled in the daytime so paid passengers could see the sights. After sightseeing, customers retired to their homes. Out-of-towners went to their hotels.

Sea Star Touring serviced a wide range of real estate. Fares went to all the larger cities from Dallas to Brownsville, then into Mexico, Reynosa and Matamoros, and smaller cities in Mexico. Hell, they weren't Greyhound; they were touring buses, not long-haul traveling buses. This late-night *touring* was another perplexing matter. Who did night tours? A tour to bars hosting a brewery crawl? Nope, this age group did not fit the bill for a pub crawl. No question had a simple answer. All the unconventional activities of this company caused his gut to tingle.

Jack watched the shed. Nothing transpired. He had his fingers at the ignition ready to call it a night when he observed a shadow walking from around the backside of the building. As the shadow stepped into better lighting, he saw him. Boyce Carter. Jack jerked his hand back from the keys. Carter was not sporting a driver's uniform or a mechanic's jumpsuit, he was wearing street clothes—a button-down shirt and dark slacks with a skinny tie.

Jack's face pinched up, thinking back to a particular day and conversation. When they made the death notification for Jamere Carter, he'd met Boyce Carter for the first time, and he'd told them he worked for Sea Star Coaches. He drove, did maintenance, cleaning, or whatever they required. It was a job, and he did what he was told, a regular blue-collar profession. Carter's appearance and behavior gave Jack the impression they had promoted him. Wow. From operator to management in a sixteen-month span. Nope, uh-uh, something did not click because Jack didn't consider Carter management material.

Boyce walked into the building, and less than twenty minutes later he strolled out with another man whom Jack did not recognize. Both fellows strode into the bus barn, dragging the bay doors shut. His surveillance was over but not finished. Not by a long shot.

"JACK, you need Visine, you pull an all-nighter or what?" Austin Reed set his coffee mug on his desk and snatched a large blueberry muffin. Unpeeling the wrapper he took a large bite, crumbs spraying the front of his shirt.

"Nope, not sleeping well these days I guess," Jack lied.

Out of the corner of his eye, Austin glanced at him as he chomped, gulped, took another bite, and dusted the crumbs off, mulling over his next words. Jack just returned, and he didn't want to lose him as a partner so soon. Losing sleep could affect Jack's job performance in the field. He required an alert, sturdy colleague who had his back if called for. Loss of sleep, or was he dealing with nightmares or flashbacks? It was not improbable to think Jack might have PTSD. If PTSD was the issue, his partner required extra time off. Austin felt if Jack had to remain on a desk for too long, eating his gun was his next step.

"Uh-ahem," Austin cleared his throat. "Uh, Jack, if you need to talk let's go for a beer tonight. In case you'd like to unload or..." he trailed off.

Jack sat listening to Austin with a huge grin on his face.

"Jesus, Reed, I swear you have a worried look for no reason. I'm fine. Hell, we have sleepless nights, you dumbass. Look at what we do for a living." Jack wadded a piece of paper and tossed it at his head.

Reed was relieved. Jack was normal, or as normal as a homicide detective could be.

Neither spoke as they dug into a list of cold cases. Any other day Jack would have bitched. Assigned to work only cold cases was boring, yes, but it kept him freed up. He grimaced as he wrote the dates for each case and the case number. Free for what, no one from the OAG or the DEA office would call. They didn't need him, they never would. It was pure BS, so why didn't he just forget it?

Crap, he knew why. Jack West—pit bull, teeth sunk into the case, gnawing and chomping until there was nothing more to chew on. Afterward, possibly he'd let go, and then perhaps not.

6

Kasper Bergman looked at his phone again, checking the time. Jack said 7:00. It was 7:45. He'd give Jack a few more minutes and drink another beer. He got Grady's attention for another tall boy. Jack could have caught a case. Who knew? He'd drink another beer then go home and call him tomorrow.

Kasper saw Jack coming from the men's room, and the detective looked beat.

"Hey, Bergman, how ya been?"

Before Kasper got one word out of his mouth, Jack got Grady's attention at the bar. "Grady, two boilermakers, please. Sorry, Bergman, how are ya?"

"Uh, I'm not gonna drink a boilermaker, that's how I am, sir, uh, Jack."

"Not for you, kid. Damn, sorry, I mean, Kasper. Boilermakers are for me. I had a long day."

Grady Quinn sat two shots of whiskey and two Heinekens down. Grady slapped Jack on the back.

"Another rough day was it, eh?" It was a rhetorical question and Grady shuffled away, not waiting for Jack's reply.

One Jim Beam down and the first Heineken chugged, Jack began sipping his second bourbon shot, alternating it with his beer.

"You find anything yet on our phantom man, McCready?"

"Your person, this fella, has never existed. There were a few Owen McCreadys. Not the one we're looking for. I dug deeper. Hope you don't mind. I took a peek at the files and—"

"How did you take a peek? I never gave you the file, and the DEA has the original files. We—"

"Christ Almighty, Jack," Kasper cut in on him with an attitude. "You're not the only one who can make friends. I assume you still see me as a damn kid. Man, I have resources too. Besides, when I get to Quantico, if I stick to working with you, I'll have more friends than I need."

In a pub with a few patrons at the bar and tables, Jack got everyone's attention when the sound of his booming laughter reverberated, bouncing off the walls. He ignored the looks, shot the rest of his second whiskey, drained his beer, and looked at the kid.

"Huh, I see, Bergman, you're full of surprises. You might damn well make an excellent FBI agent one day. Okay, keep going, what else?"

"I dug into the cigarette shop, Smokin' Hot. It's owned by a shell corporation."

"A shell corporation, huh? Impressive, Kasper. It's more than I knew yesterday. And this crap about McCready not existing solves one issue and brings another into play."

"How do you figure the man not existing solves anything?" Jack's statement perplexed Kasper.

"Now we can stop looking for a man called Owen McCready. The guy I talked to in the hospital beat to hell *is* a flesh-and-blood person. I need his name. Let's keep digging. When you have time, dig deeper into this shell company. See if it is linked to Sea Star or any other business near the Magic Market. Remember this is cloak-and-dagger? Got it?"

"Damn it, Jack, you already told me and you don't hafta remind me every time we talk. You either trust me or you don't."

"Yep, you're right. You're a grown man and a professional, and yes, Bergman, I do. Meet me here again at the end of next week, same time, unless I text you otherwise."

Jack lifted his palm to get Grady's attention and held up one finger for another boilermaker, pointing to the empty shot glass and the empty Heineken bottle.

"You got it, Jack, right after I change this keg."

Jack turned his attention back to Kasper. "If you get an idea or a feeling, follow it, research or dig because I expect you to dive in and follow your hunches, got it?"

"Sure, Jack, I can work without calling or texting you every five minutes. I'm a big boy."

Jack reached into his pants pocket and pulled out a thumb drive. "Take this and run them through the facial recognition database. Once you've got something call me."

Kasper took the drive, scooted his chair back, stood, then looked at Jack, who'd anchored himself to his seat with plans on drinking more, and alone.

"Hey, uh, Jack, don't wanna piss you off, but I want to discuss something personal."

"Yeah, what is it?"

"I've noticed you drink those boilermakers every time we meet, and you tell Grady you've had a rough day. Is that your excuse for your drinking—your rough and long days?"

"Look, Bergman, mind you're ow—"

The kid held up his hand. "Yeah, yeah, I should mind my business. I got it. The deal is we're working off-book on something with potential danger, and I, for one, need you to keep a damn clear head."

Kasper was no longer the scaredy-cat nerd. He glowered. Jack liked it. The kid admonishing him—ballsy.

"Point taken, Bergman. You're right." Jack waved at the bar, calling out, "Grady, cancel the boilermaker, get me a strong cup of coffee instead, would'ja'?"

"You want Irish coffee, Jack?"

"No, give me a cup of dark strong Columbian coffee. Hold the cream, sugar, and alcohol. Need to keep a clearer head." Jack's eyes met Kasper's in a stare.

"Yeppers, a cup of head-clearing drink on its way to ya, pronto."

Jack squared his shoulders placing his hands flat on the pub table, whilst never taking his eyes off Bergman.

"Kid, and don't get your jockey shorts out of whack for me calling you kid. You have a sensible head on your shoulders, and I admire your spunk. You're right, I have to keep a clear head." Jack coughed and cleared his throat. "Been a considerable amount of shit I've dealt with in the last eighteen months and it's consumed me. I can't change what's happened, and as hard as it may be, it's time to move on."

"Sure, Jack...I mean...I can't relate to what you've been through. I can only imagine. I pray I never deal with anything like that."

"Yeah, for your sake I hope you never do."

"As far as our future, Jack, I hope we don't get burned for working this case, because if we do, we both may drink the rest of our lives away."

Jack put his hand out. "Alright, it's a deal. If we get burned, we'll sink together in the bottle."

7

The phone rang, and he yanked it up. "West, Homicide. Be right there." He rapped on the doorframe. "Captain?"

"Jack, come in, have a seat."

He took a seat across from her desk and waited.

"Things good, Jack? Anything you want to discuss with me?" Captain Justice leaned back, her elbow on the armrests.

"Depends on what you mean by things. If you mean how I'm doing, I'm great, getting on with my life day by day. If you are talking about the assignments you have Reed and me working on, we're moving at a slow rate, but we're moving."

She moved her upper body forward, resting her forearms on the edge of the desk, never taking her eyes off his, and frowned before speaking.

"Jack, I heard through the grapevine you've been asking around about the Asian gangs who hang out at Magic Market."

"Look, Cap, I—"

"Let me finish," she stopped him mid-sentence. "This case is off-limits to you."

"I'm not working the case, Captain, just reviewing. It's important to stay informed since we get gang-related homicides," he lied.

"Great. Happy to see you're keeping yourself informed, and out of stuff you need not be working on. I'm glad you're cognizant of our expectations."

Jack stood. "Captain, I am very aware of what everyone expects of me."

He locked eyes with her and saw what she could not voice aloud: *Jack, dive in and work this case.* They'd said the DEA was all over it. Why would he need to keep working it?

"Is there anything else?"

"No, not right now. Jack, watch your six. Lots going on these days, and no one at HPD wants to step on government toes. Got it?"

Jack's jaw muscle flexed, he clamped his teeth, and anger boiled below the surface of his skin. "Yeah, don't want to piss anyone off, specifically anyone in a government agency." His fingers clutched the doorknob.

"Jack, close the door, will you?"

He wanted to bang it shut, but he checked his temper. He left, closing her door without a sound.

As he stomped through the corridor, his boots slapping the carpet with more force than necessary, his annoyance doubled. Everybody was telling him to back off the case but did not mean it. Oh, their lips forced the words out, but the words didn't mean a thing. However, the eye movements, head twitches, nods, and microscopic jerks all suggested, *Jack, do not listen to my lips, read my face, work the damn case on the down-low.* Shit!

The new message was, "watch your six." Lawmen stuck together, he figured, 90 percent of the time. The other 10 percent were men with badges who could wipe out your career or land you in jail. Trustworthy boys in blue protected each other. Would these fellas have his six when it came tumbling down?

Jack didn't know Roni Justice very well, not yet. But his gut told him she was a straight shooter and an honest cop. If her instincts said he needed to watch his six, so did Kasper, and between the two of them, they needed to ensure they didn't get sabotaged, ruined, or worse, dead.

"Jack," Reed started when he got back. "I've got a list to give Flossie so she can pull the case files we've been assigned to check into. I want to—" he stopped.

Absentmindedly, Jack grabbed a stack of three-ring binders off the edge of his desk, dropped them into the box on the floor, then plunked the lid on top. His thoughts were on her statement: *"Watch your back,"* not paying attention or listening to Reed. Jack's brow wrinkled, and he shoved his chair under the desk with a tad too much force.

Reed rattled a box of paper clips. "Jack, hey, zombie, what's up? Who pissed you off?"

"I need coffee, Reed. You want a cup?"

"No, I told you I'm heading over to the file clerk's room to give Flossie a list of case file dates. Geeze, Jack, open your ears."

"Sorry, Reed. Yeah, get the files. I'll be back. I'm going to make fresh coffee. I need a jolt."

To ease the tension in his shoulders, Jack stretched his arms outward and rested his elbows on the counter, waiting for the coffee to brew. He wanted to sit on Sea Star Coaches tonight. But he also had to rest, both physically and mentally. Damn it, he wished he could clone himself. His tenacity took a toll since day one back at work, driving himself. Could this be his plan, his way to self-destruct, or did he see an end goal working 24/7? There was no time for self-analysis. He sat his coffee down, tossed his cell and keys on the desk, and had just plopped down in the chair when his phone rang. Great timing.

"West, Homicide."

"It's Kasper. Listen, when can we meet?"

"We're meeting Friday. What's up?"

"Need to meet sooner."

"I'm guessing you ID'd the men in the photos."

"Jack, these two are bad news." Kasper reeled off the names and Jack jotted them down.

"Quinn's. Does 6:30 work for you, Bergman?"

"Yeah, see ya then."

Kasper hung the phone up. What had he gotten himself into? How dangerous would this become?

REED BANGED THE DOOR OPEN. "Jack, Flossie will bring us case file folders in the morning. I ran into Xi and Jace in the garage."

"Yeah, what's up with them?"

"They're headed to Piney Points. Robbery's working high-dollar robberies and they're shorthanded. A few fellas are out on sick leave and vacation. Captain Thompson called Roni for help, so she volunteered them. Walt Thompson is an upstanding guy. The Department got lucky with him. "

"Yeah, glad Brooks didn't run him off when the fat bastard was training him." Discussing Brooks invoked a bad aura, and Jack shook it off. He would not let Brooks control his emotions.

"Penny and Craig like Thompson. The robbery division says nice things about the man. There's also a new dick in their department too. Have you met him yet?"

"No one told me about a new guy. Who is he? Where's he from?" Jack reached for his coffee, kicking a booted foot on top of his desk, leaning back.

"Mahir Chawla, North Carolina, the Greensboro area. They say he has a super-smart wife who's overseeing the Computer and Information Science Department at U of H."

"Oh, yeah, was he in Robbery out there?"

"No, Missing Persons and cold cases. Worked a lot with their homicide department once the missing persons cases became homicides."

"Huh—Houston has a surplus of missing persons cases, and I'd venture a guess to say 75 percent of those land in our lap." Jack drank his lukewarm coffee and emptied his cup.

"Sounds about right, I'd guess. Lots of people didn't go missing on purpose." Reed began check-marking case numbers by dates to have CSU and autopsy files pulled. "I haven't met Mahir yet, but our paths will cross soon enough. Jack, you ever want to work in another department besides Homicide?"

Jack stretched out his arms, rolling his chair back. "Nope, always knew I'd be in Homicide. Homicide is like Missing Persons.

"How so?"

"We have a corpse, and the killer is missing, so we are, in fact, hunting a missing person."

"Damn if I can come up with a smart-ass remark to your reasoning. In fairness, what you've said is true, in a sick, twisted way." Reed looked at the clipboard. "Here's the list to prove Homicide has its own missing persons files. Too bad this many killers are missing."

"Yeah, be nice to shorten the list, and it works on the same principles as the Missing Persons Department files—some people go missing forever and several killers elude the law forever." Jack paused a beat. "Neither is fair, and the reality of it sucks."

8

Kasper Bergman had a seat at the back watching the front door; his anxiety went in every direction, circling him. The two thugs he looked into were bad news. He squeezed his eyes shut, inhaling, doing an eight-minute yoga exercise to calm himself. Situations as an FBI agent would be more dangerous. He needed to get a grip. Kasper exhaled and reopened his eyes in time to see Jack walk in.

"Grady, one tall boy, please, Miller Light." Jack knocked on the bar on his way to the backside of the pub.

"You got it, Jack."

He eyed the kid. "I'm not drinking a boilermaker, just beer. It's been a long day."

"I'm not your mother."

"Yeah, yeah, just don't want another scolding from you."

Tall boy in hand, Jack took a healthy swig. He set his mug down, wiped his upper lip, and looked at Kasper's attaché case. "You brought files?"

"Nah, just some stuff Art has me researching, so I'm taking it home. About those two men…they're part of a bigger organization. I—"

"I know. When you gave me their names, I looked into them. They have criminal records, drug distribution, linked to racketeering, money laundering, and even potential murder, but never charged, always conjecture. No solid proof. These two are goons for hire."

"Jack, these men are associated with the Lobos Cartel."

"Yep, I know. What did you find on the shell corporation? Who owns Smokin' Hot?"

"Not much, but I'm still digging. The cigarette shop was doing business alright, but not legitimately. McCready told you he owned it, but I couldn't find anything in the county tax assessor's files with his name. The only name is the shop's. And here is another interesting tidbit: Smokin' Hot has no tobacco licensure. The CDC controls over-the-counter cigarette sales, vending machines, the whole shebang; licenses are required and displayed in the store."

"Did you consider checking into the BBB?" Jack drained his beer.

"Yep, and nope, nothing reported. I checked into things concerning cigarette shops and owning one. I knew there were regulations. First, either you need a license—local, state, or federal depending on location. In Texas, you get a permit for sales through the State Comptroller. His shop has no permit, not even an expired permit. Now there's a catch, though, and it involves the Feds."

Jack signaled Grady for two beers, pointing to himself and Kasper. "Beer on me tonight. Now, you were saying…"

"I searched the listed database of active cigarette and tobacco retailers and Smokin' Hot is not on the list. They require every retailer who sells smokes to report the total amount of products sold via federal record-keeping. The laws state if any shop sells over ten thousand cigarettes a month, they report it to the Feds. I can't find any reports, but him owning the place for five years, he's sold over ten thousand. A higher number of smokers develop in lower-income neighborhoods, and we're not talking just cigarette smokers."

Neighborhoods with a lower socioeconomic status bred a higher percentage of smokers, and there was no arguing with statistics.

"Uh-huh, it's a ton of smokes over five years. So what else you got, Bergman?"

"If he's not reporting his sales, then it stands to reason he ain't reporting his federal excise taxes either. I can't see how he's getting away with this."

"Hmmm," Jack mused, as he pondered an idea for a second.

"Jack, what does hmmm mean?" Kasper emptied his beer mug in one long swallow.

"It means several things. What if McCready's involved in contraband cigarette trafficking?" Jack slouched with one arm draped over his chair, his eyes locking on the empty beer mug. He let the idea roll around in his head.

The kid was quiet. A movie played inside his brain. However, this was a what-if it-went-south movie. Kasper didn't care for how the movie might end.

Jack's fingers stopped. "Nah, can't be it. It's a billion-dollar industry, but it's more, much more. You get the same feeling, kid?"

Kasper let the kid thing pass. "Yeah, Jack, I do, a lot more, but shit, Jack, five years' worth of excise taxes to pay would be very pricey. We know the government is not forgiving. The interest alone would bury him, and they could also bury him in a federal penitentiary for life and the afterlife."

"Ain't no doubt the Feds would have him by the short hairs. Maybe he's working with Feds on the take. Anything is possible. We need to find the guy, only it's like he's never existed. So, what else we got?" Jack grabbed his mug, relaxing into his chair, giving Kasper the floor.

"I got to wondering about the physical building. McCready, or whoever, might have owned the inventory but didn't own the building. I'm looking for the owner or whoever handles the leases, but no luck. I called the leasing number, got voice mail. Left a message, but no one's called back."

"Don't beat yourself up looking, kid...uh, Kasper."

"Hey, I need to vamoose. Got personal crap to do." Kasper glanced at the time on his phone.

"Sure, I'll be in contact. If you get anything important, call me."

"Will do." With a wave, Kasper left Jack finishing his beer.

A can of chili with no crackers and he was outta beer. Going home didn't sound appealing. Conversation with Grady and a club sandwich was more inviting. Jack moved to sit at the bar. He ordered a beer and food, settling in for a while.

It was 11:00 when he got home. He'd nursed his third beer and ordered a second helping of fries, chatting with Grady in-between the old man's customers. He wanted out from underneath this state of feeling lost and lonely. It was now nearing the two-year mark of Gretchen's murder. He knew it was time to move on. Gretchen was gone. She'd have wanted him to move on with his life. Currently, he lived for one singular thing: the job. Deep down, he wanted more. Jack needed a life, or perhaps he needed simple excitement.

IT WAS EARLY. No one was in the division room. Perfect. Jack needed private time to research. He entered "Lobos Cartel" into the criminal database. Next, he typed in "known associates, dead or alive."

The screen populated and he scrolled through each page, finding dead, incarcerated, and living associates. Dead cartel members, which included a vast number of gang members, buried and gone, or just gone without a trace. What a shame. Half of the associates were mere boys. Young men who lost their lives for what? To join gangs or become criminals. Was it their lifelong ambition as a six-year-old? Everyone knew the two reasons you became a criminal: money and power. Whoever had the money had the power. Dying at any age for a gang wasn't acceptable. However, these young kids died daily for this cause.

Jack jotted down a few names, then added the two men he saw at Sea Star, Tweedle Dee and Dum. He let out an exasperated groan. He'd have to keep digging, layer by layer, but how deep? When was he going to have time? He was splitting himself in three different directions, on the verge of a fourth.

THE AFTERNOON WAS SLOW.

"Man, this is boring. Not catching a fresh case...crap, this is Houston, for crying out loud. Squad room feels like a ghost town." Reed propped his elbows on the desk and set his face down in his hands.

Jack lounged back in his chair, and his eyes scanned the room with a one-word response, "Yep."

He might want a fresh murder case because this was his job. However, he did not want someone to die so he could do his job. Crazy irony.

The squeaky door sounded and with it, Captain Justice strolled in.

"You two look snowed under." They looked outright bored. However, she was going to change that for one of them.

"Reed, head out to this address. Two bodies found. Luck and Webb are already on the scene. I want you to assist."

"Sure, Cap, I'm on it. See ya, Jack."

Reed signed out on the board and left, eager to vacate the dull squad room.

Who wouldn't be excited? Filtering through ancient cases to find out when it was last worked, re-reading all notes, the autopsy reports, and the findings from the CSU sweep. Not exciting. This was all a one-man job. And if you got a new lead, you still had paperwork. Paperwork was Jack's least favorite job. The cold case unit had been shorthanded for over a year, and the active homicide squad rotated to help. Jack had been on cold case duty for more than his share, but he didn't complain. Without this covert mission, he'd be pissed off if he had to sit out on a fresh case.

After Reed had vamoosed, Roni rolled out Severson's chair and sat catty-corner from Jack's desk.

"How's it coming?"

"We're through the oldest cold cases and have them checked for last date revisited. We've pulled the evidence boxes and put them in the que ready for whoever they're assigned to."

"Find any problems?"

Jack arched an eyebrow. Roni was making small talk. Why didn't she discuss the weather with him instead?

"Nothing major so far. Main one is misfiling and we've been reorganizing each book we've found. Some of the oldest cases are lacking in the reports department with half-finished paperwork."

"You and Reed, ya'll coordinate with the morgue for reports?"

"Yes, Bennie has a list. Mack is supervising the pull, in-between current dead bodies on their slabs."

"Have you—"

"Yes, we have, Roni. We've done this before, you know. Crud, for the umpteenth time in the past few months, you've assigned me to cold cases. What gives?"

"Nothing, Jack. Are you busy enough or are you bored?"

His gaze intensified as he tried to read her. What was her deal? "Yes, I'm busy enough and no, I'm not bored."

"Giving you time, Jack, without being under pressure on a new homicide. Take it slow, just day by day."

Being back on the job seven months, he hadn't taken the lead on any investigation. All he'd done was assist with three cases. Then he was assigned cold case duty—again. He didn't mind since it freed him up. It was a futile wish, but still he hoped for the call to come in.

Captain Justice wasn't sure what his silence meant. Was he unhappy, pissed off, what?

"Jack, are you—"

"Cap, I'm sorry to interrupt you. I've been back to work for seven months. Just what do you mean by this take-it-slow stuff? Geeze, Roni, how slow do you mean? I'm already standing still, so still my joints froze. Whatever assignment you give me is fine. And no, I'm not wishing for a murder to crop up, but it is my job. If I'm needed, tell me." His head was on straight. If she needed him, he wanted to make sure she saw him as capable and ready.

"Jack, I understand. I didn't mean...whatever, just never mind what you thought I meant. You've done great, and I don't doubt your ability to do the job, or your emotional state. There are things I cannot discuss or disclose. It's best you continue with what you're doing. Understand what I'm saying?" Her mouth voiced one thing, yet her face communicated another story.

Jack's eyes bore into hers. Captain Veronica Justice, her face firm, her lips in a flat line, stared back. It was a very miniscule movement, but her head tilted a fraction, her snappy amber-colored eyes narrowed, and she inhaled and held it in for a beat of two seconds before exhaling. How one person conveyed a message to another with a mere look was uncanny. The way one's eyes narrow with a definite stare, or a split-second movement of one's head, with flat pinched lines of the lips and a simple inhale and exhale—it boggles the mind.

Jack nodded. "No worries, Roni. I get what you're saying." He could have also said, *Yep, I hear what you're not saying, Cap.*

A grin tugged at her lips. "Tell me how you do that."

"Do what?" He feigned ignorance.

She winked. "Gonna let you continue cataloging cold cases."

Jack stared at the closed door. Alone in the room, he scanned the area from one wall to the other and slumped back, rocking his chair. He didn't understand how he knew what someone was saying when they didn't speak one word, he just did it—this was his superpower.

9

Ten till nine, daylight faded. Jack grabbed his binoculars. *Crime and the evil men do when the sun goes down,* he thought, shaking his head, bringing the binoculars up to his eyes.

The first returning bus let off nineteen female passengers, all of them talking nonstop. Jack wondered who was listening to whom or if they were listening at all.

His slow night dragged. Out of water, out of chips, Jack's neck and back ached, and he was ready to leave. With his key in the ignition, he stopped, not firing up the engine when another busload pulled in. Jack grabbed the binoculars and saw the Tweedle boys walk out with another man. "Joven Cazalla, damn."

Aha, this just got more interesting. Jack heard word on the streets Cazalla was no longer just a soldier; he'd made Captain or something higher.

He laid the binoculars in his lap. He ran through a probable chain of command. Callum and Mundy, his Tweedle boys, followed Boyce Carter's orders. So did Carter follow orders from Cazalla? Was Cazalla following Omar Villa Lobos' orders?

Cartels were vast organizations, with one top boss, commanders, lieutenants, hit men, soldiers, filtering to the bottom with pissants whom they called polleros—the chickens. Most were disgraced ex-convicts trying to work their way back in, men who dealt in drug smuggling, human trafficking, murder-for-hire, and expendable employees.

The crucial question was, how did this tie into his homicide case? He understood the DEA and the OAG going after the cartel. What he didn't understand was why order him to stand down?

Was the link to his and the DEA's case Boyce Carter because he was involved with drugs? There were no implications linking Jamere Carter to the cartel, only his association with the Dragons. How much deeper was Boyce Carter involved? He was associating with the likes of Joven Cazalla, who was connected to the cartel, and the cartel equaled drugs. Factor in drugs equaled gangs, which equaled running drugs—your basic cannot-have-one-without-the-other type businesses.

Jack's fingers drummed a steady beat on the armrest and he wondered if his case involved the cartel.

Was Boyce Carter connected to his son's murder and the Lobos Cartel, or was he a gang shot-caller? Gang affiliations were tight. Everybody said Jamere was not involved in a gang. Was it a lie? Was Boyce part of a gang, and his deceased son the member of a rival gang? His father had no rap sheet, at least not as an adult; however, it didn't mean Boyce Carter was spotless.

Jack needed to dig deeper and find out more about Boyce Carter and this nameless man.

"Reed." Jack yawned, stretching. "Lucky and Webb kick you to the curb?"

"No. I'm working on search warrants and witness reports. Lucky said Webb sucks at paperwork. Besides, I think Roni wants Luck to keep eyes on old Spider Webb. Yesterday at the scene he was acting sorta weird..." Reed kept talking, and Jack's mind went elsewhere, not hearing a single word.

What he knew was diddly shit. Boyce Carter, Joven Cazalla, and the two gomers he called Tweedle Dee and Tweedle Dum, Louis Callum and Carl Mundy—none of these men were anywhere near squeaky clean. Boyce Edward Carter had a sealed juvie record and nothing after he reached the age of adulthood. He wasn't clean; they just hadn't caught him. Jack wanted to see the sealed records, however, this was a problem. Sealed records nowadays would be easier for Kasper to break into because current files were scanned directly into the system. Older records created another problem too, because they'd been stored on microfiche. Poor Kasper, he would pile more on the kid. But Jack had a strong suspicion the kid loved every minute of this covert mission.

Callum and Mundy. These two knuckleheads were dangerous. They appeared to be brainless muscle, but Jack knew they were not stupid. Stupid men didn't get caught. Two thugs in this line of work for several years had decent rap sheets, but neither had served long stints of jail time. One thing was certain: both unscrupulous men were top-notch at following one order—*don't get caught*. To date, they hadn't been charged with any major felony.

"...two this afternoon. Then let's get lunch at the new Hole-in-the-Wall, you game? Heard it was a terrific burger joint and I've wanted to try it out," Austin concluded, but Jack hadn't been listening.

"What, Reed? I zoned out for a sec."

"Jesus, Jack, you didn't hear a fucking word. Man, get your head in the game. I was giving you a rundown of our case. I also asked if you wanted to try the new burger place called Hole-in-the-Wall Burgers." His voice had an edge. Reed was sick of Jack's inattentiveness. It had been happening all the time, even while they worked cold case files. His being off in la-la-land was irritating.

"Listen, Reed, don't snap at me. Man, untie the knot you have your balls in, and give me a break, you asshole. You've never asked someone to repeat themselves, have you?"

Jack's short-fused temper exploded. He felt crappy as the last word left his mouth, but Reed was pushing his buttons.

Austin Reed sat, wordless. His mouth dropped open, and an air of pure shock washed over his face. Reed had never heard Jack speak this way to a fellow detective. He wondered if Dawson Luck ever had to deal with this hostile side. Was this the new Jack since Gretchen's murder? Jack had dealt with a load of shit. Austin processed this. If circumstances had been reversed, he might have cracked or drowned in the bottle.

Jack didn't move, nor speak. He watched the range of thoughts slide over Reed's face and wondered what snide retort he had to look forward to getting, and deserved.

"Hey, Jack, I'm sorry, I zone out too sometimes. I'm frustrated, that's all."

"Man, Reed, sorry I snapped. What's frustrating you?"

"I'd rather be out there with Lucky, tracking a killer and talking to witnesses, and Skip-to-my-Lou-Webb could bug the shit outta you, because I'm sick of being cooped up in the squad room."

"Yeah, I appreciate cooped up. I was there a year ago. After I... well...just after. One difference was I didn't have to shower and shave for the day. We cool, Reed?"

"Yeah, Jack, we are. Also glad you shower and shave these days."

With a solid handshake it was back to normal in a split second.

"I'M HEADED to the morgue. Lucky texted, wants me to bring the prelims. Jack, I'll bring ya back something to eat. Whatcha want, a burger?"

Jack stood and stretched. "Nah, gonna call Flossie, ask her to bring more cold case files from the list. But thanks, I'm gonna head to the lobby and get a Subway, after I make a personal phone call."

Reed gathered his phone, his keys, and straightened his desk, giving his squad room partner a side glance. Was Jack waiting for him to skedaddle to make his call? How personal was it? Was it a woman? Reed was not a blabbermouth. But hey, if Jack wanted privacy, he was gone in three.

"Later, see ya when I see ya," Reed called back. He wondered if Jack had a new girlfriend. Shit, it'd do the guy wonders to get a romp in the boudoir, if nothing else. In Austin Reed's opinion, Jack needed the tension relief, and soon.

The door's hardware clicked and Jack dialed Tech.

"Tech, Bergman."

"Bergman, Jack. You got a few minutes to talk?"

"Sure."

"You alone?"

"Yeah. The guys are at the other end of the hallway."

"Boyce Carter has a sealed juvie file, goes back over twenty. The courts scanned all older records on microfiche. I need a peek. You have anyone in Records you can sweet talk? We're working with Robbery tomorrow night."

"I thought I heard they dumped it into a computer database. I know two people I can ask. You know anybody who owes you a favor?"

Before Jack could respond, Kasper popped off with, "Hey, Art, what's up?"

"Can you call whoever you're talking to back later?"

"Sure, it's only Zoe, in Cyber Crimes. She's picking my brain."

"We need your brains in the conference room. Robbery needs to go over the assignment for tomorrow night. Walt, Penny, Gilly, and Johnson are on their way. I need you in the meeting. Be there in ten."

"Sure, Art, be there in five." Kasper gave him a thumbs-up.

Jack was a bit impressed at how easily lying came for Kasper, and this was fantastic practice for his future calling.

"Okay, Art's out of earshot."

"Can you get into another state's criminal database?"

"Another state's criminal database, are you joking? Shit, Jack, my list is getting long."

"I need you to search for McCready—"

"You're asking me to do a state-to-state search for him? It's crazy, not to mention time-consuming. I...man, shit, this is insane. He doesn't even have a social. Having a social is not a state-to-state thing. Hell, Jack, I'm no miracle worker...and also—"

Jack let the kid rant for a few seconds. Hell, the FBI would expect ten times more, so if he couldn't handle this, he should just wave good-bye to the FBI before he even said hello.

He waited, Kasper's rant slowed to a weak grumbling and he took a breath.

"I'll see what I can find, Jack. I ain't promising anything, but I'll do the best I can."

"Just keep trying. Meet me Friday, the Waffle House off Sam Houston Parkway, 6:00 a.m."

"Yeah, sure, Friday, Waffle House at 6:00. Hey, got a question for you, Jack."

"Make it quick, kid. I gotta get off here before someone comes in."

"What the fuck are you doing these days since I seem to do the deep digging?"

"You wanna know what I'm doing these days?"

"Isn't that just what the fuck I asked you?" Kasper's nerves were unraveled.

"Okay, I'll tell you what I'm doing. The cold case unit is shorthanded, so I'm working cold cases, now ain't that fun? Cap has me looking at all the written notes, most recent leads, and people they questioned. I'm digging on our case too, when eyes aren't looking over my shoulder. Then at nightfall, I don my red cape and mask, staking out Sea Star Coaches looking for bad guys. Anything else you want to know?"

Jack's smart-alecky attitude agitated Kasper.

"I see. Glad you're active, you asshole."

"Happy you approve, kid. Look, I gotta get."

"Hey, uh, not joking, Jack, watch your six."

"I will. You do the same, Bergman."

10

"Order up," the fry cook called out, followed by a server who blared out a new order. "Pull one—bacon—drop two hash browns, in rings, mark order triple scrambled, one waffle."

Jack rather enjoyed the commotion and energy in Waffle House, dishes clanking, griddles sizzling, the women servers with gruff, gravelly voices barking out the orders in "Waffle House Speak."

"You ready to order?" The woman sat a simple napkin, fork, and knife over the half-wall partition between the booth and cooking area.

"Just coffee. I'm waiting for someone, thanks."

"You got it." She scurried off to get the coffee. On her way, another customer who needed more ketchup stopped her. She grabbed him a bottle, then headed to the coffee urn.

Someone had put a dollar's worth of quarters in the jukebox and the voice of Neil Diamond filled the air as he sang, "Forever in Blue Jeans." Jack's foot tapped along with the beat. His mind zoned in on the lyrics, his eyes fixated on the Formica table, bobbing his head to the music. Kasper slid in across from him breaking his musical journey trance.

"Jack, you order yet?" Kasper waved at the server.

Jack roused from his hypnotic state as the song faded, replaced by a rapper song, which was not his music of choice.

"No, was waiting on you."

In a mere second, his server reappeared, filling his coffee cup. The older woman whipped out her pencil and pad, looking them over. "You fellas ready to order?"

Orders in, Jack began.

"Have you had time to research the strip mall and the property?

"The strip mall, CCB, Incorporated, owns the physical buildings with a property manager who collects rent and takes care of general crap. Three partners: Nate Conover, he lives here in Houston; Bill Conover, Nate's father, is in Boston; and Luke Briggs, Bill Conover's nephew, lives in Dallas. I'm guessing Conover-Conover-Briggs is the CC and B, in CCB."

"Double plate, crispy bacon, grits." The server sat Jack's plate down. "Scrambled, scattered, smothered, crispy bacon and one waffle." She laid Bergman's plate down, refilled both cups with fresh coffee, wiped her hands with a striped dish towel, and looked them over. "How does everything look?"

"Looks great, miss. Thanks." Kasper took a bite of his eggs and grabbed the salt shaker.

She looked at Jack. "Holler if ya need more coffee."

Their waitress walked to the end booth to begin the clean-up where three toddlers had wreaked havoc for the past hour.

They ate in silence for a few minutes. After one last bite of extra crispy bacon, Kasper started again.

"I did background checks on CCB. The Conovers have the usual traffic tickets, parking and speeding, and the son has a juvie record—petty thefts, truancy, and one drunk disorderly charge, not much else. His old man, Bill, did a nickel upstate for robbery in Massachusetts in his late twenties, and he's had more than the occasional run-ins with the law. He has an excellent lawyer who's kept him from going to jail, always finding a loophole. His nephew, Luke Briggs, is trouble with capital T. The guy has a thick juvie record. As an adult, they sentenced the douche to a five-year stint for aggravated robbery. He got out in two. Then went back to jail for aggravated assault two years later, the dumbass. The guy did the two, then stayed clean for an entire year until he got pinched for running drugs. He beat the rap. The douche had an exceptional lawyer who got him off on a minor technicality. He'd have been a lifer if he'd been convicted with the three-strikes rule. Guy's a career scum-bucket."

"Sounds like you don't care for him."

"I hope he keeps his sorry ass in Dallas."

Jack pushed his plate and empty coffee cup to the side. The server laid two receipts facedown. He took them.

"I've got this, Bergman. So, this Bill Conover in Boston has me curious. McCready said he was from Boston. But everything about our elusive McCready has been a fabrication."

"I'll dig into the Boston Conover and see if anything pops when I tap into the database, but something tells me we won't find a connection."

"Fine, if we get nothing, then we get nothing."

Kasper drank the dregs of his warm coffee. "You headed into the station from here?"

"I took the day off. I'll do recon work over near the Magic Market, see what's what."

"Be careful, Jack. That neighborhood knows you're a cop."

"Yeah, but I hope to be a man unobserved today." Jack stood with both tickets in hand, and Kasper followed.

They stood to the far side of the old Waffle House building.

"Which one is yours?"

"That one. Got it from Jasper at Impound. It's connected with a drug bust. I hope nobody recognizes it. It might be trouble for me if they do."

"When you return it, tell Jasper I said hello. I haven't seen him since the toy drive last Christmas. "

"Hey, I just realized something."

"Oh yeah, what's that?" Bergman took keys out of his pocket.

"You're Kasper and he's Jasper, names for twins. Be funny if ya'll get partnered up. Kasper and Jasper, sort of sounds like Heckle and Jeckle."

Kasper's brows drew down. "Heckle and Jeckle. Never heard of 'em; who are they?"

"God, kid, and don't get pissy, but you're a kid, at least to me. Google Heckle and Jeckle. They're magpies. Just Google it, check it out and you'll see." Jack muffled a laugh.

"Nah, and I bet Jasper wouldn't go for it either, we'd take a lot of ribbing. Besides, it doesn't sound like a crime-fighting duo, sounds like a vaudeville show."

"Did I say a crime-fighting duo? I meant you two are a couple of clowns."

JACK DROVE to the gym where he had a membership, but never frequented, to change into a pair of faded jeans, a worn-out black Houston Texas T-shirt, scuffed older running shoes, and plain black ball cap. He zipped up the unlined charcoal-colored windbreaker he wore halfway to conceal his shoulder holster. In the front zipper pockets, he carried extra magazines, and he had a small 25-caliber Kimber strapped to his ankle. He closed his locker, wondering why he paid for a membership when there was a gym and locker at the precinct. *For times like this, you dope*, he thought to himself. If he went to the HPD gym, people he knew would see him and ask questions. Membership fees were a small price to pay for anonymity.

He got into the four-door 1998 dark blue Chevy Malibu and turned the key. Jasper was a true-blue sorta fellow, and Jack could count on him to keep mum. Jack revved the engine and his insides tingled. A V-6 with modifications made this a great ride. It was too bad the previous owner was in lockup at Huntsville Penitentiary for drug trafficking and aggravated assault. Jack put the car in drive and headed to the Third Ward.

He assessed the area, circling the block one more time before turning into a parking lot of work trucks and employee cars. City employees were everywhere, working on streets and other jobs. Men mowed the grass and blew loose clippings all over the place, spreading it about. Houston always had a street in repair or disrepair.

Magic Market was a short six blocks, so he slapped on his cap, pulled the bill low, and got out of the car. He hoped to blend in. No matter his attire, everyone knew he was a cop. Was it his face? Could it be his mannerisms? Who knew? He would keep his head down, slump, walk slow, not bring any attention to himself, he would act like a sloth—it might work, he hoped.

It was 9:15, the shops were open. He people-watched as he walked the first four city blocks. The public thought shit happened as darkness fell—what a misconception folks had concerning crime. Everyone assumed at nighttime criminals got out of bed to go to work —ha! One thing Jack knew was criminals worked 24/7—no sick days, no holidays, and for damn certain no two-week vacations. Each department at HPD could verify this as fact.

At the end of the sidewalk by the run-down apartments across from the shopping center, he stopped at the city bus stop. The area was littered and the old wooden bench was covered in spray-paint tags. Two men stood nearby looking down at their phone screens oblivious to anything else while two full-figured women occupied the bench, leaving enough room for an anorexic toothpick to sit between them. These hefty women were testing the tensile strength of the old wood, and he heard cracking and snapping noises as they shifted in their seats. The city needed to replace these kinds of benches. Metal benches would be a sight better and stronger. He strolled along the sidewalk past the bus stop, pulling the bill of his cap lower to avoid eye-to-eye contact with any passersby.

Jack crossed the street, strolled past the ratty apartment complex, and headed for the strip center. The pawnshop on the corner was open for business. He did a quick run-through to find it was your regular not-so-clean pawnshop with a fat owner named Walt Burch who wore a ZZ Top T-shirt. Pawnshops meant a lot of things. Money laundering came to mind.

Two empty units stood between the pawnshop and dry cleaners and next was a general store. The liquor store opened in another hour. Jack stopped in front of Smokin' Hot and tugged at the doors—locked. A *Closed for Business* sign hung in the front window. He stuck his face to the window to peek through the dirty glass, noting stock was still on the shelves. It looked as if nothing had changed. He skipped a visit to the strip center's anchor store, Magic Market. Instead he strolled to the alleyway, scanning the area, looking to see if anyone was watching him. Good. No one, not one person gave a rat's hind-end where he was going or what he was doing.

He walked to the back exit of Smokin' Hot and turned the doorknob. Locked. Had he envisioned it would open by magic? He stared down at the knobs. It wasn't odd they were empty, who'd want to set up shop here? What surprised him was a cannabis store hadn't popped up, but then again, why would they need one if they had free-flowing marijuana?

Frustrated, he stuck his hands in his windbreaker pockets, rounded the corner and headed to his car. He crossed the street and walked along the sidewalk. One last glance over his left shoulder at the shopping center, and Jack stopped dead in his tracks. A man by the front door of Smokin' Hot was talking to the fat ZZ-Top T-shirt-wearing pawnshop owner—Owen effing McCready—what the hell!

11

Jack's adrenaline pumped in triple time as he picked up his pace to a fast walk then a slow jog, trying not to attract attention. He was in his car and on the road in fewer than five minutes. Four blocks down, he pulled into the apartment's parking lot. Jack let out the breath he had been holding, relieved to see McCready. The man was still talking to the fat pawnshop owner.

The pawnshop owner's flabby arms were crossed and resting on his protuberant belly, his face twisted as he spoke. In a causal stance, McCready was leaning against the brick wall, listening. In 0 to 60, there was an abrupt change. The Irish cigarette man morphed into a badass. He straightened to his full height, poking the fat man in the chest, emphasizing something he said. Finished and irritated, McCready left the fat pawnshop owner standing alone with an incredulous expression on his face.

In the parking lot, he strolled over to a beat-up 1980 Ford Ranger single-cab truck, hopped in, and drove out the north end of the lot. Jack followed. Six blocks in, McCready stopped at a light, flipped his right blinker on, and pulled into a gas station. Jack watched him set the pump on automatic and then drop on his haunches, looking at his left rear tire, checking for something, a nail or a screw in the rubber. The wind blew and the shirt Owen wore billowed out, exposing a gun tucked into the back waistband of his jeans. Shit, the man was packing! Guess he felt safer with a gun since he got the holy shit beat outta him, or was he involved in something criminal? Tons of variables ran through Jack's head.

Back in the truck, McCready changed his course from north to south. In his rearview, he saw the Malibu as it followed him onto the feeder road then to the on-ramp. With a smirk on his face, McCready hit the Beltway full throttle once he had merged into the oncoming traffic. His blinker on, he headed to the State Highway 225 exit, punched the gas again (now over the speed limit), and watched the Chevy Malibu behind him in his rearview. He smiled as he motored along the La Port Freeway, glancing in his rearview to make sure the detective was keeping up.

JACK WATCHED the blue Ford truck move to the far right, and he moved with him as the truck made the right curve leading to SH-146. They drove another mile, and McCready turned left on East Barbours Cut Boulevard. Jack knew the area. They were near the Galveston Bay, which fed into the Gulf.

McCready turned into a large container yard. Jack passed him and drove a quarter mile, turned, and came back. As he eased into a left turn, he saw the blue Ford sitting near the main office. Jack parked next to an empty construction trailer, got out of his wagon, and stood peering past the corner to see.

McCready stood at the front of his truck shaking hands with Joven Cazalla. Jack cursed under his breath. "What the fuck, McCready? Cazalla probably ordered your beating—what's going on?"

Zooming in as close as his phone would let him he clicked a few pictures. Two more men showed up: Louis Callum and Carl Mundy.

This connected them to Boyce Carter. So McCready, how did he fit into the mix? The men disappeared through a side door.

"Fuck," Jack swore again.

Ten minutes later he saw McCready exit the main door. Three minutes later Cazalla came out walking a fast pace to catch up with McCready.

The Irish cigarette man knew Jack was nearby, watching his every move. Cazalla hollered to McCready to wait and Jack saw him turn around. Joven got close enough to McCready, and they were toe-to-toe and nose-to-nose. Whatever he said to Cazalla must have pissed him off, because he poked McCready's chest with force. McCready swatted it away, pushing Cazalla back.

Joven Cazalla stepped back up, his fists at the ready, his chest thrust forward in anger.

He waited for Cazalla to belt McCready in the schnozzola. Nothing happened, and this took him by surprise. Cazalla's fists stayed in tight balls against his sides, and Owen said something to him, causing him to step back. They squared off, staring at each other. Cazalla responded with a curt nod, then turned and walked away. McCready waited, watching Cazalla disappear inside. Jack was unsure of everything now. Was Owen McCready a victim or part of the entire setup, including the cartel?

The cigarette man got in his truck, put it in reverse, and punched the accelerator, then peeled out flinging gravel. Three minutes later, an older dark Chevy Malibu followed at a steady pace.

McCready kept glancing in his rearview mirror, watching him.

Detective Jack West—what a tenacious bulldog. All things aside, he was impressed with this detective.

He followed McCready to the Port Terminal Railroad Association outside Houston's city limits. Jack sat in the Chevy, the engine idling, and watched McCready vanish inside. Old Irish dude stayed for less than fifteen minutes, came out, and left Jack on his tail one more time.

Who did he meet with and why? Did it connect to his case? What does a Bostonian, who owns a cigarette shop, have in common with a cargo container yard near a shipping area and a railroad yard terminal? Nothing, most people would deduce. However, Jack was not most people.

Jack's phone rang. Austin Reed's name flashed and he let it go to voice mail. The dashboard clock blinked 4:02. His middle was growling, but food would have to wait. His sights were locked on a blue Ford pickup. Why was Owen McCready consorting with people who beat him? That was the million-dollar question. These people had left him for dead. He'd said he was leaving this fecking place and moving to Boston. Why hadn't he left? What a load of bullshit; Jack knew the Irish shit never really intended to leave.

The loop was murderous. Jack watched the blue truck weaving in and out of traffic, and tried to keep him in sight; however, he failed. A slowdown in the right lane had everyone moving left, including the over-the-road truck drivers hauling trailers. Big rigs were in abundance this afternoon, headed out to Interstate 45 toward Dallas/Fort Worth, or Interstate 10, headed to the San Antonio area. As the sun dropped lower, so did the light, and Jack lost the old truck in the mass chaos of weaving vehicles. The cigarette man saw the chance to exit with the cover of 18-wheelers, which blocked the dark blue Malibu driver's line of sight, and he pulled off the Beltway.

Jack cussed the drivers and Houston traffic. Constant freeway slowdowns at 5:00 in the afternoon or 2:00 in the morning, it didn't matter what time it was. His palm hit the steering wheel as he tapped his brakes once again, when several red brake lights flashed ahead of him in the turtle-moving traffic. Frustrated, he inhaled deeply then exhaled, deciding he might as well return the car to HPD's impound lot, grab dinner, and head home. The man was no longer a ghost. Owen McCready was very much alive and still in Houston.

Jack signaled to Jasper as he took the turn into the impound lot.

"Glad I caught you before you went home. Here are the keys, man. Thanks for letting me use the car; appreciate it."

"Anytime, Jack, I've got your vehicular back, as always." Jasper grinned pocketing the keys.

"Uh, and um, keep this under your hat, would ya?" Jack held his hand out.

Jasper gave him a good-ole-boy hearty handshake.

"You know me, Jack, I don't wear a hat, so it's like it never happened. No worries."

With a two-finger salute, Jack drove off.

Back on IH-225, he hit the closest Dairy Queen and ordered a Hunger Buster Meal. He was starving. While he drove, he ripped into the burger, wolfed it down with a Diet Dr. Pepper, and munched on the fries. By the time he pulled into his driveway, he had an empty cup and a squashed DQ bag. It had been a long day driving. He was beat. All he wanted was to kick off his shoes, jump into jogging shorts, turn on the radio to soft classical rock, and chill. Almost certainly nurse a few beers. Unbeknownst to him, this plan would never play out.

The wadded DQ bag in one hand, Jack fiddled with his key ring and found his house key. Thoughts of relaxing for a change filled his head. It was time to stop, breathe, and clear the mechanism for one evening.

As the tip of the key touched the lock, he stopped. Was he so tired his mind was playing tricks on him? Had he heard a noise from inside the house? He narrowed his eyes in concentration and listened. Nothing, no sounds, just him breathing. He blamed his edginess on fatigue. He unlocked and opened the door. Still holding the wadded bag, he flipped on the wall switch. A small table lamp in the hallway emitted a soft yellow glow leading into his living room. Motionless, his hand still on the doorknob, in the semi-lit hall he listened, adjusting his eyes to the low lighting. His perceptive gut said something was off-kilter. He told his gut to keep quiet, chalking it up to lack of sleep.

Jack shut the door not bothering to lock it. In the semi-darkness, he walked toward the kitchen to toss the DQ bag in the trash and grab a beer from the fridge. The hairs on his neck prickled when he glanced to his right. A shadow stood at the furthest end of the countertop on the kitchen side. Jack's right hand dropped the DQ trash, and he reached for his piece, his hand stopping short. He saw the silhouette of a gun pointing right in his face.

"Jack, you aren't fast enough to draw before I get a shot off, and at this distance ain't no way I'd miss."

He stared at the dark figure, dropping his hand still holding the Glock. Jack listened to the intruder's voice. It didn't sound familiar. He couldn't see his face.

"You have me at a disadvantage," Jack responded. "You know who I am. Who are you?"

"Slow, and I mean slow, walk backward toward your TV," the anonymous silhouette instructed, ignoring Jack's question. "Take your left hand and with two fingers, pull out the pistol you have tucked inside your back waistband, and place it on the cabinet next to your TV. Squat, unstrap your ankle piece, lay it beside your other gun, then step to your right, and sit in your recliner. You got it?"

"Yeah, I got it," he swore under his breath, "motherfucker." Jack moved his left hand steadily, taking his pistol by the butt with two fingers, holding it aloft for his faceless intruder to see, laying it on the TV cabinet. He squatted to raise the bottom of his jeans, revealing a Kimber 45. Jack unstrapped the ankle sheath, stood, and placed it next to his 9-mm Glock 22. Swear words rolled through his thoughts at how stupid he was, and he apologized to his gut who said something was wrong but he'd ignored the warning.

"I've relinquished my weapons and I'm sitting. Now, will you tell me who the hell you are? And what you want?" Jack's face pinched in anger.

The shadow was silent, creeping along the edge of the countertop to the light switch. He flipped the switch, revealing his identity.

"Yeah, I fecking will, Jack," the lilt of a Bostonian/Irish accent rang out.

He sat, eyes narrowed in anger, looking at one Owen McCready, or whoever the hell he was, in the flesh.

"Why the fuck are you here, pointing a gun at me, you bastard?" Jack was livid, wanting to leap out of his chair and beat the crap outta the man. Give him a worse beating than they'd given him that had sent him to the hospital over a year ago.

"How I found you is not important. I'm here, in your house, talking to you. Jack, we are just talking as long as you keep your cool."

"Yeah, well, since you broke into my house and were waiting for me you could'a vacuumed," Jack popped back. His rage did not diminish even with his attempt at tension-breaking humor.

It was funny. He knew Jack's anger was not a joke, so he did not laugh, but couldn't stop his lips from curling up at the corners. "I'll keep it in mind for the next time I break in."

He strode over to the sofa and perched on the arm. His eyes never left Jack's nor did he lower his weapon.

"I'm putting my gun down, and I want you to listen to me, okay?"

"Uh-huh, you put your pistol down, and what you get from me is no promises."

"Back off, Detective. Stop looking into things that don't concern you." McCready kept the revolver aimed at him. It was more than apparent how the detective was feeling. Jack was a caged animal in his own home, with a short fuse on the brink of blowing.

"You're a fool if you believe it doesn't concern me. I work homicides. Three men are dead. They beat the crap out of you. And I find you conspiring with the same assholes who ordered your beating. So again, McCready or whoever you are, tell me what you want."

"Back off before things go sideways."

"Who wants me backing off?"

"Just people, Jack, ain't gonna give you names."

McCready stood, the gun raised and aimed at the detective. He hated what he was fixing to do, but he had no choice.

With a gun pointed at his face, Jack's heart was pumping as if he had received a direct injection of Red Bull into a vein. Dying didn't scare him, but he was fucking pissed off having to die under these circumstances, at gunpoint in his home!

McCready looked down at Jack, whose hands were gripping the arms of the recliner in unadulterated hatred, his knuckles white.

He had to make it convincing, and he took two steps, letting the toes of his shoes hit against the toes of Jack's shoes, the gun still aimed at his face. His eyes on Jack, he inhaled, and with a swift fluid motion, he slammed the handle of the gun into the detective's temple. Jack's body slumped and right before it slid out of the recliner, McCready's left foot raised the footrest, and the chair reclined, taking the knocked-out detective back with it.

"Sorry, Jack, and sorry for the headache you're gonna have." With his left hand he reached into his front pocket, taking out a small folded package of white powder, labeled *B.C. fast-acting aspirin*, and dropped it on the arm of the chair. He then left behind an unconscious detective, locking the door behind him.

In his truck, he drove with his cell phone next to his ear, listening for the first ring, and then three more rings before someone picked up.

"Yeah, he's warned," McCready stated.

"Think he'll quit?" a faceless voice asked.

"No, he was mad, and he won't stop. He can't stop."

"Can't or won't—there's a difference, you know."

"Okay, he won't stop. He is driven."

"Good."

"Let me repeat orders here. I allow the man to tail me, worried about blowing cover. You want me to scare him off, but you don't want him to stop working the case. What kind of shit is this?"

"We want to find out if he is the pit bill they say he is. Can he leave it all alone, do as ordered, and stand down? The guy has been through hell personally. We needed to see if he can go the distance."

"Uh-huh, I see. Well, he was pissed as hell at someone getting the drop on him and holding him at gunpoint. Plus, he will have one major headache when he wakes up. If I ever meet up with him again, I have a feeling I'm in for it."

"Yeah, guess you'd better watch your back, with him and everything else. Now, give me an update on what's been happening with you."

The unidentified voice went straight into McCready's briefing.

12

Purple and blue with a minor gash, and a helluva headache, Jack popped another two Excedrin and reevaluated his face in the bathroom mirror. McCready was a damn bastard, if that was even his name. A man who didn't exist on paper, but he *existed.* He'd call Kasper and meet ASAP, and he needed a story to tell Reed. What sounded plausible? Shit, there wasn't very much he could tell him, and more than likely Reed had seen his share of pistol-whipped faces. He'd think of something and stick with his lie. Telling Reed the truth was another option, but not today.

Reed heard the squeak. He didn't bother to turn around.

"Jack, it better be you walking in here. Plus, you better have a flipping good reason you couldn't take my call yesterday. Reasons, oh, like you were unconscious, or you were in the throes of passion."

Austin Reed wanted him to admit being in the throes of getting some. It didn't have to be love. It could be just old-fashioned lust, which turned into sexual playtime. The man needed to move on in his personal life. Uncomplicated sex for Jack would be the prescription he needed to let off pent-up steam, and change his crappy attitude.

Huh, Jack thought, *unconscious*, well, he was, but couldn't admit it.

Jack walked by Reed's desk and Reed glimpsed his face. He saw the lump and bruises on his left temple. "God Almighty, Jack, what the heck, man?"

Jack started his lie. "I, uh, had a minor accident in my garage."

"What happened?" The concern in Reed's voice took over his prior perturbed tone.

"I was hanging new shelves in my garage and I laid the hammer on the shelf. When I squatted to pick up the power drill, I stood and hit my head on the shelf. Stupid hammer came back at me. Man, I still have a headache." It sounded lame, even to him, but he had already committed himself to this lie.

Austin squinted, trying to envision this happening. His eyes narrowed and his lips moved downward. He was having trouble seeing the playback. Why would Jack lie?

"Uh-huh, and betcha it hurt like Billy Heck. Did you get the shelves hung?"

"Yeah, it did, and crap, I'm gonna have to take 'em down. I forgot to factor parking my truck in the garage."

Austin knew he was lying, but decided not to confront him about it.

"Well, don't beat yourself in the head with another hammer taking them down. I don't think your brain could withstand another hit. You're already loony."

Austin's aim was to be comical, but his heart wasn't into it today, and once more, Jack's lips conveyed one thing and Austin's ears heard something very different. His lame story about shelves and a hammer falling was pure bullshit, but he wouldn't pry—not just yet.

"What did you call for?" Jack changed the subject, wanting to take the focus off him.

"Roni sent me on a callout, and I wanted you to meet me there, but no, you ignored me, so I got stuck playing patty-cake with fucking

Earl Nichols. Man, Dawson has Skip, Spider Webb, and I get his best friend, Good-bye Earl."

This broke Jack up and he snorted.

"It's not funny, Jack. I can't stand the guy."

"Find a copy of the Dixie Chicks CD with the song, 'Good-bye Earl' on it and play it when you're in the car together, then go to Golden Corral Buffet and after you make your plate, bring him a bowl of black-eyed peas." Jack doubled over laughing so hard he had to wipe his eyes.

"If I had the balls, like the song says, I'd slip him poison in his peas and I guarantee the only two people who would miss him would be Brooks and Skip Webb."

"Where is he anyway?"

"I sent him to run down a judge for a search warrant so I'd have a minute of sanity and peace."

"What if I bring you Antoine's subs and chips to make it up to you?"

"Fine, but you'll still owe me, so tomorrow morning, bring breakfast tacos from Gilford's, but not a box, just four for me, cuz damn if I'll share with Earl."

"Deal."

Jack liked the idea of cutting Good-bye Earl out of the breakfast tacos.

"I'm off to see Mack and Benny at the morgue. Jack, I'm looking forward to lunch, so don't forget. See ya at 1:00." Austin signed out.

Alone with no ears on the walls, Jack picked up the phone. " Tech, Bergman. Jack, man, I wasn't expecting to talk to you today. Everything alright?"

"Yeah. Let's talk, but not over the phone. Quinn's tonight around 7:00."

"Sure. Hey, you've never asked me if I have a girl or a life. I mean, you telephone and I come running."

"Well, do you?"

"We broke it off a few years ago, and I dove into work. I've been too busy for a serious relationship. I'm what you might call a casual dater if I have the time."

"Kasper, you're a blockhead. Why should I ask you about a girlfriend? Or if you work all the time, if that's what you do?"

"Well, it would be damn nice if you cared enough to know about me," he kidded, "other than my great nerd skills, and you love me for the person I am." Kasper snorted a short laugh.

"Kasper, you're a weirdo. I'm hanging up. See ya tonight." Jack hit end call and left to head on over to Antoine's and pick up Reed's sandwiches and a couple for himself for later before he dove into the old case files. He felt rotten for not picking up Reed's call yesterday. It would be nice to get a fresh case.

As soon as he strode into the front door of Antoine's, he saw his favorite counter person—a woman in her late 60s with lots of spunk left in her. Her dream long ago was to be in law enforcement, in any capacity. But her topmost aspiration was to be FBI. If this woman had been in law enforcement and he'd asked for her help, she'd be knee-deep into this covert mission and loving every second, and this thought made him smile.

"My, my, Detective Jack West, haven't seen you in forever and a day. You have a case you need my help with? Any judges you need to take down?" Her face lit up with a saucy grin, and she winked.

"Hi, Viola, not today, but who knows, huh?" The dimples in his cheeks pronounced as he winked back.

Quinn's Pub was busy and Jack stood at the bar waiting for Grady to finish. He was serving and talking to five boisterous men at the other end. Next, he stepped over to the group of young women. The chattering women had pulled two tables together, and they were eyeing the five men. The last group of people congregated at the rear, taking over four tables. It was an after-hours gathering of coworkers, letting off steam.

"Jack, Jack, Jack. You wanna have a drink before the kid comes in and gives you a slap on the wrist?" the pub owner chortled.

"Bite me, Grady, and draw me a tall boy, draft, dark lager, Sam Adams."

The man was enjoying himself. This many customers in his pub on a weeknight, and it wasn't even happy hour.

Half the beer gone, Jack saw Kasper walking in and looking around, and he lifted his hand, waving him over to the bar top at the opposite end.

Kasper sat on Jack's left, then motioned to Grady for one, and turned to Jack. "I think we need more privacy to talk, don't you?"

"Grab your beer." Jack signaled for another drink. "Let's move over there." He gestured to a back table in the far corner away from prying ears. Once he passed him, Kasper got a clear view of Jack's left temple.

"God, Jack, whose gun butt did you slam your head into?"

Kasper called him out on it.

"Yeah, so let me fill you in on yesterday's mission."

"Not good, Jack. Crap, what if he shows up after me next? You ever consider that possibility?"

Jack drained his mug and then looked at Kasper. "He ain't gonna come after you; he doesn't know about you. Hey, don't take this wrong. He'd never see you as a threat."

"Gee, thanks, Jack. I guess you think cuz I work with computers nobody would ever see me and say, 'Don't tangle with him, he's trouble. Watch out, he might hit you with his laptop.'" Kasper finished his beer, setting the mug down with a hard thump.

Jack couldn't keep from laughing.

"Not funny, Jack-*ass*."

"Yeah, it is. *What if he comes after me next*?" He mocked Kasper's whiny tone.

"Fine, you prick, but hell, what if he does? What do I do, shoot him and explain why later, and then drop your name as a reference?"

"Not to worry, not yet. You just do the behind-the-scenes stuff, and keep your head down."

"Uh-huh, I'm okay with the behind-the-scenes stuff, but why not bring me with you next time?"

"Nope. I will not put you in harm's way. If something happened, I'd never forgive myself."

"Ain't your call, Jack, it's mine. Before you get all mentor protector-y with me, just listen. I'm already in this and if it goes south, we go together. I understand the consequences and can't act like a pussy. If I can't do this, I'll never be FBI qualified. So, cut me some slack. I'm not a kid, even if you call me kid. I'm a full-grown man. Hell, Jack, I pee standing up, pay rent, own a car, and cook for myself. Got it?"

Jack liked the kid's moxie. "Noted, and notice I didn't call ya kid—kid."

A crooked grin played on Kasper's lips.

13

Walt Burch's T-shirt displayed the *GIGANTOUR* across North America in 2008, the band name *MEGADETH* done in bright green lettering in the center of the shirt. And the man's bulging fat shoved the band's name into your face. The two goons held his arms back; one had a gun jammed in his neck.

"Hey, man, I wanna—"

Joven Cazalla's fist caught him square between the A and D in Megadeth. Walt doubled over. His ribs were sore from the upper jabs, and now the dickwad was giving his middle a workout. And if the goon with the gun jammed it any harder into his carotids, blood would spurt.

"I...look, Cazalla, I was—"

"Shut up. I'll tell you when you can talk."

Walt nodded. God, stealing from the boss was a death sentence. He prayed they would give him the chance to pay back the dough and live. Money laundering was a valuable service for them, and he was one of the best at it.

Cazalla took the gun from the goon and the pressure on his neck subsided. Dread washed over him, and sweat beaded his pudgy upper lip.

Joven stepped up as close as Walt's enormous belly allowed, and a snarl curled his lips. His hot breath filled the obese man's nostrils.

"You have until the end of next week to return the money. If not, it ain't gonna be healthy for you, understand me?"

"Sure, uh-huh, I'll have it back to him, I swear." His mind raced. How could he make money? He had to; he'd figure it out somehow.

Joven Cazalla took two steps back, raised the pistol, and with the grip end, he slammed it into the plump guy's left temple. Burch saw stars for a split second before he crumpled.

"Take this fat slob to the pawnshop when he comes to. Then go to Galena. The boss has stuff for you to deliver."

Eleven Days Later

He slammed his cell on the desk hard enough to crack it, yet it did not break. Phone back in hand, he punched in the number.

"Where are you?"

"The container yard, why?"

"Time for you to visit that fat slob."

"Why?"

"He ain't got the money, for starters, and he knows too much and we can't chance it."

"*You* can't chance it, is what you mean, isn't it?" This was pissing Theo off.

"What about you? You think you can take a chance? Shit, I—"

"Man, if I thought you were threatening me, I'd be pissed. For the sake of your health, don't issue me any threats. You realize who you're talking to, don't you?"

The tone in his voice changed. "Yeah, I do. Listen, this is just a call with orders from the big boss. Dispose of the slob pawnshop owner. You're the garbage man, so take him out."

"Don't refer to me as the garbage man again or you'll be the next body they find in the landfill. I'll handle it. Just stop acting all high and mighty." Before the other man retorted, he shut his phone. The man with rippling muscles, wearing black jeans and dusty motorcycle boots, slipped his phone into his rear pocket. He turned his attention to the cargo manifest. After he'd looked over the paperwork, he signed off on it and handed it to the clerk. "Gonna be five or six fellas here to unload our container tomorrow afternoon. Sit on it until then. Got it?"

The clerk nodded. If he did his part, they'd pay him decent money. The pimple-faced boy needed the extra dough. And he damn well needed to keep away from the ponies or get his legs broken.

When the truck pulled into the alley, he saw the rear end only. Through a small crack in the doorway, he watched as a big man, wearing all black, his pant legs tucked into motorcycle boots, which appeared to be a size 12 or 13, stepped out. McCready's curiosity peaked since he'd never seen the dude, and he watched as this nameless man disappeared through the pawnshop's rear entry. It didn't feel good.

If you stole anything from the cartel, this would sign your death warrant. Walt Burch let it slip he was saving money so he could skip the country and get out of the business. His saving money was skimming off the top, which he'd been doing for two years. He took small amounts at first. Desperate to put his plan in motion, the amounts increased and so did his flapping gums. That day in the shopping strip, he'd tried to warn Walt, but nope, he was not listening. Burch hadn't said how much he'd skimmed, but it didn't matter, because stealing was stealing. McCready told him to take his losses and leave the country. Burch didn't know McCready would use this information to his advantage. He'd informed Cazalla, hoping it was a way for him to move up in the organization. His warning to Burch was to take his advice and vamoose.

Walt Burch staying in Houston was a bad move and McCready's insides tightened as he closed the back door. If the heavy guy got the holy hell beat outta him, he wouldn't take the blame, and he hoped Walt would skip town after he healed. He would if he were smart; smart—yeah, right. Not stealing from the cartel would've been smart.

He jammed his gun with intensity shoving it hard through layers of fat, poking him in the ribs. Walt Burch jumped as far as a fat person could jump with a yelp.

"You bastard, hey, you trying to break my—" He stopped when he saw the silencer on the gun barrel. Shit, his time was up.

"The boss wants a word."

Sweat beaded on Walt's upper lip. He had part of the money, not all of it. If he were dead, it meant no more money for them; he prayed it was another warning. Why had he been so stupid? He wanted out of this life. However, he knew too much and they would never let him walk away.

"Lock up and turn the sign to closed."

"Uh-huh, yeah, I'm doing it, I'm doing it." Walt wiped his sweaty lip on the short sleeve of his T-shirt. The mean bastard had him at gunpoint, what else could he do but comply? Deep down, he prayed it wasn't true, but he knew he would meet his maker soon.

Owen watched the front of the pawnshop from the far corner of a window. Once the *Closed* sign appeared, he scurried to the back door and laid a rock in the doorway to keep it from shutting. He snuck out the door to slip behind the dumpster so he could peek around the metal receptacle and watch the truck. No license plate on the back bumper. Not good.

He watched as the motorcycle-booted dude shoved Walt out.

Owen did not see the gun, but his guess was he had Burch at gunpoint. McCready watched them drive away. Another gut-wrenching feeling tightened in his middle. Walt Burch was in trouble, and he had no way to help him. Maybe he was getting his just rewards.

WALT BURCH's heart rate doubled as they drove on the loop and exited Highway 225. Mr. Muscles gave him directions, the gun lying in his lap, his index finger resting against the trigger.

Silence ensued for miles, and Walt saw the container yard. His brain screeched out, *terrific place for a murder*. He tightened his grip on the steering wheel. The knuckles on each hand turned white.

"Turn here and drive to the row of Burlington Containers around back."

Walt followed the man's instructions.

"Shut off the engine and get out."

Again, Walt complied.

"Walk to the end. The door is open. Go in, and remember I'm behind you, me and my gun."

Burch prayed under his breath, trying to make amends as best he could for his wrongdoings. He was facing death, because there was no chance the Grim Reaper behind him would let him live.

The man poked him in the ribs with brute force, and Walt Burch pissed his pants as he stumbled into the deserted humid container.

HE RUBBED the blood from his palms with a black bandana.

Why did Burch hafta fuck himself? It made no difference nowadays what sorta business you were in. You couldn't find decent upright employees. Where was the honor among thieves, thugs, and hired guns these days?

The man, wearing all black, opened the passenger door. He dropped a Ziploc baggie into a cooler. With a half-empty bottle of tepid water, he rinsed his hands. Burch's fat, chubby hand lay inside the baggie. His face pulled in revulsion at the sight. The severed hand and the blood didn't bother him. What made him sick were the big roly-poly fingers. He'd send Mundy and Callum out tonight to get rid of the body, all but this one fat hand. This was his power play. He'd make certain old skinny beak nose and the other chowderheads saw it first before he got rid of it in a meat grinder. Seeing the fat man's hand wasn't necessary, but they needed to understand his capabilities. They needed to realize he wasn't someone they should mess with.

14

OAG Agent Janet Spears took the business card. It had lain on her desk since the day she ordered the detectives to stand down on their case. Palming the card, she thought about all the times she spent wondering if he had gotten the unspoken messages. With the shabby business card in her hand, Janet dialed—it rang four times before she heard his voice.

"Jack."

"Detective West, Janet Spears here. How are you doing?"

"Hello, Agent Spears. Well, what a surprise. You haven't crossed my mind in a long while. I guess it's because you never called." Frostiness crept into his voice.

"Fine, I deserve your pissy attitude. I get it. So, if you're done being pissy, can we meet somewhere and talk?"

Jack leaned back in his recliner. One hand held the phone, the other rubbed the back of his neck. He let the silence linger as he thought.

"Detective, I, I don't have the time to—"

"After all these months? You have the nerve to call me and you imagine I've got time for you now? After leaving me in the dark for what, eighteen months, you assume I'm still interested? Look," he rushed his words to keep her from speaking, "I haven't even given the case a second thought. Other stuff has happened and I—"

"Liar. Now I'll talk and you listen. I've monitored you and your progress over the last year. My sources are vast, Detective. These sources updated me and I know you're digging into the case on your own time, so don't lie to me."

A brief silence ensued. Jack simmered at the tone she had taken with him, and her know-it-all attitude.

"Jack, I'm aware of what you're looking into, and if you want proof, I can give it to you. You have the right to pull away after I give you this proof. What's more, if you feel like I'm bullshitting you, you can tell me to fuck off and go to hell, okay?"

He'd have to be full of rage to say this to any woman. However, if she gave him a reason, he could spew out the words without a second thought.

"Yep, works for me. Okay now, what do you know? Or think you know?"

Janet smirked into her phone and he couldn't see her. "Meet me tomorrow night, 8:00 sharp."

"Fine. Where?"

"Are you sitting?"

"Yeah, Agent Spears, I'm sitting. Why do you want me sitting?"

"Good. Quinn's Pub tomorrow night, 8:00 sharp, ask Kasper Bergman to come too." She clicked off before he got a word out.

The kid kept quiet; Jack would bet his life on it. How could she know about him and Quinn's Pub?

Sophia booted up the program she needed. The chat was in five minutes. She was antsy. It had been a slow, tiring, hot, and uneventful day. Her stakeout had gotten her zilch. No, that wasn't true. She'd gotten mosquito bites; however, not one live or dead body showed up again.

If he agreed to partner up with her, she worried about the legend she'd created for him in case he showed. Sophia had no desire to make Jack uncomfortable. But there was no going back to change the story she'd already concocted.

A tiny *ping* sounded and she clicked the keys on her laptop. She watched the magic happen after she'd punched in the satellite code. It was mystic, indeed. Who would've figured in this thick-treed, remote area, with less human inhabitants than hogs or goats, anyone could be privy to a secure computer chat site? Satellite links bouncing signals off in space, making it possible for her and Janet to communicate.

The numbers rolled up, flashed, then stopped. Sophia entered the number sequence and tapped her short fingernails below the return bar as she waited. Another *ping* and Janet began the conversation.

Janet: *How are you? You hanging in there in that shithole?*

Sophia: *It's effing hot, not to mention humid, and boring for a few days.*

Janet: *No new talk, nothing—not good. Are you using an insect repellant? Damn mosquitoes carry every kind of virus.*

Sophia: *Yeah, been slathering it on, but that's not what I called about, Janet. Did you contact him?*

Janet: *Yes, I did. Keep your panties on. It's also my job to make sure you stay safe in other aspects, like health. Now, will you let me talk, uh, I mean type?* Janet snorted aloud but Sophia couldn't hear her so she typed, *LMBO.*

Sophia: *Hilarious, Janet. How much have you had to drink?* She typed back and added her acronym, *J/K.*

Janet: *Not enough, but I might pound them back when we're done here. Let's get down to business. I made the call, but I haven't told him anything; meeting him tomorrow night. Shocked him, I'm sure because*

I mentioned Kasper Bergman, which means I know he's been working the case.

Janet paused, her hands hovering over the keyboard, and she dropped her fingers and began typing.

I have to talk to his superiors after I get his decision, and I'm sure it won't go well with his new captain either. This makes it tricky cuz we cannot involve any more people. My orders are to keep our op under wraps, you understand, Sophia. Janet waited.

Sophia: *Janet, how covert is this op? Like if I need the cavalry to come in, they won't show up?*

Janet: *No. God, I for one will not leave you hanging or in more danger than you're exposed to already, I promise. People are working against us, and the fewer who know about this op the better.*

Sophia: *We have people who are playing both sides?* She typed with speed since the window for the chat time was getting smaller.

Janet: *I'd rather not go into detail. You find out how they transport, where, and get names. I'll handle stuff here, okay?* Janet's fingers flew over the keyboard.

Sophia: *When are you sending him here?* She hit send and waited.

Janet: *I expect him to be ready in less than two weeks, so hang in there. I'm also hoping Bergman agrees to be our eyes and ears here. No time to clarify, just trust me.*

The timer closed on the screen. The last thing she read was "just trust me." Sophia closed her laptop. For safety and security reasons she alternated her hiding place. She stuffed the laptop into the ceiling on a flattened cardboard box and replaced the water-stained ceiling tiles. Sophia sat on the bed, thinking about Janet's message. Kasper Bergman, their eyes and ears in the States. Only one word came to mind—why? Bergman is a technical person, not a detective. Why keep him in the mix?

Janet's words rang in her ears again. *Just trust me.* She had faith in Janet, well, at least 99.9 percent. The directive to keep the inner circle small meant someone had infiltrated or was working both sides.

Well, that was just hunky-dory. Who was she to trust if she couldn't trust her own team? Damn.

15

"Bergman, Tech." Kasper couldn't squelch his yawn.

"You bored, Bergman?"

"No, Jack, I had a late-night stakeout until 3:00 this morning. I've been here since 7:00." He peered at his watch. It was straight-up 5:00. "I'm whipped."

"Get un-whipped and meet me at Quinn's, 6:00."

"Can we do this tomorrow night? I'm not gonna be worth two hoots if I have to—"

"They've summoned us, so no, can't do it tomorrow, and I gotta go. Reed's coming down the hall. Six sharp, Kasper, be there."

After the call ended, a stupefied Kasper Bergman sat, still holding his phone to his ear and the three words lingering from the brief conversation were, "they've summoned us." Who were *they*? He felt the bile rising and thought he would be sick. Without a doubt, he was wide-awake now.

Ten minutes till six. His gut wrenched in anticipation. Kasper was waiting at a table in the back, an energy drink and one king-sized Snickers candy bar wrapper balled up, the other candy bar not yet eaten. His nerves were bouncing every direction, and finally he saw Jack walk in the door.

"That's an unlikely dinner combo, Bergman."

Before Kasper had two seconds to reply, Jack waved at Grady behind the bar.

"Grady, one Miller, and uh, a salami on rye, mustard, and sauerkraut, hold the pickles."

"One beer on the way, sandwich in fifteen," Grady called back, repeating the order. He stuck his head in the open back bar window and gave the order to his cook, a college kid working for extra pocket money.

"Caffeine, Jack, caffeine, not healthy, but damn well needed tonight." Kasper drained the energy drink then crushed the can. Jack lifted his mug and drank.

"What the hell, Jack, summoned? Summoned by who, and why?"

"Janet Spears with the OAG, she—"

Kasper cut him short in a fit of anxiety. "The Feds? Now we're dealing with the Feds, oh Mother of God, what the shit, Jack? What have you gotten me into?"

With vigor, Kasper ripped open the second candy bar chomping into the Snickers as his hand shook. That bar went quickly. Kasper fiddled with the wrapper, his nervous tension wired in a tight knot before he tossed it into Jack's empty beer mug.

Grady sat Jack's sandwich in front of him.

"Need another beer, Jack?"

"Yep, another tall boy would hit the spot." As always, Grady did not outstay his welcome. He scampered off for the beer, served it, and trotted to the bar. He knew when Jack met the kid, they were working. Grady did not get nosy; if he asked questions, they might ask him questions too. Uh-uh, it wasn't worth it at this stage of his life.

"You seem calm. Maybe I should be too, but crap, I can't afford to lose my job."

"She found out somehow we are working together, and it worries me, because how could she find out?"

"I didn't tell a soul, I swear, Jack. Could she have bugged the place?"

"Don't know. Could she have someone on the inside at HPD?"

Jack shoved his empty plate to one side propping his forearms up, his fingers tapping out a light beat on the tabletop.

"You're kidding, aren't you? This ain't like the movies, Jack."

"Art imitates life, so it could happen. Be smart, Bergman, take extra precautions when you are surfing the web or talking to me, got it? We don't want this blowing up in our faces. If it does, we'll go down together in the bottle. So are you staying in or not?"

"I'm in if you are." Kasper's mouth opened in a long-drawn-out yawn.

Neither of them had seen Agent Spears standing at the table. She cleared her throat.

Both men stood, and Janet smirked. "Keep your damn seat, guys. Chivalry died in the fifteenth century." She pulled out a chair.

"Jack." She looked at him. "You look decent for an old man."

"Yeah, I guess since the crap rolling over me like a steamroller finally quit." He reached out his hand, and she did the same.

"Good to see you, Janet. Kasper, Agent Janet Spears from the OAG; Agent Spears, Kasper Bergman, part of Houston's finest Technical Department, and a nerd with a badge," he introduced the two.

"Ma'am, it's nice to meet you." Kasper outstretched his hand.

She returned his solid handshake. "Kasper, call me Janet, not ma'am. Ma'am was my granny."

"Uh, would you care for a drink, ma...Janet?"

"It's been a harrowing couple of days for me, bureaucratic bullshit and dealing with men afraid of women with power." A tiny scowl passed over her forehead. "I shall exclude present company until you show me your true colors. Hmmm...what do I want?"

Janet didn't want them to think she was a hard, fast drinker. Well, she knew she could outdrink most men. *Oh, screw it,* she thought. "I'll have a Sam Adams, dark, and a shot of Makers 46."

Kasper's mouth dropped open, and Jack busted up.

"One boilermaker coming up, Janet." Jack motioned for Grady, gave him her drink order then filled her in on his boilermaker story, with Kasper acting like his mother. She burst into laughter, and Kasper turned pink.

"Look here, kiddo, when you're a woman in a man's world and have had some rough days, a strong beverage is in order. Just because I'm a female doesn't mean I have to stick to girlie drinks either."

Beer and whiskey in hand, she did not sip her whiskey. She dropped it into the lager, raised the glass to her lips, and chugged it down. Her entire body shuddered from her head to her toes as she let the warmth fill her. "God, I needed that." She let her shoulders relax.

"Hey, about calling the kid a kid." Jack regaled her with the story of him calling Bergman a kid when they began meeting at Quinn's Pub. When he concluded, Kasper's face was once again pink.

"Pardon me, uh, Janet, but if you two assholes could stop laughing at my expense, you mind if we get to the reason we are here? Last night was a long night. And it has been a fucking long day. I just want to go home." Kasper wasn't kidding around. Jack's brows arched. The kid would be a formidable adversary if he was not your friend.

"You've got moxie, Bergman." Janet liked Kasper. Her intuition said he'd do terrific in law enforcement, with a three-letter acronym or not. "Yep, let's get to the whys and wherefores, gentlemen."

Briefed on the state of affairs in Mexico and Medina's status, Jack wondered what Spears wasn't telling them. This flabbergasted Kasper. This was new news. The DEA was involved, and Agent Medina was alone in Mexico. This was dangerous.

"So you're telling us the HPD, uh, the OAG and the DEA, and, what, is the FBI involved too?" Kasper spouted in his sleep-deprived state.

"If we get this case solved the full alphabet might play out. Any acronyms ending in a vowel—CIA, FBI, DEA—and ones with consonants—ATF, DOJ, NDSS, DHS—hell, kid, even INS could become involved. I have no fucking clue what agencies we might work with when this all comes to a head. Does that answer your question, Bergman?"

"Yeah, I guess it does, gee, thanks, Agent Spears." Kasper's tone was a little sarcastic. He hadn't needed her to recite the alphabet.

"Owen McCready? What information do you have, Janet?"

"It's sketchy. Uh, he goes off the grid a lot. We don't know if he's involved or just a victim." Damn it, she hadn't expected him to mention McCready, not yet, and she hated tumbling over her words.

He stared into her eyes, studying her; she was lying, but why?

"What about Sea Star Coaches?" If Janet knew about Kasper and Quinn's, she knew he had been watching Boyce Carter too.

"The company is transporting drugs, or that's what we think. It might be a lot more, but that's all my pay grade lets me disclose. We're observing and nothing more for now."

"This concerns the Lobos Cartel and Omar Villa Lobos, so you have eyes on him?" Kasper joined the conversation.

"We aren't on Omar. We are watching his captains, their crews, and any gang or underlings who are loyal to the cartel," she said.

Jack knew she was lying to them.

"Not on the key man? I don't get it, why no—"

Jack cut in. "I get it, Bergman, it's fine." His booted foot pressed against the kid's to shut him up.

"Here is the sixty-four million dollar question, Janet. What do you want from us?"

"You're needed in Mexico, Jack, to work with Medina." Turning, she glanced at the kid. "Bergman, we need your ears and eyes working for us. I'll have one of our guys brief you. Afterward, Bergman, there is a new DEA agent here working in Houston. They transferred him from the Corpus office. He was working undercover and helped to bring some low-level cartel members down, but he was compromised, so they are sending him here to work with us."

Kasper's head was reeling, and he found his voice. "Me, here, eyes, ears, doing what? I mean, I don't want to become covered underneath this clump of...of...well, shit, and not come out smelling like, uh, fresh posies." He combed through his hair with both hands and it accomplished two things: messed up his hair and wiped off the sudden sweat accumulating on his palms.

"Bergman, chill a little, will ya?" Janet needed another drink and motioned for the pub owner. "Can you get me a gin and tonic, three-fourths gin, the other fourth tonic, please?"

"Yep, coming right up. Jack, you or the kid need anything?" Grady waited, wiping his hands with a bar towel.

Kasper responded without hesitation. "Yeah, a whiskey and tonic, hold the tonic, and make it a double." Jack kept his amusement to himself, pinching his lips together after he requested another tall boy. Holy smoke, he was fearful old Kasper might become an alcoholic before this ended.

She filled them in on what the department allowed her to divulge, and it was time for her to leave.

"Gentlemen, keep your seats. I've got a meeting in an hour. These late nights are kicking my butt. Bergman, take my card. It has my private cell number on the back. You'll get a call after Jack gets squared away." She looked Jack's way. "I'll see you tomorrow. Okay, fellas, I have to leave or I'll be late and I hate walking into a conference room and finding ten sets of eyes on me. I'll be in touch soon."

Jack spoke first. "I think there is so much more she ain't sharing. Look, I'm sorry for dragging you into this, cuz this could get messy, and I—"

The kid waved his hand in the air. "No, no apologies needed. I mean, if I can't work this I don't deserve to go to Quantico."

16

"He can't be in Mexico forever, Houston needs him, and I—" Roni Justice was mid-sentence when Spears cut her off.

"It doesn't matter what you think, Captain Justice. The OAG is taking this case in the interest of national security. I..."

"Don't national security me, Agent Spears." Roni's hand went up, slicing the air, a blatant gesture for Spears to shut up. "There are plenty of DEA agents to cover this, and you and—"

Both women jumped out of their chairs, facing each other in a showdown.

"Listen, Justice, I have jurisdiction over you, so don't try to—"

"Oh, the hell you do, you'd better listen, Spears, I'm not—" Captain Justice's anger increased. The ambiance in the room hit DEFCON-1 and Davis Yao had had enough.

"Ladies," he barked, "take this down to DEFCON-5. In my office, I'm in charge, and don't forget *I* am the Chief of Detectives. Sit down and both of you damn well shut up."

This took both women by surprise. They'd forgotten Yao was in the room. They stopped snarling at each other and looked in his direction. Yao's face reflected his aggravation.

"Damn women cat-fighting in my office, this is bullshit. We're on the same team. *Team*, you gals got me?" These last words roared with force.

Roni Justice ducked her head and sat. "Yes, sir, I'm sorry."

She turned to Janet. "Agent Spears, I apologize. I am aware you have an important situation and—"

"Call me Janet." She stepped in before the captain finished her sentence, and Roni's eyes narrowed. "You don't have to apologize, just listen,"—she paused— "please."

"I'm listening." Roni tried to keep her teeth from clenching.

Davis Yao, his face stony and his head ready to explode, and blood pressure up, jumped back into the conversation. "And ladies, I insist you two play nice, and after you've each stated your arguments, I'll finish it up. Then I'll get Jack in here. He needs to be briefed on the situation."

The moment Yao uttered those four words, "get Jack in here," Roni Justice pinched her face up, trying to stay calm. She thought Jack would be on this case, but working here from Houston. The Captain hadn't expected him to go traipsing off to Mexico. Plus, no one knew how long he'd be gone. If he were here, he was available if Homicide needed him. Now her department would be short one detective.

In Yao's office an hour later, Jack felt suffocated. The atmosphere between his captain and Agent Spears charged with negative vibes, and both faces showed signs of hostility. It seemed Davis had to split apart two squalling cats. Chief Yao clenched his jaw a few times. Jack tried not to grin at the COD's expense. He would've loved to have been a fly on the wall. It would have been entertaining to watch the Chief lower the boom on these two.

Roni glanced at Janet for a nanosecond and then turned to her detective. "Jack, HPD will lend you to the DEA at the behest of the OAG. It'll only be for a short period. You'll be back soon."

Spears looked at Yao, but her words were aimed at Justice. "It takes time to get an investigation completed. Everyone understands how it works I'm sure."

Jack saw Roni bristle, and he got the distinct impression these two women had a history. Had they known each other in the past? Whatever it was, he felt the hostility sizzling between them.

A growing surge of energy filled him. It was a chance of a lifetime for him. Undercover work with the DEA. It was dangerous. Add in that he'd be working with a female partner. Made it interesting. What about his legal jurisdiction? Working for the city of Houston and Harris County did not give him legal rights to work elsewhere. Otherwise, he could drive across the world playing cops and robbers anywhere.

It was like she was reading his mind.

"Jack," Janet addressed him, "I will deputize you as a temporary DEA officer. You'll have the same jurisdictional powers until the case is over. Roni..." She looked at Captain Justice. "If you will get the paperwork for Detective West's working leave of absence, and fax it to my office."

"Jack, it will be a working leave, with half of your pay from HPD, and the DEA will subsidize the rest and pay all your expenses. Isn't this correct, Janet?" Davis Yao's duty to protect the department's fiscal budget did not take this hit, not knowing the length of Jack's assignment.

"Sure, Davis, we have you covered. Jack, meet me tomorrow morning at the DEA building."

"I'll be there, Agent Spears."

"Great. They will brief you in more depth, since not everyone here has clearance." She glanced at Roni. "It's not my call, Justice."

The meeting was over. Jack rose and made to leave but Yao got his attention.

"Hey, Jack, this assignment is covert, not even Dawson, got it?"

"Yes, Chief, I've got it—covert."

Kasper crossed his mind. Janet realized he was in the loop, but

Yao and Justice did not. Spears needed to straighten it out with Clarissa and Art. With the extensive work he'd done and the tremendous amount of information he contributed to the case, Jack would not disappoint the kid.

17

Jack paced outside the DEA building at 7:50 p.m., not rested, but ready. The sound of the snap of a door lock caused his heart to pump faster. They would swear him in as a temporary DEA agent in a few days. Afterward, he'd be working undercover in a remote part of Mexico. It was an adrenaline-charged—check, filled with danger—rare opportunity. This was the change he needed in his life.

He loved his job in Homicide, and he enjoyed the tight-knit group of detectives he knew so well, but right now it wasn't enough. He was missing an element of motivation. Jack wanted more excitement. Mexico, DEA, the cartel, danger, and working with a female partner—just thinking about it was exhilarating.

"Glad you made it, Jack. Do you have a current passport?" Janet jumped right into it.

"Yeah, I do."

"First, we get the bureaucratic bullshit paperwork done. You know what I mean—waivers, confidentiality contracts to adhere to or go to jail, and so forth."

The paperwork completed, she escorted him to the SAC's office.

"Jack, this is Special Agent in Charge Jerrell Bogard. I'll leave you two to talk. Be back later."

"Janet, shut the door behind you, please."

The soft click of the door sounded, leaving them alone.

"Good to meet you, Special Agent Bogard."

"Call me Jerry. Take a seat, Jack. Let's get started, shall we?"

"Yes, sir, I'm ready."

"Spears told me about you, Detective. You've done impressive work."

"What work are you referring to, sir?"

Bogard leaned back in his plush executive chair. "Jerry. Call me Jerry, not *sir*. It was a smart move pulling Bergman in. Damn smart."

"Thank you." Bogard sidestepping his questions about his work so far he saw as deliberate, and it aggravated him.

"Once this assignment is completed, perhaps you'll consider working for the DEA, and for me."

"No thanks, Jerry. I need a change, but not a forever change. Homicide is my calling. Besides, I'd rather not deal with the crap your people deal with. And Bergman, how does he fit in?" Jack was not planning to change jobs, nor was this a job interview.

Jerry slumped in his chair, folding his hands across his chest, an expression of arrogance on his face. "The kid's not a secret to us. We know he wants the FBI. If he wants Quantico, he might as well have this experience under his belt."

Jack's eyes moved downward in thought. What other information did they have on him or Bergman? He was sure Kasper told no one about his aspirations regarding the FBI. He hadn't shared everything with them, but it didn't mean they didn't know what he knew or what he'd been through. The McCready incident came to mind.

He'd seen the movies about Big Brother watching and how the DEA, CIA, and FBI knew things. Currently, Kasper was the one person he would depend on to have his back, no one else. Next time he talked to the kid, he'd have to figure out how to keep anyone from knowing what they discussed—*no one* should know.

The SAC sat, waiting for Jack to comment, wondering if he was too smart. Janet, he could handle, however, he didn't know about this detective. This could prove a problem. He had already stuck his foot —hell, both of his legs—in the water. Now he had to drown or swim.

When Jack didn't speak, the SAC took the floor again.

"Jack, if you want the kid in, it's your call."

"It's his call, Jerry, not mine. I'll get back with you after I've talked to him."

"I need his decision soon. We have to move things along. I hope you understand time is not a luxury."

"No one in law enforcement has the luxury of time. It ain't news to me, Jerry, I assure you."

Jerrell Bogard's eyes held a faraway gaze. One more person to monitor meant he'd be running a daycare. Shit, didn't he have enough on his plate right now? Well, yeah, he did, and it was *his* problem right now, not the OAG, the DEA, the HPD, or Jack West's business.

"You think this kid Bergman can be trusted? Can you depend on him?"

"Yeah, the kid has my six. You gotta problem with Kasper?" His eyes narrowed. Something was amiss, but he couldn't put his finger on it.

"Jack, I have to count on you to do what needs to be done. It's imperative you follow orders without questioning them. Are you in or out? If you're in, fantastic. If not, thanks for stopping by. Now, what's it going to be, my boy?"

Jack looked past Bogard to the wall behind his desk as he considered his response. There were photographs on the wall of Jerry and various agents. SAC Bogard, a man with certain power. Something in Jerrell Bogard's tone prickled the hairs on his nape, making him feel there was an internal problem, and an inner voice bleeped out a warning—*exercise caution.*

He might not get his triple homicide closed if he didn't accept this assignment.

Jack was not his *boy,* nor was he one of *them.* His loyalties were to no department, no agency. His loyalties went to the victims. If he had to, he'd step on other powers to get justice. Jack had big enough boots to do the job.

"I'm in, Jerry."

18

Bergman, Quinn's, Wednesday, happy hour—need to talk.

Because this weighed heavy on his mind, he'd waited a few days before approaching the kid. Should he tell Kasper his part was over? Bergman worked in Tech, not a high-risk position. Was it fair to put him in this spot? Was he ready, or was he still too green? Jack's gut tightened in stress. An inner voice was screaming a war inside his head. Yes, no, no, yes. Just because he was working in a technical aspect didn't mean someone wouldn't come after him. But if something bad happened Jack could not handle the guilt for another person's death. Gretchen. He reminded himself, for the one hundredth time, that it was not his fault, and he needed to remember this or the guilt would consume him again.

What was wrong with him? The kid was part of HPD law enforcement and you put yourself in harm's way, even as a tech. Kasper could say yes or no, it was his choice. He'd have to do a helluva lot more if he wanted Quantico.

His fingers drummed, tapped, and bounced in a frantic rhythm, not loud and nonstop, changing from one form to another, and the beats altered. His feet did the same tapping. After he checked the time, his eyes darted toward the entrance. Was Jack doing this on purpose, making him wait and wait and wait, see if he could handle the pressure?

People were sitting at the bar jabbering as he watched Grady floating from one part of the bar to another serving drinks to a busy crowd. As of late, more and more HPD staffers, receptionists, secretaries, and clerks showed up at Quinn's Pub for Hump-Day Happy Hour. Wednesdays had stopped being an optimal night to meet, so why tonight? Where was Jack anyway?

"Kid," Grady called out, "you gonna sit twiddling your thumbs and tapping that tune or are ya gonna drink?"

"Yeah, get me a margarita, hold the marg and the rita, double shot, and a beer?"

Grady's eyes widened, and his brow shot upward. "Alrighty, a double-shot tequila and a Bud Light coming up."

"Skip the Bud, how about a Sam Adams Double Bock? You got any?"

"Yep, you want one?" Grady dried his hands with a dish towel, eyeing the kid. A double shot of tequila and one beer with 9.5 ABV was not a usual combo for the kid.

"Yeah, and open me a tab, would'ja?"

Grady nodded, went for the beer, poured a double shot of Jose Cuervo, started the kid a tab then served the drinks. Grady sat and then leaned back, staring at the kid.

"What? You think I'm gonna need you to call me a cab later?"

"Huh, if I have to I will. Don't mind at all. And cuz I know who you are and who your buddy is. I'll just give old Jack a call. Kasper, why are you drinking this way? I gotta tell ya, kid, you got me worried."

Kasper took the shot of Jose, downed it, then took a swig of his Sam Adams and let out an, "Ahhh, that hit the spot."

The old man never intervened or commented on his patrons and their drinking. His goal was making sure no customer drove drunk and killed someone or themselves. Kasper wasn't a regular patron; he and Jack were his family. It was how Grady Quinn felt about them.

"Grady, don't worry about me. I had a few hard days, nothing else. Besides, you won't have to call him cuz he just walked in."

Turning, Grady saw Jack.

"Okay, if you say so. If you become an alcoholic, we won't see each other again. I kinda like ya, kid." He winked, got up, and walked toward the bar. Grady walked past Jack, speaking discreetly, "Watch the kid doesn't drive drunk." Then, louder, he asked him what he wanted to drink.

"Get me a boilermaker, would'ja, Grady?" Jack's voice carried, and then inconspicuously, under his breath, "Get me a tall boy, I'm just aggravating the kid."

Jack sat down eyeballing Kasper.

"Geesh, I've been here for at least"—he looked down—"almost twenty minutes. Sorry, Jack, it's this cloak-and-dagger shit. The OAG, DEA, the cartel, I'm wound up and on effing edge." Kasper took another long pull of his beer.

Jack took in the shot glass and the beer. He picked it up and sniffed.

"A shot of our friend Jose Cuervo, huh, and a Sam Double Bock. Hard day at the office?"

"For your damn information, it was a double, so bite me. Now, what's the deal?" Grady sat a Miller tall boy down.

"Thanks, Grady."

"Yup, holler when ya need another, Jack." The old man scuttered off.

Kasper looked at the mug of beer. "I heard you order a boilermaker."

"Uh-huh, and you told me once you weren't much of a drinker. Guess we both didn't mean what we said." Jack smirked and lifted his mug.

"I wasn't a drinker until I started working with you, you asswipe. Now look at me. I am a bag of alcoholic nerves. Besides, if I can't drink with the big boys later in life, I might get the shit belted outta me or worse. I figured I should practice for Quantico. So what's the deal with Agent Spears and her BS?" Kasper leaned back, crisscrossing his ankles, giving Jack the floor.

"That's it—and Spears with her eyes and ears shit, whatever that means, tells me not a goddamn thing." Kasper frowned.

"Something feels wrong about this whole situation, but I haven't figured it out yet. A few days ago, Captain Justice advised me to watch my six. I don't know why yet. If this worries you and your decision is no, I'll understand. So, Bergman, are you in or out?"

Kasper held his second bottle of Sam Double Bock aloft, waiting for Jack to raise his near-empty mug. His bottle clinked against Jack's beer mug.

"You're damn skippy I'm in...and Jack, I've got your six."

19

Knowledge was power. First, you had to have the knowledge. Jack was working with DEA agent Clive Bebchuk and his skinny sidekick, Stan Cleef. Bebchuk was a blowhard armchair quarterback and bully; Cleef, a skinny sleazebag. Jack was sick of it and ready to bail but stopped himself. It had been a couple of days since he'd talked to Kasper, and he wondered how it was going for the kid. It was time they planned a beer-drinking night before he jetted off to Mexico.

Quinn's Friday night, 8-ish? Jack texted with speed, clicked off, shoving his cell in his pocket just as Clive Bebchuk walked into the conference room.

"West, here are more files. Go through these, begin strategizing a plan. I'll be back." Without fanfare, Bebchuk dumped the files in a heap on the lacquered mahogany finished table and strode off and out the door, leaving Jack with a mess of loose papers drifting to the floor.

Jack's hand came up to flip Bebchuk off as the door catch clicked. He squatted, gathering the papers. "Strategize this, you asshat." Breathy words floated into nowhere.

Jack plopped down after yanking a chair over, fanning the pages out. He organized them in date order scanning each page. These were copies of Agent Medina's reports, but not the originals. Someone had written unfavorable remarks in the margins in red ink.

Her reports were your basic, "I watched, I saw nada, the day ended." Medina was a team of one there to gather intel, nothing more. From the notes in the margin, Clive Bebchuk demeaned her abilities. His remarks were malicious, pointing out she was a worthless expense for the agency, and a waste of time. They'd created an op to pacify another useless female agent.

This had him hating Bebchuk even more. Women were outstanding officers and detectives. Females who made it to the DEA, FBI, or CIA deserved to be there. Jack stretched his neck from side to side, sitting back. He felt the sudden vibration and pulled out his phone.

Yeah, 8-ish works, Quinn's tonight.

Jack shoved the phone into his pocket, wondering if the kid had gotten his own arrogant, know-it-all Clive Bebchuk to deal with.

The door opened. Jack did not look up; he just kept flipping through pages.

"I thought I'd find you in here, Jack. Are you reading files, Bebchuk's files, and side notes?" The name Bebchuk was pronounced with loathing leaving a bitter taste in her mouth.

Relieved to see Janet, he set aside the reports. "Yeah, and can I be frank with you?"

She pointed to the back of the room and walked past the conference table. He took her lead and followed.

"Be as straightforward as you want. It'd be refreshing." Her tone hushed, and his brow dipped as he looked past her and around the room.

He matched her low tone. "Huh? They got the place wired?"

She shrugged. "Don't know for sure, but I'm not chancing it. Alright, Jack, be frank and don't sugarcoat it either."

"First off, I thought you and I were working together. Why was I stuck working with a blowhard cocky dickhead? And believe me, those are the nicest things I can say about Bebchuk. His skinny sidekick, Cleef, is no better. What they have me doing is—"

She cut in. "Reading inconsequential reports and files and being smug. Jack, you're gonna deal with it and play nice with them, and I'll explain why."

Jack stretched his long jean-clad legs out, crossing one cowboy-booted foot over the other, folded his arms, and stared at her.

"Why do I have to play nice with the likes of Bebchuk and Cleef? I'm not obligated to stay because I didn't hire on with the OAG or the DEA. I *will* work for you and I *will* adhere to all disclosure clauses. Nothing says I *have* to work for you. *Will*, Janet. I am not forced to work for you, get it? And work—work on what? I'm not working on a damn thing of any importance."

"Okay, let me tell you what we have, and then I hope you'll feel differently."

He held her stare with his own, pressing his lips together in thought for a minute.

"Alright, convince me."

"I am gonna preface what I am about to say with one word. That word is conjecture. We have no solid proof. Your ears only, so do not discuss this with anyone."

"Understood."

"We suspect there are individuals working both sides."

"What makes you think so?"

"Because we can't get one step forward before the cartel is five steps ahead of us." The heavy breath Janet emitted from her lungs was a mere fraction of how beat-down she felt. "These are the reasons we had to slow our operation. We've had to be selective about what, whos, whys, and wheres. Agents are suspicious of each other and unwilling to work cohesively. Truth be told, I'm afraid to talk to anyone inside the agency except Sophia, and a few higher-ups, but even then, I get jittery."

"You have nothing, just assumptions, because the cartel is one step ahead of you? That's it?"

"I do not have the proper clearance to disclose more. What I can say is this: we're concerned about the loyalty of agents who've been on this op for an extended period. Other anomalies have turned up which have my boss's and his boss's boss concerned as well. So, you can see why I need an outsider, someone who has zero predisposed notions regarding our operation or our people. You come in on a clean note. They want you to sift through the garbage. Look for what everyone else can't or won't see."

"Janet, the thing for me is this. I'm a homicide detective, not a sit-in-a-conference-room detective reading stupid, unnecessary case files. Right now, I feel useless. Why not let me work the triple murder?" He saw her body language; she was about to cut him off, and he rushed his words. "Wait, before you say anything. Then I'd report back to you, and Dawson and I

could—"

"Uh-uh."

"What, why not, because we—"

"Listen, you are *not* working the homicide case. If you walk away and forgo the job with us and we catch you working the case...Jack, don't make me threaten you, because I can make your professional life hell."

Jack sat up straight, his eyes never leaving her face. "Me combing through redacted files, which mean nothing, working with people who block me at every turn. All I have right now is shitty information and a pile of rubbish, which proves my point. Crap, no one can work a case or an op without proper information. And your threats, Janet, are empty. We both know that. Just let me be a homicide detective and do the job I do best."

"Jack, will you just listen, please?"

"No, Janet, stop feeding me bits and pieces because if I don't get a complete story out of you, I'll walk. Then you can count on this: I'll work my case on my time and nothing you can say or do will stop me."

"Jack—"

"Uh-uh, Janet, I'm not finished. Don't threaten me. You have no jurisdiction over me as a private citizen, and if you try, I'll slap a harassment lawsuit against you and your agencies, and you don't want that kind of notoriety, now do you?"

"You need to get your shorts out of a twist, Detective! It's my turn to tell you I don't appreciate being threatened. Besides, you wouldn't get anywhere with a lawsuit against the OAG. Those are just empty words. Are you ready to listen to me now?"

"Yeah, I suppose, if you have anything to say."

Janet gave him a brief rundown, and *brief* was an understatement. She watched him. Was the detective ready to blow a gasket?

"Before we get into what you didn't tell me, why is Medina alone in the field?"

"Not my call, DEA call. It was Bogard's decision."

"And was it his call to include me? "

"No, my boss, DDoFO Remi Walsh, it was his call to get you onboard."

Jack did a facial shrug.

"Okay, so far you've divulged nothing. You've said there are various people, anonymous agents, and other non-agents on your radar. Not one blasted name, just unspecified people. Here's what I'm guessing. None of them are nameless. I need you to disclose who you're watching and who you suspect, so give me names. Janet, give me meat, or I'll walk and I'll take Bergman with me."

"Those were my orders; I was to give you no names. Tell you to figure it out with no gossip, no conjecture, nothing. That's the entire message from them to me to you, end of story."

"What in the, oh, cripes, Janet, this is ridiculous. How am I gonna check into anything? When I am investigating a murder, I can find at least one suspect to get the case going. You've got people you suspect, but can't tell me who. This is a guessing game. I hafta guess who to dig into more closely. This is a joke, right?"

"There are things I cannot divulge, Jack. You understand how it works."

"Yeah, I do."

Janet gnawed at her bottom lip and hesitated, and he saw her brain working something out.

"Detective, exercise caution with the people at work. And I mean everyone you work with, got it? Rely on your instincts."

The door flung open.

"West, are you—" Clive Bebchuk stopped in mid-sentence when he spotted Janet. "Spears, what are you doing here?"

"Nice to see you too, Bebchuk." The timbre of her voice changed. Her hostility was clear, her smile fake. "I stopped by to chat with Jack. Wanted to see how it's going."

"Visitation over, Janet, so, if you don't mind..." His words trailed off as his head bobbed toward the door.

"Sure, Clive, I was leaving anyway. Jack." She turned sideways to see him. "How about lunch, tomorrow in the cafeteria, you free?" Her gaze darted to Bebchuk, waiting to have him decline for Jack for any stupid reason he could muster.

"Sure, Agent Spears, I'd enjoy having lunch with you."

"See you tomorrow then. Bebchuk."

"Spears."

Small non-goodbyes said, Janet was out the door.

"Watch her, West, she's trouble."

"Sure, Agent Bebchuk, I will because I've got my eye on everything." His eyes narrowed with the word *everything* leaving his lips.

The expression on Bebchuk's face turned into a deep scowl. He hadn't liked the way Jack West sounded.

20

"Your eyes only, Jack." Janet passed him the folders across the cafeteria table.

"Yeah, along with the other crap Bebchuk gave me to read."

"Roll with it and remember what I said."

"Yeah, I will. When this is over, I'll tell ya what I'm gonna do. Punch Bebchuk in the chops. I'm not a twenty-year-old kid who started in the academy yesterday. Not to mention I've had eighteen plus years in and Clive Bebchuk is an egotistical prick."

"I agree. He's always been arrogant, and Bebchuk hates me."

"He does, I can see, but why? Is it because you're a woman?"

"Yes, for starters. It goes like this. The OAG has jurisdiction over the DEA. I have more authority than he does. Add in that I am a woman. He's chauvinistic. Thinks it should be like it was in the 40s. A time when women wore aprons, cleaned house, and cooked for the man. When females were submissive to the nth."

"What are these files anyway?" Jack turned the overstuffed extra-large manila envelope over—no markings or labels attached.

"Incident files and copies of Sophia's reports, the correct ones she sent to me. Bebchuk and Cleef never saw these because she sent bogus reports to them. Before you get pissy, because you will, they've redacted names and several events. Sorry. That's how it has to be." She sounded sincere.

An aggravated sigh heaved from his chest. "Fine, Janet. You know there's a TV game show which mirrors all this crap; it's called *To Tell the Truth*. There are three people on the panel. Two are lying and only one is telling the truth. Can we get to the freaking part where at least one person is telling me the truth? Jesus!"

Jack arched his shoulders back, raking his hands through his hair; he was getting a massive headache.

She couldn't get mad at him. She'd feel the same way and be a lot more verbal about it. "Are you ready for other news?"

"It depends. What is it?"

"You are leaving Sunday for Mexico. I got the orders this morning from my director."

"Janet, you should've started out with this news. Then maybe my head wouldn't be pounding so hard."

"Take two aspirin and suck it up."

"Right, you're all heart. Bebchuk and Cleef, are they aware of my destination?"

"The two of them are on a need-to-know. The powers have decided they don't need to know."

"Well, what did you tell them? I'm curious?"

"We're sending you to Corpus and then to San Antonio to train with other DEA operatives doing surveillance. I told them you're gonna be training with the guys running the drones. It was great. You should have seen their faces."

"I like it. That's a little satisfying, them being jealous of me, a lowly homicide detective."

Janet thought a minute, weighing her words. "Satisfaction comes in many forms, Jack. Somewhere down the line, I feel you'll get more gratification than you expect."

Jack regarded her as he mulled over those words, and nodded. Maybe, and then, maybe not. Time would tell, he figured.

"Thanks for lunch, Janet." He held up the envelope. "Thanks for this too. I guess it's better than a blank page."

"Jack?"

"Yeah?

"You're an honest cop. Few trustworthy guys left."

His thoughts went to Brooks, Webb, and Nichols—and these men were neither honest nor trustworthy—but the other men he knew were 100 percent honest.

"In my world there are. Janet, I work with honest men."

"Your world is different than mine, Jack. You have occasion to live a normal life. Crud, I haven't had a regular life in forever. I sort of miss that. Look, I've gotta scoot, got a meeting in ten and can't be late."

"Yeah, see ya."

Jack stayed at the table, his elbows propped up, his face leaning into his palms and he stared into space, thinking. Life. Two years ago he worked and was in a relationship. It took him over twenty years to find that special woman, making his life seem normal. Jack, like Janet, missed having any normal in his life.

He got home well after 6:00 and his brain hurt from the rubbish Upchuck and Creep had him sifting through. He strolled into his living room with a package of Fritos and a cold beer. Things were not adding up. He thumbed through and found the file he wanted then sat back, his sock-covered feet propped up on the coffee table. He read, then reread, looking for an anomaly in any report. He arched and stretched his back, feeling discouraged.

There's more than meets the eye. What are you missing? he thought. Taking the file from the bottom, he began working backward, starting with his triple homicide. With pen in hand he wrote:

- *Triple homicide. McCready-beaten–left for dead —disappears.*
- *Owners of the strip center—CCB, Conover-Conover, and Briggs. Involved?*

No. He crossed them off.

- *Trong flies off to Vietnam right after the homicide.* He put an asterisk next to his name. Trong wasn't involved, although the poor man had issues but not cartel issues.

Jack munched a few Fritos, emptied his bottle of warm beer, and went for a cold one.

Back on the couch, he jotted notes:

- *McCready re-appears; is seen talking with Walt Burch, then goes to a container yard. Meets with Cazalla, Callum, Mundy, and the unknown man, heads to Port Terminal Railroad. Then the bastard got the drop on me in my freaking house.*
- *Walt Burch—he bet ten ways to Sunday he was involved. Hell, pawnshops were the perfect way to launder money. Did this connect to his homicide investigation?*
- *Where was Omar Villa Lobos? The DEA had tabs on him, and nothing more. Cazalla had a loyalty to the Lobos Cartel and Omar. So how did he fit in if Villa Lobos was not their target?*
- *Why was Cazalla at Sea Star with the Tweedles and Boyce Carter?*

His head was throbbing. So much was happening. A crime series played in his brain, but the episodes were out of order. You had to start over to understand what was happening. Watch episode number one, then go in order. He scoffed, grabbing the files shoving them all into the large envelope, and tossed it on the desk. If you watched *The Godfather Part III*, then watched the first one it would confuse you. Watch the second one last. Then you wouldn't know your butt from a hole in the ground. This was how he felt about this darned case—lost. But what connected it all?

Jack headed to the attic, his spirits despondent, for reasons not involving his case. He hadn't had an occasion to pack since the last time he'd traveled. With heavy feet, he trudged up the stairs. His last trip was to Colorado, where he met Mr. and Mrs. Benson for the first time on the day they laid his love, their daughter Gretchen, to rest.

His gaze locked in on the hiker's backpack and the large duffel bag lying on his bed. A sense of sadness overcame him and he forced it down. As he closed his eyes, he filled his lungs as full as he could muster, and then expelled all the air in one heavy long sigh. Tonight he would pack away his memories. He also needed to let go of this past. The sweet memories he would cherish, but the ones which haunted him needed to be put to rest. A new goal was devised, and it meant moving forward and getting on with his life.

The duffel bag filled as he shoved in shirts, pants, underthings, personal hygiene, and shaving gear. Next, he filled his hiker's backpack with what he might or might not need. Stores weren't an option in no-man's-land. More was better. He packed his carry-on gear last knowing that he would not be required to run this bag through a scanner at Hobby Airport, courtesy of the DEA. He filled it with ammunition for both his Glock and his Kimber.

Tomorrow was Friday. Sunday he was flying out of the country on a mission—dangerous and covert—so covert they might not acknowledge him or Agent Medina if they called for help. Jack needed to fill Kasper in because he was the only person he felt he could bank on.

21

"Boilermaker, Grady, start me a tab, please. Bergman, what's your poison tonight?"

"Sam Adams Double Bock, with a double shot of Jose. Start me a tab too, Grady."

"Nah, one tab for the booze, my treat. You fatten us up, Bergman, and spring for dinner. I'll get us drunk."

"Yeah, sounds like fun, but not drunk. We're the police, Jack. Grady, I'll take a Reuben, heavy on the mustard and sauerkraut, with fries. Jack?"

"Yep, Grady, make it two."

Grady put their order in. He came back with both drinks and two glasses of ice water. "You boys need anything else. Give me a shout." The old pub owner trotted off. Four new customers just bellied up to the bar.

"Let's drink, Bergman, to liars, OAG, and DEA agent douchebags, all of whom have us running around in circles chasing our asses."

"I'll drink to that." Kasper raised his shot glass, tapped it to Jack's, and both men tossed their shots back, then took a drink of beer before wiping their mouths.

"So, what's new, Bergman?"

"Other than the OAG pissant I've been dealing with, nothing. And I'm serious, not a damn thing. The OAG peon Spears has me training with is a kid, a pimple-faced brat. Seems his father is someone of importance and I could give a rat's hind end. I spend the day listening to him drone on about nada and trying to put in plain words technical crap he can't explain to a hole in the effing ground. God, it's like I have a textbook with eyes and pimples slapping me in the face with nonsense any beginner tech could understand. It's pissing me off and today, well, today I met a—" Kasper stopped when Grady delivered their food.

"Looks great, Grady. Didn't realize how hungry I was." Kasper's stomach rumbled on cue.

"Yeah, pup, I hear your stomach talking right now telling you to feed it. More drinks, fellas?"

"I'M FLYING out of Hobby Sunday night, heading into unfamiliar territory, brother."

"Uh-huh, Janet dropped the news on me this morning. After zit-face finishes bending my ear like a droll college professor who has a leg and a half in the grave, I'll be working with a different DEA agent. Janet brought him over so we could meet. Theo something-or-other, can't remember his last name. Guy reminds me of the Hulk, a tall dude with a big bag of muscles. He has a computer science degree, and his specialty, from what Janet told me, is undercover surveillance. It floored me because he looks like a damn biker, hit man, not the computer nerdy-looking type."

"So techs got a type? You mean to tell me muscles and nerds don't go hand in hand?"

"Yeah, everyone in Tech looks like Clark Kent during the day and at night becomes a hunky, husky superhero. You ain't the only one with a cape and superpowers." Kasper snorted, and Jack pinched a laugh back.

"What's his story?"

"He transferred from Tucson, Arizona, to the Corpus Christi office two years ago. Since the Houston office supervises Corpus, the powers that be sent him here. Janet told me he's been instrumental in the arrests of a few mid-level gorillas linked to the cartel. They were getting deals for information, but there's been a snafu of sorts."

"Yeah, what snafu would that be?" Jack moved his empty mug back.

"These guys aren't talking, not anymore."

"So, no deal in the works any longer, I take it."

"Dead men don't need deals."

Jack looked at Kasper, his lips pursed in a frown. "Shanked before they could talk?"

"Yep, you nailed it. They found one guy dead in lockup, strangled, and he was alone."

"Inside job I'd reckon. I'd think whacking someone in prison might be easy to do. There are plenty of viable suspects. It could be easy to get away. They all say the same thing. None of 'em saw anything. But I've never worked a prison homicide, at least not yet."

"I'd think that might be a touchy case, Jack, don't you?"

"But it would be interesting."

"Yeah, it might be. So this new agent, Theo, whatever his last name is, Styles or Stack. Seems the Corpus SAC thought he would be helpful on our assignment. They say he is an expert in reconnaissance and has experience with the cartel."

"Sounds like he'd be useful."

"Dunno, Jack. Something ain't right about him. I just haven't figured it out, at least not yet."

"Stay on your guard. If the shit hits the fan in Mexico, I need someone here who won't hesitate to send in the troops to get us." Jack reached for the bag he shoved under his chair, pulling out two burners. "I've entered the numbers; we use these phones from now on. Don't call me from HPD or from your cell."

"Got it. Anything else I can do, since I'm the nerd?"

"Yep, there is. Create two new email addresses. Secure them and lock them down, like as in NASA secured."

"Yeah, easy-peasy, have it done in the morning. I'll have dummy accounts we can attach untraceable disposable emails to. You want me to—"

Jack butted in, "Text me the email addys on the burner. Starting tomorrow, these burners and emails are our principal lines of communication. I'm leaving my phone on vibrate and if I don't answer right away don't get jumpy and send in the National Guard. Send them if I don't respond, at least by the next day."

"Jack, you worried things will get bad?"

"I'm not sure. All I know is these men play for keeps. I'll be in a remote area in the mountains soon. Not your optimal area to call in for backup. One female agent as my backup, and I—" The expression on Kasper's face had Jack pausing and staring at him.

"Listen, Bergman, I'm not a sexist pig, but even a powerful woman in law enforcement cannot come out smelling like a rose when three or four mean hombres come at her. Medina isn't *Wonder Woman* or *The Bionic Woman* any more than I'm *Superman* or *The Six-Million-Dollar Man.* And I...what, Bergman? What's that look for?"

"What's a *Bionic Woman* or a *Six-Million-Dollar Man*? Jack, I've never heard of those. *Superman* and *Wonder Woman*, yeah, Marvel comics superheroes, but I—"

"God, and you wanna know why I call you kid, kid? Google it when you get home. Old television shows from the mid-to-late 70s." He motioned to Grady.

"More drinks?"

"No, Grady, just the tab, thanks, man."

Outside, Kasper looked at the burner phone and then crammed it into his pocket.

"Contact you sometime Sunday, keep your burner with you cuz if all else fails, you're my backup, kid."

"I won't let you down, Jack, I swear. Just don't go get killed in Mexico or I'll get pissed."

"Be working on staying one step ahead of these bastards and dodging bullets best I can."

An authentic sturdy Texas handshake bonded them.

"Be careful out there. Use lots of mosquito repellent. Don't come home with malaria or with bullets in ya." Kasper's lips curled in a lopsided grin, but it did not mask the worry in his eyes.

"Will do, and, uh, listen, watch your six. Can't have my contact here getting knocked off the grid, got it?"

"Roger that. Safe trip, Jack, be waiting to hear from ya." Kasper Bergman did a tiny salute good-bye and walked around the corner to his vehicle.

Jack didn't leave right away. He relaxed and leaned against the building, watching cars traveling both ways. It was late. Ten-forty-five, traffic still busy, not congested, just busy. Car headlights and streetlights illuminated the night. All the sounds and smells of the city, and the city itself, spoke to him in odd ways.

He took a walk down the sidewalk, stopping at an empty bus stop and sat down on the rickety bench. The buildings were older. Behind them sat established neighborhoods with people of every race and ethnicity, age, and marital status. Kids played in the parks here and went to schools. Children raised to be part of the community and the city. The good part, he prayed.

A bus pulled up, and the driver stopped. He opened the doors and people got off, heading in different directions. Houstonians heading home after work. Some were heading *to* work.

He people-watched for a few minutes, thinking about his journey to Mexico in two days, dealing with dangerous men. Jack didn't want to come home in a box. He loved Houston—the people, the history, and the life.

22

Volaris Airlines was not rocking many travelers, departing or arriving. Sworn in for his temporary stint with the DEA, he was eager to get to Mexico. Jack's nerves were on edge, but he was still excited. He patted his pocket, feeling for his cell and the burner phone, his HPD badge and his temporary DEA badge.

Under his coat, he carried his 9 mil and on his ankle his Kimber 45. The entire bureaucratic BS dealt with for his carrying concealed weapons onboard.

"Once you've touched down in Guanajuato, you will be met by the Federal Ministerial Police. An agent will drive you to checkpoint one. Jack, the Mexican agent and our agent are not your backup, understood?"

"Yeah, it's clear, if our asses get in a vice lock, they can't help us."

"Sorry, Jack. If push comes to shove, they'll get word to us and we'll send in the troops as fast as possible, I promise. We could call the Mexican authorities. But we don't know who is on the take. "

"Understood."

"We're sending you in as a tourist so we can bypass the

hullabaloo. Our people don't want to deal with the local Federales. The agency wants you on your way without red tape, armed and dangerous and none the wiser. Marcella Ágулia, a flight attendant onboard, is our American contact. She is expecting you and can interpret since you don't speak Spanish."

"This woman's DEA?"

"Undercover. Just a little over two years now. She came over from the Mexico side."

Janet pulled the car up to the curb at the departure gate.

"Jack, I'm not seeing you off. When you are wheels down in Mexico, you won't need to contact me, I'll know. Do you have means to communicate with Bergman?" One eyebrow arched as she asked.

"Yeah, Agent Spears, we both have cell phones, he's got my number and yours, and I got yours and his. You got any other way in mind for me to communicate with you and Bergman? Ham radio, telegraph, Morse code, pigeons in flight?"

"Don't be a smart-ass, Detective West, I know what you have. I know you know I know, you know?"

"The answer is yes, as confusing as it sounds." He opened the door. "Pop the trunk so I can get my gear, would'ja?"

Bags in hand, he stood at the curb. She rolled the passenger door window down halfway, leaning toward the open space.

"Take care, Jack. I'd hate to get in a verbal war with your captain if something happens to you and I gotta tell her."

"Yeah, about that, Janet... When I get home, how about you tell me the story between you two?"

"No story to tell, just two strong-willed bullheaded women, that's it in a nutshell."

"Huh, now who's the liar? Catch ya later." He tossed the two-finger salute, turned, and headed for the terminal to Volaris Airlines as a sworn-in DEA agent. Anticipation tightened his gut and excitement filled his senses.

"Now boarding for Guanajuato, Mexico," a woman's thick accent carried over the loudspeakers. *"Will passengers on rows one through six please report to terminal D, gate thirteen."*

He was on row fifteen, so he waited.

"Rows fifteen through twenty now boarding for Guanajuato, Mexico," the thick accent spoke again. It was time. Taking his ticket out of his breast pocket, he made his way to the gate attendant. His adrenaline pumped faster. Two hours from now he'd land in Mexico, meet his contact. Afterward he'd be off to find Agent Medina in a third-world town. Jack was ready.

Long legs and airplane seats do not mix well. Pushed into a tight frame, ready to pop, Jack felt like a squeezebox would feel. When the passengers had boarded, the pilot came over the loudspeaker. The stewards went through the preflight instructions and takeoff speeches that lasted forever, as his long legs stayed cramped up. Once the seatbelt light blinked off, he popped the catch, thankful he had an aisle seat. Jack got up, stretching and rolling his shoulders, and rose on his toes, extending his calf muscles before sitting. He gave the older couple beside him a friendly nod. The older man nodded back. "*Si, lugar estrecho para piernas largas,*" he spoke in Spanish, and the older woman's lips turned up crookedly. Jack's Spanish was marginal, composed of words not fit to say in mixed company. Words Hispanic gang members repeated in interrogation rooms. These words he knew by heart. However, they weren't conversational words, so he nodded politely, not knowing what to do, much less what to say.

"He says tight spot for long legs." Jack looked over his right shoulder to see a flight attendant standing there with her pushcart of drinks and snacks.

"Yes, it is, ma'am. Sí, muy, uh..." He glanced at the man, and then looked at the attendant. "How do you say cramped?"

"Estrecho."

Jack turned to the man. "*Sí, señor, muy estrecho.*"

The old man nodded. His wife patted Jack's hand.

"You have *tipo*, uh, kind eyes, and uh, a nice *sonreír*, uh-eh, smile," the elderly woman said, her English stilted.

"Thank you, *muchas gracias*."

The flight attendant took the man and wife's drink order in Spanish, asking Jack the same, but in English. Their drinks were poured, with a bag of chips for him and two small bags of popcorn for his seatmates. In Spanish and then in English, she informed them who she was.

"My name is Marcella. I will assist you on this short flight today. If you need anything, press the call button."

She signaled to him to make his way to the tail of the craft with a side glance and an eye movement to the rear. Jack waited until she finished serving the passengers on the last row.

"I've got it, Jenny. Take this to the cockpit, please. Marcella handed her two bottled waters and a clipboard.

"Yes, I'd be glad to."

Not at all hard on the eyes, Jenny regarded Jack strolling down the center aisle headed their way. He wore jeans that fit him to a T and a blue button-up dress shirt, with a light camel-colored sports coat, and black cowboy boots. His dark thick hair brushed the top of his shirt collar, curling a tad on the ends. Jack had neglected to shave on purpose the past four days wanting to appear scruffier for the assignment. His face of stubble had shaded in and looked extremely sexy on him.

As he got closer, she saw a tiny dimple peeking out when he was almost smiling. She returned what she thought was a smile for her, fluttering her lashes as her insides did flip-flops. Tall cowboys and Harley bikers were her weakness.

"Ma'am, excuse me," Jack addressed the younger flight attendant.

"No problem." Jenny turned sideways to pass. Jack knew a young girl's dreamy-eyed gawk when he saw one, and he ignored it with an undetectable sigh. His life had a huge void without a female companion. A fleeting thought of Gretchen filled his head. It was not the moment to deliberate his love life. Besides, finding a woman as wonderful as Gretchen was gonna be a long haul. When this assignment ended, he'd work on that phase of his life—maybe.

"Detective West," the woman spoke in a hushed voice. "No one suspects I'm DEA. Let's keep it that way."

"Yes, ma'am, I understand and it's good to meet you, Marcella." He extended his hand, and she took it.

"I'll be filling drink orders while we chat."

He nodded, leaning his hip against the counter and crossing his arms, watching her.

"Once we land and the other passengers disembark, Agent Espinar will meet you at the ramp. He'll check your weapons and take you to the security office and I'll meet you there once I'm finished. Here comes Jenny. Follow my lead."

"Sure."

"Oh, yes, if you have the time. Go see the Museum of the Mummies of Guanajuato. It's a wonderful place to tour if you like history."

"Giving another lecture if you have time to go to Guanajuato, Marcella?" Jenny slipped in behind him, standing too close for comfort.

"Well, these mummies sound very interesting and I'm much obliged. Thank you." He gave Marcella his best smile and then turned to Jenny.

"Ma'am." He did a head nod as if he were tipping his hat to her without the same type of smile he'd given Marcella and went back to his seat, praying he'd dissuaded the young girl from flirting with him.

Marcella shook her head at her coworker.

"What? Geeze, are you dead? He is a hunk, a tall cowboy hunk. *Mm-mm-mm*." The tone of her voice emitted a dreamy note as she ended her statement with a heavy, wistful sigh.

"Jenny, you need a steady beau. Now, get busy and gather the passengers' empties."

The young woman pushed her cart to the front and turned around. Jenny walked back, stopping every few seats to gather trash.

At Jack's seat, at first she gave him a serious stare, her brows crinkled in a slight frown. In a split-second, she put on her best flirty smile. He shot her down with one disapproving expression, causing her to huff. Jack chuckled. The score: Houston Homicide Detective Jack West—one. Flight Attendant Jenny Martin—zero.

23

The landing was bumpy, and it felt wonderful to get wheels on the ground. Once the first-class section departed the plane, rows 1 through 27 began trudging out, hauling carry-on bags and kids. Jack remained seated near the window, letting the older couple leave first. After the last passenger sauntered by, weary-looking, Jack grabbed his carry-on out of the overhead bin. Before exiting he glanced back in the galley's direction, giving Marcella a vague nod before taking his leave.

"Jack, Jack West?"

As Jack walked off the gangway and into the physical airport, he spotted the man who'd called his name. Jack gave him a stern once-over and then relaxed.

"Yes, I'm Jack and you must be Agent Espinar. No uniform? I thought all Federales wore uniforms."

"I am a plainclothes *policia*, like your homicide detectives in the States. You have luggage?"

"Yeah, I'll need to go to the baggage area."

Espinar sidestepped the check-in conveyer, passing the metal detector with a minuscule head nod to the airport security officer, and received a slight nod in return. They bypassed all security checks, getting Jack through with his weapons intact as well as not checking his carry-on bag. At the luggage carousel, Espinar spoke to a baggage attendant.

"Have someone drop Mr. West's luggage behind the desk of the main lobby."

"Sí, señor, de inmediato." (Yes, sir, immediately.)

"*Gracias.*" He turned to Jack. "We'll wait in the security offices and once Marcella arrives, we will be on our way."

Jack eyed the man. "What about my firearms, Agent Espinar? Shouldn't you take possession?"

"Something tells me I shouldn't make a big deal out of it."

"Aha—your intuition says you can trust me, is that it?"

"It is what you call an...uh, *a sensación de la estómago,* uh, stomach feeling."

"Gut feeling."

"Oh, yes, a gut feeling, *a sensación de la tripa.* Sometimes my English gets twisted up."

"Well, don't feel too bad. Americans butcher English most of the time, and it's our primary language."

Less than an hour later, Marcella opened the door, finding them chatting like old friends.

"You two ready?"

Jack sat in the back, his mind on his destination and the meeting with Agent Medina, a woman he knew very little about. The unknown weighing a ton on his mind, his adrenaline pumped to a new high, as did his heart rate. This assignment had become real, very real.

THE RIDE WAS QUIET, and Jack watched the city, buildings, travelers, residents, and the town disappear with every mile. The further Miguel drove the flatter the land became, with dead long stretches of road ahead. Passing homes in different states of neglect, trash, and no apparent amenities like central air or heat, indoor water, or toilets. The area didn't have enough buildings or people to call it a village. What or who was up in the mountains ahead—now this was another mystery.

There was nothing for the next eighty miles but road and land. Miguel took a road onto what appeared to be the Sahara Desert of Mexico. Dust billowed behind them as the tires rolled, crunching dirt and teeny pebbles, and the background scenery blurred in a billowing cloud behind the car.

"Looks like no-man's-land. Geeze. Does it ever rain here?" Jack watched out the window at the land dotted with trees and very little green; dried-up weeds in patches of rock and dirt passed by.

"Yes, it rains, and when it does, it downpours hard in the mountains. Look over there." Agent Espinar pointed. "The Secretariat of the Interior plans to build a new Policia Municipality, a training center for new officers and agents. They have twenty acres, housing three barracks, a physical fitness course, shooting ranges, and more. It is a school much like your Quantico."

"The Mexican FBI, I like it."

"The Ministerial of Federales and the AGO of Mexico are discussing military training. Every prison guard will be trained there, free of distractions. Each man, student, or teacher will have a thorough background check. Because of what we are trying to accomplish, Sanchez Guadalupe, our Secretariat of the Interior, decreed background checks will be *instrumento*, uh, implemented on all *inmediato*, immediate family members. Should there be any *contratiempos?*--I think this means hiccups in English—it will keep a man out of our training facility." Espinar gave Jack the rundown.

"Hiccups, like what?"

"Traffic violations, drunk and disorderly, getting fired from a job, to bad credit; this will put the brakes on."

"Finding men and their families who are squeaky clean will be a tough job. It would be near impossible in the States. So, how many maximum security prisons are in Mexico?" Jack watched the land roll by from his window.

"Three-hundred and nine State prisons and there are nineteen Federal prisons. All are overcrowded. Killing each other makes room for the next group of murderers." Miguel shook his head. Never would he understand this.

"Prisons are the same everywhere. The one difference is location and language." Jack was of the same opinion and he'd never understand it either. For the rest of the drive, Miguel talked shop and Jack listened, wondering why Agent Águlia was so quiet. His first impression of her had been positive, but her side glances and tense facial expressions on certain subject matters concerned him. Maybe one-on-one in the open, she would feel freer to speak. With all this cloak-and-dagger, maybe she didn't trust Miguel Espinar. He wasn't an American DEA; he was the Mexican Federal policia. Mexican police, Federal or State, were often corrupt men. Jack's smart, intuitive gut said use caution.

Marcella and Jack walked into a building the size of a double-wide construction trailer. Two desks faced the door and on the side wall were three metal filing cabinets, a table with a fax machine, a tabletop copier, two-way radios, one shortwave radio, and several walkie-talkies. When the door opened, they saw a man standing behind the desk.

"Jack, this is Umberto Vega," Marcella introduced him.

He offered his hand, and after shaking Umberto's hand, Jack felt a powerful urge to wipe off his hand, but he resisted.

"What is it you do, Agent Vega?"

"I am not an agent, Mr. West. My position is a contractor for the government and the Federales. My job will be as director over the men training the new military students." Umberto shot a slanted glance Marcella's way. Jack did not miss her expression of displeasure.

"So, when are you breaking ground on this new facility, Mr. Vega?"

"It was to begin two weeks ago, but there have been delays. They plan to start up sometime next week."

"Training new military students, so you are ex-military?"

"I have enough experience." He didn't like all these questions. "There is work I must do." Umberto ignored Jack as he turned to Marcella. "The paperwork is finished, Agent Águlia. I believe you will find it in order, so I will leave you to entertain your, uh, guest." His tone was brusque and disrespectful, the words aimed with dislike toward Jack. He didn't know the man, just met him. So what was his problem?

Without a word, Umberto turned on his heels banging the back door shut.

"He's got an attitude. I don't like it." Jack did not tolerate rude people.

"Never mind him, Jack. We need to meet Espinar."

Outside the building, Jack looked around, trying to picture a facility similar to Quantico, and it was hard to envision.

"You were silent on the drive, Marcella." He noted she had not jumped into the conversation, not once.

"Oh, huh, I didn't even notice. Once Miguel starts about the new training center and the infrastructure that Sanchez Guadalupe and the Ministerial of Federales Carlos Ayala has been planning and how they will run it with an iron hand, I sorta zone out."

"You're not interested. I mean, as an agent, I would imagine you would be."

"Jack, I know this information inside and out. The first time I heard the story I was excited."

"Fair enough, I suppose. Let's get to business then. What can you tell me?"

As Jack listened to her, his anger rose. Not because of what she told him. It was what she wasn't telling him. Marcella briefed him on nothing, just as Janet had briefed him. It was the same briefing he'd had with SAC Bogard. The same crap—nothing leading him to any conclusions except for two questions living foremost in his thoughts, questions he needed answers to:

1. What was the real story of his assignment?
2. Was this assignment for show?

There was no agenda, no direction. Were the good guys bad guys? People hiding behind their agency's three-letter acronym? Nothing made sense.

24

"That's it? You're joking, because there has to be more."

"I'm sorry, Jack, but it's all I am at liberty to mention. So, you ready to go?"

"Guess so. Let me grab my gear."

Inside, Jack offered Umberto his hand. "Good to meet you; perhaps we shall see each other again."

The Mexican man stared at Jack's outstretched hand ignoring it.

"She will take you to your checkpoint." Umberto turned. He left banging the door shut.

Jack processed the man's odd behavior, grabbed his duffel and other gear then followed Marcella out the door.

"What's his deal?"

"Mexican police care little about real policing. Their government is corrupt." She ignored his question.

Jack shifted his duffel to his other shoulder and hitched up the hiker's backpack.

"Yeah, it's a shame words like *trust* and *honesty* aren't in any government or law enforcement's vocabulary. This ain't news to us law-abiding guys. So, tell me about Umberto. What's his deal?" He wasn't ready to let that go yet. He needed answers.

Agent Águlia stopped walking, and so did Jack. They turned facing each other, her eyes steady on his. Jack was a smart man. However, there was only so much they could keep hiding. Disclosing information regarding Umberto and his direct ties to the cartel was old news, just not news Jack had been told. Perhaps relating this info would placate him, especially if he thought she was spilling details the DEA wanted hidden.

"Jack, I'm going beyond my pay grade to get you up to speed on what I'm comfortable telling you," she lied.

"I appreciate it, Marcella. Be nice if at least one damn person was a straight shooter."

"Come on, it's not far. Let's talk and walk because Miguel is waiting. And, Jack, you got none of this from me, got it?"

"Sure, Agent Águlia, I understand."

"A group of men overthrew Villa Lobos' Cartel a couple years back." She saw him stop in mid-stride. "No, keep walking, Jack."

"Yeah, yeah, I'm walking, so you keep talking."

"Villa Lobos went underground, and we lost him. He has resurfaced a few times. We've learned he is strategizing a plan to regain his power, but nothing more than street talk. He was on our radar and isn't any longer, or it's what the higher-ups in our organization tell us. The real truth is the OAG has him on their radar and we get the secondary reports."

"Odd, seems to me the DEA would have more interest in watching Omar, but we can discuss this later. So, how does Umberto Vega fit into this picture?"

"Vega hates men of power in his country. He thinks women are weak, plus he despises what he calls 'superior Americans.' Here I am, a Mexican American with a powerful job at the DEA. Add in that I'm a woman. This has him seething. "

"Yeah, I could tell there was no love lost between you. It doesn't explain how he fits into everything."

Marcella pondered only a second. "Vega's family was from a very poor little community outside these mountains, migrant workers. A few years back—"

"Wait. Sorry to interrupt you. But you say *was,* as in past tense, you mean they're no longer there?"

"Villa Lobos tried to strong-arm the families in the village, but they wouldn't work for him and fought back so he killed them."

"All of them, the entire village?" Jack's heart broke and the anger he felt burned deep.

Villa Lobos spared a few men and a few women and children. Umberto was spared because he was gone. He and thirty other men were away working on farms in the North. They returned to find the village in ruins. Their dead lay out and left to rot. The people who lived fled and their families could not find them. The men joined the Federales. Their plan was to get revenge on Villa Lobos, thinking they could make it appear legal."

"How were they planning to get revenge by joining the Federales? The cartel pays off several Federales, so it'd be hard to identify who they could trust without getting themselves killed."

"Well, it didn't matter anyway. They refused Umberto's application."

"Why?"

"He wasn't a high school graduate, and he had a misdemeanor. Men who did not pass muster to become a Federale formed the Mexican Security for Civilians. Theirs was a group of angry militants with weapons, looking for revenge."

"Villa Lobos is still alive, so they didn't exact their revenge, did they?"

"It's not revenge like you'd think, Jack. They wanted him alive and powerless. This is a fate worse than death for Omar Villa Lobos. Have you ever heard of the Mata al lobo de México?"

"No, who are they?"

"Vega and his compadres broke away from the Mexican Security for Citizens group, added members who were like-minded, and formed Mata al lobo de México, which means 'kill the wolf of Mexico,' and they overthrew Omar, sending him underground. "

"The cartel is huge. The group had to be smart."

"Sometimes, Jack, if you know the right weak spot or have support from one special person, you can accomplish more than you realize."

"Villa Lobos' Cartel is no longer in action, which means one less cartel, albeit a large one."

"The drug trade means a lot of pesos, so several people here need this drug trade to continue. It's how they earn a living, for some a better living than working crops. Here is a strange truth. They didn't want to destroy the cartel, all they wanted was to destroy Omar. Umberto hated Omar for killing innocents in his village. Jack, these migrant farmworkers like him have nothing if there is no work. Presently, there has been less and less farm or orchard work. To protect their families and earn money, Umberto and his men would have worked for Omar, but they didn't have the choice once Omar showed up while they were all gone."

"Aren't the cartel and Omar Villa Lobos the same?"

"You would think, but no."

"A cartel is a cartel, someone in power, someone to fear. What do you mean?"

"The men who formed the militia wanted a different leader. Not a man as ruthless as Omar. They wanted someone smart enough to know dead men were useless. Dead men cannot run drugs, sell drugs, cook drugs, and most of all, dead men do not collect money. At the rate Omar was killing men, his cartel was shrinking. These men are now loyal to another leader. Only we don't know who it is. We are hunting a nameless, faceless man."

"I understand now why Janet said Omar was not on their radar. There is one thing I'm not clear on. What is Umberto's connection to the DEA and the new facility being built?"

"Umberto led a group in the takeover and it got bloody. He didn't want to run the organization. It's too much responsibility for a man like Umberto. He is not smart enough to run a cartel. Vega is pretty insignificant in the scheme of things. He wouldn't have a large allegiance of followers. The job to overthrow Villa Lobos was a huge undertaking, and even though he could rile the troops, he had plenty of powerful help."

"Help? Like, what kind of help?"

"Someone or several someones from the United States, maybe even our own agency personnel. Jack, I don't have to tell you how disturbing this is. To both the DEA and OAG."

Jack cast his eyes down. His booted foot swished the dirt from side to side, a cloud of dust rose then settled, and he repeated the movement as he thought. Agent Águlia had no reason to lie to him. But there it was. He had just met her and knew nothing about her background or her character. Okay, he'd go on blind faith and trust her for now or until he felt he couldn't.

"Any clue who's the new boss of the cartel?"

"Nobody knows, Jack. We have no clue if it's run by a Mexican National or a US citizen. One thought was there are two individuals working together. We don't know if it is even being run from Mexico. Someone might call shots from your country, we just don't know. This has everyone baffled."

"Why am I even here, then?"

"Several reasons, Jack. We need intel on methods of transport, dates and times, and locations. We feel this will give us insight on the new head of the snake."

"Medina and I have a lot on our proverbial plates, don't we?"

"Yes, you do. You'll be pulled from every direction. This concerns me about what you will accomplish."

How skilled or smart was Sophia Medina? Marcella knew little about the woman. Jack West, however, was a different story—from what she'd heard about him she'd learned he was not one to give up. Would he keep going until he got to the root of the evil? Or would his doggedness get him killed and Agent Medina too? DEA Agent

Águlia was uncomfortable with it all. Her worry was for very different reasons, ones she could not and would not share.

Agent Espinar waved when he saw them.

"Well, hot damn, I was not expecting this." Jack surveyed the area, quite impressed.

A helipad and an outlying building sat in the middle of nowhere. He'd figured they were going by ground in a jeep or truck.

"You will not expect I am your pilot too, huh, Detective?"

"No, I wouldn't."

"I will fly you to the drop-off location. There is a vehicle waiting for you."

Marcella stretched out her hand. "Jack, these people play for keeps, as in dead, so watch your back."

He nodded, taking her hand. "Of course."

It was in her eyes. What was it he saw? Fear, worry, or a plain I-don't-give-a-shit-what-happens. Jack didn't know her well enough to read her.

Seat belted in, flight-ready, Agent Espinar checked his gauges, flipped switches, and turned on the headset. "Ready, Jack?"

With a stiff affirmative nod and thumbs-up indicating a go sign, Jack inhaled, ready to take off.

Miguel's heart was heavy as he fired up the engine. In the remote area, he would drop the detective off. He realized it was just Jack and Sophia with no backup. He prayed no harm came to them. These men were dangerous and would kill anyone they deemed a threat. If policia or Representante Federales were close, and the cartel found out the law was on their trail, their bodies would disappear. With zero proof of their murders, no one would pay the price for taking their lives.

Sin un cadáver no hay asesinato. Without a corpse, there is no murder.

25

In a clearing the size of a football field, surrounded by brush and dotted with small trees and weeds, Miguel brought the helicopter to the ground.

"Wow, my first helicopter ride, nerve-racking and exhilarating!" Jack spoke into the headset still attached to his helmet, as the rotor blades were whirring overhead.

"The first time, I felt the same. But now it's...how you Americans say it...old cap, right?"

The edges of his mouth tugged upward. "You mean old hat."

"*Si*, yes, old hat. English sayings sometimes do not come out right for me. Jack, grab your luggage while I explain what's next because I do not want to be here too long and attract attention."

With his hiker's backpack, duffel bag, and carry-on gear, he jumped out, setting his baggage on the ground, and Miguel handed him two large manila envelopes.

"Inside are the maps you will need and the coordinates. Mexican police reports on drug traffic connected to the northern and southern sides of Mexico. The other envelope has money, and your temporary resident visa along with bogus paperwork, but it looks official enough.

Included are documents for your business and personal property ownership. The work visa lasts 180 days. You need both visas. In the event your case goes over 180 days, you just need to renew the work visa."

"I hope I'm not here for four years, Miguel. My captain will have Janet Spears' head." A huge grin landed on his face. Another catfight between her and Roni would give Davis Yao more than a simple headache—it would cause his head to explode.

Agent Espinar was silent for a moment, and Jack cleared his throat to wake him from his hypnotic state.

"Oh, sorry, Jack. I was wondering if I should toss in my two pesos or not."

"I'd appreciate it, Miguel."

"In the past, cartel leaders live a plush lifestyle here, guarded, protected, and well hidden, but the Southeast Cartel is not run from Mexico. It's being run from within your country, Jack; Marcella mentioned this to you, didn't she?"

"She mentioned something like that."

Marcella's exact words were, *"They didn't know if it was being run in Mexico, or from the States."* He kept this to himself. What she'd told him sounded like double talk.

"*De todos modos,* I mean, anyway, there are several smaller groups who've broken off from the North and South Cartels and become problematic, not just to us but to the cartel operations here in Mexico. I'd say it has spilled over into your country too."

"So we have outside forces in modest numbers working to grow and gain more power, and this causes internal wars within the cartels. This could prove useful." Jack's mind was on how inner turmoil inside the cartel helps them on the outside.

"Detective, how do you mean?"

"They fight each other, eliminating their enemies, who are our enemies too. We need to locate one or two of these idiots to turn them. Maybe get them on our team. Promise them immunity or protection if they give up information."

Miguel nodded. "It is something for us to consider, *si*."

"Why does everyone feel the Southeast Cartel is being run Stateside?"

"No name, no face, and no sightings. The cartel is here without a leader. There is a person second-in-command, following a leader's orders, though. Also captains with many soldiers, but I assure you, the leader is not in my country, Jack. When the leaders ruled from Mexico, there would be dead bodies hanging, beheadings, and such. But there have been none in the past sixteen months."

"I'd say that's good, good for your countrymen. Do you have anyone on the inside, Miguel?"

"No, we pulled our undercover policia two-and-a-half years ago. There were eight undercover men. Three disappeared. They're never coming back. We know this with certainty. The other five we had to extract are going through physiological screenings; a few are even in drug rehab. It took an emotional and physical toll on them. Detective West, we've lost too many good men."

A frown rolled over Miguel's face. He stared at Jack with worry. He didn't want another honest man to be taken by the cartel.

"Hey, Espinar, don't worry. I have every intention of getting back home to my regular job, in one piece with my sanity intact."

"Remember, there are no control officers to contact, and no radio callouts. Nobody will fly in to save the day, Jack. It's just you and Sophia."

"Then we'd better make an excellent team."

It was just them. No way to call for help. Man, this wasn't an optimal situation. He wondered what the powers that be had been thinking.

"You should find everything you might need loaded into the vehicle. Agent Medina will be extra happy to see you." Espinar's words held a mischievous note, but Jack ignored it as he thought about the situation at hand.

"So no contact on the inside, huh? No confidential informant? Not even an undercover agent from the US?"

"Ask your people, Jack."

"Okay, then there is someone, so enlighten me."

"I guess I let that cat out of a sack."

"It's cat out of the bag, and yeah, I guess you did. Why not tell me? Who am I gonna tell out here?"

"My apologies, Detective, but I cannot say who or where to keep them from being compromised."

Jack blew out a sigh. "Well, shit, we won't know who to trust, will we?"

Espinar gave him a hard stare. "Trust yourself and Sophia, and this is all I'd count on right now. *Malditos bastardios*—this means, uh, fucking bastards. They claim to be on the true side of the law—nameless, faceless people. Unless you're positive you can trust them, don't, not with anything." Miguel glanced at his watch. "Jack, I've been here too long; time for me to get out of here with my *pájaro que zumba, helicóptero,* my, how you say, whirlybird, helicopter." He pointed behind Jack. "Follow the dirt trail for a quarter of a mile. You'll see a path to your left. Follow the path until you find the hidden vehicle and take this." The guy pulled out a compass from his front shirt pocket. "Didn't know if you brought one, but you're gonna need one out here to get around, I promise."

"Is there a specific road to follow once I get the vehicle?" He saw hills, trees, and a thicket, with low-lying gullies for miles. The only cleared patch of flat land was this clearing for Miguel's helicopter.

"Not to worry. You will find your way. Here. In this envelope, you'll find keys, cash, and a map of the terrain. As well as separate documents you will need." Miguel proffered his hand. "We won't speak again, so good luck, and be safe." *We won't speak again*—words that were truer than either man could ever imagine.

"Will do. Take care yourself." After hoisting on his hiker's backpack, Jack grabbed his duffel, stuffed the manila envelopes in, and swung it up on his shoulder. He then picked up the carry-on bag. With a nod, he turned and headed toward a path he knew would lead to danger.

26

Jack plodded forward, the copter whirring overhead, and shielded his eyes from the sun, catching one last glimpse of Miguel, the helicopter pilot, which had been a definite surprise. A light glint on the metal rotor blades reflected and vanished into the sun. Jack looked from left to right. He glanced over his left shoulder, next his right, then straightforward. No real road, only a narrow path loomed ahead.

"Huh, well, they got a vehicle in here, so I damn well should be able to drive it out," he voiced aloud.

Moving through trees and brush, he used his duffel bag and carry-on as shields against the small limbs and scratchy overgrowth. The duffel pushed it back out of his way as it swished at his thighs. His carry-on gear kept branches from scraping his forearms when the pathway narrowed. As the path ended, he found_himself_in a dense section of prickly shrubs, with a pile of dead tree limbs butted against a thick cluster of bramble. He regarded the stacked limbs and brown brush entangled at the underside of the heap, almost like a weave. Jack began pulling the largest section of undergrowth away to reveal the entire front section of a vehicle, and his grin turned into a full smile, lighting up his face. He thought of an old movie, *Romancing the Stone.* The two main characters needed a vehicle. When they asked around, the townspeople tell them about a man who has a car they can use. When they arrive, the drug lord says, "You mean my little mule, Pepe?"

Pepe turns out to be a souped-up Ford Bronco. It wasn't a Bronco, though; he'd uncovered a black two-door Jeep Wrangler. The doors were locked. He opened the envelope and shook out the keys, unlocked the door, and pulled the hood release.

"Hot damn, a V-8." A low whistle emitted from his puckered lips.

After shutting the hood, he examined the tires. Large 37-inchers —extreme terrain tires, for rougher terrain—like where he was now. He peered inside the back window. A cover matching the gray interior was pulled over the storage area. He unlocked the rear door and snapped the release to roll the cover back to reveal his treasures.

Expensive-looking camera equipment and the works lay in front, along with several boxes marked, *Nonperishables,* and water. Thank God, getting Montezuma's revenge on an op was not something he'd considered.

Something was hidden at the very back. Jack reached in, his knee propped on the edge of the inside of the backend. He raised the end of the canvass cover and a long low whistle escaped his lips. He had uncovered the actual treasure chest. Two Remington 870 pump shotguns with sawed-off barrels, Taser stun guns, a Kevlar vest, a load of ammo, two sets of night-vision goggles, *"and a partridge in a pear tree,"* Jack sang under his breath. He recovered the guns, locked the back door, tossed his duffel and hiker's backpack into the back seat and got in. He sat his backpack in the passenger's seat and turned the motor over. Jack revved the engine, closing his eyes loving the noise a V-8 made. It was the sound of power.

A few miles out he had to stop and shed his sports coat, and rolled up his shirtsleeves past his elbows. He squared up his shoulder harness, unsheathed his gun, pulled back the slide, and chambered his first round, for a "just in case of an emergency"—wildlife or man.

And for Christ's sake, he hoped Medina had a plan; he was getting to the party late.

FINALLY PAST A FEW BARRIERS, such as fallen trees and rockslides, he stopped to stretch his legs and consult the map again. There were steeper mountains ahead. The coordinates took him straightforward with no turns, just forward and into the mountain. Crap.

He scrounged in his hiker's pack and fished for his field glasses. Flipping off the lens covers, scanning up then down, he noted flatter land, which could mean a road was up ahead. Back in the monster Jeep, he forged onward, with the sun descending behind him. Damn, he hoped to get to his destination before nightfall. Camping was not an option he'd considered. Having bottles of water and assorted nonperishables—chips, jerky, and canned rations—he wouldn't starve. The damn Jeep had headlights, so why couldn't he travel at night?

"Nope, not a great idea, Jack, you'd be putting a target on our back if you do, and then they'd have the Jeep and the contents, leaving me with nothing, right, bud?" He talked to himself, mindful of one straightforward fact—he'd have a shallow grave, that was, if they buried him at all.

Maneuvering over small brush and a short hill of boulders, the Jeep cleared a fallen tree. Jack stopped to examine the map. He stuffed the map into his back pocket and forged on until the mountain had him turning right and driving on a steep incline for about fifty yards. The incline dropped off into an abrupt downward slope, and he braked and downshifted to keep from overturning the Jeep.

"Holy hell, mother of pigs," he swore, both hands gripping the steering wheel, and his right foot tapping the brakes. The Jeep rattled on the rocky hillside, bumping and pitching for 100 yards into a small clearing between hills of rocks only four feet tall and a large clump of trees on the opposite side. After braking to a complete stop, he wiped the sweat off his face with the sleeve of his shirt.

He took another gander at the map to get his bearings. The directions made him drive around another mountain. By his calculations, it was another ten miles out. The X marked the spot for his ultimate destination. It was on the other side of the mountain, in a low-lying valley area, on the southeast side of the Sierra Madre Occidental. He headed northeast, where there was nothing on the map. All he knew was Agent Medina was in a modest, less-than-rural city. An area time forgot, and no one bothered with.

"Well, Jack, you signed up for this, so better haul your ass."

TEN MILES GAVE way in his rearview. Headed now due north, he swerved east, watching the compass needle as it pointed northeast, and he followed flatter ground for five miles before happening onto a wider road. The sole reason he knew it was an actual road were the ruts—grooves created by vehicles driving this way over the course of time. He let the Jeep idle, sitting at the mouth of the road. With his binoculars, he scanned the area. There was nothing to see, not yet. According to the map he was in the right spot. It was the only road, which to him meant it was the right way.

The sun fading, he needed to forge on. Jack put the Jeep in drive and pressed the gas. It was showtime.

27

Two miles later, the road descended and the drive became a roller-coaster ride. Jack's foot pressed the brakes on the long haul down to keep the Jeep from picking up momentum. He reversed his actions, pressing firmer on the accelerator to go back up once he'd hit a low spot. The powerful V-8 scaled the steeper incline. It got him to the top where the road leveled off. He was peering down on what appeared to be a small town. A hidden valley, or more appropriately, a town obscured. He viewed dim lights and proceeded with caution.

Poles in various spots lined in a zigged manner and spaced-out supported strings of clear Christmas tree lights. Electricity up here, nah, it had to be gas-powered generators. There were a few barrels with lit fires inside as the smoke and flames flicked skyward. Four men sat at an ancient wooden picnic table, where a run-down food truck was parked. Three tired beat-up trucks sat helter-skelter, rusted, and dented, with missing tailgates parked in front of the only business open. Chairs were on a wooden deck where four men sat drinking, smoking, talking, and laughing. Past this, he noticed other buildings. Small sheds in dire need of paint and undoubtedly extra nails. Without lights, it was hard to see.

He parked the truck, shut off the engine, and let his eyes get accustomed to the dim lighting. The sounds of Tejano music played, but not exceptionally loud. People were laughing. The building supported traditional slide-up wood-paned windows with screens. Each panel was a full section of wood flipped up and latched. When unlatched, each wood pane covered the opening. What was out here to steal? He tucked his gun at the back of his jeans, thinking it was comical. Out of the Jeep, he sauntered without purpose to the wooden porch, where four old geezers sat, staring a fiery hole into him wondering what this gringo was doing so far off the beaten path.

"*Buenos noches.*" Jack nodded to the old guys before stepping through the doorway into a full-fledged bar-beer top counter with stools, tables, a bartender, and patrons—men and women. Must be the entire town, he mused. A crowd gathered around in the back, encircling a table, blocking off its occupants. Was it an arm-wrestling contest or what? Who knew what was going on? Jack's eyes widened once he'd nudged a guy over so he could see past the crowd. Never would he have guessed she'd be the entertainment, yet there she was. Agent Sophia Medina sat at the square wooden table across from a rather sizable Mexican man and in the middle of the table sat an almost empty bottle of tequila gold.

Nine overturned shot glasses sat in front of the hefty man, who had one filled glass hovering at his lips. In front of Sophia sat ten overturned shot glasses stacked in a pyramid. The woman had a smirk on her face as she waited for him to shoot his tenth shot. His large, sweaty hands shook. He was unstable. She, however, was upright, hands resting atop the table, looking sober as a judge.

The group was quiet, anticipating the outcome of the man's tenth shot.

"Well, damn, the woman can hold her booze," someone said in English.

Her head popped up, and she glanced over her right shoulder, searching for the face of a tall Texas cowboy called Detective Jack West. He was here.

She caught his eye, grinned, gave him a diminutive head bob with a tilt, and a slight eye signal. He returned her nod and took a few steps back from the crowd. From the looks of her opponent, he was about to slide out of his chair, onto the floor, and if his protuberant gut managed it, underneath the table.

Sophia downed her eleventh shot, flipped the glass, stacking it on her pyramid. Her eyes bore into the plump man's, her back straight, hands steady. She did not waver as she shoved the bottle to him.

With a shaky hand, he poured tequila into his shot glass, but the tumbler hit the tabletop before it reached his lips. He puked on his sweaty, grimy shirt, falling sideways out of his chair. The crowd moved with precession, leaving enough space to watch the man slither onto the floor as they laughed, snorting, and hooting. Sophia sat, smiling, took the near-empty bottle of Cuervo, drained it, plunked it down with a thud, and stood.

This fat buffoon would never learn. No matter how many times he tried to best her, he could never do it. The bartender walked over, slapped her on the back, and lifted her arm.

"Nadia deja de beber a esta chica, el gordo pierde de nuevo!" The crowd clapped and roared. Sophia, Jack knew, spoke fluent Spanish, but he glanced at her as she turned to the barkeep for translation. His English was a bit broken, but the message was clear: "No one outdrinks the girl, fat man. Again he loses."

Sophia grinned, handing the bartender 2000 pesos, equaling around $100, and the bartender beamed. She moved backward, looking down. The slob had passed out in his own vomit. No more bloody tequila shot contests with this doofus. Next time, if there was a next time, they would drink vodka, and she'd still whoop his ass.

Her eyes searched the crowd and her face lit up when she saw him. With a sidestep between patrons gawking at the passed-out drunk, she shouted, racing up to him, "Jack, you're here!"

In an instant she flung her arms around his neck, pulled his face down to meet her own, and planted a long wet tequila-tasting smooch on his lips, running her fingers into his hair. Sophia had to pull him tighter to keep him from jerking away. Once she removed her lips from his, she nuzzled her head into his neck, purring, her voice a mere breath of wispy air.

"Please follow my lead. I'll explain later." Her words not slurred, her body to a degree unbalanced, but not much. Cripes, the woman threw back eleven tequila shots, why wasn't she drunk on her ass? She was a buck-twenty-five soaking wet, and in great shape. How was she able to toss back that amount of tequila? Taken by surprise, he nodded, and his innards jolted and stomach clenched. Gretchen was the last woman he'd kissed, and that was two years ago when he touched his lips to her warm yet dead lips.

When the young flight attendant Jenny flirted with him, it hadn't surprised him. The younger girls at HPD all flirted with a handful of the detectives including him, even the married ones; however, this was the biggest shock ever. Sophia Medina just kissed the socks off him!

She stepped back, her hand still on his arm, giving it a little squeeze. Sophia winked. Then, in a low voice she said, "Say something appropriate for the crowd, Jack."

"Sophia!" He swallowed hard, his heart racing, sweat accumulating under the backside of his collar. The woman rose on tiptoes and pecked his cheek, burying her face into his sleeve, mumbling words he alone could hear.

"You haven't seen me in months, so look at me with love and desire and sell it, Jack," her voice muffled against his shirtsleeve.

Jack pushed her back so he could pull her around to face him. His eyes looked into hers. As a slow sexy smile crept across his face, he bent taking her lips in a soft warm kiss, his tongue just grazing the tip of hers—at first.

Not expecting this, Sophia's heart rate jumped and her breath caught in her throat. As Jack deepened the kiss, her arms slipped up and around his neck. She let her fingers glide through the back of his hair, pulling his head down, and kissed him. An eternity passed. She ran her hand from his neck, to his shoulder, to his forearm, and she squeezed, moving her right foot back, pulling away. She held onto his arm to steady herself. Not just the tequila had her dizzy; his kiss had rocked her to her toes, or it was a combo. Making a mental note, drinking and smooching Jack was dangerous. She'd better not do it often, at least not the kissing part.

As they separated, the crowd hollered out in Spanish. She understood it all.

"Get a room!"

"Get her naked"

"Holy shit, what a kiss!"

"What a hot cowboy, lucky bitch!"

Sophia did not know how much Spanish Jack understood. The phrases, "get a room and get her naked," were embarrassing.

Agent Medina looked at Jack, then the bartender, and she did the flirty shrug, her eyes twinkling.

"Jack, meet Hector Secada. He owns this bar, and it's also the general store."

She turned to the barkeep speaking in English and taking her time.

"Hector, this is my uh, fiancé, *mi prometido*, Jack West. He is the photographer, uh, *fotógrafo* for the magazine."

Hector Secada, the one person in this shithole who tolerated her, offered his hand. "Hola, Jack. M*ucho gusto,* is nice seeing you. Sophia tells stories. She is, uh, how you say it, much pleased to see you."

"I am ecstatic, uh, *emocionado,* Hector."

Holding hands, she guided him past the table where the fat man lay. Jack saw the pistol tucked into his back waistband where his T-shirt had risen, exposing a roll of fat his gun rested upon.

"You realize he's carrying, right?"

"Yeah, I know, and when he drinks, sometimes he talks."

"You have drinking contests here regularly?"

"Nah, this is the second time. I went head-to-head with the fat slob after I arrived. Dang, after a few tequilas his lips got loose. Hell, he told me in Spanish because he thought I didn't understand. When he mentioned tunnels of white powder, it gave me a lead, and hope. Tonight, he wanted a rematch. No luck with his spilling any vital info, but one never knows in our business when a slip of the tongue will happen." She blushed. "Well, uh, not that kind of slip of the tongue. I mean, not what just happened. Well, oh shit."

He ignored her comment, smiling, with his palm lifted to the barkeep. "*Por favor, una cerveza, Pacifico, o un Sol.*" (Please, one beer, Pacifico, or a Sol.) The barkeep nodded.

Sophia, happy not to have him comment on her own embarrassing comment, looked at him in amazement. "Hey, you speak Spanish. That's news to me."

"I don't. But important phrases, like what beer you want or where is the restroom needs to be conveyed in Spanish."

Hector set a bottle of Pacifico down staring at her. "*Usted?*"

"Bottled water for me, *por favor*."

Nodding, he trudged to the room behind the bar to a cooler where he stored bottled water under lock and key. Bottled water was a huge commodity because no one, not even the residents, wanted Montezuma's revenge, and drinking the piped-in water was for bathing and washing items, never for drinking.

Jack took a hefty swig. The icy beer went down, hitting the spot. He took another deep pull, savoring the cold brew as much as the taste. Sophia watched him from her peripheral vision. She had thrown him off with her amorous greeting, or thought she had. He hadn't pulled away, and the kiss he gave her, mamma mia! Had he kissed her with so much passion to pay her back, or was he...uh...what was she doing? God, she was analyzing the kiss. Why? With closed eyes, she shook the thoughts out of her head. They were here in Mexico on a mission, undercover, playing parts because the life or death aspect of the mission was real. The people they hunted played for keeps. There were no fucking take-backs.

"Are you listening?" He tapped his knuckles on the tabletop.

Well, no, she wasn't because she was in la-la land. Her mind was on their stupid fake make-out session.

"Uh, no, Jack, sorry, fuzzy brain, not focused. Must be the tequila. What did you say?" She lied.

He scooted closer because repeating it the second time worried him. These people spoke little English. But even they could fake it. Medina did it in reverse, faking not understanding Spanish. Her heart skipped a few beats as he leaned his head in to speak. God, no more tequila while he was here, she promised herself.

"I said, I hope you have a suitable place to stash weapons, ammo, and shit. Your people supplied me with serious camera equipment for my new vocation as a photographer too."

"Yeah, cameras are great. We need pictures."

Preoccupied, he knew she was not listening. Again, where was her head?

"They gave me plane tickets to send you home and told me you'd be on administrative leave, desk work only—"

"Home? You're kidding me, I am not going, and if those fuckers fucking try to—" Her face turned bright pink once the words left her mouth, and she sputtered an apology.

"Whoa." Jack sliced his hand in the air stopping her. "Hell, Medina, I just wanted to see if you were listening."

"Sorry about my language, Jack, it wasn't very ladylike. I guess there needs to be a waiting period once two people meet before one becomes a foul-mouth sailor."

Jack lifted his Pacifico, draining the bottle. "Yeah, it happens in our field of work, Medina, no worries. I've heard people spit out words and phrases that would make a sailor blush, or even cry."

"Give me time and I'll blurt out something even more unladylike to make you blush fire red." With an impish expression, she winked. Good. She had her head back on straight.

Jack motioned for one more beer. It just felt terrific to sit and relax for a minute. Sophia propped up her elbows, her chin in her hands, her eyes scanning the area. Most of the locals were gone, leaving a few stragglers. Not a rowdy crowd. Two or three unfamiliar faces at the bar top, avocado pickers passing through, hunting for work.

He stared at his hand wrapped around another cold beer, mulling over his feelings about how he felt kissing another woman...not about her kissing him, but the way he had responded. He felt guilty, like he was cheating on Gretchen. She was dead and no amount of wishful praying would bring her back. First, it was her smooch, and next the passionate smooch he gave her in return—and she without a doubt returned his with fervor. Damn it, it felt...well...it felt real. Would Gretchen like Sophia and approve? Was she watching, happy he was moving on? Was...Jesus, what was he doing? The kiss was a ploy to build a believable legend for the operation; however, it had thrown him. Well, someone could'a warned him.

Jack chuckled when she yawned and he stood, looking at her with a glimmer of mischief in his eyes. "We gotta get outta here. Oh, and Medina, as far as unsavory language making me cringe or blush, I've heard it all. A few of the gals' mouths at HPD can make your toes curl. A couple of 'em have embarrassed a few of the men with their obnoxious, smutty language. As for you embarrassing me, let's see who blushes fire red first. I'm betting it won't be me."

"You're on. Whoever blushes fire red first buys the drinks next time. Deal?"

"Deal, and I like my beer icy cold." He pulled out paper money. Not sure what to leave, he dropped 400 pesos. Jack walked out the front door. Sophia followed, wondering what Jack West had up his cowboy sleeve.

28

The road was rock-strewn and narrow, and with every roll of his tires he felt as if he were forging a wider one. He followed her for fifteen minutes before she broke off to the left and changed directions. Good thing she knew where she was going, otherwise he would've missed the road. In the shadows of pale moonlight shone dim yellow lighting which did not appear inviting or habitable. It was neither a motel nor a hotel. As he got closer, he realized it was a rundown hacienda. What would the inside be like? He squished up his face in disgust. Sophia turned into the half-dirt, half-rock parking lot, tapped her brakes, and crawled to a stop, cutting her engine. Out of her vehicle, she walked to Jack's while he eyeballed the place.

"This shitty hacienda is where we're staying?"

"Yes, this shitty hacienda is our home away from home. Grab your gear."

"All the gear?"

"Yep, all of it. Oh, and don't worry, I have places to stash it all."

Three trips later, they stood inside the room, now piled with camera equipment, a box which had been loaded with flak jackets, night-vision googles, Tasers, shotguns with plenty of ammo, and Jack's personal luggage, leaving only the gas cans in the Jeep.

Sophia dove into the box with the cop toys. She let out a whistle when she saw the sawed-off shotguns. Her lips formed a frown while picking one up, sliding the pump action, racking the shotgun.

"Those bastards didn't give me shotguns, sawed-off or otherwise. I love the sound of a shotgun racking. *Cha-chunk*! What a fantastic sound, gives me a, well, it makes me, uh, it gives me a rush."

With a straight face, Jack said, "Yeah, gives me a hard-on too." He broke out in a loud hoot at her expression, even though she had not blushed. It surprised her because she snorted out a laugh and covered her mouth to muffle the sound.

"Okay, okay, I'm not embarrassed, but I'll buy the beer. Nice one, Jack, you got me."

"You're set with a 9 mil, or are you a wheel gun girl? And ammo, you got plenty I assume."

"No wheel gun, I like my semiauto 9 mil, Sig Sauer. As for ammo, I'm loaded for now—and don't make a joke about the tequila." She snickered.

Jack looked around and peeked out the one small window.

"This place is a hotel, is it?"

Not your standard hotel, not like back home. As you can see, they don't leave the light on, so it ain't a Motel 6." She snickered at her own joke. "They installed walls and doors creating several small rooms in the interior, subpar construction at most. Long ago, the place was a thriving hacienda, at least that's the story. First owners kept a large orchard of avocados, growing tobacco on the side."

"What happened?"

"Heavy rains, flooding, and hurricanes within a five-year period ripped the area apart. Guess they never recouped. That was over thirty years ago, and the crop workers lost their jobs. There were hundreds of them. Nomads, traveling from place to place as migrant farmworkers. They went to the same places yearly. The new owners were relatives of the original ones. Something like twenty-first-removed cousins. Place might've been grand once. Now it's just a run-down piece of real estate."

"It looks it, but it's convenient, so I guess it's better than camping out in the open. So they remodeled, did they?"

"Yeah, if you wanna call it remodeling. They built in a few walls, added extra plumbing, and doors to make rooms to rent. From what I understand, the man and wife who own the joint went to Ciudad Valles working their way back with a few bobtail trucks, stripping out whatever they could from abandoned houses—doors, toilets, sinks, anything useable—and presto, you've got a patchwork motel."

He sat the duffel bag in a corner. Plopping down on the bed, he closed his eyes and stretched out his legs, yawning. "Medina, I'm bushed. I need to rest before we hike through the mountains tomorrow, or whatever you have planned, so..." trailing his words off. He didn't want to pop out with, *hey, get out so I can get shuteye.*

Sophia's mouth became dry. "Jack, this is my room too."

His eyes popped open, rather startled at this news. His mouth opened and then closed as he stared at her.

"Jack, we're engaged so we need this legend to seem as real as possible." She thumbed toward a side door he hadn't noticed. "Through there is an empty single room and no bed. I told the owner we might need extra room for your camera equipment. The other room doesn't have an attached bath. And well..."

He rolled his eyes with a laugh. "Fine, Medina, I can sleep on the floor, no problem. Besides, I like the convenience of having an in-room toilet." Jack stood, tossed his bag on the bed, then unlatched the top to get clothes and his shower gear out.

"We can take turns sleeping on the floor or we can share the bed. It's a queen size and I can handle myself. That is, if you promise to not cross any lines either, then we'll be fine. Besides, the bed is a smidgeon more comfortable than the floor. I've already tried it."

"I'm in total control, Medina, so you're safe." He gave her the Groucho Marx eyebrow wiggle. "Now, let's discuss my half of the closet..."

29

"Damn, these mosquitoes are vicious." Jack swatted them from his neck. It was early morning, but the humidity enveloped him like a cocoon to a caterpillar.

"Yep, they are. Did you use repellant?"

"Yeah, I did, and I brought the can with me. Okay, Medina, what's the plan?"

Sophia shrugged her shoulders. "I guess we monitor the entrance, watch for activity. Stay close to your left. It gets slippery and narrows a bit, so be careful. I have pictures of the dead man." She stepped in front, leading the way through a denser brush area.

"Right, I'm on your heels, uh, a figure of speech. Did you get anyone to run him?"

"The pictures, nah, I didn't send it to anyone."

"Look, Medina, why are you holding his photo back? Why not send it to Janet, get her to run it, get a damn lead?" This annoyed him.

Sophia stopped short and Jack almost ran into her backpack, nose-first.

"What the hell, Medina? Warn a guy when you're gonna stop on a dime."

She turned with a cross look on her face, squaring her shoulders at him; she let out a tremendous groan of exasperation.

"I did not send it to anyone because I have issues."

"Issues. Just what does that mean?"

"It means I have trust issues and I don't trust anyone. That's what the fuck it means. Look here, I...let's get one thing straight between us. Right now I hafta trust you because I've got no one else, and don't make me regret it either. Second, with the way my own people have treated me, I have zero confidence in them a-holes. Part of me doesn't trust Janet or SAC Bogard. Something's going on. I damn well know there is, uh, well, shit. Never mind."

"Christ Almighty, Medina. We should've talked about all your issues and what you know. It'd be nice to know what you know. Or what you think you know. Then I can know too. Know what I mean?"

Sophia could not help it; she sputtered a laugh and her bad temper disintegrated to almost nothing.

Jack's forehead creased and his eyes squinted near shut. "What do you find so amusing?"

"You, Jack, you're amusing. Plus, how many times can one person use the word *know* in a sentence?"

Well, Janet had used the word at least five times in a sentence when she dropped him off at Hobby to catch his flight. Right now, he wasn't in a humorous chitchatty mood. His face was hard, and he let out a frustrated groan. "God, woman, you had better start trusting me, 'cause if you don't then I'm leaving and heading back to Houston. I volunteered, so get this straight, Medina. I *have* to abide by the disclosures I signed, but I can damn well leave anytime I have a mind to, understood?"

Surprised by his sudden anger she went on counter defense. "Fine and dandy, Detective. I read you loud and clear. So right now we're good until we aren't. But, Jack, I'm warning you, if you cross me, it will be me telling you to get your ass back to Houston, or me cuffing you and waiting for our people to come and take your butt back." She gave him no time to respond. Instead, she threw him a question. "You've met Bebchuk and Cleef I take it?"

Jack took a single step backward, relaxing his stance, and softening his expression a tad. He responded to her empty threat with one of his own empty threats. "That goes the same for me. And I will not wait for someone to come get you, Medina. I'll take your tough little butt back to the States myself. And, yes, I've met the two dickwads. All they do is lie. And as for Janet and Bogard, let's just say the jury is still out."

"Huh, I'm trusting you a little more, or at least your instincts." Sophia pulled at her backpack, regaining control of the weight, and then turned around, jerking her head for him to follow. "Let's get back to it, then."

"Right behind you, partner. And for your information, I have someone else I trust. His name is Kasper Bergman, and he has my six, which means he has yours too."

Back at the hacienda, they were tired, hot, and sweaty, with zilch to show for their long butt-whooping stakeout; no activity, not even a cliff chipmunk, a mammal known to inhabit this region, had appeared.

"How do you and Janet communicate?"

She gave him the scoop on how Janet and she talked and why she never again reached out to Bebchuk and Cleef. Medina gave him a brief insight to the inner workings of her own, her coworkers', and the DEA's internal issues. It showed trust on her part and it was a step in the right direction.

"Yeah, I worked with Bebchuk; he was nothing but a narcissistic blowhard, and his girlfriend, creepy Cleef, is just, well, creepy."

"Well, there it is, Jack. I like you more with every derogatory remark you make about those wieners." Sophia got up on a chair and fished out her laptop.

"Forward me the picture of the dead man. I'll shoot Bergman the photo, have him run it. Here's my number."

Medina dug out her burner phone, keyed in the number, and sent Jack the pictures. "I have your number. Here's mine."

He keyed her number into his phone.

"Don't put my name on the contact page."

"Damn it, Medina, I'm not a rookie. Cheese and rice on burned toast. I put you in as Betty Boozer."

"Cheese and rice, you actually said this? Jack, you're funny. Betty Boozer? Huh, and I wonder where you got the idea for that name?"

"You're joking, aren't ya, Tequila Queen? And will you be asking me why I gave Kasper the contact name Ghost?"

"Nah, no need, that's a given. I gave you the name Boxer Joe." Her lips tugged upward.

"So, you heard about me giving my captain a punch in the face and it doesn't bother you knowing I punched out my superior?"

"Nope, I heard he deserved it."

"Well, see there, Sophia. I like you more and more too." He repeated her words. A slight *ping-ping* noise sounded. Kasper sent a message: *Got the pics, now what?*

Jack typed in a message: *See if this dude has a rap sheet. Get back to me when you have something.*

On it, Kasper responded, and then texted, *Work safe.*

30

"Hell, two days and nothing. Well, shit, not nothing. I've got skeeter bites and tree branch scratches, a damn sore neck, and chapped lips." They were back to where they'd stashed the Jeep, and Jack was bitching.

Tired and frustrated herself, she groused back. "I had hoped your ghost man would get something. We gotta have something to work with. Damn it, I thought he was Mr. Miracle."

"If there's something to get he finds it. He's a smart kid, skilled, and still working HPD stuff cuz he ain't sitting around twiddling his thumbs. Besides, from what I've learned about him, Kasper digs, and digs deep, and gets good intel, so don't worry."

"Yeah, yeah, I get it, I get it; keep my britches on and be patient."

He wondered if she would let him take point or would she pull rank, her being DEA?

"I'm going to take point for a while."

"What the fuck can you do differently or better, huh? It's a macho thing, right?" Grouchy, hungry, and needing a shower, her nose got outta whack, and it pissed her off he was implying he could do a better job.

"I ain't saying I can do better than you. Shit, woman, stop being defensive. You've been alone sitting on an entrance not going any further for safety's sake. Now it's time to go in, search for the exit, take initiative, and—"

"Nowhere to run and hide, and then what, Jack, get shot and dumped? I was there. No way to get further and not get caught."

"They teach you how to do this at the DEA—don't take chances, play it safe?"

"Damn it, no, they don't, and I've taken chances, just not yet on this fucking case. I'm telling you, we can't—"

"Wait..." He felt the vibration and pulled out his burner. Clicking on the screen, he opened his message.

"Well?"

"Don't know. I need to check my email."

"Oh shit, you guys are using your regular email? Are you crazy?"

"For your smart-ass information, no, we aren't. We have locked-down secured email; I told you Kasper has skills. Let's head back to the shithole we're living in."

Jack was often cavalier. But that went out the window. He was not moving aside to let her go first. And he sure as heck was not about opening the damn door for her. Her moods bounced everywhere, and two things came to mind. She had a case of burnout, or it was that time of the month. Shit. Maybe it was a combination.

THEY WORKED IN SILENCE. He went through the steps to his secured locked-down email. He took the codes Kasper gave him, and clicking them into the system, Jack traveled through several screens before his private email page appeared. This was the closest to surfing the dark web he'd ever been. The subject read: *Nameless dead man has a name.* Jack read.

Sophia, no emails, her usual since Upchuck and Creep left her out of her own loop. She didn't care. She hated them both, but not hearing from Janet made her mad. Entering Janet's email address, on the subject line, she typed, "No report for today." With her curser in the email body, she began her message:

> *Janet, why in the heck aren't you emailing? No hey, how are you, nothing? Shit. Anyway, since yesterday, the day before yesterday, and five days before that—nothing, zip, and nada has changed; there is nothing to report. I will not send a formal report. Tell Butthead and Creepo too. Upchuck will alter my report to make me seem like an idiot. Jack told me what he did to my reports. WTF, Janet, you let him get away with doing this?*

She hesitated and then began deleting, from *"Tell Butthead"* and ended her message with, *Be in touch soon.* Sophia hit send, clicked out of the programs, shut the laptop then sat crossed-legged watching Jack work.

WITH BIG YET DEFT FINGERS, he keyed in his own special code, and the program he built to monitor all computer traffic, emails, and whatnot outside of the office. No one was on the tech floor. He had the place to himself. Perfect.

His big fingers began tapping his keyboard. He read Medina's message knowing there had to be more, especially if West was there. Why was she holding back? He found it humorous she and Janet were both oblivious to the fact that someone was reading their emails and had either altered them or deleted them. No matter how professional, girls got pissy with each other for lack of communication. A grin spread across his face, knowing he was creating a breakdown between these two. Per his inside resources, he'd heard Janet was lacking confidence in Agent Medina, and Medina was pissy about Janet's lack of communication—perfect.

Done, Jack closed his laptop and leaned back, the gears in his head turning.

"Kasper get us anything, Jack?"

"The dead dude is Julio Ramirez, 33, he, is, uh, *was* I mean, affiliated with the T-288 crew."

"Are those the delinquents running Sunny Side, south of Houston Proper?"

"Yeah, Kasper found out they've gotten in deeper with the cartel. He got ahold of someone we trust in Vice, who told him the word is they run meth labs but not in Houston or Sunny Side."

"Where are they running labs?"

"The intel they have points to McAllen and Reynosa, Mexico, with a smaller gang as the go-between. Word is the T-288 crew is moving supplies there to teach them how to run a lab, and getting part of the booty in either cash or drugs."

"So this means the T-288 boys work for the cartel?"

"Vice can't find a direct contact between the two, but hell, anyone in the drug trade works for one cartel or another. Kasper told me Vice is surveilling the top-tier T-288 members. So far what they've discovered is they ship product out every second week, and where it goes is anyone's guess."

"Might need to get a few DEA agents coordinating with HPD Vice; it's an idea. You learn more about the dead guy?"

"Uh-huh, the dude had a jacket, and it reads like an interesting crime novel. Drug use, drug sales, B&E, assault, petty theft, robbery, but not the felonious type, a shitload of juvie arrests, and two months ago picked up on unpaid speeding tickets, and they found him with a kilo of pure meth and an unregistered gun. He's out on bail, or *was* out on bail, fifty grand."

"Well, someone lost their fifty grand. Jesus, a full key of pure meth is serious bucks."

"I imagine he got in over his head. This idiot didn't come by this kilo of dope by buying it. Betcha fifty bucks he was pilfering and got caught."

"Which begs the question of why didn't they kill him in the States? Why bring him here? The cartel has no boundary lines for murder. There are hired killers looking for work in the USA too. Why come to Mexico?" Sophia uncrossed her legs, swinging them to the side of the bed, wiggling her feet to get the blood flowing again.

"I was wondering the same thing, and I'm wondering how this Julio the Dead Man got involved with the T-288 crew."

"Why? Kasper told you he had affiliations with that gang."

"Your dead man's connected, but not as a member of the T-288 crew. Bergman can't locate a gang he was loyal to. He divided his time between several gangs, from what he could find out."

"Who does that? Never heard of anyone bouncing from gang to gang. Seems like a huge conflict of interest. We know for a fact one gang ain't friends with another gang. Crap, they hate each other."

"Agreed. But nothing should surprise us, Sophia. Not in our world, nor the underbelly world of these lowlives. I asked Bergman to dig deeper on this dead man, see if he filed tax returns. I mean he was 33, he might have had an actual job-job, before crime was what he did for a living 24/7."

"Tell him to contact Janet; she can get the information—hell, scratch that. You told me the kid can dig. Let him get it on his own." Sophia did not like the fact her faith in Janet was wavering. She damn well wanted to have faith in her. But if Janet kept letting Clive Bebchuk mess with her notes making her seem stupid, she drew the line. Her trust had wavered to not having any.

"Okay, so if Ramirez wasn't a gang member, what gangs was he affiliated with?"

"Besides the T-288 crew," he ticked them off, "the Brown Cobras, the Dragons, *Soldados de México,* and the Westsiders. If we were to dig a lot deeper, I'm betting the Bloods, Crips, and the MS-13 have seen his face a time or two."

"*Soldados de México*, Soldiers of Mexico—who are they, a new bunch? Never heard of them."

"Yeah, not a large organization yet. I hear tell from a buddy in Vice they are a branch of the Brown Cobras but not in Houston, something akin to a charter gang, following the Cobras' orders. God, can you believe gangs have rules and laws, mantras, a working tier of hierarchy? Guess instead of human resource departments they have inhuman resources and not a payroll department but a payoff division, so all they need now is a health insurance plan and a tax ID."

"Oh, they have health insurance. It goes like this: steal, be disloyal or rat out a fellow member, lie to the Boss or go against the organization, you're ended—as in dead. It's the only insurance or assurances you have in a gang. Problem is none of the above have a cure."

It was funny, yet not funny because it was a fact. Gang life numbered your days for various factors. These boys never considered once you were in, it was for life. As short as your life might be after that.

Jack hid his laptop in the ceiling in the far corner, while Medina hid hers too. His mind was on everything except sleeping or eating, and he needed to eat; sleeping was merely an option.

"Medina, have you done any nighttime patrolling since you've been here?"

Her hip jutted out, she crossed her arms over her chest. Her brow furrowed and her eyes narrowed with sharpness as she inhaled and then let out a slow and deliberate exhale, reeking of resentment, before she spoke.

"Are you accusing me of not doing my job thoroughly enough, *Detective West*?" His name rolled off her tongue with a touch of annoyance, her hands moving to her hips in a stance he knew all too well. "Those pricks, Bebchuk and Cleef, asked me the same question. Two freaking macho assholes. Spears warned me to be cautious cuz she didn't want my damn death on her hands. So marching into the dark with no one having my back is ludicrous. A fucking man might do that. God, you men! You dipshits think all of y'all are an effing bag of macho chips. Besides, guys are stupid enough to believe they are invincible." She was a steamroller going a hundred miles an hour, her voice growing louder. "Well, I—"

Jack's hand came down in a thunderous *thawaap*, hitting a small Formica top table. "Need to shut the fuck up!"

Startled, she jumped back and stopped talking.

"God Almighty, woman, you're insane. Stop squawking and listen. First, I am not one of those sons of bitches Bebchuk or Cleef. Just your putting me in the same class as those two weasels insults me."

Her eyes widened in surprise as he let out a guttural sound, still reading her the riot act.

"Secondly, some of the finest cops and detectives I've had the privilege to work with have been women. So get the hell off your pity party, cuz I am not letting you get away with that shit. You are a special agent of the D-E-fucking-A and can handle yourself in the field or you'd be parked at a desk, or you'd be home cleaning toilet bowls and making a man his after- work martini. I want you to know—"

Jack went headlong into his own heated tantrum and Sophia rushed him. It only took three quick steps, and she was close enough to reach up and grab him by the neck. She pulled his head down to hers and planted her lips on his, shocking him speechless.

He responded for a second or two before taking his palms and pressing against her shoulders, making her take a step back. Time zoomed by and the silence became overwhelming until he spoke.

"What the hell, Sophia? Are you going to make kissing me at the oddest moments a habit? I'd like to know so I can be on my guard." He sounded angry, but at who? Was he mad at her for her outburst and not shutting up, or because he caught himself responding to her overture? Damn it.

She took a few extra steps back, plopped down onto the bed, and cleared her throat nervously.

"Sorry, Jack, I wanted you to stop your rant and other than screaming at you, I thought it was the best way to shut you up," she lied. Jack gave female cops and agents props with the comment that women deserved to be in the field. He's said these women were some of the finest he'd worked with. Sophia wasn't mad in the slightest that he had screamed at her to shut the fuck up. She found what he said refreshing and sexy as hell. God, he was right, she was a lunatic.

"Next time, throw something at me, hit me in the head, I'll stop talking at least long enough for you to get a word in edgewise."

"Throw something at you? Something besides throwing myself, is that it?"

His expression was hilarious.

"I get it, Jack, I understand." Falling backward, she lay on the bed looking at the water-stained ceiling tiles, embarrassed but not embarrassed. "I've been here alone too long. And then you, and, well, never mind. Chalk it up to the heat of the moment, okay?"

"Sure, no worries, Medina, forget it. Here's what I was thinking. We have the night-vision goggles—" He paused, shaking his head to keep her from talking when he saw her lips form an O shape. "It was a good decision not going without backup. Your backup is here now. I've always said nighttime brings out the deviants and devils. Oh, they do work in the light of day too, but under the cover of darkness, well, you get my drift."

"Food first, and while we eat, we can discuss. Come on, Jack, I know where they make damn tasty authentic pozole, tamales, refried beans, and exceptional homemade tortillas."

"Here, at this shithole? You mean we don't have to eat the food rations we brought?"

"They have a man who cooks. All we do is order, wait, and carry it to the room. After we've finished, we take the dirty dishes back and drop a few pesos to cover the food and leave a tip. Come on, I'm starved."

31

Her hair in a ponytail, she turned her ball cap backward and slipped the headgear over it. She tightened the chin strap around her head, and then she flipped the hands-free eyewear down over her eyes. Moving the toggle switch to on, she activated her goggles, testing them. Jack did the same.

"Now we can see. Come on, Jack, let's hoof it." Sophia took point, Jack bringing up the rear as a lone coyote howled in the night.

It had been an hour and a half and nothing, not one sign of life, just the lonesome yowl of a mountain dingo. They moved along the border of the mountain, the ground rocky, hard, and unforgiving. Dense underbrush, weeds, and broken tree limbs underfoot, he was glad he had the proper boots and wore thick socks. Again, he reminded himself, he needed to get to the gym more often.

Searching the area a few miles from the tunnel entrance, the terrain became flatter covered by sparse brush. Her head down, she walked twenty paces ahead of Jack. Her eyes followed ruts made by a horse-drawn cart or something similar. The cart had carried a heavy load; the ruts were rather deep.

"Jack," she called glancing over her shoulder.

"You got something?"

Sophia squatted. "Not sure."

Her fingers plucked up a few larger particles, and she stood, holding her palm out.

"Blue crystals. Looks like we have a rolling meth lab."

Sophia took out a small envelope, dropped the crystals in, and sealed the flap.

"Check the map, Jack. What's in that direction?"

Jack pulled the map out unfolding it. "Nothing for miles, but it gets you to Highway 70."

Sophia looked at the map. "Tampico is in that direction. What, they produce the meth out here with no one watching? My guess is they transport it somewhere in the mountains before they smuggle it into the USA."

"Let's assume they ship product, trucking it from here to trains, boats, other trucks, individuals driving in cars across the border, or they are using mules to smuggle it across."

"I follow, so whatcha thinking?"

"Not sure, Medina, thinking aloud. Want to figure this out. Why make product out here, then take it elsewhere? Why do they need this tunnel?"

"Great question, and one I can't answer. Product storage, or their hideout, hell, who knows, but it'd be nice to find out where this damn tunnel ends."

Jack nodded, turned, and looked out into the darkness, knowing it wouldn't be dark much longer.

"Hey, Medina, we need to boogie outta here. Us out here with night vision, Kevlar, and guns. Be difficult to explain. We can't lie our way out. Especially with all this gear, don't you—"

Jack turned to see her walking away, leaving him there talking to no one. He took long hurried strides to catch the speedy pace she'd set.

"Hey, you gonna just leave me talking to myself, Sophia?"

"You made an excellent point, Jack. Getting caught is not a good idea. Wouldn't that make Bebchuk's day? I'm not gonna get killed and give him or Stan Cleef any satisfaction."

Both had a semi-warm shower. After they got a few hours of sleep, they woke hungry.

Jack waited for her to bring back food, breakfast tacos with some strong coffee to energize and gear them up to go back out again that night.

The smell of chorizo, crispy potatoes, and eggs drifted into the room once Sophia walked through the door. She set the plates down, then handed him a cup of hot coffee. Coffee grown in Mexico, rich and robust, he savored the hot drink.

"Best coffee I've ever had, hands down."

Sophia nodded. "Yeah, coffee's been a commodity grown in Mexico since, oh, somewhere before the 1700s. Here. These breakfast tacos are delicious too."

For once, they enjoyed the quiet, eating in silence.

Sophia broke the tranquil hush after draining the last of her coffee.

"Jack, what did Janet share with you at your briefing?"

He shrugged, taking the last drink of his lukewarm coffee, and stayed silent. What he knew was sketchy—no names, no leads, nothing substantial to run with—so he was just spinning his wheels. Janet told him there was a traitor; however, she never implied Sophia was a person of interest. His silence spoke volumes.

"Look, Jack, this works two ways. You share, I share. I don't blame you for being cautious. I would be too, but my instincts say you're an okay guy and I should trust you. What's your gut's opinion of me?"

"The same, I suppose, since it ain't saying anything negative, so fair is fair. If we spill what we know maybe the truth will come out. So here goes. Janet told me she suspects there are double agents or just scumbags working both sides, however, all of it is conjecture with no tangible proof."

"And did she say who she suspected, Jack?"

Medina had to have her suspicions. Hanging the two weasels out to dry wasn't a problem for him.

"Bebchuk and Cleef for starters, and if they're involved, it might implicate a few higher-ups, and Janet said—" He stopped. "Nope, it's your turn."

"We have a man inside. He's been undercover for several years. The higher-ups are wondering about his loyalty. They say an honorable man could be turned, but I don't see him turning. He's a good man."

"Who is he? Where is he?"

"Uh-uh, sorry, Jack, can't say until I have clearance from Janet."

"Look, Medina, all this information in bits and pieces is wearing me down."

"Nope, Jack, not this info, so drop it."

"What can you disclose? Or is this it?"

"There's not much we have proof of. Like Janet told you, it's all conjecture. She has her suspicions but didn't open up to me, which leads me to believe it goes up the chain of command—like top people involved."

"Well, just saying top people are involved gives us nothing. Crap, Medina, there are too many people who have more authority than we do. You'd think Janet would be privy to better intel. This information must be over Janet's pay grade. If we knew who to trust, we could bypass her. Go to the upper echelon of bosses. No one talking to no one sucks, and we can't do our jobs unless we are in the loop. We should find out who knows more."

"I know Janet hasn't told me everything, and it doesn't mean she won't. She may be waiting for the go-ahead to brief us in full, who knows? Do you tell me everything? All the crap Kasper tells you, do you tell me?" All this crying about who didn't tell who what was getting on her last raw nerve.

"Yeah, I tell you because you're my partner."

"Glad to know it, and don't do that, Jack."

"Do what?"

"Give me the puppy-dog eyes. I still cannot tell you about the undercover agent."

Jack would let it go—for now.

"Fine, so what Kasper told me, it's not much, and I am not holding back, I swear. He told me he's been working with a new DEA agent from Tech, a Theo whatever, but the kid said this guy's off. His gut says the dude ain't right."

"Don't know a Theo. But we have tons of agents all over the state, hell, the country. Just what did Kasper say about this guy?"

"He can't pinpoint it, but he's been watching his back. Bergman said the dude is out a lot. Gone for long stretches of time and never explains where he's going or why. And not once has he discussed the surveillance on the cartel, nothing. "

"Well, Jack, if the guy gives him the creeps, I'd watch my back too. So, speaking of creeps, Umberto Vega, do you know much about him?"

She bit the insides of her bottom lip. Had anybody mentioned Vega to Jack, or had she possibly just stirred up a dust storm?

"Yeah, I know about him."

She arched her brows. "You do? How, and how much do you know?"

"As much as Agent Águlia would tell me, and after meeting him and hearing his story, I gotta say that shit disquiets me. He loses his family to a cartel, yet he wants a cartel in Mexico. I don't get it."

"Well, he's on my list of people I have a bad feeling about too, so we agree."

"It makes him dangerous, playing up to the Federales like he is on their side when revenge is his game."

"Miguel has connections with the local Federales and a few snitches. So if anyone knows more about Vega, we can ask him to dig for us. I'll get a message to him."

"Good idea." Jack pursed his lips in thought. He would have one more go at her about the unnamed undercover agent. "So, about your mystery agent, what freaking harm would it do to tell me? Besides you, I have Kasper, who by the way can keep a secret. Who else do I talk to, huh?"

"Nope, Jack, and stop asking because until I have clearance to disclose who this person is, they stay anonymous. I'm sorry."

Sophia looked sincere, but this did not dispel his annoyance. It was her responsibility to keep any covert agent anonymous and protected. Besides, this agent's location wasn't an issue, she hadn't been told. They had put her on a need-to-know only. How could she have predicted her unidentified undercover agent would introduce himself to Jack soon, with a humorous and dramatic flair?

THEY'D clomped around in the humid mountains, ending up at the tunnel entrance. They sat, waiting for someone to show, or perhaps several someones, from nightfall until almost sunrise. No wild animal activity—excellent—no human activity, not what they had hoped for.

"We'd better start back, Medina. The sun will be up soon."

"You're right, let's boogie." Sophia turned and started out at a jog, Jack bringing up the rear.

Slowing to a stop and bending her hands on her knees she inhaled and exhaled, catching her breath. Jack stopped behind her, also bent over, breathing hard, then rose, rolling his shoulders and arching his back. The backpack was full of needed essentials like jerky, water, extra ammo, bug spray, Sani-wipes, and flashlights, with extra batteries. The Kevlar they wore added another twelve to fifteen pounds to jog with, and they were feeling the pain as they each shook off a few kinks.

Ahead, he saw the familiar spot and the marker.

"Medina," he huffed still catching his breath, "we're here." He pointed.

A countenance of relief flitted across her tired face. "Transportation, thank God, my feet are killing me. Time for four walls, a tepid shower, food, and forty winks."

"Sounds fantastic, and we'll flip for who gets the first shower. Just because you're a woman doesn't mean you go first. I'm not letting you run roughshod over me. Got it, Medina?"

"Yep, I've got it, Jack. You are a Jack-ass, but hey, if I can't call my new partner names, who can?" Without another word, she climbed into the 4Runner and started the engine.

Jack got in, slammed his door shut then turned to her. "There's a long list of people who refer to me as Jack-ass. Get in line. Now, let's get outta here. I wanna shower, eat, rest, and contact Bergman to see what news he has."

He did not repeat himself. Sophia floored the accelerator, ready to eat, rest, regroup, but shower first, before Jack—she wanted to win the coin toss.

32

She won the coin toss taunting him a little.

"You shower. I'll stay out here, give you your private time."

"Great, and after I'm cleaned up, I'll get breakfast. Then, shit, I've got to sleep."

A tired and stove-up Jack watched her disappear through the side door. The sun was up. It was almost 7:00. He would give her time to do whatever females did. Men were low maintenance. In the design of things, women were complicated. And this was in every aspect of life. A few were just mega-divas. Gretchen hadn't been high maintenance, and he'd appreciated it. So many things he had enjoyed regarding her, and so many things he missed...his heart tugged, aching for a fleeting moment. He could hear her speaking inside his head. *Jack, focus and stop daydreaming. Let me go. Live your life. Get me off your mind. Stay safe on this mission.*

Hands in his pockets, he walked the length of the building before rounding the corner and saw several vehicles parked willy-nilly. A Mexican orchard thrived here a long time ago. Jack imagined what it looked like back then. But now this had the earmarks of an inconspicuous place to do drug business. Sequestered near the Sierra Madre Oriental Mountains, close to a town, which wasn't an actual town, and one thing he was positive of, nobody came here on purpose.

Outlying buildings, two with thatch roofs, and one structure that may have once been a barn sat further out back. An old beat-up 1970-ish Ford pickup backed into the doorway with the hood up. Several crates were stacked and against the wall. Old cans and bottles sat in piles next to them. Jack looked under the hood. Parts lay on top of the engine, with ratchets and wrenches. It appeared the truck wasn't running, but somebody was working on trying to fix it. The makeshift garage smelled of oil and gasoline. Rusted toolboxes, four of them, sat in the dirt, opened and piled with greasy tools, all in a jumbled mess. Buckets of oily rags, shovels, rakes, and various lawn and garden tools sat in the truck's bed that had no tailgate, and the front bumper was missing. It had to be a joke getting Ford parts out here. Did Amazon deliver by truck or drop by plane? His head moved in a short indiscernible shake as he left the squalid garage with the nonfunctional truck and the smell of a 30-weight oily dirt floor garage.

A gust of wind keyed him in on farm animals. The smells of a farm, with horses or cows and fresh hay weren't bad; however, out here it was a unique case. Real farms didn't have animals fenced in so close to their living quarters. The pungent odor slapped him in the face. He saw one pen housing eight pigs of varying sizes, and chicken coops nearby with a dozen chickens scratching and pecking the ground. He knew these smells, and there was an added aroma—goats. Six goats roamed, unfenced, heads lowered in a continual eat-eat-eat, drifting headfirst to reach whatever they nibbled on, and their feet followed their mouths forward, eating, without looking up. Past the pigpen, the chicken coop, and goats, he found flatter land at the backside of the hacienda. He walked back the way he came, taking his time, kicking pebbles with the toe of his boot as he thought about nothing for a change.

Jack had killed an hour and fifteen minutes wandering around, and if it wasn't enough time for Medina to shower, dress, and whatever, then tough, she'd just have to learn to speed it up.

He knocked on the door before opening it. All he saw was an empty room, but he heard water running. Lord, he hoped she left some hot water. Exhausted and grubby, Jack's mood teetered on the verge of out-and-out foul. Jack took his service weapon out from the waistband of his jeans and laid it on the stand next to his duffel, leaving one chambered. Hell, he was in Mexico, and shit happened.

Jack sat on the only bed in the room, falling backward to lie across the saggy mattress. He shut his eyes, crossing his arm over his face to block out any light. Ten more minutes, that's all he'd give her. Then he'd pound on the door until she came out. Or he'd bust in and drag her out—either way worked for him. Jack lay there with his eyes closed. A yawn escaped him, and he shuddered. No sounds of running water. It was his turn, thank God.

His body rolled up on the bottom of the bed. Jack sat with his back facing the bathroom door. With an outstretched arm, he reached for his bag to grab clean clothes and personal gear.

The door creaked open. A man's voice called out, "Hey! What the hell!"

The hair on the back of Jack's neck bristled. In a split second, he stood, yanking his service weapon from the table, swinging around, his gun aimed at the intruder.

Both men, eyes wide, one dressed, tired and holding a gun, and the other with wet hair, wearing boxer shorts and a towel wrapped around his neck. They did not speak; they stared, shaking their heads in disbelief. They were eyeing each other experiencing a surreal moment, while time stopped for a second before Jack's brain woke first.

"McCready, what the fuck? How did you get into my room? Better yet, why are you in Mexico?" His eyes narrowed, his nostrils flared, and his fingers tightened around the Glock.

"Whoa, Jack, get a grip and calm down." Owen McCready took a half-step and reached out, but Jack halted him.

"Stop there, McCready. Step back and pull the towel from your neck and toss it to the floor; keep your hands where I can see them." He jerked his head in the general direction, and pushed the gun out toward him. "Don't make me repeat myself."

With a jerk, he slid the towel from his neck then flicked it to the floor.

"See, nothing under the towel, and no gun hidden in my boxers." A low laugh bubbled up. "I've got some female companions who might argue that fact with you. Hey, but we can talk about it another time, over a few mugs of beer."

"Funny, real funny. You're a standup comedian now, are you? I know you aren't a *fecking* Irish cigarette shop owner and after your visit to me at my damn house, I don't know who you are."

"Can I grab my pants?"

"No, no pants, and move over there and take the straight-backed chair, sit." Waving his Glock in the chair's direction, his eyes on McCready every second, he turned his body at an angle, taking a step back as he plopped down on the bed. Where the heck was Medina? Was she hurt?

His legs stretched out, his bare feet crossed at the ankles, and his arms rested on his lap. McCready's posture screamed out calm, not at all bothered by the fact a gun was aimed at his face. A tiny chuckle slipped from his closed mouth.

"You find this funny, do you? When you had me at gunpoint, in my effing house, you said I needed to stop or things might go sideways."

"Yeah, I did."

"What will go sideways?" Jack crossed one leg over the other, the gun in his right hand held steady at McCready's chest. He was getting worried. Where was Sophia?

"Lots of shit going on, Jack. Be careful who you consort with and don't turn your back on anyone."

"Don't give me that bull. I see who you associate with, goons like Joven Cazalla."

"Yeah, he and I are fecking drinking buddies. He loves Irish whiskey." The Irish brogue came and went as he talked, and it aggravated the piss outta Jack.

"You and Cazalla are drinking buddies. You drink with the bastard? I gotta say if he's a friend of yours you aren't a friend of mine, and by the way, are you even effing Irish?"

A snort of laughter burst from the man in the boxer shorts. "Uh-uh, but I worked on the accent a lot, so I enjoy using it, especially when I'm talking to a new woman. And my reddish hair, light hazel eyes, and lighter complexion seals the deal I'm Irish, no?"

Jack did not give a rat's ass what he looked like. Or if he was or wasn't Irish. The truth was he'd liked the dude better when he was black and blue, swollen eyes, broken jaw, because he thought Owen was a victim, not a prick.

"Why are you here? To finish the job you started at my house?"

McCready leaned forward, slapping his bare leg in amusement, and the movement had Jack's hackles up. He uncrossed his legs, planted his feet, his back ramrod straight, ready for McCready to jump him. It didn't happen.

"No, Jack, not to—"

They glanced over at the door opening. Agent Medina walked in, carrying a medium-sized plastic crate, with boxes letting off steam. The aroma of tacos, Mexican spices, and menudo hung in the air. Jack smelled the homemade tortillas; he was famished.

She was surprised to see him, not knowing he was in Mexico. The man sat in the chair, half-naked, wet hair and the towel on the floor. Next, she looked at Jack, sitting on the bed, his body rigid. There was a cold dark glower in his eyes, his gun out, proving this was indeed a charged situation. Her black eyes intensified with anger, looking at the smiling man in boxer shorts with the pattern of yellow and red fish. Sophia Medina pinched her lips together, closing her eyes. Her body went slack as she sighed. Sophia reopened her eyes, looking from one man to the other.

"Damn it, Jack, put your gun down. Caden, wipe the smile off your face and put your pants on."

Jack's jaw dropped, and so did the hand with the gun. A look of delight filled Caden's eyes as he retrieved his pants from the floor. He pulled them on, returned to his seat, smiled at Jack, and then turned to Sophia.

"The food smells great. Hope you got enough for three."

Jack rose from his seat, his face screwed up, and he found his tongue. "Wait, just damn well wait a damn minute here." His baritone voice took on a strong vibrato as his confusion and anger rose. Were they having a go at him? Why had she called McCready, Caden, and not Owen?

Sophia removed the containers from the crate, setting them on the rickety table. She then dug out plates and plastic silverware. Turning to Jack she pointed. "Sit, you need to eat, and afterward we both need to rest."

"Uh-uh, not yet, not until I get answers." He brought his gun up again and aimed it at this man she'd called Caden. "Don't make me hold the food for ransom. One of you better spill the truth before I get any madder, and y'all don't want to see me mad when I am hungry, grimy, and tired. Now y'all fucking tell me what the fuck is fucking going on!" Pissed off didn't even come close to describing how mad Jack was.

"*Jeeesssuss*...stop yelling." Sophia had her hands held up, palms out, trying to calm him down. "Put the gun down. Sit."

"Fine, I'm sitting, and you, Caden, Owen, Irish Fuck, whoever you are, stop grinning cuz you're pissing me off even more." Jack laid the gun down and sat on the bed.

"Yeah, yeah, God, man, get a grip."

With a weighty sigh, Sophia was choking on the enormous amount of male testosterone floating between these two men.

"Detective West, I'd like to introduce you to DEA Special Agent Caden Ward. Caden, Jack West, Jack, Caden."

Caden Ward grinned, rose, and took a step forward, his hand held out.

"Nice to meet—"

Jack half-stood, his arm coming up as his fist swung, catching Caden in the jaw, sending him sprawling to the floor in a heap.

"Jack! Why on earth did you do that? Holy shit, are you okay, Caden? Jack, goddamn it, step back." Sophia took a step toward Caden and stopped when she heard laughter rumbling in his chest; he was shaking his head wiping the blood from the corner of his mouth.

Jack stood over him, looking down. "Let me give you a hand up."

Rising off the floor, Caden took ahold of Jack's outstretched hand. "Alrighty, Detective West, we have officially met. Are we squared up now?"

"Yeah, although I owe you one whale of a headache, so I'll owe you another punch. Now, fill me in. I'd like to eat, shower, and then take a well-deserved nap."

Caden Ward had been undercover for years.

"That's a long time, Agent Ward. And in the Fifth Ward, dealing with the gangs and other riffraff, how did you stay sane?"

Caden lifted his shoulders and shook his head while he chewed the last bite of a taco.

"Who says I'm sane?" He snickered, but Jack's expression was a clear statement that comedy hour was over. "Sorry, Jack. Uh, for a few years, my shop, Smokin' Hot, was the hub."

"Your shop was the hub—the hub for what? Look, McCre—, uh, I mean, Ward, stop dicking around and fill me in. Would that be too much to ask?"

He liked Jack, and he sorta enjoyed getting under his skin. "Shipments used to come to my store twice a month. Several crates and two or three heavies came with them. I never got to open them. On shipment days, my shop was padlocked. I didn't have a key. Plus, I wasn't allowed back in until the next day. They didn't sweep up well, and I got samples of the powder for our lab. It was pure meth, uncut, lots of it."

"Who took the crates?"

"The Dragons and the Brown Cobras did. For the last twenty months the T-288's started showing up."

"Your shop is in Dragon territory. Why would they let the B.C.'s or T-288's just waltz right in on their turf?"

"Cartel business."

"So the cartel is running the gangs?"

Caden shrugged. "The cartel is a large organization, and if I were a gang, I'd work *with* them, not against them. Healthier if you get my drift. The gangs deal with their own internal crap. Everything else is run by whoever's in charge here for the cartel."

"Okay, what did you mean *used* to come to your place, they don't anymore?"

"No, they moved the hub after your triple homicide last year, and no one will tell me where."

Jack had an idea where the new hub was located.

"Why'd they pick your place?"

Sophia spoke up. "The DEA created a detailed legend about Caden and his criminal actives. Then we rousted him a few times."

"Yeah, they did, and I'll have to say they made it damn well realistic too."

"Don't bitch, Caden, you volunteered for this assignment if you remember. Anyway, Jack, it took a few months, but they approached him about using his shop."

"Who approached you? Was it Cazalla?"

"Yeah, him and his left and right arms, Mundy and Callum."

"Yep, know 'em, two shitbags. Are the pawnshop, Magic Market, and the other stores involved?" He wondered how the triple homicide fit in, but he'd hold those questions for now.

Caden Ward blew out a breathy grumble. "The pawnshop is. The other stores are being extorted by gangs. You know how it is too, they are all afraid to talk."

"Is the pawnshop owner Walt Burch laundering money for the cartel?"

"Yes," Sophia supplied. "Burch and several other pawnshops are laundering. There are heaps of different businesses spread out over Houston with their hands in the pot. A few of these places are respectable. The company that owns the strip center, CCB..."

"Conover, Conover, and Briggs."

Sophia's brows arched. "You know them?"

"Yes. Kasper dug, and..." He stopped and a laugh popped out. Their expressions said it all. "I guess you two think you know it all, don't you?"

"Well, let's compare notes, and then we will be caught up."

"Not quite, but I'm catching up to you shitheads, not to worry."

Jack smirked, leaving out information regarding his stakeout at Sea Star, and a few other tidbits. It was best to have an ace up your sleeve. Especially when you played poker with people who cheat.

Caden Ward, aka Owen McCready, was impressed as he listened to Jack. Most cops didn't impress him, but Jack wasn't most cops either.

"CCB has no involvement; at least we can't connect them to the cartel or drugs. They are no longer on our radar," Sophia disclosed.

"I wouldn't mark CCB off any list of wrongdoers, cuz my gut says so, but right now they're on a back burner. I have a question for you, Caden, and it will be odd calling you Caden instead of Owen."

"Yeah, I suppose so. But don't forget to call me the right name. Mainly in front of the right people because I'd like to stay alive. What's your question?"

"You got the living shit beat outta you and were left for dead. What I want to know is why and who. Isn't it too dangerous to go back? They tossed you out like garbage. I'm thinking you were lucky they didn't kill you."

"Well, Jack, my buddy. Things went to hell the day after you came by and visited. The kids who broke into my shop took more than just inventory. Part of a shipment went missing. I wasn't involved, but they didn't care."

"This is the reason you got a near-death beating?"

"Not just because of the theft, Jack. Also because you and your partner came waltzing into my shop. You two overstayed your welcome. They wanted to make sure I hadn't talked. So I took the beating. Been meaning to tell you thanks." Caden Ward's posture stiffened and sarcasm dripped off of the word *thanks*. "Being undercover, it happens in our line of work. Listen, Jack, I can't put all the blame on you, but it proved two things to them."

"What two things?"

"I'm loyal, and I can take a beating and keep my mouth shut."

"Sorry, man. It could have played out differently. If we had been in on who you were." They looked at Sophia, who glared back.

"Don't you, either of you, go there with me, got it? I do not call the shots, you turds."

"Just checking to see if you're awake, Medina."

"Fuck off, Jack."

Their laughing pissed her off more, and her forehead wrinkled in the *I am not amused* frown expression.

"Look here, you two shitheads, you're pissing me off. Now, back to what we were talking about. Jack, I'm going to be honest."

"Well, there's a first, Sophia."

Her expression had him apologizing again.

"Alright, fine. I can't say you've been lying to me, you just haven't told me everything. Sorry."

"Thanks. About your triple homicide, from what we've learned on the street it was just an unfortunate incident of robbery."

"Why would gang members who are dealing with the cartel steal from them? All it does is sign their death warrant. I don't see it."

"Word on the street is your three dead men were not connected to any gang. So, there was no actual gang member involvement. There was rumor of a pending robbery, and Smokin' Hot was the target."

Caden jumped in. "The robbery was planned the night after the shipment arrived. Jack, I got a look at your homicide files, and—"

"This is total horseshit. Y'all should've never ordered me to stand down. Jesus, Joseph, and Mary, this is crazy. Why can't the police and the three-letter acronym agencies ever work together for the greater good?"

"Jack, let it go. You're here now working with us." Sophia's voice was calm and her eyes searched his. "We—you, Caden, and me—need to work together without resentment. Please?"

He heaved a sigh. She was right. In the future when told to stand down, he'd have this case for reference on why he shouldn't.

"Fine, I will this time, Sophia. But if the DEA or OAG come knocking again, I'd better not get pushed aside from my case, agreed?"

A grin tugged at the corners of her mouth. "I'll do my best; it's all I can promise."

"That's all I'm asking, Sophia."

He looked at her and Caden Ward saw it. There was a spark between these two. It wasn't a tiny spark either; it was more like a small flame.

"You two finished with this nonsense about working together, not working together, and all that bullshit? Cuz we *are* still on a case."

"Sure, Caden, you shit, now tell me about my homicide file."

"One of your victims, the kid, Robert Thompson, had a mini Uzi, with a fifty-clip load, so they were looking for trouble. They know stealing from the cartel is a reckless and very dangerous move, but hey, the mentality we deal with is on the brink of stupid. People hear things. Most of the time it's never good news, so I'm positive word leaked out. We've heard on the streets that it wasn't a planned gang hit, but somebody hired a gang to pull the trigger."

"You think the cartel ordered a hit, then?"

"Yes, because the cartel's presence in the centralized area of the Third and Fifth Ward, trickling down to Sunnyside, has grown exponentially. Gangs are following orders, not calling shots, especially for big hits like this."

Jack gave an almost indiscernible shake of his head. "This puts a new spin on my homicide now, doesn't it?"

33

It was after 1:00, and the food had been eaten. Jack yawned for the second time, and Sophia's eyes drooped. "Caden, you haven't told us why you are here." He muffled a third yawn.

"Yeah, Ward, what gives? All this drama and other crap, it slipped my mind." Sophia yawned, and her eyes watered.

"I had to make a trip here."

"That did not answer the question, McWard," Jack combined McCready with Ward.

"How did you know we were here and who sent you?"

"My handler said you were here. And as far as who sent me here, well..." His voice got lower as he shifted uneasily in his seat. "Cazalla sent me."

"That just beats all, Ward, and you didn't answer the first question. Why are you here? Oh, and by the way, what's the deal with you and him at the shipping yard? You remember, the day I followed your ass, the day you pistol-whipped me?"

Sophia's eyes widened. "Caden pistol-whipped you, Jack?"

"It's a story I'll tell you later, Sophia. Caden, answer the questions."

"Cazalla sent me to check on a shipment, which seems to have gotten off course. When I checked in with my handler, I found out you two were here." Caden lifted his shoulders, and then let them sag. "I've been hanging with the pond scum of the world. Thought it would be a nice change of scenery. Besides, did either of you consider the chance I'm taking being here?"

"Understandable." Tired, Sophia gave a one-word response.

"Yeah, guess you are, but hey, it's your ass. You didn't have to show up. I've got more questions, Caden, and you'd better be upfront this time."

Sophia looked up. She was dead tired and frowned, and so did Caden. "More questions, Jack? We're headed out again tonight. We need sleep. Tired agents do not make safe agents with quick reactions. It could mean getting you or me dead."

Jack was catching a second wind. He kept his eyes on Caden, waving her off. He planned on taking advantage of Agent Ward, aka Irish fuck, being here in person. This was his chance if the man didn't stonewall him like everyone else associated with the DEA or the OAG had been doing every time he asked questions. He'd already been warned to watch his six, not trust anyone, and this included DEA Agent Caden Ward.

"There's no time like the present to talk, and I'm wired. So, Ward, you told us back when we were working the triple homicide that you owned Smokin' Hot for what was it, five years? You've been under a long time living a legend, especially with no repercussions."

"That ain't a question, Jack, it's a statement."

Sophia stood, stretching. "Listen, fellas, you can keep at the Q&A, I'm gonna get a few winks." She walked toward the extra room.

"No bed in there, Medina," Jack said, keeping his eyes on Caden.

Sophia grabbed two pillows, then snatched the thin worn blanket off the bed, shuddered, and yawned.

"The floor is fine, Jack. I'm exhausted. I don't give a shit as long as I get a little sleep."

Out the door, Jack knew she'd be asleep in a matter of nanoseconds. Not him, though, because he had a renewed burst of energy.

Jack sat in a ratty chair beside the small wooden table with his head lowered, watching Caden's feet rocking. He wanted to kick out the back legs of the chair sending the bastard to the floor. Getting the butt of a gun slammed into his head still pissed him off. Not to mention the shithead breaking into his house. Jack figured he might hold a grudge until Agent Ward saved his life or did something heroic to even the score.

"Aren't you gonna need sleep, Jack?" Caden tilted the straight-back chair against the wall and it teetered on the back legs, rocking backward then forward.

"Nah, I'm not tired. Got a second wind. I'm guessing it's adrenaline."

"Suit yourself, man, but it'll be a weeklong day for you later." Caden dropped the chair back on all four legs. "Come on, bud, let's have it. I see it all over your face."

"What you see on my face is a fifteen o'clock shadow with bags under my eyes and yeah, I've got crow's feet too. Ward, when's the last time you looked in the mirror? Shit, man, you looked healthier the day I saw you over at Ben Taub. Black, blue, and grayish-yellow, those are better colors for your face."

Caden's face had a *ha-ha-ha funny* look, and he spewed a tiny laugh.

Jack found nothing comical. He glowered as he held the gun, pointing it at the wiseass wannabe Irishman who was an agent for the Drug Enforcement Administration. Had his loyalties turned? "I want to know why you cracked my skull with your pistol. Why not just tell me who you were?"

"No, I couldn't give you any details. I couldn't tell you anything. *My* job was to keep out of sight. And you, you shit, are a helluva detective, like a dog with a bone. So, blowing my cover was not an option. Sorry, Jack."

"I'll let it slide, but I still owe you a real punch. You slamming a gun upside my head ain't the same as a punch in the jaw."

"So, you owe me another punch and I'm thinking I won't see it coming. Do whatcha gotta do, Jack."

"Have you met the boss yet? You have a name for us? Seems if you're following orders from a top man like Joven Cazalla, this gives you a doorway, doesn't it?"

"After all this time you'd expect I would have. But no, I haven't. Just because I've been in deep for a while don't mean a thing. It isn't like the movies, Jack. Shit."

"Yeah, I get the point. You aren't Donnie Brasco or Joe Pistone; you're more like Austin Powers or Gracie Freebush."

"Who the hell is Gracie Freebush?"

"You never saw the movie, *Miss Congeniality*?"

"Jack, if you think I think you're funny, you'd better think again."

"You hear me laughing?"

Caden didn't respond. He stared at Jack, waiting.

"Joven Cazalla is as high as you've got. I ain't buying it. The DEA sent you in. You aren't a rookie, man. You've gotta be convincing to go under and infiltrate, and stay there this long. So what are you doing?" His tone of voice eked out an accusation, one Caden did not appreciate, and Jack could see he was getting to him.

"Yeah, pal. Find any agent who's been in a while. Call Joe Pistone or the other dude, uh, Jack Garcia. Why dontcha ask them to enlighten you on just what it takes to get to the boss. After that, get back with me."

As Caden Ward stood, his hands pushed the seat of the chair back and it hit the wall with a resounding thud. "Stop acting like a pussy. If you want to accuse me of something, West, do it. Yeah, I've been under for a while and yeah, I have been with scum, vile scum, damn mean and unscrupulous men. I've taken my fucking beatings and so what if it's taking longer than expected? My not pushing myself or them has kept me alive, you fucking bastard."

The men locked eyes, one fuming, the other mulling over his

opponent's words, reading his emotions. Jack's stare passed through Caden's inner soul and he saw it; it was just a flash, but he saw what he needed to see. His being a DEA agent was more than a job. Agent Ward had a story, a real-life story. Perhaps one day he would share it.

Caden Ward wanted to know why Jack was pushing. No one ever accused him of crossing the line, not once.

"Okay, Ward, sorry I came at you so hard. It's just that I needed to see who you are. Us, our job, this job, life-or-death kind of stuff, you gotta be on top of who you can trust. You understand, right?"

Ward nodded. Yeah, he understood all too well. Their eyes locked once more, as their hands clasped.

"Brothers in blue, Jack. I've got your back."

Jack regarded him, realizing if he let Agent Ward in, he would have three people he could count on—him, Kasper, and Sophia. His gut said it was the right move.

"You let me down or cross me, Ward, and I swear you will regret it, and it'll be worse than getting a gun smashed upside your head. I'll kick your fictitious Irish butt all over Houston, back to Boston, got it?" Jack narrowed his eyes and stared at the other man, not a trace of humor in his voice.

Their hands still locked in a firm grip, Caden bobbed his head.

"Yeah, I do, I fecking do," he let the Irish accent flow and smirked. So did Jack.

THE REST of the afternoon flew by. Jack was keyed up, but he caught a little shut-eye. He spent the time on his laptop, reading, while waiting for his partner to wake and return to the room.

Sophia stretched and yawned, rolling her neck. Nothing worse than sleeping on the floor. She tapped her fingernails on the door as she turned the knob. She peeked in to find Jack awake, on his computer, and very much alone.

"Hey, where's Caden?"

"Gone."

"Just out or not coming back?"

"He had a flight to catch back to Houston. Listen, I—"

She didn't let him finish. "You get any sleep, Jack? I hate to say it, but you look like hammered hell."

"About forty winks. I'll be fine; my adrenaline is pumped up." After shutting his laptop, he stood and jiggled the kinks out of his legs. "Let's get some grub and black coffee. I might say I'm fine, but black coffee and lots of it won't ever hurt." He winked and headed out the door, her on his heels. She didn't argue with him. They needed both food and lots of caffeine.

Night-vision goggles on, Jack stepped around the pile of dead brush searching the ground.

"What are we looking for?"

Before Caden left, they mended fences and shared information. Boys keeping secrets, playing games, and she was on the outs. It was bullshit and infuriated her.

"Effing boys just piss me off," said Sophia, her words not articulated loudly. Not watching where she was going, she plowed into the back of him.

"Medina, hey, watch where you're going. You mean Bebchuk and Cleef, those boys?" He knew it wasn't, but she was cute when she was mad.

"You know I'm not and why do you feel you can't trust me? Give me one damn reason."

Her grousing tone fading, she was no longer behind him. He stopped and walked back. Sophia stood still, hands planted on her hips, her face stony. It was the universal female stare. The face women had when they expressed anger, hurt, and stubbornness. It took a mere five steps, and he was face-to-face with her. A single tear fell to her cheek before she could swipe it away.

"Medina, Sophia, I...look, I'm sorry, I..." Jack changed his mind and kept his mouth shut.

With a suppressed sigh, her eyes shut, and then she reopened them studying him.

"Sorry, Jack, when I'm tired I get emotional. I know everyone's kept you in the dark from day one. Your triple homicide sits unsolved, and it eats at you. We and the OAG don't tell you anything important. Bebchuk and Cleef are useless asswipes who gave you zero reasons to trust them. I also know you've got your doubts about SAC Bogard. Then you meet Caden, who is a monstrous shock. You belt him in the jaw, and now you boys are best of freaking friends."

"Hey, it's not—"

"Uh-uh, let me finish." Her head shook as she wagged her index finger back and forth.

"All of this crap makes me sick, all you men make me sick. Maybe I don't have a penis, but I'm a damn good agent. I've taken all the shit I am going to take off men, including you. If you feel left out, imagine how I feel. Hell's bells, these are the people I work with, people I'm supposed to trust. I got sent here alone waiting for a backup team, and I got you. No offense, but you are one man, not a full team."

"Yep, and like you, I am damn good at my job. Too many people have made my gut twist up. Shit, Sophia, my back is against the wall. The one person I trust is in Houston, and that's Kasper. Out here it's you and me, and now Caden. I haven't known you long enough to know you very well. And—"

"Now damn it," she butted in, "I am not, let me repeat, *not*, crooked, not going to stab you in the back,"—she snorted an irritated half-laugh—"or shoot you, although right now I'd like to punch you in the nose, you bastard!"

His stare was hard and unyielding. "Medina, you have my six?"

"I am not Upchuck or Creep, not Janet or SAC Bogard. I am always gonna be straight with you, you dickwad. It is us, you and me and no one else, so yeah, fucking-A, I've got your six." A pissy look settled on her face, and she huffed. “Now, you gonna let me in on what Caden told you, you prick?”

West liked this woman, he liked her a lot, and it bothered him. This was neither the time nor place. Besides, liking another woman didn’t fit in his life; neither did a woman who worked in law enforcement. With a head jerk, he motioned her forward.

“Come on, let’s walk and talk.”

34

"We're looking for an exit Caden told me about. He said he overheard them talking about moving product from one end to the other. You found an entrance, and he told me about an exit. It has to be the beginning and end of their underground system. The entrance you found...I can't see them unloading product from that end, can you?"

Sophia looked around. "No, but we're at least two miles from the entrance. You think they dug this far?"

"Same thing I asked Caden when he told me the general area to search and he doesn't know. Remember, we're not going in an exact straight line either."

"It makes sense, sort of. But it's a long tunnel. How long would it take to dig? This is like almost two miles."

"Sophia, it's the cartel, and God knows they have an abundance of workers, and not all are volunteers."

The frown lines between her eyebrows squished up together.

"How did Ward come by this information? He told us earlier he wasn't any closer to the top tier than Joven Cazalla."

"Cazalla talks when he drinks. When they drink together, Caden buys, so Cazalla drinks with him a lot. I tailed him one day when I thought he was Owen McCready. Him and Cazalla—"

"You tailed him?"

"Yeah, I was watching the strip center, working my homicide case, and I saw him there talking to the pawnshop owner. I followed him to a container yard and him and Cazalla had a heated argument. In all honesty, it looked like Ward was the shot-caller."

"Did he explain?"

"Yeah. After his beating he got verbal, in a nonviolent way. Walt Burch was skimming off the top, so he snitched and Cazalla told him it wasn't news to him. Caden wanted to know why Burch didn't get a beating for stealing, so he got into Cazalla's face about it."

"How did Caden learn Burch was skimming?

"The idiot smarted off about getting his piece of the pie in small amounts. He wanted out, but needed cash to get the hell outta the country."

"We should put a tail on him."

"Yeah, only Caden said he saw a man behind the pawnshop a week later. He hasn't seen Walt Burch since. Ward called the man 'Old Motorcycle Boots' since he has no name for him. Said he felt bad for snitching and figured they needed Burch for money laundering, so killing him wasn't an optimal idea, but making an example out of him was. I'm betting no one hears from Burch again. Ward said the same thing. "

"Walt Burch is fish food, nothing we can do about it now. So, about these tunnels, what else did Caden tell you?"

"They have shorter tunnels elsewhere in small towns under houses, close to the border and the waterways. People living there are forced to do as the cartel orders. These particular houses were chosen because they are en route with UPR—that's Union Pacific Railroad."

"They have multiple underground systems, in the mountain and under houses, leading who knows where. Damn, Jack, this beats the hell out of El Chapo's tunnel system, doesn't it?"

"Uh-huh, and transporting product by railroad means the cartel has employees at Union Pacific de Mexico and Kansas City Southern Rail on their payroll who let them load and look the other way."

"Paid employees, or threatened. There are times honest people do bad things to save themselves and their families."

No one would disagree with her; it was more truth than fiction.

"Trains stop in El Paso, Eagle Pass, Laredo, Brownsville, and Corpus, and here's a kick-ass piece of news. Caden told me the cartel is not only transporting drugs, they've included transporting humans into their criminal enterprise."

Sophia's hand came out stopping Jack from speaking, a forlorn look in her eyes. "Illegals. The cartel is now in the coyote business, smuggling people across the border?"

She would never understand how the cartel could treat their countrymen so deplorably.

"It's much worse, Medina, it's human trafficking. Caden told me they kidnap women and teens—boys and girls—Hispanic and Caucasians, then sell them. The play is they sell illegals to wealthy Americans, who turn them into underpaid slaves. Caden says these people stay quiet, so no one calls INS. Caucasian women sold in Mexico or other parts of the world aren't as lucky. They get them hooked on drugs and make them turn tricks, and I can't stomach the story about what happens to the teenagers."

"God, Jack, this makes me want to hurl. Is the FBI involved?"

"Caden got word to his contact, and they're looking into this aspect of cartel activity."

"We do not have enough people in law enforcement to cover the criminal activities these people are involved in. What else did he tell you?"

"There's a small town close to the Panuco River with working fishing boats, and a few boats catering to tourists. They use several boats to transport via the Gulf keeping the product moving and hidden. The Boss and his lieutenants know which boat the product is being shipped on. No one else is told. At nightfall, they transfer product from one boat to another, to mix it up. Not sure how—"

"Jack, they must have people on their payroll in the Coast Guard too. Damn it, the cartel can buy people from every agency and we wonder why our own county is falling apart. Jesus."

"We need one person involved outside of Mexico to flip. Afterward, we put them in a secured facility. Maybe the DOJ will consider WITSEC if they turn enough State's evidence to make a case stick. But I'm thinking no Mexican National is going to flip—too dangerous for them if the US doesn't grant them asylum."

"Jack, it needs to be solid evidence from a source we can trust. And it has to be verifiable. There is no truthful criminal. Hell, they don't trust each other, not really."

"Since there's a great possibility our people are working both sides, it makes it damn hard to know who to trust. I think our motto should be 'trust no one' until we're positive they can be trusted."

"Jack, I swear I've got your six. Come on, let's find a way we can hurt their business. Or at least slow it down. "

Sophia's foot caught in a tree limb and she stumbled; unbalanced, she fell sideways. "Oh, damn it to hell."

"You okay?" Jack stopped when he heard her curse.

"Yeah, I tripped over my clodhopper feet. Hey, wait, would'ja?" Sophia shucked off her backpack, opened it, and dug inside until her hand came out with a folding spade.

"What's up, Medina? You find something?" He sunk to his haunches.

"I'm...well...this dirt seems too soft and loose, like somebody's been digging." She drove the tip of her shovel into the ground with ease scraping away soil. "Get your gloves on, Jack, and help me dig." Her heart raced, and her stomach filled with a heavy foreboding sensation.

They'd dug two feet down and a hand appeared, followed by an arm. With bare hands, they started pushing the dirt away and the upper portion of the dead body began revealing itself. On her knees, her hands dropped to her sides. She closed her eyes, expelling all the air from her lungs, and a small whimper escaped her lips.

"What the hell, son of a bitch!" Jack spat in anger, gritting his back teeth so hard he feared he would break them off.

Agent Miguel Espinar of the Mexican Federales stared at them with lifeless blank eyes, his face smeared with blood and dirt. The hair on his head was matted, a gunshot wound in the middle of his forehead. They had tortured the man; his face was bloody, his eyes black and blue and swollen to just mere slits. On the hand she'd uncovered, his fingernails had been pulled off, his fingers bent and broken. An eternity passed before Jack spoke.

"His body has been here less than forty-eight hours."

Sophia nodded, not able to speak, needing to compose herself before she fell apart.

Jack worked his hand underneath the body to the back pocket, looking for his wallet or ID, needing this information to pass on to the officials. Her movements were automated. She took pictures at several angles, carrying out her business duties and once finished, squatted and began covering his body with Mother Earth again as her tears fell into the dirt. Jack kneeled to help her, and once they'd reburied the murdered Mexican agent, he placed his hand on top of hers.

"Medina, saying a prayer over Agent Espinar I feel is the right thing to do before we leave him."

She nodded, closing her eyes. She prayed in Spanish. Jack did not need an interpreter; he felt every word she prayed, his hand squeezing hers, because losing a fellow law officer hit home hard.

"Help me mark the area so we can find it again. I want to make sure his family gets his body for a proper burial." Her voice was tight. She was steeling herself to stay strong and power on in the face of finding a murdered compadre. They marked the area so his body could be found without too much difficulty. Sophia peeled her latex gloves off, wadded them into a ball, and stuffed them in her pocket.

The numbness she felt inside was heavy, pulling at her heart, and she walked ahead of Jack in silent automation.

"We've got to inform someone, Sophia. "

"It'll be up to Janet. She'll decide when to let this news out and to whom."

"My gut says Vega was involved. What do you think?"

"Hard to say, Jack, but I think this goes deeper than we've imagined."

"As in, people are working both sides? Is that what you mean?"

"Yes, it is. Honestly, I'm not sure I want to tell Janet. Jack, I'm not sure who we should trust."

"I am going to loop Kasper in; he is part of our team."

"Alright, Jack, let's head back." Sophia swiped one last tear away.

Holy shit, Jack! Kasper typed back after he read the latest news.

Listen up, Bergman; this is going to sound odd. Hope you get the messages, Jack typed.

At his desk, Kasper shrugged as he typed, *I'll try.*

UPR—weed out staff. Got that?

Kasper's brain clicked, and Jack waited.

Yep, I get it. What else? Kasper hit send, and his fingers tapped the keyboard as he waited for Jack's response.

Jack nodded as he typed. *Good. Check transports—ways, whys, hows, and uh, wheres. Any transports to big buildings and match up—SSC, see if troublemakers are there. Check associates#, are you getting this?*

Yeah, I think so. What else? Kasper asked.

Jack smiled. *I need this ASAP, all of it. Ask JS for help, get AW onboard if you need to. We can trust him, and he'll do it without a lot of yapping.*

ASAP, on every damn thing, you think I work miracles? Kasper typed in a hurry. Their window of time was closing in.

That's why I said get AW, geezers, don't you read?

Fuck that, I got the time and I am a miracle worker. Besides, since I don't have a life, this has become my life. I am on it, TTYL. Kasper ended the session without a 'good-bye' or 'talk to you later', knowing it would miff Jack, because he wouldn't get the last word this time.

With a lopsided grin, Jack clicked off, secured it, then shut his laptop. Kasper surprised the hell outta him and made him laugh. Score one for the kid.

Sophia felt the energy in the room change and she glanced at Jack from her own work. His face was set, and she could see the wheels in his head rolling at breakneck speed after he stuffed his computer in its hiding place.

"Kasper is on it. I hope he got my code, he—" His burner vibrated, cutting into his thought process. He looked at the message and grinned.

Check into Sea Star employees; check police records and associates and Union Pacific Railway employees; cross-reference all staff, search for trucking companies—schedules and warehouses in the area—and I'm going to add in any waterways, Jack, I get it all, but why the code?

Jack showed the text to Sophia, laughing. "Yeah, he got the message, smart kid."

He texted back: *Good, and Bergman, watch your six. The walls have ears, or so we think. Take extra precautions. Send me part of the text and the other part to Sophia's burner—mix it up so we have to decipher, but we will, don't worry. Take precautions, stay low, and don't let anyone see what you're digging into.*

I will, Jack. Call you when I can. Kasper ended his text.

Jack pocketed his phone.

"He's a smart one. Glad he is on our side."

"Yeah, me too. Maybe he'll forgo the FBI and come work with us," Sophia said.

"Nah, he's without a doubt FBI material. Hope he makes it. Now tell me about this place, Sea Star Coaches. What's the deal?"

He went into detail, beginning with his triple homicide case and everything he's seen while sitting on Sea Star Coaches—Carter, The Tweedles, and Cazalla.

"So, they're transporting meth or whatever using old people as a cover?" Her brows knitted in disgust.

"It's what I think and makes sense. Since Smokin' Hot got looted, I'm almost positive this is the new hub. At first I thought these old folks liked the trip closer to Mexico to get their prescription meds cheaper. After I saw Joven Cazalla, I changed my thinking to cartel involvement since he is an associate of Villa Lobos."

"Yeah, but Cazalla's changed loyalties to a new boss." Sophia opened a bottle of tepid water. It was not cold, but it was wet and her throat felt parched.

"Just how do you know he isn't working for Villa Lobos in secret? Men in the top tier of the cartel are thick. These guys are thicker than family and loyal as fuck. I'll tell ya I'm having a hard time believing Omar just let him walk away. Spill it, Medina, and shit, stop fucking keeping things from me, cuz this is grating on my last fucking nerve."

Jack's anger was justified. It wasn't a matter of needing to be straight with him; she had to be straight with him. If Janet got her panties in a wad, she'd just have to live with wadded-up panties.

Sophia blew out a sigh. "We've been watching him for the last few years."

"Who, Cazalla, you've been following him?"

"No, Villa Lobos, and he is not in Mexico or the United States."

Jack's face twisted up, getting a tinge redder. Janet lied to him. Everyone was lying to him. This would end now.

"Shit! Medina, Janet told us no one was tracking Omar. I didn't press her, but I am you, so start talking."

He was right, they needed to let him in on *everything,* and starting now, she would not hold back.

"Alright, just get a grip, Jack. Marcella told you about Umberto and how he and a militia he formed ran Villa Lobos underground and shoved him out of his own cartel, right?"

Jack nodded, his arms folded across his chest, his feet planted in a semi-wide stance. He was locked down, not moving a muscle until she got every word of her story out.

"You look like a statue, Jack. Sit down."

It took a few minutes before he took a step back, grabbed a chair, and sat, his eyes narrowing, his lips pinched. "I'm sitting."

"First, I wasn't keeping this from you on purpose, I swear. Omar is not our target."

"Yeah, well, why not just humor me? Tell me stuff I don't need to know. Or better yet, tell me the stuff the fucking DEA doesn't want me to know."

"Jack, I told Janet you needed a full briefing, but she told me Bogard told her you didn't need info on Omar because even though he is a DEA target, he has nothing to do with our current operation."

Again, he stared at her with tight lips, waiting for her to continue.

"Villa Lobos is being tracked by us, uh, the DEA. He's been traveling the coastline of Venezuela, Columbia, and Ecuador, and other parts of South America along the Caribbean coastline. His activities involve drug-running, murder, and terrorizing smaller towns that refuse to assist or obey him. All we have is hearsay; we don't have documented proof, pictures, records, or a turncoat to talk. Villa Lobos is not running the cartel, and we don't know who is. When he went underground, things took a drastic change."

"Why is the DEA tracking him if he isn't running his cartel any longer?"

"We've heard he is gathering an army to get his cartel back. Jack, if he does it means war, and he'll stop at nothing to wipe out every person who was part of his overthrow or gets in his way."

"Revenge is another word for war. The only revenge these people understand is killing their enemies. Here's a question, Medina: Who is the person running his cartel and if you know, damn it, you'd better talk."

"I swear all we know is whoever it is, they are not in Mexico. They are conducting all cartel business stateside. If they moved the hub from Smokin' Hot to Sea Star Coaches, I'd like to know why.

Jack, you were watching Sea Star because of your triple homicide, right?"

"Yes, because I was watching Boyce Carter, but seeing Joven Cazalla changes things. Does my homicide link or not? Were my three victims connected to the cartel? Or, were they plain ordinary thieves who the cartel whacked as a warning, steal from us and die? Or was this a planned hit for other reasons altogether?"

Sophia titled her head back, closing her eyes, rolling her neck, thinking about it all.

"If we get leads for your homicide, Jack, maybe it will point the DEA in the right direction, or vice versa."

"Yeah, maybe. Time will tell, Medina. Let's discuss going into the tunnel."

35

The kid was talented. He'd give the kid props, but he was less experienced. One day the younger man would surpass him, but not today. He connected his earbuds to his laptop, typed in code after code, his fingers flying, and voilà! Reading emails under a cloak of invisibility was useful.

Espinar's murder was trouble. Hell, he didn't whack the guy, and he didn't give a fig about the dead agent; however, now a red flag waved, damn it. Umberto Vega. What a stupid, greedy fuck, and a mean bastard on a long list of mean bastards. The thing was, he liked Umberto, because he *was* a despicable SOB and he figured he was the one who'd offed Espinar, but on whose orders? He made a mental note, he'd kill Umberto later; whacking him now would wave one more red flag. Two red flags were two too many. Shit.

On his cell, he dialed a number committed to memory.

"Hello."

"It's me. Meet me tomorrow, in your office. I'll be there early."

"I, well, I guess—" Clive heard the dial tone; his caller had left the conversation. This was not good, not at all. Sweat beaded his lip.

IT WAS A DANGEROUS GAME. People thought there were two sides. One side was local police, government agencies, and Mexican Federales. The other side was the dethroned cartel boss, who still had loyal followers. The third and last side involved a new cartel leader. Here was the deal. He was playing all sides, and it was dangerous as well as exciting. Two of the three sides paid rather handsomely. After he'd amassed what he needed, he was out of here. Never to be seen again. He didn't worry about Mexican law enforcement. Having friends in low places was beneficial. If his face were to end up on the FBI Most Wanted List, he didn't give a fuck. Even if an agency of the United States found him, he'd picked places with zero extradition treaties. He just needed to bide his time. Soon enough he'd be sitting on a beach in Taiwan or on a beach in Maldives, somewhere off the coast of Brazil. No matter where he was, it would involve a beach, lots of beautiful women, and him, with alcohol in hand.

A FEW KEYSTROKES were on his keyboard, and he caught it from his peripheral vision. He leaned back and lifted his hand off the mouse, staring at the screen. It blinked, the tiny white dot at the bottom left corner. It continued to flash off and on, and Kasper propped his right elbow on the desk, his eyes glued to the white dot. He ran his forefinger across his top lip before resting his face in the curve of his palm, his eyes never leaving the flashing dot. "Hmmm, seems we have a visitor now, doesn't it?"

Once again, he lowered his hand and his fingers flew across the keyboard. As he began typing a code, then another—nothing magnificent happened. Okay, he thought as he arched his neck, straightened his back, and flexed his fingers. Both hands went to the keyboard, and he typed, hit enter, and waited. Frustration built, pouring out between his eyes, and his gut tightened. Whoever was in his system had skills. Strike that. They had exceptional skills.

Kasper's shoulders sagged; he felt drained and shut off his monitor after an hour. Glancing to the left bottom corner, the dot sat blinking, taunting him. Crap, so much for secured emails. Jack had been spot-on to send him a coded message. At home, he would double-check all security he put in place, copy every email he had onto a thumb drive, and wipe his emails off into oblivion. Then he'd hunt for the bastard who had hacked into his system. It was late, so he locked his desk, picked up his computer bag, grabbed his phone and keys, and headed to the parking garage, all the while thinking. He ticked off twelve people in the loop of this so-called clandestine mission and out of these twelve, who could *not* keep a secret? Sworn to secrecy, hell, people were human. Not everyone had the confidentiality gene. A scowl darted across his face as he backed out of his parking space.

If his plan was going to work—going head to head with this extremely capable hacker—he needed to dive in. It was time to swim in the murky waters, surfing into the darkest corners, places people fell into the spiraling abyss.

"BERGMAN, YOU LOOK LIKE HELL." The man rolled a chair over next to Kasper's desk, then plopped down, resting his bulgy forearm on the edge. "Did you party too hard, drink too much, or what?"

Kasper's head was pounding. He had spent all night searching for his backdoor guest, with little luck, and he didn't have time to play Twenty Questions.

"Nope, I didn't stay out drinking all night. I didn't sleep well. Besides, Sykes, what's it to you?"

"Ain't my problem. Want to see if you're on your game, that's all. I've got a briefing at 10:00 with the OAG. Afterward, I'll be at my other office."

"Well, don't let me keep you, tear your ass."

The larger man stood, pushing the chair to the adjoining cubicle.

"Bergman, you're fun to aggravate." He turned back. "Oh yeah, forgot to tell you, I'll be on a field assignment for two days just in case you miss me or my brain."

Kasper ignored him and Sykes shrugged it off and left, leaving Kasper a happier man. Douchebag gone, even for a short time, was good. His luck was changing.

This DEA goon of a geek had rubbed him the wrong way since day one. Kasper Bergman disliked Theo Sykes and did not trust him. Deep down in his gut he felt it, but what *it* was, he couldn't pinpoint. "Field assignment, huh? I hope they send you to Mexico and you get Montezuma's revenge and shit yourself on the flight back home." Words mouthed softly to no one as he booted up his computer.

Last night he thought he'd found his computer interloper, but it was just a chat room linked in and attached to three more chat rooms —a computer smoke screen. There had to be a miniscule footprint. Even a speck, and if he found it, it's all he would need.

Kasper's fingers flew across the keyboard and after a few tries, he hit his fist against the desk in frustration. He got out of the chair. Popping his neck from left to right, he loosened his stiffened joints, knowing he was far too young to be stove-up. He'd been hitting it hard for two hours nonstop. What he needed was a caffeine jolt. It was time for a break.

"Fresh coffee, great. I need a shot of caffeine."

Art Walsworth poured a cup from a fresh pot. "Yeah, midmorning wake-up, and great, someone brought mini-muffins. Hope these are banana, not blueberry."

Kasper grabbed a cup, filled it, and took a tiny sip. "Ah, just what I needed, nectar of the gods."

Art pulled out a chair to sit, then propped an elbow up, reaching for a muffin.

"So, Bergman, how are you and Sykes getting along?" He bit into the muffin. Banana-nut, just what he wanted.

Kasper leaned on the counter, thinking about what to say. He'd never been one to speak ill of his coworkers, but Sykes was not an HPD coworker. The man was on loan. Besides, he worked for the DEA; he did not work for the HPD.

"Art, I don't like the guy. Something is off about this dude. I can't put my finger on it though, not yet. I'm glad the pimply face brat is gone. Now I wish the DEA would call Sykes back."

"I get it, cuz he gives me a bad feeling too, but hell, I just met the guy. He might be an alright dude. Maybe we should just get to know him better." Walsworth crammed one more mini banana muffin into his mouth, took a napkin, and wiped his face.

Kasper reached for the coffeepot, walked over, refilled Art's cup, and topped off his own before speaking again.

"Thanks." Art took a sip of hotter coffee.

"Art, have you ever had anyone hack you, watching you, and no matter what you did, you couldn't find any digital footprint?"

"You think you got a person spying on you?"

"Nah, it's a hypothetical question only. I was reading an article the other day, and it got me wondering where someone would head to find a ghost? I mean, other than the obvious places?"

"Word is, Bergman, sometimes you gotta search in your own backyard. If your search is wide, pull it in tighter, start small, and widen as you go. Get what I mean? "

"Start at home and work outward, you mean?"

"Uh-huh. There were times the answer was right under my nose and I never saw it. It happened a lot until I realized I needed to look under my nose first." Art let out a laugh and stood. "Bergman, I'll be glad when your special DEA assignment is over. I got a smart staff, but you are one of my best."

"Yeah, Art, me too, and thanks, that means a lot."

Art bobbed his head upward and left Kasper pouring another full cup of java before returning to his desk with one thought in mind—search in his backyard and neighborhoods close by. Okay, he felt renewed. It was time to find that bastard who had tapped into his computer and was reading over his shoulder.

The caffeine gave him a jumpstart and his talk with Walsworth renewed his attitude. He flexed his fingers; it was time to cast a wide net. Admittedly, he was all over the place in his search, and he needed to tighten the parameters of his search area. Reining in his negativity, Kasper typed, not as frantically as before, but with purpose.

In an hour, he whittled down a few facts. He knew where the IP address wasn't. This helped, but it still frustrated him. Kasper got off his chair to stretch his frame. Bending, he touched his toes, rolled his neck backward in a circular motion, and repeated the same in the forward motion, his eyes closed in thought. What was he not seeing? He plopped into his chair, and the conversation at Quinn's popped into his thoughts. Janet mentioned people on the inside in her department, or perhaps the DEA office. She was not positive. Was this it? Should he be looking for somebody on the inside?

Kasper tightened up his search range adding more specifics, traveling to another server. He tapped into the OAG, where he found several generic IP addresses, linking no names, just searches. He got the same from a DEA server search. One issue was the number of IP addresses, used and not used at both agencies. If anyone was smart enough, they could dive deeper, create a new VPN, secure it with another VPN. A good geek could become a ghost if they had the skills. Just add on a couple of bogus IP addresses and scatter them haphazardly. After that, begin the process again, taking one specific IP address to use which would hide on a confidential VPN, created within a matrix of bogus VPN addresses.

Only a nerd would understand this process. Few people, nerds or not, had the patience. This was the deepest way to hide. Not even scammers or regular hackers needed to use this deep security. Whoever was doing this was exceptional and intelligent. Kasper was certain this person was dangerous.

With a smile, he cracked his knuckles, then flexed his fingers, ready to dig deeper. The person he looked for didn't know anyone was searching for him—good. It would be easier for him to cover his tracks since this person was not watching his own backdoor. Brainy people were sometimes overconfident, and this element of human nature benefited him. It would keep him hidden while he searched.

Besides, he was on the DEA and OAG's time clock; today they would get their money's worth. Fingers on the keyboard, a man in his element, Kasper typed as he smiled.

36

"Is Bebchuk in his office?"

"Yes, sir, he is and he—" The junior secretary didn't get to finish her sentence. Theo Sykes barreled past her and flung open the inner door to Clive's office. The door bounced back and Theo stopped it with a slap of his hand then banged it shut.

"Sykes, can't you act like a person and not an animal for once? Why do you make a big production out of everything?"

"Why do you gotta act like a pussy?"

Clive ignored the name-calling. "Why are you here and not over at HPD babysitting that nerdy kid, Bergman?"

"I got it under control. Don't worry about it. What needs to concern you is the two dead bodies. Medina found Julio Ramirez when she discovered the tunnel entrance and now, per an email to Spears, she and Jack found the body of Agent Miguel Espinar. I'd also like to know who offed him. You shithead, two dead bodies are two too many to deal with."

"I'd be concerned. But these deceased men are in Mexico, and Ramirez is untraceable. No corpse, then no murder. Besides, it's the Mexico law enforcement problem, not ours."

"Well, if the director makes it the DEA's problem, then it becomes your problem, and you'd better have one or two solutions."

Bebchuk's eyes squinted as he leaned forward and lowered his voice. "You do not give the orders, and you're not my boss. I have a message for you from S.C. too. Stop going rogue and follow the damn chain of command or it's gonna come back and bite you in the ass."

Christ, Sykes was bad enough to worry about, but to piss off S.C., well, Clive knew the consequences; pissing Theo off was safer, yet still deadly.

"I doubt it, since I don't leave a footprint. You're a different story. The man has you in so deep it's like quicksand, pulling you in till it's almost over your head, ain't it?" Sykes let out a hushed, ominous-sounding laugh. "Besides, you realize who I am dealing with and who decides, so fuck off and get outta my business." Theo Sykes had an enormous secret. This knowledge was power, but it wasn't time to wield his power, not yet.

A phlegmy cough escaped Clive's throat. "Ahem, well, you might think you know everything, but you don't and besides, it's my business, not yours."

"Wrong. It becomes my business the minute it interferes with what I am doing, or told to do. Get this straight, Upchuck—it won't matter. Even if you or S.C. try covering your digital footprint, I can still find them, not to mention I've got enough information under lock and key implicating you, him, and a few others who are playing a dangerous game with both sides, just like you. So don't play your stupid 'I am better than you' card, you asshole, cuz you ain't." Theo held up his hand, his index finger jutting up, his eyes boring a fiery hole into Clive's. "Be careful, you prick. You and S.C. got nothing you can hold over my head, but I do both of you, and I'll be happy to play my trump card to the higher-ups." He stood, shoving the chair back, placing both palms flat, leaning in until his face was mere inches away, and Clive Bebchuk could feel his fiery breath. "When it all comes to pass, you'd better hope you aren't in the tornado's path, cuz if you are, it's gonna swallow you and S.C. up."

"Is that a threat, Sykes?"

"An effing promise, my man, a bonafide promise."

"Fuck you, Sykes, you aren't my boss, I should—"

"Stow it, Upchuck. You might get squashed underfoot, like six feet underfoot if you decide to cross me, and I ain't scared to pull the trigger, capiche?"

DEA Agent Clive Bebchuk nodded, gritting his teeth. He hated and feared this scary asshole. No tangible proof, only stories heard on the street. If you needed a person whacked, Theo Sykes was the man to call. Yeah, he was a scary person alright. The scariest person he knew this side of the border was not Theo. It was S.C.—his own partner, Stan Cleef.

A MAN STEPPED out into the hallway, dropping his keys and his phone, trying to hold onto files and a cup of coffee.

"Shit." He bent down, setting the files on the floor, got his phone and keys, and stuffed them into his inside jacket pocket. Once upright, he turned, finding himself nose-to-nose with Theo Sykes.

"Hey, what the fu—Sykes, what are you doing here?" The SAC cleared his throat and his back became rigid.

"Talking to Clive and reporting in, so you got a minute?" The expression in his eyes was unmistakable.

"No, I don't have time. I've got a meeting." Jerry Bogard made to sidestep him, but Theo blocked his way.

"Make time." The words hissed, and the hairs on the back of Jerrell Bogard's neck bristled.

"Can't it wait until this afternoon? Damn it, Sykes. I said I'm off to a meeting. If I'm not there, they'll come looking for me."

Theo stared at him, searching for a lie. Jerry Bogard was a terrible liar, but he wasn't lying. Sykes did an insignificant head bob, then spoke, his voice quiet, yet menacing.

"Sure, Jer, go to your meeting. When I come back later you'd better have time for me, got it?"

"Sure, Sykes. After the staff has gone home, will that work?"

"Yep, see you later, Jer, oh and we've got a lot to talk about, so make coffee." He saluted with a smirk then turned. Theo Sykes vanished out the door, headed for the stairwell.

Theo scared the shit out of him. Hell, he scared everyone who knew him. Not just who he was. But what he was and what he could do. No one crossed him, no one except Stan Cleef, who considered himself the man in charge. Stan was an imbecile, and this would be his downfall.

Bogard inhaled and wiped the sweat from his brow. How he had crawled into bed with this monster he'd never figure out. He was in too deep. This was the mother of understatements. No time to mull over this dilemma. It would have to wait. Right now he had to get to this blessed meeting. It was essential to keep his keister covered.

No KNOCK, no nothing, and Bogard's door opened. Theo Sykes walked in, pushing the door closed. The SAC's blood pressure rose and his heart rate sped up. He hated this man. Hindsight was twenty-twenty, and it was too late to back out.

Sykes pulled the office chair up positioning it at an angle, resting his elbow on Bogard's desk and stretching his legs out. Neither he nor Bogard spoke. Time passed and Jerry Bogard's patience wore thin.

"Look here, Sykes. What is it you want?"

"Ah, well, Jer, there are plenty of things I want."

He straightened, turning his body to face Bogard, propping his bulgy forearms on the desk, rising from his seat a bit and leaning in closer, and the door swung open. Sykes moved backward, settling down on the chair.

"Gentlemen, glad I caught you together."

"Stan, glad to see you, we were just—"

"Cut the bullshit, Bogard. You aren't pleased to see me." Stan Cleef looked over at Theo. "Sykes, you happy to see me?"

"Well, it depends on whether you're going to stop me."

"Once I find out what it is you're trying to do, I'll decide." Stan took a seat, crossing his legs with a haughty *I am so important* look on his face. Theo wanted to punch Stan in the nose. Better yet, he wanted to shoot the guy in his face. Blow off his arrogant expression to show him who was in charge. He let it pass, for now.

"Just what do you want from good ole Jerry, Theo?"

"Send Bebchuk to our Brownsville office."

Stan nodded. "Yeah, it's a good idea. He'd be onsite to handle the intercepted shipments."

"That's what I was thinking. And, it's time to get Ralph Foster out. With that goodie-goodie out we can loosen up security." Theo hated Ralph Foster. He was a man who stood by his principles, and Theo knew he couldn't turn the guy.

"Shit, Stan, he can't do anything with confiscated shipments, you know that." Bogard's head was pounding.

"Jerry, Jerry. He just needs to make it easier for the boys to steal the stuff back." Stan stepped over and leaned against the credenza behind Bogard's desk.

"Well, if that happens, Stan, they'll have me fire him, so what, one shipment gets through? Then what?" His head was about to explode.

"Let me worry about it, and you're not gonna fire Bebchuk. If you do, your ignorant ass will be on the line, got me?" He glanced at Theo, then back to Bogard. "Or worse, got it?"

Jerrell Bogard nodded and felt the perspiration running off his neck. If one of the agents under his command let a gang waltz in and steal a confiscated shipment of meth, how could he not fire him?

There was not a damn thing they could do about it. Unless any of them wanted one of two things—to be in prison, or dead. They were puppets of Stan Cleef.

37

Two Days Later, Back in Mexico

"Go a foot to your right."

"Watch your step, Medina, it's slippery."

Jack pushed the brush aside, got on his knees, and peered inside. He rotated his flashlight around, keeping the beam aimed downward so he could see the dirt floor.

"No signs of the living or dead. You ready, Medina?"

Sophia lifted her gun out of the holster and stuffed it in the back waistband of her jeans. She dropped to her knees beside him, then pulled on a pair of work gloves.

"Let's do this."

Sophia turned on her stomach and slipped her booted feet into the opening. With caution, she stuck her foot into the first crevice, easing herself into the hole, steadying herself at the rim. Her gloved hands clutched the crevasses formed for climbing and she descended. Once her feet struck the ground, she turned with speed to keep her back toward the opening; she faced the dank, dark entrance into the underground passage.

In one fluid motion, Jack was in the tunnel standing next to her. The passageway amazed him.

"Cripes, I'm six-one and have room to move in, Jesus, it must've taken years to get this thing dug."

"Don't let this impress you much. You're gonna have to hunch over the further we go into the tunnel."

"Medina, you want me to take point?"

She ignored him and flipped on the night-vision goggles; she was fine with taking point. Besides, he was right there on her heels and for Pete's sake, she was no candy-ass.

"I ONLY MADE it this far before finding my dead guy, so anything further I haven't seen." Her voice was low, not knowing what was ahead of them.

"Guns."

Jack took the gun from his waistband chambering a round and Sophia did the same.

He nodded for her to go.

Impressed was how they felt moving deeper into this underground passage—astonished was more like it.

Jack hunched over. In a couple of places, he didn't have to stoop at all. As the tunnel walls closed in and became narrower, his boot hit something solid. He shoved dirt away from whatever his boot had collided into and he crouched.

"Well, now, what's this?"

"Shush, lower your voice, and what's what?" Sophia squatted to see.

Jack had uncovered tracks, and steel railing. On his knees, he moved forward, his hands on one part of the track, following as it continued. He got up, walking back a few steps, searching where the tracks started. The steel rail ended about fifty feet back.

"This is the beginning or the end. I think this was a mine at one point. But why would the tracks end or start here? It also explains why the tunnel is deep and goes on endlessly."

"Back in the 1700s there were silver and ore mines. I did some research on this area, Jack. Most of the mines caved in during earthquake activity, and it was years ago, even before the 1985 earthquake that blasted Mexico City."

"Yeah, story goes it was the earthquake that kept giving, even all the way into April of '86."

"Must've not done too much damage in the area. Doesn't mean this place is stable."

Jack prayed Mother Nature was not in a bad mood today.

He reached into a side pocket of his backpack and grabbed two glow sticks.

"Take this and let's switch off our flashlights. Too risky the further we go. If we hear voices, shove it under your shirt, under the Kevlar, which will conceal the glow, got it?"

Sophia shut off her flashlight, hooked it on her belt, and broke the glow stick, and he did the same.

"Now, onward, my lady, and hope we don't run into an ogre on our path."

"Humph, ogres or trolls I can deal with, killer drug runners, not so much."

THE MINE SHAFT WAS NEVER-ENDING, and the sweltering heat unforgiving. Sophia stopped and looked at Jack over her right shoulder.

"Aren't you concerned about how far we have walked without finding an end in sight? Shit, Jack. We have to get out of here, back the way we came in, because we don't know if there's another exit. How far do you figure we've gone?"

"Around two-and-a-half miles, give or take a few feet, I guess."

Leaving hadn't crossed his mind, but she was right. They had to get out. Should they turn back now?

"Hey, I—" Her brow furrowed, and she cocked her head. "Do you hear that?"

Voices, faint, almost inaudible, but it was an indistinct murmuring sound. Jack nodded shoving his glow stick under his Kevlar, motioning for her to do the same. A surge of excitement ran through his veins, and his heart rate kicked up a notch. Sophia's insides pulsated with a spurt of energy and fear in one fell swoop. Her hand went to her back pulling her Glock 17, and she glanced at him.

His Glock 23 at the ready he stepped closer to her. "Nowhere to run or hide, Medina, so let's keep close to the wall and wait."

She dropped her voice. "Nope, let's move forward. We gotta find out what they're saying. Besides, if we move or don't move we have no place to run. Who knows, maybe we can get the drop on them."

"Not knowing how many we're dealing with...gotta say you've got balls, girl. I go first with you watching me, agreed?"

"Fine, hotshot, I'll watch you, but it could be you need to watch me, you shit." The words hissed from between clenched teeth.

"We gonna get into a pissing contest right now, are we?"

Sophia Medina's top teeth bit into her bottom lip to keep a smile from springing onto her face. "Nah, we can have a contest later if you want to." She winked; he smiled and signaled with a head jerk to move forward.

With slow deliberate steps, they walked with their shoulders rubbing against the dirt wall, cautiously. They'd walked a mere fifteen yards when the path curved to the left, and they could no longer see ahead, so Jack stopped.

Jack put a finger to his lips, then touched his ear, a signal to listen not talk, and she nodded her understanding.

The voices became more distinct and were speaking Spanish. He stepped backward, forcing her to step back as well.

Her face registered, *What, what now?*

"Get in front and listen," his voice only a thin breath of words, "they're speaking in Spanish."

He let her move ahead of him and Sophia stood where the dirt wall turned at an angle, trying to make sure her nose wasn't showing, and she listened. Jack stood behind her, his breath on her neck. When the man was close, she acted flaky. But right now, she didn't feel those sorts of goofy feelings. Her nerves were jumping for other reasons altogether.

Sophia overheard a conversation regarding handling a shipment: who, where, when, and how much. She heard separate Hispanic voices and was about to hold up four fingers to signal four men. Another voice sounded out, and no interpreter was required because he spoke in English. Five fingers rose. There were five men, or at least five voices. Jack's lips next to her ear, "Five against two, and we do not know how much firepower they have. Not the odds I like, Medina."

She angled her head coming nose to nose with him. "Yeah, so let's not get caught." Her heart was in her throat, between the danger they could face and him being so damn close—her heart beat out a perpetual, *boom-thud-boom-thud-boom!*

"Hey *maricón*, watch what you're doing."

"*Si*, and don't call me no queer."

"Just load the shit and shut up, and watch what the fuck you're doing. We need to pick up the pace. This has to get to the rail before we miss our window."

"Me gustaría tirarte por una ventana que mierda." (I'd like to throw you out a window, you shit.)

"What'd you say?"

"I said okay."

The men who spoke Spanish laughed. The non-Spanish speaking American did not laugh. He didn't care what the asshole said because he was running the show.

Jack crowded behind her, tapping her on the shoulder. She angled her head back to see him make a hand gesture to switch places with him. She complied. Now he wasn't so close. She wished her heart would stop pounding against her ribs in *that way*.

Jack craned his neck left, hoping to get a look. Luck was on their side. The craggy wall jutted out enough to give him an advantage to see them without them seeing him.

Two men he knew, Umberto and Carl Mundy, which meant Louis Callum was nearby, joined at the hip to Mundy; one was never without the other. Further down he saw ten or more men loading packages into box crates, then stacking them on an old mine cart. Nobody talked and not much guesswork went into the contents of each package—one word, one product—meth. Once they'd seen Mundy, this left no doubts about Sea Star Coaches and Boyce Carter's involvement. His right foot lifted to take a slow step backward when he stopped and did a double-take. Jack closed his eyes, reopened, then blinked and refocused. *What the hell, I can't believe this.*

West looked on as Stan Cleef walked into the opening, Clive Bebchuk on his heels. Unexpected was a clear understatement. He recalled when he and Janet had lunch. She'd voiced her suspicions, but this was much more than even she imagined.

"What is taking so damn long? Umberto, tell your guys to haul ass and be quick. We're on a time limit," Carl Mundy carped.

Stan Cleef stepped into the other man, his skinny face drawn up in an ugly sneer.

"Mundy, I am not gonna keep reminding you to stop acting like you give the orders around here, so back off." He turned to Clive Bebchuk. "Get the list for Umberto. Tell him which Union freight cars he needs to load onto. Get the list of trucking companies that are picking up. Mark which crates we want sitting in Customs and this time don't fuck it up. You fuckers pissed Beck off because there were thirty crates missing when his boys came to get the shit." Stan jerked his head toward the exit and smirked at Bebchuk. "Haul your fat ass, Upchuck."

Jack pulled back and took out his burner; he clicked on the camera, squeezing closer around the curve to get the best angle, snapping shot after shot, knowing he had to get lucky and get a few clear pictures with the crappy ones. Too bad he couldn't record their conversation; however, the pictures were solid proof. It might be his ace in the hole. Maybe they would roll on each other. They'd have something substantial to work with if one of them was worried about saving his keister.

Sophia watched him snapping pictures. She stood a few feet behind him with her gun raised to cover him should someone fire.

Jack backed up and turned, motioning for her to let him in front and to follow so they'd be out of hearing range, keeping their voices lowered.

"Well, Jack, who's there, doing what?"

"Umberto and ten or more loading and hauling out packages. It's gotta be meth or coke."

"Umberto's participation doesn't shock me. I didn't think he was trustworthy. I think he was involved in Miguel's murder too."

"Yeah, so do I. Here's more for you. Mundy and Callum, Cazalla's goons, are here, and you want another huge surprise?"

"Why not? Seems like there are a lot of fucking surprises these days."

"Cleef and Bebchuk are here too."

"You're kidding?"

"Uh-uh, and you want another shocker? Stan Cleef is calling the shots. The guy is not the limp dick, brainless person under Bebchuk's thumb that we thought he was."

"What the hell? Let me see the pictures."

He pulled the pictures up, clicking through them, looking with her.

"Jack, those three,"—she pointed them out—"they don't look like locals, do they to you?"

Clicking on the picture, he enlarged it as much as he could to scrutinize the image. "You're right, they aren't. See the B.C. on his neck? He's a Brown Cobra, from Houston. Shit."

"Now what do we do? We are outnumbered; it would be suicide to go in guns blazing."

His forehead rose, and a teeny tiny flicker of a grin flashed.

"Why are you staring at me that way, Jack?

"You are going to defer the plan to me. Are you serious? Ain't gonna try to one-up me saying you have higher rank?"

"You're an absolute jerk and no, I'm not, because I see the wheels in your head turning, so why bother? Just tell me what we're gonna do."

First, we leave the way we arrived. Second, get Kasper on this. We need to find out where this mine ends. It might intersect with the railroad. I'm gonna have him check into the trucking transportation in this area associated with the railroad."

"We need to inform Janet what we've found out about Cleef and Bebchuk."

"No."

"What the hell, Jack? Why not? We have picture-proof evidence."

"No, Medina, we aren't saying shit until we go back to Houston. I'm not about to chance letting this out over airwaves. Crap, we've chanced enough."

Sophia kept her mouth shut. He was right. What was the matter with her brain these days? Common sense dictated in person was better. What was her rush? Oh, she knew the reason. This job needed to be finished. Jack was getting into her private space—he had become rooted in her existence and this could end painfully for her.

"Come on. It's not safe. There are just two of us."

No matter how badly he wanted to round the jutted corner, gun in hand, and take their asses down, he wouldn't. They were outnumbered and out-gunned. However, his primary reason to step back into the shadows was Sophia. He would not risk her life with these bastards. If they got the upper hand, she would suffer to the nth. One woman he knew suffered at the hands of a monster. Jack wouldn't let another woman suffer the same fate. This time, it would not be in the hands of one monster, but many.

38

"I'm glad Bergman won't be able to see us, because I'm betting we look stupid, Jack. You dork, I can't believe you lost your headset."

To conduct a three-way call with Kasper on speakerphone wasn't a brilliant idea since one never knew who might be listening. So they shared Sophia's earbuds.

"Hey, us being cheek to cheek, Medina, keep your lips on your side."

Sophia's mouth was full of water. His comment made her laugh, and water spurted through her nose.

"Hey!" He turned in time, avoiding a spray of "nose water."

"Funny, Jack, I mean, you're hilarious." She wiped the water off her face.

Their camaraderie was like they'd known each other for years. If anyone was watching them one might imagine their relationship was far more than it was. Theirs was a relaxed working relationship. Had either of them admitted to wanting more, it would have ruined everything. Up to a point, that is.

They each stuck an earpiece in as Jack clicked on the number and hit call.

"Hey, Bergman, we're both on the line. What were you able to find?"

The proximity to Sophia sped up his pulse, and he attributed it to being a red-blooded man. Well, she was a beautiful woman, brave, smart, and funny. *Focus*, he told himself, and pushed his personal thoughts back.

Sophia liked the man a lot, perhaps too much. Jack West could impress any woman with his looks alone. Once you got to know the man —the cop and the detective—you realized how easygoing he was, and funny with a dash of intimidation. It would be easy for any woman to fall under his spell. Get this nonsense out of your head, her brain said.

His shoulder touching her shoulder, her head near his had her wishing or hoping. *Stop entertaining these ideas. This will create nothing but trouble*, she warned herself one more time.

Kasper's voice broke into both of their thoughts, bringing them back to reality.

"And the ore mine closed over thirty-odd years ago. I found a large logistic trucking hub around thirty miles from the outskirts of a small town called El Tomaseño. It's about a hundred and twenty miles from y'all." Kasper shifted in the front seat of his car, looking over his shoulder every few minutes.

"Got a name for this hub?"

"Yeah, Logística de México, or Logistics of Mexico."

"Who owns the place?" Sophia jotted notes.

"Shipping Inc. in Mexico, the physical address is bogus; this company exists on paper only, but the hub is real."

"Any railroad activity connected to Logistics of Mexico?"

"A few spots between El Tomaseño and a town named Cruillas, which is a small rural area. These people are poor and if the cartel forces them to work, no one would look at them twice."

"Sophia, do you think the Federales would look into it?"

"Yeah, I guess. If we can find anyone we can trust."

"I'll contact Janet, she can—"

"Guys, you two wanna discuss this later, geesh, I got other crap to talk about and I ain't there in person, so—"

"Yeah, yeah, okay, Bergman, what else ya got?" He smiled. Kasper kept them on point; he liked his work ethic and his drive. Heck, he just liked the kid, period.

"UPR has a section of track close to Logística de México. From there, trucks can go freaking anywhere. One trucking company goes from the hub straight to Reynosa, and they unload at Customs, and then return to the hub. Other trucks haul to San Fernando and in areas toward the Gulf. I looked at the trucking companies. They haul flour, cornmeal, tobacco, and alcohol, but not sure from where exactly; there are several places. There are a few loads dropped off that seem weird."

"Weird, weird like how?"

"No one claims them, and the crates sit unchecked, no paperwork. After two weeks, another trucking company comes to pick up the load, and then they haul it to an undisclosed destination, but it appears to stay in Mexico."

Their foreheads wrinkled, looking at one another from the corner of their eyes, and she shrugged. "What the heck, Kasper?" She found it odd the shipments stayed in Mexico. "Why would the cartel need to import into their country? The stuff is already there. Besides, they are exporters 99.9 percent of the time."

"Beats me, Sophia, but I'll keep digging and hafta get back with y'all."

"Bergman?"

"Yeah, Jack?"

"See who you can find in Customs, land, air, or whatever. I'll be damned if I can find anyone we can trust. Also, what about the employee list for Sea Star?"

"Uh, Jack, I haven't had time to investigate that yet. As it is, I'm worried about this entire phone call because I've had an issue and I didn't want to tell you guys, at least not before I had proof with more details. I mean, and in the interest of your safety...hell, my safety too, I hafta take care of this and—"

"Bergman!" Jack barked. "Get a grip, man, stop rambling. Now, take a deep breath. Good. Now begin at the beginning and explain."

Kasper coughed, clearing his throat. "Well, to the best of my knowledge, no one's tapped into our burners, which is good news. But, uh, my computer at HPD was hacked, and whoever it is has been reading our emails. Two days ago, when you were telling me what you wanted in code...oh, uh, by the way, good call, Jack."

"Yeah, uh, thanks. Now back to your voyeur. How in the hell, Kasper—"

"Whoever it is found my private VPN and bypassed my security and firewalls, all of them. Not to brag, but I'm superb at this crap. However, this person is brilliant. Hell, I'd be envious of their ability if it weren't freaking the shit outta me. And to top it off, with you there, I've got no one I trust watching my fucking back."

His mind whirled. If anything happened to Kasper, he would never forgive himself.

"Jack...Jack, you still there? Sophia?"

"Yeah, we're here, Kasper. Listen up. Better to not talk over the wire. Even now it's chancy with burners. If your mysterious intruder has superpowers, well, what's to say he stopped at computers? Keep your back against the wall. Do not take any risks, got it?"

"Yeah, Jack. Now, what else do you need from me?"

"Information on the shipments left at Customs. Find out why these shipments sit." He scratched his chin covered in stubble and got quiet.

"Jack?"

Sophia's head twisted to see his profile, her cheek close to his and her breath hot and whooshing as she exhaled, causing his heart to thud a little faster. Two things went on in his head. First was, what was their next step on this case? And number two was Sophia.

"Jack, Kasper is waiting on you."

"Yeah, we need to hurry and finish. Art will be on the warpath. It makes no difference who I'm working for. Art still wants to see my smiling face and on time too."

Gathering his wits, Jack shook off whatever he felt when his body was close to Sophia's. Cripes, he needed to squelch these feelings, or perhaps face them head-on. He cleared his throat and resumed giving orders.

"Get names of trucking companies who use Logistics of Mexico traveling to and from Brownsville, McAllen, Laredo, Eagle Pass, and Del Rio, then cross-reference those establishments. Find out which trucks go to these places and what they haul. Before you say anything, I realize it can be all kinds of merchandise, but look for foods, frozen fish and meats, coffee, dry staples as your top picks. Keep digging for your computer interloper; no way to change what he or she might have read. Don't want ears either, so we talk in code on our burners."

"I'm on it, and my computer eavesdropper may be a worthy opponent, but so am I." He crossed his fingers.

"Kasper, I'd take you as a partner any day."

"Uh, thanks, Jack."

"Yup."

Kasper pocketed his phone and got out of his car, the one place he felt safe to talk. A renewed drive surged inside of him—he would *not* let Jack down.

THE SINGLE EARBUD out of his ear, Jack distanced himself from her so his heart would stop beating in allegro tempo. It helped, a little. He had to shake this.

Sophia bit her bottom lip in thought, her ankles crossed, one foot jiggling back and forth. "We should send Janet the pictures."

"No. After Kasper's announcement, it's not safe. Besides, we need more proof so we can nail these bastards, especially for Espinar's murder, and Walt Burch's murder too."

"Yeah, you're right. So, what are you thinking, Jack? These towns and the trucks are drop-off points from other border towns?"

"Uh-huh, and find out what DEA field offices are near these towns. With Creepo and Upchuck involved, perhaps others are too. McAllen and Reynosa is a hot spot. Especially since the T-288 boys taught the new gangs how to make meth. You can bet the cartel has control of these two new gangs."

"You're thinking like a true DEA, Jack. From Matamoros to Brownsville, the number of people to sell to is phenomenal. They are either users or pushers; there are too many of them. Just running the borders from Texas to Mexico you can reach out and touch the cartel's hands, yet still be in Mexico."

"I'd like to slap cuffs on the wrists of those hands." His forehead puckered in thought. They needed more proof, concrete evidence, but how were they gonna get it without walking right into the hornet's nest?

Sophia stood stretching her arms skyward. She bent her neck backward and yawned. Sleep. Lord, she wanted to doze at least for a few hours. Then maybe her brain wouldn't be so damn fuzzy. Alert and rested they could discuss how to go about getting more proof.

Jack sat across the room, his eyes following her movements. Her toned body, the way her gun holster rested against her hip, the arch of her neck as she stretched, the way her T-shirt pulled against her—holy shit—Jack stood. His insides quivered a split second. He was a mere six steps from her and in a dreamlike state, without pause, his feet traveled toward her.

Sophia's head lowered and her hands moved to rest on her upper thighs as she pulled back in the opposite direction, stretching. Standing upright, she was face-to-face with him, literally.

"Hey Jack, why don't—" Her words cut off in utter surprise as his eyes stared into hers, and she lost the ability to speak. Her heart raced, as did his, and time froze.

Sophia found her voice. "Uh, Jack, what..."

Her words cut off as he slid an arm around her waist, drawing her in, lowering his mouth to hers. As the kiss intensified, his other arm came in and drew her body closer and the heat between them blazed. Sophia's arms raised and without orders from her brain, her hands slipped to the nape of his neck, grabbing his collar-length hair, pulling his body closer to hers. Jack moved his lips from her lips, trailing soft nibbles down her neck. He relaxed and his hands traveled from the small of her back and upward. Sophia's body moved in, fitting her frame into his like molten lava, smooth and hot. His mouth moved again taking her lips once more, and the kiss filled with intensity, then sweetness. He pulled away, ending the kiss with an abrupt movement, stepping away from her. Sophia's eyes opened and she looked at him. Uncertainty filled her head, and he waited for her to say something. Anything.

Her heart pounding, her insides melting, she did not know what should happen next. It flashed in her head that working relationships never lasted when romance or sex occurred. It always ended up with one person getting hurt and in most cases partners could no longer be partners. Lord! She wanted to get naked with the man. That was a terrible idea. It was imperative to keep it professional; they made too good of a team to ruin it with one fleeting mistake.

"Sophia, I'm, uh, not sure what came over me, and I apologize for overstepping—"

"No, please don't apologize. It was a shared moment. I mean, I didn't stop you. Hell, I, my...well, crap, I kissed you back."

A laugh bubbled, and she looked at him. He was grinning.

"You did indeed, Medina, and wow."

"Uh, well, I have an idea."

One brow shot up, and his heart gave a double beat. "Oh yeah, and what might your idea be?"

His thoughts ran the gamut of seductive French kisses, caressing, foreplay, and where it all led to. But she was about to disappoint the red-blooded man; however, she would arouse the detective.

"I wanna get in touch with Caden Ward. I think we should talk to Joven Cazalla."

"Alright, Medina, you have my attention. Whatdaya got in mind?" He was disappointed. Their ideas hadn't matched, but he figured it was for the best anyway.

It was down to business. They had to keep the recent liplock from hanging over them.

Jack needed distance, so he sat on the opposite side of the room. This was not Tinder. He was at work. Not swiping left. He had to shut it off. Not a good time to get intimate with a female partner. Nor was it a super idea. This had happened once at HPD, and he heard it turned sour quickly. Problem was it didn't wipe out what he was feeling. It'd take more than a squirt gun to extinguish the fire he felt.

Oh, hell no, she would never forget the kiss. One day, maybe not soon, she would address his response and attack it head-on. Aroused hormones combined with occupational anticipation, her heart still pitter-patting like a drummer. Whew, she would have to force these libidinous feelings down, deep down. In her heart, she knew what she wanted—what they both wanted. But not now, not here; but then again, no. Swallowing all this "wanting Jack" down, Sophia began.

"Alright, Jack, before you shoot me down, let me explain."

"Well, since we aren't going on a stakeout, and we have nothing else to occupy our time, fine." He winked at her; she blushed but did not comment.

"From what we know, Joven Cazalla was one of Omar's top men. Loyalty is huge with these people. What makes you think a new boss would trust him?"

"Excellent point, and I can't say why."

"Wasn't Cazalla talking with Boyce Carter at Sea Star Coaches? And you were watching Carter because his son was a victim in the triple homicide?"

"Yeah, yeah, and where are we going with this, Medina?"

"From our intel everyone thinks the new cartel boss is stateside.

I'm thinking Cleef and Bebchuk are players only. You said it looked like Stan Cleef was in charge. You think Cleef is running Bebchuk?"

"It looked like Stan was calling the shots."

"Wait, didn't you say Cleef said they'd better not be pissing Beck off again?"

"He did."

Things were adding up. What he hoped was, it went like this—two and two is four, not two and two equals nothing.

You wanna tell me what's rolling around in that pretty head of yours?"

"Cazalla still works for Omar, or that's the story I'm rolling with because once loyal, always loyal. An ex-cartel boss can have you executed with a snap of a finger, and it wouldn't matter one iota if Villa Lobos was in deep hiding or not. If Joven Cazalla had switched his loyalties, he'd be dead by now."

"You can't know that for sure."

"Yeah, I think I can, Jack. Because Cazalla knew things about Omar others didn't know. Things a kingpin like Villa Lobos would rather not bring to the surface. We know what big league criminals can do from behind bars. Ain't much difference, hiding incognito or behind bars, Omar has power and people."

"You have a point, but loyalty and trust don't happen overnight either."

"True. It's difficult to know who's loyal. I say we start from the inside and work our way out."

"Like go after Cleef and Bebchuk. Then figure out who shot Agent Espinar. And find out who is responsible for my triple homicide?"

"Yes—and..." Her brow dipped in thought.

"What else is there...and...and what?"

"Didn't you say you heard Cleef saying they pissed Beck off once so they better not fuck up again?"

"Yeah, and your point is what?"

"You heard of anyone named Beck, Jack?"

"Not that I recall, why?"

"The name Beck, what's it short for, Beckett, Beckman, or Beckley, does it ring any bells?"

"Medina, I've met no one named Beck, shortened or otherwise. Wait. Hold on a minute."

Jack shut his eyes, digging back, then he opened his eyes, smacking the table with an open hand. "Boyce Edward Carter, son of a bitch—BEC—that's our Beck and Joven Cazalla is working with Beck. Well now, kiss my ass."

"Tempting, but first things first, Jack." A small smile played on Sophia's full lips.

39

Back in Houston

Kasper blew out a nervous breath, wiping the perspiration off his forehead, before moving onto the next screen. His neck was sore, his back ached, and even his fingers were cramping up from the abnormal amount of keyboarding he had done in his search for the technical intruder. Shifting his butt in the chair to ease his discomfort from being more sedentary than usual, he clicked the mouse to move to the next screen. He closed his eyes stretching his arms overhead and rolled his shoulders, then opened his eyes and stared at the screen. The numbers rolled up in sequence. Numbers in batches of twenty with two empty lines to follow until the next twenty rolled up.

As the numbers slowed and began reconfiguring, Kasper watched the screen closer. A back door—he was in. Being able to go incognito was one issue, but he had a workaround. Kasper Bergman had built a fabricated code name—The Ghost—burying himself under layers of dark websites before unleashing The Ghost into the cyber-world of HPD, the OAG, and DEA. He was a flea on the dog. And with speed and precision, his computer persona was jumping from place to place, doing this before his secret cyberstalker got smart enough to get a flea collar. Once he'd figured out how to infiltrate and be unseen for a little while, he'd laughed at his analogies.

His flea stopped bouncing in rapid progression. It slowed to small hops from one number to another. It searched out three precursor numbers. Once these numbers were secured, it began the same process over again. From these first three numbers, it locked onto three more. Then several dots later, three more, and more dots between numbers. Multiply by threes with dots in between until it ended with the last six. Promising.

Kasper's heart rate increased as did the sweat accumulating that had trickled down his neck, although the room was in fact cool. This cyber intruder was in three places. Or was it three people? The secured IP addresses were from three separate entities: HPD, DEA, and the OAG offices. He did a print screen, moving it to his personal file to copy onto a thumb drive. Bergman could wipe out his history of searches, making them disappear without a trace. He'd saved the program code he built, securing it in a safe place. One day when he was FBI, he might need it again.

He spoke to his computer screen in a low voice. "Shit, who the hell are you? How many of you are there?" It was almost noon. He needed to stretch his legs and take a breather for just a minute to clear his head. The entire tech staff had taken Freddie to lunch. Today was his last day before he moved out of state. He'd begged off saying hard work to catch up on, so he wished Freddie farewell and good luck. Kasper thought the floor would be deserted.

He heard someone in Art's office, but it wasn't Art talking, and he didn't recognize the voice.

Down the hall, on his laptop, sitting in Art's office he watched the numbers roll and then the screen went dark. "Damn." It wouldn't be long before it blew up in his face. He had to act quickly because time was running out. He picked up the phone and dialed.

"Sea Star Coaches, may I help you?"

"Let me speak to Mr. Carter. Yeah, I'll hold."

"Boyce Carter."

The office door was wide open. Shit, he was slipping.

"It's Sykes. Give me a minute to close the door."

The door shut before Kasper reached it, and he stealthily inched up. Laying his ear against the doorframe, he listened. The voice was hushed. He'd never been able to distinguish voices well. As he listened, warning bells sounded. The words were muffled and he strained to hear.

"Shit, Sykes, I told you not to call me here."

"Shut the fuck up, Carter, and listen."

Kasper heard the unnamed person say Carter, and he'd bet his last paycheck it was Boyce Carter on the other end. His heart rate zoomed, and he kept his ear to the door, hearing merely one part of the conversation. The man spoke again. He wasn't whispering, but he wasn't talking loudly either; the voice was not registering in Kasper's brain. It dawned on him who it might be...but no, it couldn't be... could it?

"Yeah, well, I don't give a damn." The speaker hissed. "Get this straight. I've got Bebchuk and Cleef under control. You just monitor Cazalla and those other two idiots."

The man inside the room stopped talking. Silence. Kasper's heart skipped a beat. He hadn't realized he'd been holding his breath until the man spoke again. Kasper pressed his ear against the door and concentrated.

"I don't care. Burch had it coming. Besides, no one would ever think of pinning it on me, now would they? I've got you four by the balls and I'm not letting go. And you threatening to get Villa Lobos to side with you, you'd better think again, you puss-bag. I've been on here jabbering with you way too long as it is, so stick to the plan, and if I suspect you're gonna double-cross me, it'll be the last thing you do, hear me?"

Kasper waited, ready to bolt when the conversation was over.

"No, call Bogard. Tell him I said get those two fucks back to Houston, pronto. What, who, Vega? He's no longer a worry. I've seen to that."

"You don't want to know. So, like I said, don't worry about it."

Theo clenched his jaw as he listened.

"No, I don't want you running an old folk's tour. I want you picking up product, then have the women we have stashed in Brownsville brought in. I don't give a rat's ass, just do it today."

Kasper heard Art's chair squeak as it rolled back. A silent thank you went to Art for not getting any WD40. It took two minutes. Kasper was out the door headed to the parking garage. Whoever was in Art's office sounded familiar, but male voices all sound the same to him. This sucked.

He had referred to Bogard, Bebchuk, and Cleef, saying he had all of them by the balls. All of whom were DEA. This was big...and dangerous.

Kasper hurried to his car, started the engine, backed out cutting the wheel, moving in reverse to the last row. Putting the car in drive, he slowly pulled up watching the stairwell door as he turned into his parking spot. Surges of fear, panic, and adrenaline bounced inside his gut when the door opened, unmasking the face of the nameless voice.

With calm hands, he opened the car door and slid out, hit the key fob to get his *beep-beep* sound, locked the doors, and with sure feet, he headed straight to the stairwell, toward the unfamiliar voice.

"Bergman, you back from Freddie's farewell lunch?"

"Yeah, and you, are ya headed to lunch or back to your other office?"

"Gonna go to Three Forks. They got great steaks. Have you ever eaten there?"

"Not in a while." Kasper was trying his level best to stay calm, not act jittery or in a rush.

"I'd stay and chew the fat with ya, but I'd rather be chewing the fat off a T-Bone. See ya later, kid."

Kasper stayed calm, his voice steady. "Sure, Agent Sykes. See ya later."

Sykes heard the click of the stairwell door and he glanced back. Nice kid, but he'd stepped into a situation that could get him killed. Theo Sykes climbed into his car, hoping it didn't come to that, but if he did, one thing was positive: Theo Sykes was not the squeamish type.

40

As one foot hit the stairs, Kasper took them running, three at a time, headed to the sixth floor. Just inside the stairwell door, he stopped to catch his breath and compose himself. "Stay calm, don't panic." His lips moved, but the words were inaudible. No one in Homicide knew Jack's current 20. Kasper didn't know what the men in Jack's department had been told. His mind was reeling.

Three heads turned when the door opened.

"Hey, Bergman, you lost?" Dawson Luck swiveled his chair around.

"Not really, Detective. Good to see you."

Lucky grabbed Kasper's hand, pumping it.

"You know these fellas, Austin Reed and Earl Nichols?"

"Detectives, good to see you again; it's been a while and several murders ago." Turning to Lucky, he lowered his voice. "Can I have a private word?"

"Sure. Let's go to the common room. We can talk there."

"Close the door, will you, sir?"

"Hey, call me Lucky, not sir. We're colleagues. I'm not your boss. Have a seat."

Lucky pulled out a chair, gesturing for Bergman to sit.

"You're wound up. What can I help you with?"

"This is going to sound weird, but can I borrow your cell phone, and you not ask me questions?"

"You in trouble, Bergman?"

"No, Detective, I'm not in trouble or anything. It's just that, I, well, uh, it's private. This call cannot be on my phone records, I—"

Dawson Luck sprang up, pushing his chair back, shaking his head. "Listen, kid, I am not gonna involve myself in any underhanded dealings. I'll try to help if you've got a problem, but not at the expense of my career."

"What if I told you I am doing a favor for your partner?"

"How well do you know Skip Webb? And let me warn you, bragging about it will not win you any popularity contests at HPD."

"Not Webb, I'm talking about Jack West."

"Jack?"

"Yes."

"What's going on with him? It's all been so hush-hush, like he's training to be super detective or whatever." Sarcasm dripped off his tongue. Not in the loop again, Dawson Luck's big nose was outta joint.

"Jack's right, you can be an ass. Man, I can't give you any details. Wish I could, but I can't. So, you gonna let me use your phone or not? If you aren't, then fine, I'll figure out another way."

Bergman knew Jack would check an incoming text then he'd take the call from Lucky's cell.

"Yeah, alright, keep your panties on, geezers." Dawson Luck yanked his phone out of his front pocket and handed it to Kasper. "Now I suppose you need privacy?"

"Yes, if you don't mind. I need to, uh..."

Lucky walked out and down the hallway. Kasper followed.

As he pushed open the half-closed door, Detective Luck flipped on the light switch, waving his arm in a sweeping motion.

"Here, the room's all yours. Best empty office in the house for private trysts, clandestine phone calls, and all that shit."

Kasper surveyed the smaller room, seeing a few beat-up file cabinets against the back wall and a scratched-up broken-down wooden desk and old folding chairs against the adjacent wall. A box of pens and telephone message pads sat on top of the desk, and the room smelled musty. "Storeroom?" He looked at Lucky.

"No. I call this Jack's hush-hush room. Seems like a shitload of mysterious crap happens here and for odd reasons, Jack's name is always in the mix. Bring my phone back down to the squad room when you're finished."

Dawson Luck left, shutting the door, pissed off at himself for still having his big honker out of joint. It wasn't Jack's fault, and when the dust settled, he knew Jack would tell him about it, or at least a little to satisfy his curiosity.

KASPER SENT a text to the burner: *Calling your personal cell using Detective Luck's phone — Kasper.*

"Jack."

"Kasper, why the devil are you calling from Lucky's phone, and where is Lucky?"

"He's in the squad room."

"Where are you then?"

Kasper looked around the room. "In a cluttered musty storeroom, Detective Luck calls it Jack's hush-hush room. Why's that?"

Jack didn't laugh, no matter how funny it was to him, it was not funny to his ex-partner. Dawson's nose was still twisted out of shape. He hoped with time, Lucky would let it go.

"That's a story for another day. So, why are you calling me on my personal number from Lucky's phone?"

"I won't take a chance with our burners. Too much at risk. After this call, we talk in person. The search for my computer voyeur is over. I've got other news as well." Kasper recapped the conversation he'd overheard and revealed the name of his computer voyeur.

"Sykes, as in Theo Sykes, he's your hacker? You sure?"

"Yeah, after matching up IP addresses for offices here, the DEA, and OAG, I'm sure."

"And it was him you overheard in Art's office—you're positive?"

"Yeah, Jack, I'm positive. No one else was on the floor, and he came to the garage."

"And he mentioned Bogard, Cleef, and Bebchuk. You positive that's what you heard?"

"Yes, Jack, I'm not deaf. It's what I heard. He mentioned a fat pawnshop owner and they couldn't pin it on him, so you think he killed the guy? This ain't good, Jack."

"Hold on, Kasper, don't hang up. I need to confer with Sophia."

"Yeah, no way I'm hanging up right now."

Three minutes later he was back.

"Bergman, here's what you do. Go to the OAG. Speak with Janet, and only Janet. Make damn sure you are alone. Or better yet, be outside in the open because they might have bugged offices."

"What do I tell her, everything?"

"That you were in contact with us, nothing else. Tell her to send someone to come get us. Give us five days to tie up things here. Tell her it's a ten-hour drive into Mexico City, and we want to fly out of Mexico City. Other than Janet, just the pilot needs to know our flight plan. Have her meet us at the hangar once our wheels are down in Houston."

Kasper nodded and waited.

"Did you hear me, Kasper?"

"Yeah, sorry, Jack. Shit, Sykes read our conversations. He knows I'm working with you guys. Maybe he thinks I know too much. What if he, well, what if..."

"Hang tight, kid, keep your cool. You just do what you do best. Got me?"

"I'm acting like the nerd I was the first time we met. Sorry, Jack. I've got it together. What do you need me to do?"

"Start with monitoring his email, under the radar, which I know you can do. You're smart. Second, for the next four days follow him, see what he does, where he goes, who he talks to. Remember, kid, you want FBI, so think FBI, and get ready for a shitstorm!"

41

"Go to where? Are you kidding me? You're going to have me transfer out to the Brownsville office? Why would I consider a relocation? This is for shit."

"You need to be there to intercept and move product. This is my call, Clive. Don't get all pissy. Bogard and Theo agree with me. You go there, contact the T-288s and set it up. Once you have the shipments in the bonded warehouse, contact Vega."

"Damn it, Stan, I don't like this shit, not one bit. You're asking me to pull up stakes and leave Houston, my home, and, well, my life. I am tired of being under your fucking thumb." Clive Bebchuk hated this skinny weasel.

"Don't forget I have you by the balls, and I ain't gonna let go. My own balls are in a vice grip, so pal, we're in this together."

"I ain't gonna transfer, Stan. I won't. Give it your best shot; see if I give a damn."

"She was sixteen, you were what, thirty, and yep, she was a curvaceous, big-breasted, mature-looking sixteen-year-old, but, shit, Clive, sixteen. How many times did you fuck her brains out at that fleabag motel? " A tsk-tsk'ing noise slipped from his wafer-thin lips.

"And your wife, Clive. Shit, man, Carla Bebchuk, Attorney at Law, what will this do to her? There are no statutes of limitations in the State of Texas for statutory rape. The law will consider this a sexual assault on a child, and—"

"You think I'm stupid, Stan? Damn it, I know the freaking law." Bebchuk set upright planting his palms on the desk, leaning in. "That was twenty-odd years ago. Go ahead, keep trying to blackmail me, whatever it is you're gonna do, and I will—let me repeat, *I will*—come back and get my retribution. I can confess to the wife; I'm not concerned about that. All these years I've worried about losing my job or going to jail. This shit,"—he waved a hand over nothing—"this shit we're doing is worse, and I am sick of it, three years sick of it, understand me?"

Stan Cleef remained seated. He was silent. Clive was tired of it all. He needed out. If he confessed everything to the right people, perhaps he could save his own ass.

"Well, it ain't that simple for me. I tried to get out, but I'm in too deep. If I don't keep bringing those leg breakers cash, I'll be swimming with the fishes. "

"Get 'em paid. Then put in for a transfer, leave Texas, and join Gamblers Anonymous. You—"

Stan butted in. "It's easy for you to say. You don't have a flipping clue about how much I'm in for. There's other stuff, but damned if I'll tell you anything else. I won't take the chance to be maimed or dead."

"Yeah, Stan, I get it. You gotta do what you gotta do, can't blame ya." Bebchuk didn't want to hear any more.

Stan stood, straightening his jacket, pulling at the ends of the sleeves, and adjusting his ugly multicolored tie. "You'd better think hard about any double-cross to take us down and save your ass. But we all gotta agree to let you out including Sykes and Bogard. They might, since it'll be more money for all of us. But just remember, I got all the information I need on your sexcapades, capiche?"

"Of course, I understand. I'd never rat you guys out. Hell, I was too involved and don't want my ass burned either. Give me time to set the paperwork in motion for an early retirement. I'll leave the state after that."

"I'll notify Bogard and have him stop the transfer and explain."

Cleef stuck out his hand. "It was good while it lasted, huh, Upchuck?"

"Yeah, Creep, all these years, been a wild ride. Sorry I have to get off the merry-go-round." A nervous crackle surged through Clive's voice.

"Later, dude, see ya in the funny papers."

Clive Bebchuk watched Stan disappear down the hallway. All the life drained from his face. Stan hadn't ranted or raved, nor did he argue the whys and wherefores of the situation. His bailing out when this involved men such as Theo Sykes, Jerry Bogard, and Boyce Carter was too easy, way too easy. He knew they wouldn't let him out. Now he'd put two more lives at stake, his wife and his son. Clive Bebchuk's only thought was to save his family—WITSEC—that's the deal he wanted in exchange for information.

"Sykes, it's Cleef. Bebchuk just bailed. Me? Are you crazy?" Stan stopped after rounding the hallway corner and stood at the stairwell exit. His head bobbed, and a heavy frown line dipped between his eyes, so deep it looked as if his face would split in two.

"You can tell him we gotta keep our hands clean. That's imperative." The words hissed between Theo's gritted teeth.

"Fine. God, he'll be pissed cuz he thinks he's the man. Jesus, Theo, he thinks he is pulling the strings."

Theo Sykes closed his eyes, rolling them in his skull. What a moron. Stan Cleef was an arrogant asshole.

"Let him think what he wants. We know the truth, Stan, don't worry. Make the call. I gotta go."

Theo hung up. The pot was boiling and when it blew, he hoped he was long gone.

"Mr. Carter, please."

"Of course. May I tell him who's calling?"

"Tell him it's Stan."

"Hold, please. Mr. Carter, I have a Stan on line two."

"Stan, what's going on?"

Carter listened, his eyes narrowed.

"You're joking, right?"

"No, and when have I ever effing joked with you, Carter? Now, back to what I was saying. You need to make the call. It's your call, Theo said..."

Boyce Carter ran his hand over his short, cropped hair. "Theo said, Theo said. I am fed up with hearing what Theo said. Stan, have you forgotten who is calling the shots?"

"Shot-callers have counsel, Carter. Just consider me and Theo your counsel, and take the advice. The man is a loose end. Theo, Bogard, and I cannot have any footprint on this, none, got it?"

"Huh, you want my footprints all over this just like the boys. I gave the order to kill them. For the love of God, Stan, my son was one of them boys."

"Carter, get a grip. It wasn't personal. Sorry it had to be your son, but Jamere was stealing our product from the cigarette shop, and until they identified his body, we didn't know who it was. And you weren't too torn up about it, were you?"

"Fine, I'll make the call."

Carter hung up with a thud. No, he hadn't cried over his dead son. He'd figured the boy would die young because he was a moron. Only an idiot would steal from the cartel, brag about it, and try to steal from them again. Jamere Carter was a fool, and he'd involved his best friend, Lyell Taylor, and that dumbass kid Robert Thompson, who thought Jamere hung the moon. All three dead boys were idiots.

The man in the office who'd been listening to only one part of the conversation spoke, thus taking Carter out of his trance.

"Who was that?" Jerrell Bogard uncrossed his leg, straightening in his chair, keeping eye contact with Carter.

"Cleef. They want Bebchuk dead. They've ordered a hit."

"Seems to me they ordered you to order the hit. Listen to me, Beck, it wasn't your call. It was theirs—they're in charge, not you. Can't you see that?"

"No, I am in charge, Bogard. It's you who can't see it. If it weren't for this place and me, there'd be no way to move merchandise of every kind, I might add. Since I got the owner to cooperate and have free rein here over these tour buses, that puts me in charge."

"You scare the shit out of the owner, and so do your boys. If you weren't extorting them, the owner would still have you working as a grease monkey on his buses."

I damn well controlled the gang activity in-between Sunnyside, the Third and Fifth Ward. The Dragons are my alma mater; I've had connections with them since I was eleven years old. So yeah, I'd say that puts me in control too. And who was it that talked Joven Cazalla into working with us after the robbery at the Irish fuck's store? Me, that's who, so, nope, you got it wrong, Bogard. I'm in charge."

"Well, I can tell you this. You're not in charge of Sykes. No one is, not even Stan. No matter what that skinny craggy-faced asswipe thinks."

Boyce Carter was irritated at having to defend his position with Bogard. He took a toothpick out of his pocket, rolling it between his forefinger and thumb, wishing it was a dagger. If it were, he'd plunge it between the man's beady close-set eyes.

"Theo Sykes is a hit man. He's skillful with computers and has ties with the cartel from his time in the Corpus DEA office. And Cleef's a mean prick who's in debt to bookies all over the world, struggling to stay ahead of them but can't stop his gambling. And you, what about you, Bogard? I'll tell you what it is. Cleef has blackmail he's holding over your head or you wouldn't be sitting in that chair. He pulled you in, not me, and that's your bad luck. My damn bad luck was calling in a hit and not knowing it would be on my dumbass son. I had to let go of that and look at it as just business cuz I couldn't bring him back to life. It was him and his friends who were trying to steal from us."

"Steal from Omar you mean? "

"No, Bogard, you fuck. We put a lot of man-hours into this business, and we work with the cartel, not for them. "

"I guess you'd see it that way." Jerrell Bogard stood. "Yep, you're running the show, Carter, no doubt about it."

"What did you come here for, Bogard? To pull my chain and piss me off?"

"I wanted to warn you to watch out for Bebchuk, but since Stan called, guess I don't have to now," he lied. What he wanted was one person on his side. Why he thought Carter would side with him, he hadn't a clue. Carter was an idiot, and this conversation proved it.

"Huh, thanks for having my back." Carter eyed him. What the fuck was Bogard up to? This was something he'd have to worry about later. He had other pressing issues to deal with.

Bogard left Carter to his whims and delusions of grandeur.

Agent Clive Bebchuk

Clive waited two days before telling his wife everything. He'd spent the better part of the night repeating it over and over. As an attorney, Carla had been relentless, asking the same questions repeatedly. He kept telling her the same story. Once she stopped being the smart female attorney and became the victim, she was left feeling hurt and betrayed, with good reason.

"Honey, I swear, however long it takes to make this up to you, I will spend the rest of my life trying to, Carla. I promise."

"I love you, Clive. I always have and right now even though I love you I hate your guts. Do you understand?"

"I can put in for early retirement or transfer. How about a

position in the Florida office, be closer to your family? Then you and our boy can set up a practice there after he passes the bar. Hang a shingle, Clara Bebchuk and Son, or Bebchuk Law Office?"

Clive Bebchuk was a humbled man, pleading for a second chance to set his life right. It would have impressed Detective West. The man Jack met was a prick. It was a shame Jack would never know this changed man. This was the person who'd laid dormant inside the body of DEA Agent Clive Bebchuk. It was a damn shame.

42

They'd spent the last two days trekking in the mountains getting pictures of everything—the tunnel entrance and inside the tunnel. And luckily, no human activity, which allowed them to photograph the exit. Sophia pointed out the footprints.

"Jack, it'd be a long shot, but take photos of any footprints. Here, take this."

After pulling out paper money, she handed him 50 pesos. "I don't have a US dollar on me. Use this for a footprint-size reference."

He took the bill, nodding and went back to taking pictures, moving the 50 pesos bill to each photo.

Finished with the photos, he turned to her. "We have to go, Sophia. It's important to photograph the area, coming and going, check our markers, and plant a few more."

Her eyes closed before she spoke. "Fine, then, let's get this done."

Tears stung her eyes when she saw the marker. With reverence, she walked to where Agent Miguel Espinar's body had been buried. She got down on her knees, bowed her head, and prayed a silent prayer over the lifeless agent. Jack snapped pictures leading up to the area from both directions, letting her have this quiet time.

Sophia stood, wiping the dirt off her hands onto the sides of her pants, and then straightened her shoulders before using her shirt to wipe her tears. She was not ashamed of crying; women cried, including female DEA agents. Weeping was just a part of living. Jack had lost the woman in his life at the grip of a murderous monster. He'd sobbed over her death, Sophia had zero doubts, and she figured he wasn't embarrassed about crying, because Jack West was a real man.

Day four, they took off, left the hacienda, and headed to the helipad. Sophia followed Jack's Jeep in her 4Runner. They knew no one was there since Espinar was dead, so they gathered what they needed—log books, flight plans, and paperwork they felt might be essential—and headed to where Umberto Vega was posted.

The outlying building where Vega stayed was quiet, too quiet. There were dump trucks, excavators, and bulldozers, but no men.

"What's this, Jack, do you know?"

"Yeah, Miguel told me a new facility was to be built. It looks like construction was started but stopped. Wonder why?"

Sophia shrugged. "I don't know because no one told me."

"One way to find out. Let's find Umberto and ask."

Umberto Vega had been dead for days. The scene reeked, making them what to vomit. Vega's head was missing, his body tied to a chair, his right hand devoid of fingernails. Although the body was past the putrefied state when the nails would have fallen off, it was clear they had been pulled off with pliers, which sat on the desk next to the body. His left hand was missing his fingers, and the skin was sloughing off. There were gaseous smells oozing from his decomposing body.

The door at the back was shut. Jack nodded toward the exit, took his gun out, and chambered a round. So did Sophia. At the door, he signaled, then he shoved the door open with a hard push, letting it hit the wall. She went right, he went left. The room was empty except for Umberto Vega's decomposing head propped up on a table, his eyeballs lying beside it in a puddle of gross eye fluids.

"Oh, holy shit, Jack." Sophia stepped back, her stomach lurched. "I've got to go outside. Give me a minute."

"Agreed. I'm right behind you." Jack prayed his face was not as green as his stomach felt.

Outside, bent over, Sophia gulped in deep breaths of clean air. Jack did too, trying to keep that urge to hurl from happening.

"We gotta go back in, Jack. We need photos, and all the information we can gather. Everything we think is credible evidence. Here." She pulled out two oversized bandanas and handed the navy blue one to him. "Wrap this around your face; it might help with the damn pungent smells."

Jack reached into his pocket and pulled out earplugs. "I carry this with me too. Shove a set up your nose; it helps. Learned this from my first homicide partner, been using them ever since."

"Yeah, we need all the help we can get so we don't have to breathe that shit in."

Noses stuffed, faces wrapped up making them look like bandits, they reentered, this time as their own CSU team.

Inside, Sophia reached into her backpack, pulling out a small plastic bottle of baby powder and a small palette of eye shadow.

"Medina, what are you doing?"

"See if you can find some Scotch Tape, will you, Jack? Check in the drawers and filing cabinets. Also, see if you can find anything like notepads, message pads, anything that would have a thicker binding or paper. I need something for my instant do-it-yourself fingerprinting."

"Got it."

Bent over the desk, Sophia dug out a mirror compact from a

narrow pocket of her backpack. A Swiss Army knife appeared from her front pants pocket. After sprinkling baby powder on the opened mirror compact, she began scraping a small portion of the darkest purple shadow, mixing it into the white powder. Again, she dug into the backpack pulling out a makeup brush to use as the duster. Amazed, Jack watched her go through these steps, all the while thinking she could be a contestant on *Let's Make A Deal*. What else did she have in that backpack? And who was this woman, a female MacGyver? A resourceful Sophia Medina was making her own fingerprint powder. An astonishing—beautiful—special woman. Sophia Medina was extraordinary. She pulled out two pairs of Latex gloves and handed him a pair. Jack smiled, stuck his hand in his pocket, and pulled out a pair of his own.

"Don't have eye shadow, baby powder, or a makeup brush, but otherwise I am prepared."

"See? A female partner is a plus, at least for times like this. Jack, let's get busy so we can get the hell out of this death stench."

Jack found the Scotch Tape. Sophia dusted and printed several areas, using both the dark and the white powder mixtures. She lifted prints with the tape, then stuck the tape onto the front and back covers of spiral notebooks that Jack found. Bloody prints were easy to see. Jack got a lot of photos.

Sophia worked steadily on automation, like she had at Espinar's grave. Jack listened to her breathing out of her mouth in huffs, trying not to inhale the odor of the decomposing body. Her training kicked in. Taking her knife from the sheath on her ankle, she stepped up to the headless body, and he saw her shudder before taking the loose part of the duct tape that held the body in the chair. Pulling a decent length, she cut off a piece.

"Jack, take the plastic cover off the front of the fax machine. Check in the restroom. Look for some paper towels to wipe it off with."

With a slight shrug, he did as she'd requested.

"Here, now what?"

Sophia took the length of duct tape she'd been holding and placed it sticky-side down on the clean plastic. "Here, hold this. Don't touch the tape. I'm hoping we can get prints off this tape by superglue fuming. It's iffy, but since we have no CSU team here, we'll do the best we can." She cut tape from around his ankles and repeated the process, then looked for an empty copy paper box. With extra care, she laid the fax cover with the duct tape in the box. Gloves still on, she opened her backpack and dug, pulling out two individual bags of pretzels, and Jack laughed.

"Really, Medina?"

She shrugged; opening the bags she dumped the pretzels in a waste can. With the paper towels Jack found in the bathroom, she wiped each bag out first with a wet towel and then dried them.

"Hey, gotta use what I have, and I don't have any evidence bags."

Sophia slipped the bloody knife into one pretzel bag and the pliers in the other, laying them in the box along with her homemade fingerprints. They would contact the Mexican Federales as soon as they got back to civilization.

Jack was impressed. If her DEA superiors didn't know how good she was in the field, they needed a reminder. Men like Bebchuk and Cleef couldn't hold a candle to this agent.

THEY LEFT the Jeep and the 4Runner in the airport parking lot. They stored all extra equipment in a special vault onsite for the DEA procurement and logistics staff to collect then filter back into the system for other agents to use when needed. It was a whopping 100 degrees, and the humidity made the air thick and sweltering.

A DEA plane would touch down in two hours. He paced, his boots treading along the small carpeted area where they waited. Kasper had said after this call, it needed to be in person.

Uh-huh, that was what he needed alright: an eyeball-to-eyeball meeting with Theo Sykes, SAC Jerrell Bogard, Clive Bebchuk, Stan Cleef, and Boyce Carter.

Sophia was going to contact Caden once they returned to the states. The idea of contacting Joven Cazalla, to elicit Villa Lobos' help, was still on the table. Jack was not comfortable about this; however, the words *for the greater good* kept ringing in his ears.

After boarding, they stowed carry-on luggage overhead and Sophia plopped down on a seat, leaned her head back, letting her eyelids droop. "Most comfortable thing I've sat on in the last four months."

"Being home will be nice. Can't wait to take a hot shower, sleep in a cozy bed with the air conditioner on high, and no mosquitoes."

"Me too. It'll feel like heaven. So, I was thinking. How about we —" her words cut off when a voice called out.

"Agent Medina, Detective West, I am glad to see you both."

Janet Spears walked up the aisle from the rear galley, a smile on her face and her hand extended to welcome them aboard.

"Janet, this is a surprise. No one mentioned you were coming to fly back with us."

"I knew you wouldn't be expecting me. How do you like our transportation, Jack?"

"A Gulfstream G100, very nice ride, sorta pricey for me though, on a detective's salary. The agency must pull in a sizable haul, cuz this baby is a million or two, I'd guess."

"Yeah, it's a pricey plane alright. Costs enough to keep it flying. The upside is we didn't buy it. Let's just say we got it through a cartel estate sale. When Kasper asked me to bring y'all home, I thought I'd come and fly back with you. Once we're off the ground, you will update me on what's been happening. We have fewer ears up here."

The pilot's voice sounded overhead. Preflight checks were complete, all systems were ready to go. They'd be up in twenty.

"Please fasten your seatbelts and stay seated until the green light is on. Then you may leave your seat and walk about the cabin."

Seatbelts fastened, the plush captain chairs swiveled to face each other. Jack and Sophia sat next to one another, Janet across from them, and before the pilot fired the engines up, they began filling Agent Janet Spears in on everything.

43

Keeping to himself, Clive Bebchuk arrived at work in silent contemplation. Every day he considered speaking with Director Kelli Slater. He thought about spilling his guts, being smart enough to come clean and strike a deal. It would mean going into WITSEC with his wife and son. It was Carla's life too. Before he made a rash decision, he had to discuss it with her. They'd had a long night, but he'd owned up to everything. WITSEC was his only choice. Looking over his shoulder for the rest of his life was better than being dead.

"Clive, yes, you need to make a deal. Do you think for one second Cleef, Sykes, or Bogard wouldn't try to negotiate to save their asses?"

"It means several changes for you. Danny, he's gonna hate me."

"Worry about Danny later, and no, he won't hate you, Clive. He has always been proud of you."

It had been one of the hardest decisions they'd made as husband and wife. Tomorrow morning, Clive Bebchuk, future ex-DEA agent, would meet with Director Slater, Sophia Medina, and ask Detective West to sit in too. A weight had been lifted. It was the best he'd felt in years.

CLIVE OPENED the Suburban's door, tossed in his briefcase and jacket, and slid in behind the wheel, feeling better about his situation, yet knowing it would be a long haul. Pulling the door shut he stuck his key in the ignition and turned it. Nothing. After another twist of the key, he picked up the muffled sound of a *tick-tick-click-click*. He knew the sound and fear grabbed his chest, squeezing it in a vise. It was over. There wasn't anything he could do to stop it from happening.

The bomb blew out the roof of the Suburban, blasting a hole through the metal garage door, flames igniting inside the large vehicle with Clive Bebchuk still at the wheel. His right hand sat beside him on the passenger seat, his left dangling by the skin hung up in the turn signal arm, and bits and pieces of his face spattered on the dash.

The explosion was so close, she froze where she stood, her mind working to comprehend what had transpired. As the initial shock passed and time moved again, Carla Bebchuk flew out the front door, screaming.

"*Clive*! Oh my God, *Clive, no, no,* this cannot be happening, God, no!" Her cell phone slipped from her grip and she ran to the Suburban and retreated knowing another explosion could happen because the fire might hit the gas tank. Doors on the street flew open. Residents ran outside to see what had happened. A few stood glued to their spots, standing in a trance with mouths agape, watching as a neighbor's body burned inside his vehicle.

Scrambling on her knees, divorce attorney Carla Bebchuk found her cell and dialed 911. After the first two rings, she heard the operator say, "Nine-one-one, what is your emergency?" In the distant background sirens wailed, headed in her direction.

The FBI and ATF sealed off the area around the Bebchuk home to everyone but the residents. Sophia Medina arrived on scene to mass chaos. Fire trucks, the bomb squad, an ambulance, and the Deputy Fire Marshall crowded the street, parked askew. People like ants in an ant farm, all going ten different directions, asking questions, taking measurements and getting pictures at every angle. ATF operatives collected every tiny piece of everything in, on, or near the scene for the investigation. Houston's Medical Examiner's office collected the body and body parts, while a shocked Carla Bebchuk stood in the background.

"Carla." A hand touched her shoulder, and she jumped, startled. Turning to see Agent Medina, she broke, and in seconds Medina had a sobbing Carla Bebchuk to console. Once calmed down Sophia asked her a few questions. The woman was in shock. Sophia wasn't sure what Carla knew, or how much Clive had told her, but right now wasn't a good time to flood her with questions.

"Thank you, Carla, that's all for today. I know they'll want you downtown, so why don't you go splash your face with water, get your purse, and I'll get a patrol car to drive you."

Carla Bebchuk just saw her husband of thirty years blown to bits in a burning Suburban. Even though she didn't want to drag her husband's name through the mud, Carla Bebchuk knew Clive's blackmailer was connected to this bombing. And unless she had to, she would say nothing about the twenty-year-old incident involving her now-dead husband and the sixteen-year-old girl. Until she was fully composed, she would keep the entire story to herself.

"Medina," a male voice called her name, then cleared his throat. "Ahem, can I have a word?"

Sophia's antennae went up. Bogard was a man of interest in her investigation. He was the last person she expected to see at this crime scene.

"Agent Bogard, of course," she called back.

"Over here, out of earshot if you will, Agent Medina."

Sophia stepped over to the Fire Marshall's car at the curb, away from the others.

"Yes, sir?"

"I'd like to meet with Director Slater, Agent Spears, and you. Also, if you will, ask Detective West to be present too."

"Meet about what, sir?"

"To give you information, valuable information, and I need to cut a deal. This needs to be soon." He glanced over at the carnage, his voice tight. "I don't wish to have an unfortunate accident."

Sophia glanced at the scene—an unfortunate accident, this was Clive Bebchuk's fate. The roar of a V-8 sounded. Turning she saw Jack pull up to the curb.

"Detective." She proffered her hand, and he reciprocated.

"I heard what happened on the police scanners."

"Jack." Jerrell Bogard acknowledged him by offering his hand.

"Agent Bogard." His voice curt, he ignored the man's outstretched hand then turned to Sophia. "So, what do we know?"

"Not much. The FBI has taken the case. The ATF will try to get involved or push the FBI out. Either way, we will not be included in the investigation."

Her phone buzzed. "Agent Medina. Yes, ma'am, I understand. Of course I will, no problem."

Sophia glanced over at the crime scene, nodding in concern as she listened for another two minutes before hanging up.

"I need to speak with the FBI's Special Agent in Charge to set up a debriefing with our office. Jack, a word, please. Agent Bogard, please excuse us for a moment."

"Of course, and please set up a meeting as soon as possible, will you?"

"I'll be in touch, Agent Bogard. Jack, walk with me."

Bogard took his hand out of his pocket, zipped up his DEA jacket, and crossed his arms, staring at his feet. He looked down at the sidewalk with cracks running through it and weeds popping up between the gaps. Bogard glanced sideways, looking at Medina and

Jack in his peripheral vision, aware he was the subject of their conversation. Before he could avert his gaze, Jack glanced over at him. The older DEA agent caught the detective's expression of contempt as his brow furrowed. *Get used to that expression,* Bogard told himself. *Everyone will stare at you with a look of disgust. At least until you're in a place where no one has ever heard of you or seen your face.*

44

He pressed the microphone into place. Attaching the wire and maneuvering the body of the recorder, he hid it. It was a futile setup, but he'd overheard Theo asking some unidentified person to meet him in the garage of the Rubicon Building. He wanted to tape the conversation. It could be nothing, but somehow his gut said it was more than nothing. He'd parked his car between a truck and a minivan. It was less noticeable. After lowering the car windows for breathability, he hopped in the back seat and lay down to wait.

Dress shoes clicking against the concrete floor caught Kasper's attention, followed by the clomping of heavy boots.

"Best place to talk. No one's out here. Slide over to this side. Get out of the security camera's view. It'll look like you just walked into the building." Cleef stood at the front corner of his car, and Sykes slid over, bypassing the camera, and leaned on the front passenger's door.

"Did you tell Beck to hire a man to plant a bomb, you dillweed?" Theo's jaws clenched and unclenched and a guttural sound rumbled in his throat.

"I said to get rid of him. What difference does it make on how, as long as it can't be traced back to us?"

"Makes a big difference, because now we have to worry about the FBI, you dolt."

"Christ, get off my back. I'm thinking blowing you to smithereens is sounding like a great idea. Whatdaya say to that?" Stan flicked his fingers in Theo's face.

Theo reacted and grabbed Stan's hand, bending it backward from the wrist, far enough to induce pain but not break a bone. "Cleef, don't threaten me. It's dangerous to your health, got it?" Theo let go of Cleef's wrist.

He bobbed his head, rubbing his wrist. "Yeah, Theo, I got it. You touch me again and I'll have the living hell beat outta you, and I swear you won't see it coming. You'll get a beating worse than McCready got. Understand me?"

"Sure, Stan, of course. We're both stressed, that's it."

"I agree. We should be glad HPD isn't involved with the investigation; this gets West off our back. The FBI has the case. They'll look at the cartel first. Maybe they'll see it as the cartel sending a warning to the DEA."

"They might. The investigation just started, so this is up in the air," Theo said.

"Umberto Vega is another loose end with blood on his hands. Shit, Theo, Umberto knows who we are, what we do, and how we do it, so he's a liability to us. Espinar was getting too close, and Umberto took it upon himself to see what he knew. No one ordered him to torture Espinar or kill him; at least I didn't make that call."

"Let the Mexican officials handle it if they ever find the body. It ain't our worry since it happened there. Besides, Espinar wasn't an American agent. As far as Vega is concerned, he's no longer an issue."

Stan gave Theo a hard look. "Vega's out of the picture?"

"Yeah, I called in a favor. Now, let's discuss Bogard. He might be a problem since you blew Bebchuk to smithereens."

The skinny man stroked his scrawny chin. "Things are too intense, and Bogard's a whiney pussy, I don't think he's gonna cut it. But I can't discuss this today."

He glanced at his wristwatch. "Remy, Deputy Director of Field Operations Walsh, expects me for a meeting in fifteen minutes. The Inspector General, Gavin Kemper, wants us to dig into the cases Bebchuk and I've worked. We've been told to brief the FBI. He thinks something could pop regarding Bebchuk's murder, so I gotta play along. We'll talk later, Sykes."

Stan Cleef walked away acting like the boss of bosses, and without a bye-your-leave, he darted into the stairwell. As the door shut, Theo Sykes flipped him off. "I 'm looking forward to blowing your fucking skeleton head off your boney-ass shoulders, you freak." His words bounced off the concrete walls and faded.

Theo Sykes' motorcycle boots trudged to his car; he got in, slamming the door. Stan was one of the dumbest men he knew. How he'd become a DEA agent was beyond his intellectual comprehension. The second dumbest man he knew had to be Boyce Carter. Ex-gang member without a high school education. Add in Bogard and Bebchuk and you had four clowns. One clown down—three more to go.

Theo's car engine faded and Kasper waited three more minutes before retrieving the tape recorder. Parked in the HPD garage he stayed in his car, inserted earphones, and listened. Their conversation was not long, however, it was informative. Kasper rolled his fingers on the steering wheel several times in thought. Okay, no one- or two-party consent to record this conversation, and no legal warrant. He needed a loophole. The parking garage was a common place for several entities. Offices leased to lawyers who specialized in oil and gas, multiple oil field companies, as well as domestic law, and the Justice Federal Credit Union. Out here no conversation was private. Thus it was not against the law to record a conversation. It was his one and only loophole. Now was the time to call Jack.

Bebchuk's Murder Scene

"Bogard wants to meet, says he has info and wants to make a deal."

Another ringing phone suspended their conversation and Jack pulled out his cell.

"Kasper, I'm gonna have to call you—"

"Jack, no, we need to meet." Kasper peered over his shoulder when a car door banged shut. Paranoia had him on edge.

"Can it wait until later? We have a situation here and I'm not free."

"It's important, I—" Kasper almost jumped out of his skin when someone rapped on the driver's side window. "Hold on." Kasper hit record, slipping his cell phone in his front shirt pocket without hanging up. He knew Jack could hear everything, and everything said was being taped.

"Hey, Agent Sykes, you scared the living shit outta me."

"Did I disturb an important call? Were you talking to a girlfriend or what?" Sykes leaned against the car door, parking himself to block Kasper from exiting.

"Nah, a friend of mine who lives up in Corpus called. He's been trying to talk me into surfing, or at least trying it, but I'm not much of a water person unless it has a solid bottom and chlorine with a diving board. That's my kinda water."

"Surfing, huh? Sharks, I'd be worried about sharks."

"Yeah, don't like sharks, or any kind of predator."

"As a computer geek colleague, how skilled are you at unlocking back doors?"

Theo Sykes was one predator Kasper abhorred. If he didn't suspect someone was spying on him, he would not be asking these questions. Kasper was sure of it.

"Why, did you lock yourself out?"

The man said nothing. His eyes locked on Kasper's and the kid was not intimidated.

"What the fuck do you want, Sykes?"

"You need to listen to me, kid. I'm gonna warn ya—be careful whose back door you sneak into. It might bring you a lot of pain and misery, got it?"

"Sykes, are you threatening me, cuz if you are I don't appreciate it. Now move so I can open my door."

Kasper rolled the window up, grabbing the door handle and pushing the door outward to get Old Motorcycle Boots to move. Theo stepped back, allowing him to exit the car.

"I'd be careful of what and where you're looking. It could get you in trouble with a few fucking mean-ass people." Theo blocked him from stepping to the rear of his car.

Jack, listening in on the open line and hearing everything, gave Kasper a surge of confidence.

"Step back, motherfucker, and don't threaten me. If you have something to say, spit it out. If not, then get the hell out of my way. I've got work to do."

Agent Theo Sykes stepped back and over, sweeping his arm for Kasper to pass, and the kid walked by, knocking his shoulder into Theo's on purpose. It was a bold move.

"Watch your back, kid, cuz I heard through the grapevine you've got people watching what you do." Sykes held up his hands, palms upward. "Not me, I ain't been watching ya."

Kasper turned and faced him, a guy twice his size and more than twice his age, a man who could kick his rear-end all over the concrete garage floor and not blink an eye or break a sweat.

"Yeah, Theo, is that so? Well, you bastard, I'd be watching over my shoulder too. Seems you've got several associates in low places. And some of your buddies are singing." Kasper put his palm to his ear. "Hear that? The vocals are getting louder. Sounds like a Johnny Cash song. You're familiar with the song about Folsom Prison, aren't you?"

Kasper turned around to leave and saw Art Walsworth walking toward them. He glanced back at Theo, and his face broke into a grin.

"Hey, fellas, why are y'all goofing off out here?"

Art looked at his watch. "Meeting in twenty for the new tracking devices we're setting up for Robbery. Come on, I'll buy you both a cup of Joe." Art held open the stairwell door.

Kasper swept his hand. "Age before beauty, so after you, Agent Sykes."

Following him, with a voice low enough for just Sykes to hear, the kid sang, "I hear the train a' coming, it's rollin' 'round the bend..." Taking his cell phone out of his shirt pocket, he kept singing, "It's time to say good-bye." He hung up the call to Jack without another word.

When the click sounded signaling Kasper had disconnected the call, Jack laughed, then filled Sophia in on the conversation. Score one for Bergman. Smart kid.

"It's all coming to a boil, Jack. I've got a feeling—"

"Me too, Sophia, and it ain't good, but we'll have to discuss later. Here comes your FBI buddy."

Theo Sykes, agitated at not getting in the last word, had pegged it; Kasper the little twit got into his email. He'd cleared his emails, but the kid was proficient at digging deeper to find what most others could not. People trained in cyber shit had the savvy and smarts to dance in a software system with their eyes closed. Kasper Bergman was exceptional at what he did.

Theo admonished himself for his stupidity. He hadn't figured he'd needed to worry about this. Too late now; he needed to work damage control.

45

Only a few patrons were in attendance at the pub. It was quiet for the dinner hour on a weeknight. Jack sat a back table nursing a tall boy, wishing he could shut his thoughts off. His unsolved homicide was now at the two-year mark and so was Gretchen's murder.

Gretchen had been a woman who made his heart race with the tiniest of innuendos. She was forward in a soft, sexy way. His memories of her no longer caused him as much heartache, and he would never forget this extraordinary woman.

Sophia aroused feelings he'd thought were forever buried after his beloved Gretchen had died. Sophia, like Gretchen, forward and brazen, but for different reasons, because she was playing a part, right? That was right, wasn't it?

Gretchen kissed him into the throes of passionate, hot, sweaty sex many times. A smile slipped across his face recalling how seductive that woman was and his insides stirred.

Sophia kissed him because of the job, not because she had feelings for him. Uh-uh, nope, there was more to it than blowing their cover after that first liplock.

The kisses...shit, she'd kissed him and then responded to his with no pretending, he felt it, and he reacted a few times with the enthusiasm of a lover. Her lips had caressed his with passion. Like a woman, hot for a man. Yikes...he was that man.

Again, his thoughts turned to their shared moments. Pretend or not, feelings he'd thought had died had switched on. He looked intently at the tabletop, in deep thought, and the chair scraping against the wood plank floor woke him from his trance.

"Hiya, Jack, Bergman on his way? Did you order food?" She sat, hooking her purse on the chair, leaning back and letting out a huge tired sigh, then grinned, a tired grin.

"He texted he's on the way, and no, no food. I've just had a beer. You okay, Medina?"

"Yeah, it's just this bombing and Bebchuk. Shit, Jack, I detested the guy, but would've never wanted him blown to bits. Carla, his wife, she's a mess. I had her come downtown to give me a statement, and she fell apart and told me the entire story about his—"

Bergman pulled out a chair joining them. "Sorry, didn't mean to interrupt."

She shrugged with a face pull that resembled the "no worries" expression.

Jack nodded to Kasper with a "Hey, pard."

He waved over to Grady, who brought back three beers—Bud, Miller, and one Corona with lime for Sophia, then took their food order.

"Food will be out in ten. If ya need anything else just holler." The old guy darted off. Grady knew crucial stuff was happening because he'd gotten wind of the news regarding the bombing. News like this could never be contained.

"Okay, back to what you were telling us, Medina. He came clean to his wife. Was it about the drugs?"

Sophia filled them in.

"So he was being blackmailed by Cleef, was he?"

"I'm betting Bogard is too."

Kasper scowled. "This is all horseshit. DEA agents blackmailing each other, and now one of 'em wants to seal a deal so he won't go to jail."

"By the way, man, you handled yourself like an FBI pro, and it was smart of you to leave your phone on so I could listen. So, tell us about this conversation you and Sykes were having. Sounded like he was threatening you."

Sophia looked at Kasper, then Jack, and back to Kasper. "Sykes? What's up with this? What threat? Was there a confrontation between you two?"

"Yeah, there was."

Kasper pulled out his digital recorder and set it on the table just as Grady came with the food.

"Enjoy your dinner and call me if ya need anything." Grady left quickly. The pub owner never wore out his welcome.

"This is the first recording."

"First recording. What do you mean? There's more?" Jack picked up his mug and took a swig.

"Yeah, this is what I was calling you about before nimrod interrupted my call."

"Nimrod? Who's that, Kasper?" Sophia squeezed her lime into her bottle of Corona and took a long pull.

"Theo Sykes. Got an interesting conversation recorded on my cell. Jack heard the entire conversation too."

Kasper hit play, so they could listen.

While he ate his Reuben, he watched their faces. He saw their mouths drop open and the look of sheer disbelief as they listened to the conversation he'd caught between Cleef and Sykes.

The tape stopped and Kasper reached over shutting it off, then set his phone on top of the recorder, hit play, and popped the last bite of sandwich into his mouth.

"Kasper, this is great. And now—" Sophia stopped to pick up a few fries, shoving them in and chewing.

"Uh-uh, Medina, it ain't." Jack drained the last of his tall boy.

"It ain't what, Jack?" The last of the fries gone, Kasper wadded his napkin and dropped it onto the empty plate.

"Admissible in court. It's good info, maybe for some leverage, but..."

"Jack, come on, man." Kasper looked at him, then her. You didn't think I thought about it? They talked in a public parking garage, so it damn well is admissible. People come and go from the building. Not just DEA personnel either. I thought about it and this is our loophole. It's a bit on the underhanded side. But it will still fly in court." With a shrug, the kid drained his beer and held up the empty mug, making a circle with his index finger, signifying another round for all.

Plates, empty mugs and bottles cleared, fresh drinks in hand, they resumed the conversation.

"Jack, Kasper is right. This recording can be admissible; it's a gold mine. He had a similar conversation with Sykes. Do you think Art might have overheard them in the parking garage?"

Kasper propped a forearm up, leaned in, and looked at her. "If he heard, he didn't mention it or call me, so I'm guessing he's in the dark. Besides, Sykes confessed nothing. He just issued a weak threat."

"I have to say, Bergman, I like the way you handled the situation. You going surfing in Corpus with a pal? Superb lie and believable. Not to mention you stepping into Sykes without a second thought showed your FBI colors. I hafta say I enjoyed how you did it with humor."

"Yeah," Jack joined her, "you might have an unusual second career, Bergman."

"Oh yeah, what second career, Jack?"

"That voice, wow, kid. You ought to go into the studio; you sounded like Cash in his prime."

He couldn't carry a tune in his pocket much less sing one. Jack was a goober, but he didn't say it aloud. He just grinned.

"On second thought, nah, step away from the singing, it don't suit ya. Besides, I have never heard of a singing FBI agent."

"Perhaps not singing, Jack..." Sophia's closed mouth muffled out a laugh. "But it's been alleged we had an FBI cross-dresser in the department back in the day."

They busted up, and it felt nice to laugh, relieving work tension. It was short-lived as the three of them jumped straight back to business. They needed a plan and to set the meeting up with Jerrell Bogard. They all had to hear his story. The man wouldn't be the SAC after this ordeal. Oh, he'd be a SAC alright, a sack of shit.

"Jack, I'll text you once I have a time to meet with Bogard. Kasper, you want to join?"

"He might not want me there, but hell yeah, I'd like to come."

"Bergman, you show up. He doesn't like it, then too bad."

Jack would not cut the kid out. Kasper was part of the team.

46

Sweat accumulated, and he wiped his brow for the second time with his handkerchief. He felt his pocket for the cassette. Yes, it was still there. He had other copies in case he needed them, if things went sideways. Even if they helped him he'd still keep his copies for added safety. There was also the letter, but that would wait—it was his final card.

The door opened. Agent Medina stepped in and Jack followed. One more person walked in. Kasper Bergman was with them. Why?

"Where's Director Slater?"

"Director Slater will be apprised later."

She looked around his office and saw two medium-sized boxes on the floor. Bogard had already begun clearing out, ready to vacate and move on.

"You called this meeting, sir." Agent Medina's tone was clipped with frostiness, her posture rigid. Angry eyes stared, waiting for him to begin.

"Please take a seat, if you will. Ahem." He produced a phlegmy, guttural, throat-clearing sound. Bogard drew in a deep breath then let it out. His shoulders sagged, his once pompous arrogant ego crumbling because of his own idiocy. The high-powered men whom he had protected would never reciprocate the favor. This left him to hang alone for his sins, or if given the chance to bury his sins, he could start a new life. He prayed he got the chance for a new life. The old guy's body hunched forward, and he set his clasped hands on the desk, looking at them. His stare moved from one face to the other and he launched into his story.

"There was a sensitive situation fifteen years ago involving well-known people. This involved a get-rich scheme. We could have swept it under the rug, but when issues of bank extortion and money laundering came into the pubic light, we couldn't ignore it. People were expecting a small slap on the wrist. But other elements involving government agencies factored in. I can't say who or what. It didn't involve me then, and it doesn't involve me now."

"You're talking about the Radcliff, Olsen, Montgomery, and Addams case, aren't you?"

Jack looked over at Bergman. "You know this case, Kasper?"

"Yeah, I read about it, can't recall where, but it was a big case... ROMA, uh, the initials of the four lawyers' last names, right?"

Bogard nodded and went on with his story.

"Radcliff and Montgomery, the older senior partners, arranged their last names to spell out ROMA, as in The ROMA Law Firm. Jesus, all four of these guys were narcissists and—"

Sophia halted him mid-sentence. "This is all interesting, but is it related to your current situation?"

"Let me continue. Our agency was called in to investigate possible drug money being laundered through ROMA's clients, so we had our finger on the pulse of the situation until the FBI took over. Once the FBI began investigations, they found bank fraud and shell corporations to legitimize other funds, but nothing concerning drugs."

"Just how does this involve you, Agent Bogard?'

"I'd been working the investigation for months, and that's when I got friendly with Olsen and Addams. Those two had rich, sleazy clients. I discovered a little too late these two jerk-offs were just as slimy. Don't judge me, though. I thought they were good guys. They were generous, showing people—including me—a good time, but it was only so they could use them for their own, uh, whims. They were using me too, but I didn't think it was doing any real harm and I was getting plenty of money, so I ignored a few things. Months into the FBI investigation, a bit of damning evidence surfaced about Olsen, and of course, Addams came to his rescue with my help."

"What do you mean, Bogard? What did you do?" Sophia's eyes narrowed.

"Addams paid a very hefty amount of cash for me to alter evidence. It happened years ago. I don't know how it happened, but someone found out. They have copies of original documents, and the ones I altered. They've been blackmailing me for years. I know this is a lot, but if I give you information, I gotta go into WITSEC."

Bogard gave details on why looking into the ROMA situation was useless. Even if they reopened the incident, what would it change? Scott Radcliff and Alan Montgomery were dead. Radcliff had lung cancer and died ten years ago; Montgomery bought it from a massive stroke seven years ago; Ben Olsen died in a car crash three years after the indictment was dropped; and Russ Addams had a snow-skiing accident six years ago. He lay comatose in Red Garden long-term hospital near his family up in Ohio. None of this mattered to Sophia.

"Who's blackmailing you?" She narrowed her eyes, studying his face, seeing him in another light. Bogard was nothing but a worn-down, sad old man. Poor career choices and getting in bed with the wrong people had created his stressed-out grayish pallor, making him seem ten years older than he was.

"Stan Cleef. He was blackmailing Clive too. I suppose it doesn't matter since Clive is dead. I'm next on the list of loose ends to tie up, and if I turn witness for the state, I need to be protected."

Bogard slouched down. His hands shook. He looked from her to Jack, and then Kasper. His eyes landed back on her face.

"What information could you possibly have that would make me want to help you?"

"A taped conversation I had with Cleef and Sykes. They didn't know I was recording, and I know how that works, but regardless it gives you information to dig into. And if anything happens to me, contact my attorney, Richard Durrant. He has the extra copies under lock and key."

"You are aware I can't cut you a deal. It's not my call. Director Slater will get this information. Afterward, she and the OAG will handle this. Give Agent Spears a call."

She glanced at Kasper and then back at Jerrell Bogard.

"Kasper has a tape recording too. You need to listen, and once it's done, you need to tell me everything you know, because you're holding back, we both know you are,"—she paused for a split second, and then uttered, "sir," begrudgingly.

The worn-down DEA agent angled his head toward Kasper. "Let's hear what you have."

Kasper took the digitized recorder from his pocket, laid it on the corner of Bogard's desk, and hit play.

As the tape played, the older agent's eyes widened. These bastards were coming after him next. Bogard felt sweat run off his balding head, then down the back of his shirt as panic gripped his insides.

Kasper hit stop, and the room was silent.

"You need to put me in a safe house, Medina, or I'm gonna be dead. Cleef and Sykes will not stop until all loose ends are tied up. Plus, I've got the cartel to worry about. I don't think you understand what Sykes is capable of. He, well...you have to put me in a secured safe house, and soon." He stared at her. Her lips were in a straight line, no curve, no muscle movement, no twitch, nothing. She made no comment.

"Medina, I need to know what you're gonna do to keep me safe so I can help you." His voice faltered with a panicky pitch change.

She stood, smoothed out her slacks, and checked her badge,

making sure it hung straight on her belt. Adjusting her shoulder holster underneath her jacket, she pulled at the ends of both jacket sleeves before looking up. Agent Sophia Medina turned her attention to the other men, speaking to them first.

"Jack, Kasper, we need to go."

Bogard stepped out from behind the desk. Walking toward her, she turned to address him. Sophia was nose-to-nose with the old, sad man. Contempt oozed out of her pores, and a cold blanket of disrespect shrouded the room. She spoke her voice low yet forceful.

"I'll put a security detail on you until they decide what to do about you." She glared as she inhaled and her shoulders squared up at him. "You'd better listen, and don't forget what I am about to tell you. Understand?"

"Yeah, sure, Medina, what is it?"

"It's *Special Agent Medina* to you. Never call me Medina again. We are not buddies or friends. I don't even like you. You're a world apart from me and what I stand for. I guarantee you one thing and you can take this to the bank, you slimeball. I'll never call you SAC Bogard or sir again because you are a discredit to the badge you carry. Detective West, Mr. Bergman, it is high time we take our leave. "

With confidence, she turned on her heels, Jack and Kasper close behind. Respectable Agent Sophia Medina strode out of the office of a man who had disgraced the DEA. Jerrell Bogard would bring scandal crashing down on his head and the agency's.

In the parking lot, Jack put his hand on her arm.

"You were great back there, Sophia. Strong, professional, straightforward, you didn't rattle at all."

"Yeah, well, we'll see how this plays out. Ain't gonna be good for the agency, Jack. They'll have a hell of a lot to clean up. Reinvestigating all the cases Bogard, Cleef, and Bebchuk worked —shit."

"It will pass in time. Keep your chin up and keep doing what you're doing."

She nodded, looked up at him, and laid her hand on his.

A smile slipped from him to her, one of those kinds of smiles, and it did not get past Kasper. He not only saw it, he felt a spark between them.

"Hey, guys, so what's the next step here?"

They turned to glance at Kasper. Both had forgotten he was standing there and her heart raced, glad she hadn't made the move she had thought about making—to stretch up and give Jack a soft peck on the lips. She was no fool; she knew any soft innocent peck between them could ignite into an *I want you* kiss.

This was her show. Jack waited for her to speak.

"First, I'll catch Director Slater up and ask for a security detail for Bogard."

"What about Ward? You plan on bringing him in on this?"

"I'd prefer he stayed undercover, at least for now."

"So you changed your mind about using Cazalla and Omar?"

Sophia tightened her lips in thought. "No, not completely, I don't think. And it might not be my call."

She saw him frown, and she held up a hand. "I know how you feel. But we do what we have to do. It's all for the greater good, Jack."

"And Umberto, you damn well know his murder had cartel written all over it, and I'm betting Villa Lobos called in the hit."

"Yes, it appears so, and since it happened in Mexico with a Mexican National, then the Federales handle it, not us."

"You feel about Espinar the same way? It happened there, so we don't care?"

Leave it to the Federales? Umberto Vega was a piece of shit. But he didn't deserve the torture they put him through, or to be dead."

Kasper watched them bantering back and forth. The intensity of the situation rose.

"Detective West," her tone harsh, "you know damn well how I feel. I feel just like you do, and you're right, Vega didn't deserve what happened to him, but what do you think I can do about it, any of it, even Espinar's death?"

"Talk to the State Department, talk to the Federales, the Special Mexican police. Hell, I don't know." Jack's voice rose, as did his frustration.

Irritation covered her face as they stared at each other, Kasper a quiet spectator still watching.

"We're not gonna argue about this, Jack, because we can't change anything. Let the Federales work in their backyard. Don't you think we have enough in our own backyard to deal with?"

"Cazalla and Omar, whose problem are they? The DEA's or Mexico's? Or do we leave them to the Columbians, Venezuelans, to the officials of Ecuador, or just South America?"

"You are not being fair, Jack."

"Sophia, you for one should know nothing in our world is ever fair."

She nodded. Jack was right. Not a damn thing was fair concerning good versus evil. *Evil* seemed to win the race leaving *good* in the dust—-for decades.

UNDER THE CIRCUMSTANCES, SAC Bogard packed up and vacated his office, tendering his notice to leave the DEA—it was an immediate move. When word came down about his resignation, Sophia scoffed. What a joke. Jerrell Bogard would soon be stripped of his privileges, his pension, everything, and no resignation letter from him would matter.

Bogard made countless calls demanding to be set up in a safe house, and his demand was a burr under her saddle. Sophia ordered an around-the-clock security detail while WITSEC was arranged. This would take time. Until then, he was to lock himself in his house and not leave. Anything he needed would be brought to him.

The man's kids were grown and gone—two boys, both living

abroad. He was divorced and his ex-wife had been dead for twelve years; the man had never remarried. His job had been his life.

Bogard's new existence was being sequestered in his home, alone, peeking out the windows, fearful of his life. For a fellow once held in high esteem, not one soul in the department felt sorry for him.

"Sophia, we need to make a move."

"I agree, Jack, but what do you propose we do? Not a lot we can do with the FBI breathing down our necks."

He pondered for a moment as he arched his shoulders, not jumping in with a quick answer.

"Jack?"

"Yeah, I'm thinking, give me a second. Let's look at..." He stopped when a stressed-out Kasper Bergman walked in.

Jack felt his panic. It was palpable.

"Bergman, what's up, kid? You look like a demon is chasing you."

"Here." Kasper handed him a plastic sealed evidence bag with a flat piece of paper.

"What's this?"

Kasper dropped in the chair next to Sophia as he watched Jack read.

While he read, the corners of his mouth tugged downward.

Better watch your back, kid, shut up and stop digging, or we will dig a hole for you. We want the original and any copies of your recordings and Bogard's—all of them. If we don't get them soon, there won't be enough of you left to identify. Erase all documents, files, conversations, and emails—dump them so no one can ever find them. We know you can do this—cooperate or else. Mail the tapes to us in a plain brown packing envelope, to this PO box, and don't get smart trying to trace the PO box—we know what we're doing.

Jack scooted his chair closer to the conference table, reaching out to hand Sophia the note to read.

"You think this is from Sykes?"

"Yeah, it'd be my first guess. The man is batshit crazy." Kasper's eyes rolled up into his head.

"It could be Cleef. We don't know all the players who are working both sides." Sophia handed the sealed note back to Kasper.

"Hey, Sophia, you've got security on Bogard. Who has authority to see him, talk with him? Does Sykes?"

Jack saw where the kid was going and he followed his lead. "Bebchuk was a liability, and he's dead. Bogard resigned, but he's still a loose end."

Kasper's frown intensified. "Yeah, and as soon as the news about his rather sudden resignation hit the grapevine, tongues were wagging at HPD. I'm sure the tongues are wagging furiously over at the OAG and the DEA."

Sophia picked up the phone on the conference table, punched in a number, and pushed the button for speakerphone so the guys could hear too. A man's voice sounded out.

"Larson, this is Medina. Has anyone seen Bogard today or talked with him?"

"No, ma'am."

"And when did you see him last?"

"Last night. Pizza was delivered to his house. Why, what's up?"

"Did you document his visitors? Time in and out?"

Agent Brad Larson looked at his partner and shrugged. "Yeah, Medina, we did, it's protocol, so what's up?"

"Larson, stop being a pain in my ass. Tell me who you fucking documented." There was no doubt about the stress in her snappy retort.

"Wednesday and Thursday he had—"

She was aggravated and snappish. "No, Larson, just last night. Other than the pizza man, anybody else show up?"

"Agent Sykes did, around 9:00. He stayed for close to an hour and then left. I gotta ask ya, why are me and Whitson on babysitting detail for this old fart anyway? We don't know shit. You wanna fill us in, Medina?" Brad Larson got snippy.

"Shut up, Larson, and just listen. Go check on Bogard. If he doesn't come to the door, breach his house, got it? We're on the way."

Brad Larson's smile faded. His body stiffened and her authoritative tone made him sit upright and bristle.

"Agent Medina, what the fuck is—"

She hung up not giving Larson time to complete his question. Doom filled the pit of her stomach. Her face etched with worry.

"Jack, we're gonna take your car and you need to use the siren."

47

"I can't believe this, I can't," Brad Larsen repeated himself. "I thought it was a fluff assignment."

"Brad, you couldn't have known. Why don't you and Whitson head out? I'll handle it from here. Let me have your files. And listen, Brad, until it's announced, whenever that is, this is not to be common knowledge. Got me?" Her voice was again authoritative.

"Yes, ma'am, we've got it. Come on, Whitson, let's head back to HQ."

Sophia watched the two men leave. Brad Larson was shaken to the core. No one had ever died on his watch. And to make it worse, neither Larson nor Whitson knew the reasons for the security detail on Bogard.

"It's my fault. I should have put him in a safe house and better informed his detail."

"Jesus, Sophia, you couldn't have known this would happen. Sykes is bold and dangerous. Better keep our voices down." From his peripheral vision he saw the Medical Examiner, Bennie Guay, Vince Stoner, and Suzy Wong from CSI all walk into Jerrell Bogard's house, booties and gloves on.

"Yeah, well, Bogard let the man in. You figure Sykes had a gun on him?" Kasper watched as two dark sedans pulled up to the scene.

"It's what I'd think. Bogard had no choice. He was forced to let him in." Sophia frowned.

"Fuck, now Sykes is in the wind. Isn't that just terrific?" Kasper shoved his hands in his pockets.

"He might be hard to find. I think we need to talk with—"

"Jack," Sophia cut him off, "not now. We can talk later." Sophia watched the man walking up, dark suit, sunglass, the effing FBI.

Without taking off his shades, she could tell he was staring straight at her and it unnerved her, but she didn't let it show.

"Are you Agent Sophia Medina?"

She stuck out her hand. "Yes, I'm Agent Medina."

He did not take her hand. "And you two are?" He waited.

"Detective Jack West, Houston Homicide, and this is Kasper Bergman, HPD Technical Unit."

Jack did not offer his hand to the SOB who acted like his shit didn't stink.

"Right." One simple word, a rude "go fuck yourself."

"Medina, we're taking over this investigation. Like Bebchuk, Bogard is—was—a federal employee, so it's our jurisdiction."

"Of course, you're taking over—again." Her tone clipped.

The man stood straight as an arrow, his arrogance oozing, his nose tilted up in a show of superiority, ignoring her tone. "After the scene's locked down and processed, my office will contact you about a briefing. Get the reports, evidence, anything connected with this alleged murder. Have it boxed and sent over to the federal building, understood?"

"Yes, I, we, understand, Agent...uh..." She didn't know his name, he hadn't introduced himself.

"Crawford." Not another word came out of the dark suit, sunglasses-wearing prick. He walked away, dismissing them with a wave of his hand.

The three of them stood, mouths agape. What an arrogant

bastard. He'd pushed them aside with a condescending demeanor, as if he were the director of the FBI. What a jerk.

"And you're telling me you want to work with pricks like this, Bergman? Men who brush you off like the lint on your slacks? The, 'oh, I am a great powerful G-man?' Are you looking to be that guy?"

Sophia sputtered a short laugh. "I don't like being pushed aside either. Didn't you feel the same way? You know, when the OAG and DEA ordered you to stand down, Jack?"

He looked at her, then back at the suit-wearing asshole spewing out commands to the Medical Examiner, Bennie Guay, CSI's Suzy Wong, and Vince Stoner, stopping them from going any further with processing the scene. Jack watched the butthead with Bennie Guay, wishing he were a fly hovering about to hear how that was going.

"Hey, you guys didn't jump me at the scene and rip it from us like ripping a Band-Aid off a fresh wound, that's all I'm saying."

She bit her lip to keep from breaking into a full-fledged smile.

"I hope you and I are still friends once you become a G-man, Bergman, unless you turn into a sunglasses-wearing prick." Jack turned to stare at the kid.

A shrug lifted Kasper's shoulders. "Well, Jack, I don't intend to become a prick, unless it's in the handbook—then what choice do I have? I gotta follow the regulations." He wiggled his brows with an under-his-breath kind of snicker.

Jack stared him down and flipped him off, laughing as he did.

"Alright, fellas, guess we aren't needed here. But I've got another idea to keep us in this investigation, cuz I'll be dammed if the FBI is going to shut us out."

Jack liked the sound of that, so the three of them walked back to his car and headed to the one place they knew they could talk—Quinn's Pub.

"Yes, may I help you?" The young doe-eyed receptionist smiled, and he smiled back.

"Mr. Durrant is expecting me." He glanced at his watch. "I'm early. Can he see me now?"

"I'll ask him. And you are?"

"Jack West."

In less than four minutes, Richard Durrant walked into the room.

"Detective West," he said and proffered his hand, "it is nice to meet you. Let's talk in my office."

Richard Durrant shut the door, and Jack took a seat.

"Thank you for seeing me on such short notice, Mr. Durrant."

"Detective West, I was shocked when the OAG's office called to tell me Jerry's dead. What happened?"

"All information is being withheld. I'm sorry, I don't have clearance to tell you more. As it is, this is not to be discussed outside your office with anyone else."

Durrant nodded. "Of course, it will be kept under wraps until you get this cleared up, I understand." The attorney shook his head. "I've known Jerry a long time. This is quite a shock. I'm guessing you are here about a recording and a letter I was holding for him, in the event he passed."

"Yes, I am."

Now, this was interesting, he only knew about the recording, not about a letter.

The older man with salt-and-pepper hair stroked his chin nodding, staring at the top of his mahogany desk.

"Let me say something first, if you'll humor me."

"Of course I will, sir."

"Jerry was stressed and worried. I asked, but he wouldn't tell me why. All he told me was he needed to prepare his will and ensure that his personal matters were in order. It vexed me, but in my line of work, nothing is a surprise anymore. Detective West, I knew Jerry for over thirty years. He was my friend. When he came to see me, he refused to explain anything. Jerry told me it was to keep me from being complicit."

Jack stayed quiet.

The attorney puffed out a short laugh, which blew out his nose.

"Complicit. He used the word *complicit* like I was involved, which I am not, in whatever it is, I can assure you. As his attorney what was said between us did not make me complicit, it made me knowledgeable."

"Are you worried that I'm here to arrest you?"

This got a hearty chuckle out of Mr. Durrant.

"Oh, hell no, boy, I'm not worried, I'm lily-white and follow the law. Jerry Bogard was a respectable man for years at the agency. And before he got caught up in something bad, he did a lot of good. It was too bad this other stuff came back to haunt him. What I'm saying is I would hate to see his memory tarnished, or his sons dragged through hell."

"Yes, sir, I understand. The DEA will want to keep a lid on this and not publicize their...shall we just call it their dirty laundry?"

The salt-and-pepper-headed man nodded pushing the envelope across the desk.

"Good. I know a little of what happened back then. Let me also say, Detective, there is no need to dredge up old wounds. I'm talking about the men from ROMA. Dead or comatose, it wouldn't change anything if they reopened the case, now would it?"

Jack stood, envelope in hand, and he nodded. "I'll pass the word on, but you understand I don't control any of the decisions on what scuttlebutt gets fed to the media."

"Detective, I appreciate your trying to keep Jerry's memories in a good light. He did plenty of positive things in the past thirty-two years, for his town, his state, and his fellow man. It'd be a shame to flush it all down the crapper because he'd been a fool in his younger days. "

"Yes, sir, I understand, and if I need anything I'll call you. If you need to reach me, here's my card."

The man looked at the card, then at Jack. "Fine, and if you find yourself ever in need of legal advice, Jack, I hope you'll call me. I'll let you show yourself out."

THEY READ THE LETTER TWICE. A trove of information—all conjecture, not proof-positive except a tape of two conversations, neither admissible in court. One tape they already knew about, the second was new.

"I cannot believe this, can you?" Sophia stopped the tape recorder.

"Bogard didn't say a damn thing about recording his conversations with Boyce Carter, just his conversation with Cleef and Sykes, and I'm wondering why?" Jack couldn't comprehend what Jerrell Bogard was thinking.

"The thing is this. Carter didn't realize he was being recorded. It's not admissible in court either."

Lila, the Special Agent in Charge, spoke up. "Since we have the intel on the setup in Mexico, I'll assign other agents to work this ASAP. Sophia, you stay on Stan Cleef. Nail that bastard." She turned her attention to Jack. "HPD has a murder suspect now. I'm leaving that up to you, Detective, and I recommend you and Medina continue to work together to get both cases wrapped up."

"And Theo Sykes, ma'am, has there been any word?"

"None yet, however, we're monitoring all State and international travel. The likelihood Sykes is already out of the country is pretty high."

"I'd say you're right. The man is capable of anything though. He might be too confident he won't get caught." A frown crossed Sophia's forehead. Sykes was dangerous. "If he's still in Houston, he's a major threat."

The Acting SAC nodded. "Yes, he is, and I would advise you to take precautions while pursuing Stan Cleef. The only information we've let out is we found Agent Jerrell Bogard dead under unusual circumstances, and the FBI is handling the situation. With the FBI boys in the loop, the media frenzy will be their problem. Our position will be 'no-comment'. "

The meeting was over, and Lila Beaumont dismissed them. Her plate was full with her new duties as the Acting Special Agent in Charge. It had been one thing taking over Bogard's responsibilities once he had hastily resigned. But now, the man was dead, thought to be murdered by another DEA agent. This was a huge Pandora's box. Until the dust settled, her life would not be her own.

48

They sat in a dark metallic-gray 2012 Cadillac CTS–V, a car Jack borrowed from Jasper at the impound lot. With a 420-horsepower twin-turbo, the car needed no modifications. This was a bitching car that went from 0 to 60 in 4.4 seconds with 430-pound feet of torque.

Sophia's eyes scanned the interior. Dark charcoal leather seats were still in spectacular condition, the carpet not too matted. The dashboard was simple, nothing cracked or ripped, with bucket seats, and the shifter head had been switched and replaced with a skull-shape-shifter knob. The car didn't smell new, but at least it didn't stink. She saw the tachometer and mmm'd, and Jack glanced her way.

"What, Medina?"

"Zero to 60 in what, 4, 4.6? Badass car."

"Yep, it has a 4.4, with a 420 twin-turbo. It's a leave-you-in-the-dust kind of vehicle. A few years ago, a T-288 crew member got busted running with ten keys of meth in his trunk. He ran a red light and when Patrol caught up with him and pulled him over he was high as a hot-air balloon. A pusher and a major user of his own product. The kid was one crazy hopped-up druggie. HPD's patrol cops, John Lancaster and Ollie Richmond, stopped him. Ollie was running his plates when the lunatic bastard pulled a gun on Lancaster and if John hadn't been wearing his vest, he'd be a name on a plaque in the lobby of HPD headquarters. The dude got two rounds off. John took one in the right shoulder before Ollie tased the little fucker."

"Where is he? Still locked up at Huntsville?"

"Nope, guy got shanked two years in. He had a beef with the Skinheads. Guards found him in the laundry area with a whittled-down toothbrush pushed through his carotids. And you know how it is; no one saw or heard a thing. "

Yeah, she knew how it was, gang life and drugs. It was a damn shame these were the reasons she had a job.

Sophia yawned, and Jack glanced at his phone. After five hours of sitting and watching, they'd got nothing, not even a peep. Three buses came in and one left. No more buses due in, nor any passengers or buses waiting to go out. The marquee lights were turned off two hours ago, the front door locked and the closed sign flickered in red neon.

"No Carter, no Cazalla, and nothing suspicious. I'm thinking nothing is gonna happen tonight, Jack. What do you think? Should we call it a night?"

Jack rolled his shoulders, arching his back to stretch, glancing between Sea Star's front office and the side door of the bus barn.

"You up for a bit of legwork, Medina?"

"Oh, Jack, I thought you'd never ask. I love skulking around with you in the dark."

A chuckle slipped out as he shook his head. "You are a smart-ass, Sophia. I like it. Come on. Let's go on a sneaking and peeking adventure."

Sneaking to the back alley behind the bus shed, Jack's voice was low. "There's a door on the other side. Head that way. It is possible the door will be unlocked. If not, I can pick the lock."

"Great, we can set off the alarms. We're gonna look cute in matching orange jumpsuits, Jack."

With a jerk of his head, she followed, good idea or not.

Walking the length of the backside, they rounded the corner, staying close to the physical building and in the shadows as much as possible. They were in-between the bus barn and the main office. It was dark, not much in the way of overhead lighting illuminating the area.

Sophia was at his back. She saw a light under the door.

"Jack," her voice was low. Had she not poked him, he would not have heard her.

"Yeah?" He twisted his head to see her.

"Someone's in there. I saw a light flicker. On then off, it was quick."

Jack nodded. They crept to the back alleyway, slipping across and behind the other building. They edged up the side wall to the main door. Jack held up a fist, signaling for her to stop. Carefully, he laid his head against the door to listen. Quiet—no noise came from within. He gave it a minute and then heard it. It was a scraping sound, very slight, and then a grunt. Another thud and a second grunt along with more scraping. It sounded like heavy stuff was being pushed across a concrete floor, and voices mumbling. He looked back at her and pointed to his ear, letting Sophia know there were voices. He motioned for her to back up, pointing to the alleyway.

"What, Jack?"

"There were scraping noises and voices. Sounds like they are moving boxes or crates."

"As in two people? Could you hear what they said?"

"No, but sounded like three people. Let's get to the car."

They closed the doors as quietly as possible and Jack started the car. Without turning on his lights, he moved further down the parking lot. Getting as close as he could, he parked by the dumpster sitting at the last empty shop with its windows boarded up.

"There isn't a clear view of the front door. We're gonna hafta go on foot. See those donation boxes? We can hunker beside them so we can see. Come on."

"So we can see? Jack, there aren't enough lights out front. How are we going to see? It's too dark from this angle." Sophia scowled.

"Woman, I came prepared." Jack walked her to the trunk of the car and popped it open. Inside were night-vision googles, a Remington pump-action shotgun, zip ties in place of cuffs, and extra ammo in a box next to the shotgun.

Sophia elbowed him. "Oh, Jack, you got me a shotgun, is it because the sound of a shotgun racking turns me on?"

His heart kicked up a beat, and then he elbowed her back. "When this is over, perhaps we should go shooting together?"

She hesitated. "Yeah, sure." Her heart lurched, wondering if *go shooting* was a euphemism for something altogether different they could do together. She let out the breath she had been holding.

"You good, Sophia?"

"Yep, Jack, never better. Come on, let's get going."

THE SHOTGUN LEFT in the trunk, they crouched beside two larger donation boxes for the needy. It was not an ideal place. It smelled like a rat or critter had crawled in and died.

"Geeze, Louise, we smell dead rotting bodies and now we hafta put up with the smell of a dead animal carcass. Great."

"Oh, stop bitching, Jack, we, uh...Jack, look." Sophia's tone changed and his ears perked.

She saw two men step out of the office between the buildings. Neither man looked up or in their direction so they could not identify them, but they watched them disappear behind the bus barn.

"I didn't get a clear look, but my hunch says it was Callum and Mundy."

She bit her lip in thought. "I've got an idea. How about we follow them when they leave?"

Jack nodded, his face furrowed in concentration. "Well, I heard three voices. So one person is still in there, alive I hope. If not, it'll be another murder to add to the list, and I'd rather not add on to our already full plate."

Sophia did a mental checklist: Espinar, Vega, Bogard, and Bebchuk. Add in the three homicide victims Jack had, and this equated to seven dead, the body count escalating.

Back in the car, they waited in silence, eyes focused on the alleyway exits, Jack watching the south end and Sophia watching the north. He drummed his fingers on the console. The sound was padded by the leather, but in the quiet it resounded.

"Nervous, Jack?" Sophia put her hand over his fingers to stop them from drumming.

He looked down at her hand, and it was like she'd been burned. She yanked it away.

In a clear, normal voice, he answered, "No, I'm not, just impatient. So, are you scared, Sophia?"

She let out a sound of aggravated disbelief, her voice still low. "Huh? Uh-uh, I most definitely am not. Why would you ask that?"

"Then why are you whispering? No one knows we're here. We're in a car, with the windows rolled up. Parked across the street, more than oh, what, at least three-quarters of a football field away?"

Sophia looked at him like he had three heads. Then she grinned. "Shit, I don't know why. Guess I'm edgy, kinda like you drumming your fingers, which I assume is a nervous habit, right?"

"Could be. I guess I never thought about...hey, they're on the move, buckle up. We can talk about nervous habits later."

Sophia buckled up, focusing on their target, a dark colored car. It looked like a 2012 Buick Regal or the same year Ford Fusion.

Jack followed in the center lane, leaving a three-car distance between him and his subject. With Sophia as a second pair of eyes, they weren't likely to lose him.

"Jack, he's moving over. Looks like he is exiting."

"I see him. He's not exiting, he's just following the road leading to State Highway 146, and I know where he's going, Sophia." Jack did not blink, he moved over, keeping his three-car distance, and then slowed down to avoid looking like he was following.

"You do?"

"Yes, East Barbours Cut Boulevard. There's a large container yard and shipping port. Whoever it is, they are headed to the container yard, the same one I followed Caden Ward, aka Owen McCready to. If I were a betting man, I'd bet they run drugs from there and God knows what else."

"Being it's close to Galveston Bay, bet you're right."

"Yep, and we don't want to be caught or we'll be in one of those containers rotting until we're fish food, so get your game face on."

Sophia pulled out her gun, chambered a round, shoved her gun back in the holster, checked her clip, and then did a sideways glance toward Jack. "I'm gonna want that shotgun out of the trunk, and not just because I like the *cha-chunk* sound either."

He nodded as he exited, following what he knew now as a charcoal-gray 2013 Buick Regal, a car with a large amount of trunk space. Enough for a dead body or two.

49

The shipping container yard was peaceful at this hour. No real activity to get excited about. Most of the personnel operated from 7:00 a.m. to 7:00 p.m. The terminal container yards, railroad cars loading and offloading, and ship docks were locked down and quiet at night, but there were employees carrying out duties which had to be performed during nonworking hours. Ships, trucks, railcars, and heavy operating equipment or machinery needed maintenance and had to be completed before the next day. It's possible a few poor shmucks were still laboring after hours.

"It's a dirt road about a mile up. Main hours are from 7:00 to 7:00. I'm cutting the lights. We need to go in dark." Jack parked the caddy, pulled out the keys then his Glock, and checked his round.

"Open the trunk, Jack. I'm taking the shotgun with me." Sophia wasn't playing around this time. Who knew what might happen? Plus, they had zero backup, with no idea what they were up against.

"Don't see the Buick Regal, do you, Jack?"

"No, but they could be parked anywhere."

Jack scanned the area. "Over there, Sophia." He nudged her with his elbow, his head jerking in the direction he wanted her to see. "Did you see that?"

"See what?" She looked across the road. Huge metal boxes stacked in rows, in heights of three or more. Just what had Jack seen?

"Come on. I swear I saw a flashlight beam and there's enough lighting here, so why use a flashlight? Let's go check it out."

Once across the street, Jack hoisted himself over the chain-link fence. Sophia grabbed hold and did the same. Her pant leg caught in a loose piece of the fence wire, and she tugged, ripping the material, scratching her leg.

"Oh shit, I liked these pants. Damn it."

"Come on. The DEA can buy you six more pairs. Let's get over there." Jack pointed to a triple stack of yellow and red steel containers; Sophia nodded, on his heels.

She stood at his back with her left hand on his left shoulder, keeping her balance. Her head craned around him. She watched into the night with him.

"There it is again." His voice was low.

"Yeah, but it's not moving in any direction, just sorta side-to-side."

Turning at a slight angle, Jack quietly pushed her with his shoulder, causing her to take a few steps backward before he faced her.

"We're going in—"

"Oh, no, we're not, Jack, are you—"

"My God, girl, will you let me finish one damn sentence?"

"Sorry."

"Okay. We're moving in closer," Jack emphasized the word *closer*, "to get a peek. That's it. We aren't gonna go charging in."

"Okay, sorry, sounds like a plan. Let's go." She let him take the lead.

They moved up to the tanks closest to where three big-rig trailers sat, without the trucks attached. The doors were open to one container, and they watched as the Tweedle Brothers went in and wheeled out a pallet loaded with cartons every ten minutes, on a hydraulic hand truck, loading them into the back end of an unmarked 18-wheel trailer.

They weren't whispering, besides, who'd be out here listening? Answer: Detective Jack West and DEA Special Agent Sophia Medina.

"Stop with the fucking light, you fool, we don't need you shining light, we got the yard's lights."

Carl was pissing Louis off.

"There ain't a soul out here to give a rat's ass." Carl waved the flashlight over the ground.

"That stupid pimple-faced clerk said he'd been doing night work out here. The kid's learning how to weld. Plus, the railway crane mechanics work nights." Louis Callum drew up his lip in a nasty-looking sneer.

Carl Mundy hocked up a loogie and spat on the ground. "Sure, and they're three lots down, wearing welders' masks, running a torch, and don't give a flying fuck about a little flashlight beam. Hell, Louis, and if they did, we'd make certain they stayed quiet, pay 'em off or rub 'em out, makes no never mind to me."

"You do it without orders and it'll be you who gets whacked, you idiot." Louis wasn't about to be careless.

With a flick, Carl switched off the flashlight and shoved it in his back pocket.

Jack took his phone and zoomed in as tight as possible, snapping a few pictures. Maybe Kasper could do something magical.

They snuck behind the next stack of containers and got closer. Sophia stood in front of him, her head craned around the huge steel box, with his six-foot-tall frame looking over her shoulder.

"Wish I had a night-vision camera, damn it."

"Take a few more pictures from here. We're a little closer."

Sophia crouched down so she could see past the metal box as he leaned forward, his phone in hand clicking more photos.

Finished, Jack pulled back too sharply. His elbow hit Sophia in the skull.

"Ow!"

"Shhh!" Jack stepped back so she could stand and resumed his position behind her, peering around the container. "My bad. Are you okay?"

"Yes, shit."

"Well, I hope—" He stopped mid-sentence, and they both held their breath when they saw someone walking toward the two men. The person was one of two things: either a woman with short hair or a skinny man.

"You two gorillas stop the yammering and get the pallets moved onto the trailer. Also, y'all are on standby. I may need a job done sooner than later. Got me?"

"Yes, ma'am, gotcha," Mundy's voice clipped.

It was a woman. But who was she?

"Good. Now, get back to work and hustle. Those pissant gang thugs are on my shit list for not showing." The unidentified lady scanned the truck's trailer numbers, flicking through the pages on the clipboard. They had more trailers to fill, but not tonight. Those two brainless beasts couldn't do it all before the shipyard opened. Fishing out her cell she scrolled to the number she needed and hit call.

Three rings in, a man answered.

"Yeah?"

"Those douchebag Cobras and Dragons never showed up. All I have is your two buffoons. I'll be damned if we are going to postpone delivery again. Also, if those asswipe gang members don't stop messing with the girls, I'm gonna cut off their peckers. I am not happy about this, not one bit, Theo."

"Fine, you aren't happy. What can I do about it? I'll answer my question. Nothing. Not a goddamn thing, so stop bitching. As far as the girls, I'll take care of it. I'll get Beck to handle the Dragons and I'll visit the Cobras. Look, I've got my own problems to deal with."

"Whatever, that's on you. But I want you on top of these issues tomorrow. Get those asshole gang members out here. Tell them to be on time. Got that?"

"I'll handle it. When?"

"Eleven o'clock Saturday night."

"Why not tomorrow night?"

"I have a flight to work. I'll be gone for a few days, and I need to talk to them, that's damn well why."

"Fine, I'll pass the message along." Without one civil word to end the call, Theo hung up. He damn sure wasn't gonna tell her about his problems. If they realized someone from HPD was breathing down his neck, they would all freak out. Nope, this was his problem. He would take care of Kasper on his own later. Right now he had enough worry on his plate about Bogard's death. The old codger's babysitting detail, Larson and Whitson, could identify him. And he didn't know if anyone else came to see him. Otherwise, he was the last person to see him alive. In retrospect, this had not been his smartest move. He sat down to think.

THEY HAD HEARD ONLY one side of the conversation.

"Jack, Dragons and Cobras, looks like they're working for whoever the big boss is, and Theo Sykes has to be the Theo that person was talking to, dontcha think?"

"Yep, I'm betting you're right. Caden said the Dragons and Cobras were handling shipments from his store, and I'm guessing they are working directly with one of the capos, whoever that is. "

"Uh-huh, and it's a woman. Not that it makes it right, but finally a female in charge, and frankly, I find it disturbing that it makes me happy."

"Equal opportunity criminals, is that what we need now, Medina?"

She shrugged. "I wish she would turn this way. I'd like a look at her."

"She doesn't have to turn around. I know who she is."

Sophia averted her eyes to see Jack. "You do?"

"She mentioned working a flight. " He stared at the back of their suspect, his mind on the first time he'd met her.

She elbowed him out of his trance. "Jack."

"It's Marcella Águlia, the DEA's in-flight undercover agent."

"Wha—oh my God, Jack, are you positive?"

"Yes, I'm positive." He nudged her arm, and Sophia craned her neck to look past him.

DEA Agent Marcella Águlia faced them.

They inched back soundlessly, moving back to the tail of the rusted-out ocean-blue painted container, to hide between it and the faded red steel box.

"You think she saw us?" Sophia faced the end of the box they had rounded, gun at the ready.

"No, but we gotta get outta here."

"Yes, and it's time we nail these DEA bastards. I cannot believe I had to say that. Can you? Me being DEA, and one of the good guys, I can't believe I'm after my own people." Her teeth clenched so hard, Jack heard her jaw pop.

"Come on, Sophia, time to dig another layer on Agent Águlia and strategize. My house is in Deer Park. I wanna stop and get a change of clothes. Then you can drop me off at the station. I'll get a few winks in the overnight task room. Take the car, head to your house, clean up, and rest. Meet me at the station around six-ish, okay?"

"Yeah, let's get moving, time's a'wasting."

In the darkness, they slipped out, exhausted yet emotionally invigorated.

50

"She has a brother."

"Well, good morning to you too, Jack." Sophia set down an extra-large coffee cup from the gas station, a file folder, and pulled out a chair. The squad room was vacant, sans them. It was still early.

His face planted into his paperwork, he looked up. "You look refreshed, Medina. How do you feel?"

"Okay. A little draggy, but the shower helped. I feel like a person again. "

He rubbed his jaw and nodded. "As well as a shave; now I feel almost human again too."

"So tell me, who has a brother?"

"Agent Águlia, she has a famous brother."

"Very interesting. So who's this famous brother of hers?"

"Omar Villa Lobos."

Sophia Medina almost choked on the large gulp of coffee she'd taken.

"Shut the front door. Are you serious? How did that not show up in her background check? How did you find this information?"

The squad room door creaked open, and she turned at the sound.

"Hey there, Kasper. Okay, Jack, now I know how you found out."

"Hey yourself, Sophia, nice to see ya."

Kasper pulled up another chair since Sophia had taken his, and set down two giant coffees, one for him, one for Jack.

"Thanks, man." Jack savored a sip of fresh coffee.

"When Jack told me who y'all saw at the container yard, I started digging. If you know where to dig, sometimes you can strike gold."

Sophia, coffee in hand, leaned back sipping her warm brew. "Alright, what's the skinny on what you've dug up?"

What Kasper found was truly amazing. Omar and Marcella were brother and sister, but not biologically. Her family was from Veracruz, Mexico. Omar's biological family lived in a small fishing village nearby. In 1961 there was a large storm in the Gulf of Mexico, which never hit land but took down several fishing boats. Marcella's parents were part of a group of citizens who formed a search and rescue. Omar's entire family—mother, father, sister, and two brothers—were drowned or lost at sea when their boat capsized during the storm.

"Holy cow, how did he survive?" asked Sophia when Kasper recounted the story.

"He was only four and was with his maternal grandmother. His siblings were older and were helping on the fishing boat. When the grandmother identified the bodies, she had a stroke. The stress did her in. Three days later she died, leaving Omar an orphan with no other family to speak of."

"Are you about to tell me that Agent Águlia's parents adopted him?"

"That I am, and get this. She was a baby when this happened. He became her big brother, in every sense of the word. "

"Well, I'll be damned; this explains a lot, a hell of a lot." Sophia crumpled her Styrofoam cup tossing it into the trash can. "And Kasper, how did you, I mean, what, did someone write an unofficial autobiography on one of them?"

Jack jumped in. "Hey, Medina, I told you he was good and he can dig. You think I'd lie to you?"

"I found interesting reading when I began looking into her life. It seems she had a very loyal bone and protects him," Kasper went on.

"I assume she does his protecting via DEA? Is this right?" Jack was impressed with Kasper's digging abilities.

Sophia was nodding her head. "It makes sense now. This is how Omar can stay a few steps ahead of us. She's the reason he has been so elusive."

"Sophia, have you got any word on the prints from Vega's crime scene?" Jack's booted foot came up to rest on the corner of his desk.

With a smile, she nodded, leaned in, and picked up the folder she'd brought. "Yeah, I stopped by my office on the way here this morning to get my messages, and interoffice mail and crap. And there it was, the reports from the DEA lab on the prints we found at Vega's homicide scene."

"Hell, Sophia, that's important news. Why are you sitting on it?" Jack's brow furrowed in question.

"Cuz I got caught up with your statement, 'she has a brother,' and Kasper's news flash, okay?"

"Fine, sorry. Now, tell us about the prints; anything worth mentioning?"

"From the prints we got off the knife, and the ones I pulled from other various places, we got several hits. Of course Vega's were there, and Miguel's. So were Marcella's and yours too. Since we can run the prints through IAFIS, we got hits and one cartel thug stood out. Joven Cazalla."

Jack sat up, both boots planted to the floor. His face registered a question she knew he was about to ask.

"No, Jack, they weren't there."

Kasper glanced from Jack to her, and then back to Jack. "Uh, who wasn't where, Sophia?"

Jack didn't give her a chance to answer. "Our fake Irish cigarette shop owner, undercover agent Caden Ward's prints. He told us he was in Mexico doing something for Cazalla when he showed up at the hacienda unannounced."

"The prints that were lifted off the knife, Jack, those were also interesting. " Sophia tapped the folder.

"Not Cazalla I take it?"

"Uh-uh. Would you be surprised if I tell you they're Omar Villa Lobos' prints?"

Kasper whistled. "Wow, so he's resurfaced in Mexico again, huh?"

"Also, I picked up a secure message from Janet regarding Espinar's murder site. She sent it up the chain and straight to the FBI. Not only was Espinar a Mexican federal agent, Jack, and I didn't know this, he was also Homeland Security working with the Border Patrol, undercover."

"I thought he was a Mexican National."

"He was, but he carried a dual citizenship and was actually raised in Laredo."

A wistful smile hit Jack's face. "Well, I'll be damned. He played his part perfectly. The man made several English blunders, and I was an idiot, correcting him."

"Janet got word from the Mexican government after they worked Vega's crime scene. Their coroner put Vega's TOD maybe a day or two before we found Espinar's body, which means Miguel had been dead two days before Vega."

"Well, the timing fits. Villa Lobos' reason to kill Vega was revenge for running him out of his own cartel. Why kill Espinar though?" Kasper's brow knitted in thought.

"Vega, trying to save his own ass, gave Espinar up as an agent, I'm betting. That's why they tortured him too, I suspect, since Miguel's fingers were broken and his nails torn off. Villa Lobos wanted intel, DEA and Border Patrol intel."

"I'd say you were right, Jack, since they found Miguel's DNA in the building Vega worked in."

"That means nothing, Sophia; he worked that area and was in the building like the rest of y'all were."

"No, Kasper, I mean his blood DNA. When they worked the room for Vega's murder, they found unidentified blood. It was Miguel's. So now they're working two separate murder scenes but at the same location. The Mexican forensic lab has gone back out there to go over the scene again. Luckily no one else has been there, so nothing has been disturbed."

The three of them were quiet for a minute, letting it all soak in.

"What about the shoe prints?" Jack asked.

"Shoe print data came back too. From the pictures of bloody footprints you took at Vega's murder scene, Jack, there were at least four people walking around that office tracking dirt and blood. They aren't clear prints, not all of them anyway. But there is a smaller set, might be a woman's prints. Problem is those prints don't seem to intersect with any blood. Hard to prove she was out there at the time of the murders."

"Didn't you get footprint photos from the tunnel?"

"Yeah, Kasper, I did." Jack looked across the desk at Sophia. "Did they compare shoe prints?"

"Yeah, and two sets matched. All we need are the shoes to match —easy, huh?"

"Yep, like matching hairs from the barbershop floor—a cinch." Jack had the needle-in-the-haystack thought, but needed a better way to describe it and this was all he could come up with quickly. He was a dork.

Kasper's brows furrowed looking at Jack.

"Jack, did you really think Agent Ward could have had a part in torturing or beheading Vega?" This surprised Kasper.

"I felt the same way, Kasper, at first. I'm just glad his prints were nowhere on that scene." Sophia, too, was relieved Caden had not been party to this heinous act.

"Bebchuk, Bogard, Cleef, Sykes. I'm sure there might be more. We thought these were law-abiding agents out to get the bad guys.

People I would've trusted with my life. Scares the bejesus outta me now when I'm not sure if you got a knife in my back while you're smiling in my face, ya know what I mean, Bergman?"

"Yeah, I guess I do, Jack, since I know Theo Sykes is gunning for me. We know he's the one who murdered Bogard and was probably involved in Bebchuk's bombing. So, yeah, I feel that knife poking me in the back, and it brings me to this question. What should I do now? Wait for Sykes to get the drop on me, or are we gonna go after these bastards?"

"We have enough to get a warrant for Cazalla and we know he's in Houston."

"We do, Sophia? How do we know this?"

"Because, Jack, Caden called, and we talked."

"He's in town? When did he call you?"

"I got a text from him after I dropped you off at the station. He's off the case."

Kasper watched them talking back and forth like a tennis match.

"Off the case? Why, and who pulled him?"

"Someone higher-up did; we conference-called with Janet last night."

Jack stood and shoved his chair back. "And you didn't think it was important? Or maybe I'm not important enough to include, is that it? Shit. Here y'all go again, pushing me the fuck out." He ran his hand over his head, then down his face in complete aggravation.

"Jack, relax and sit down, please. First, it was in Caden's best interest to get out. He'd been in too long, and as heated as things are right now, it's too dangerous for him. Bebchuk and Bogard are both dead. What we have is Sykes and Cleef to worry about. Look, Jack. These guys are DEA, and we don't know how far up this goes. Directors Walsh and Slater pulled him and he's gone. He'll come back when he's needed to testify."

"Where is he?"

"Jack, I can't tell—"

"Yeah, right, you can't tell me. I get it. It seems your agencies can't ever tell me a damn thing."

"I cannot tell you because I have no idea where he is. You're a shit, Jack. " She blew out a long breathy sigh. "Can we please get past this petty crap?"

The frown between Jack's eyes deepened then lessened, and he nodded. "You're right, Sophia, and I apologize. Wherever Ward is, I hope he's safe. Guess I'm frustrated, but that's no reason to get pissed off at you."

"Apology accepted, Detective."

"Okay, kids, y'all done with this squabble?" Kasper felt the tension ease up.

"Sorry, Kasper, we promise to behave. Okay, Sophia, what's next**?"**

"We'll find out tomorrow. A meeting has been scheduled in the DEA task force room. We are all invited. And I'll tell ya what I think. This shit is about to get real."

"It's about time," Jack said, and Kasper nodded in agreement.

51

Sophia, Jack, Janet, SAC Lila Beaumont, and Senior DEA Agent Craig Bower sat in the large task force room at the DEA office.

"The Violent Criminal Task Force picked up Joven Cazalla last night. Captain Loomis took him in, and he's been in holding since early this morning," Janet said.

The door opened and five heads turned.

Kasper Bergman and the OAG's Deputy Director of Field Ops Remy Walsh walked in together, followed by FBI Agent Perry Crawford, and a new player, Captain Lee Scottsdale from Customs and Border Patrol. Bringing up the rear was a representative from the Mexican Federales, Officer Tony Sanchez.

Craig Bower stood to greet the newcomers. "It's like a convention. We have people representing the HPD, DEA, OAG, FBI, and now Customs and Border Patrol and the Mexican Policia. It's nice to see you again, Officer Sanchez. Now, all we need is someone from the ATF to round it out."

Kasper whispered, "Well, Jack, the entire alphabet is coming into play after all."

After introductions, Deputy Director of Field Operations Remy Walsh took charge.

"FBI Agent Perry Crawford will now brief us on the Bebchuk bombing and the murder of Jerrell Bogard."

"Thank you, Deputy Director Walsh." Crawford moved over to the podium. "Regarding Agent Clive Bebchuk's murder, the ATF is investigating the bombing. They've begun sifting through parts and materials trying to reconstruct, to follow the money. We are looking into blackmail allegations on both the Bebchuk and Bogard murders. I will conduct one-on-one interviews with all who've worked with these two dead men recently, Agent Medina, Detective West, and Agent Spears." He looked over at Walsh. "Remy, my boss will contact you later today. We will need to gather all of Bebchuk and Bogard's personnel files and a list of case files they closed within the last ten years."

"It will be ready within a few days. Thanks for coming, Perry."

Nods and good-byes were said. FBI Agent Perry Crawford left the task room.

"Okay, that's out of the way." Deputy Director of Field Operations Walsh picked up a file. "We are working an operation at our DEA field offices along the Texas/Mexico border with the help of our border patrol contact, Captain Scottsdale. Lee, the floor is yours."

Captain Lee Scottsdale went into detail on the plan they'd hatched in Customs to get legal hold on shipments held unclaimed and sent back to Mexico. They would also, with the help of the Federales, close the meth labs that had popped up near Matamoras and Reynosa, along the Texas border. "Our CIs here in Houston and Mexico have recently delivered names, dates, and places. The intel has checked out. We aren't coming to this party late; we've just kept our part under wraps." Lee Scottsdale looked over at Tony Sanchez. "Tony and I have been working round-the-clock surveillance and have solid evidence of cartel involvement with some top capo names."

Tony Sanchez spoke, "Our main concern has been the human smugglings. I'm not talking about Mexican Nationals trying to come over to the States illegally. We've got good intel on how they are running the human trafficking business. I know our police force has a bad reputation for being untrustworthy, but I assure you we are vetting these men by watching their financial activities."

"Lee," Janet spoke up, "are you still working with the FBI on this case?"

Lee Scottsdale nodded. "Yes, Janet, we have a new joint task force with them and the DEA senior staff at the offices in McAllen, Brownsville, and Laredo. We also have a large presence near Eagle Pass moving up toward El Paso."

"Working with your border patrol and DEA offices has been an enlightening experience, and a pleasure working with honest men," Federal Agent Tony Sanchez announced to the group.

A few comments such as, "you bet," "absolutely," and "glad to hear it," were made in response, back to Agent Sanchez.

"My flight leaves in three hours, so I must take off." Agent Sanchez stood, looking first at Sophia, then Jack. "After you question Joven Cazalla, if you get names and evidence we can use to find out who murdered Agent Espinar, contact me ASAP. Miguel was a good friend. He was also a respectable man."

"Absolutely, Tony, and if we can, we might just extradite Cazalla, give the scum back to Mexico. Then you guys can lock him up."

"Thanks, Medina. That means a lot." Sanchez grinned.

Once again, so-longs and good-byes were said, leaving the HPD, DEA, and OAG offices represented.

"Alright, folks, let's get down to business. Lila, as acting SAC, you have the floor."

"Thanks, Remy. Craig, I want you to let Sophia have a run at Cazalla, and Jack, you sit in, back her up," Lila said.

"What about Callum and Mundy? I'd think using these two as witnesses for the State is our best bet," Janet said.

"I agree, Janet. Not much we have on them. Transporting drugs, they'd be out in no time. I've got agents out looking for them, and we're gonna bring them in for questioning." Craig Bower stood. "I need to get to another meeting. I'll touch base with you later this afternoon, Lila, update you on our search."

"Oh, and Craig, once we find them, I want them to know we have Cazalla. Call me this afternoon,"—she looked at her watch—"before 3:00, or if you locate Mundy or Callum."

Another round of good-byes and the group was shrinking in size.

"Janet, I am going to leave you in charge as my liaison for the OAG." Deputy Director of Field Operations Remy Walsh got off his seat. "Lila, I know the way you moved up as the new SAC was a shitty way to get here, but congratulations. You deserve the break; you'll be a great leader."

Lila Beaumont stood and accepted the congratulatory handshake offered by Deputy Director Remy Wash.

Janet Spears smiled, and Deputy Director Walsh didn't miss the look of appreciation she gave him. He smiled back. "I am not the chauvinistic pig you thought I was. Am I, Janet?"

Jack, Kasper, Sophia, Janet, and SAC Beaumont were the last five left in the room.

"Well, here we are. Seems we are all the original players. Almost, that is."

SAC Beaumont shrugged. "Sorry to disappoint you, Janet, that I am not Bogard."

"No disappointment at all, Lila. Better you than that old fart, may he rest in peace."

"I know you have Cazalla in holding. Is he here?" Jack jumped into the business of business. "We need to get this rolling." Hashing crap out in meetings wasn't his idea of working a case.

"Jack, they are bringing him for county right now." Lila's cell buzzed, and she answered it. "Right, yes. Thanks for calling. Yes, hold them. I'll send agents to collect them." She ended the call. "Seems the HPD caught up with Callum and Mundy. Vice Detectives Tormo and Sparks brought them in on a drug bust. Now go figure, we can hold them indefinitely or until they lawyer up. I want you two ready for Cazalla. There is one thing I need to impress upon you both."

"And that is what, Lila?" Sophia gathered her files ready to get to work.

"No mention of Agent Ward, nothing at all, understood? He was under for several years and we have a lot of debriefing to do."

"We understand, right, Jack?"

Jack nodded. "Now, let's go get some answers. Whydaya say, Medina?"

"Okay, guys, y'all have your assignments, uh, what about me? What do I do, wait for Sykes to show up and kick my ass, or worse?" asked Kasper.

SAC Beaumont chucked. "Sorry, Mr. Bergman, I didn't mean to pass you over. No, you don't wait for that other shoe to drop. One of our agents will get you set up in an office. We have a computer for you and any databases you need. I've made sure you have proper clearance. Here." She handed him a folder. "These are the classified case file numbers you will need to begin a wide net search for Sykes. There is a list of known associates, dates, and activities we've been tracking. Dig, Mr. Bergman, get more, all you can find."

"Kasper," Janet addressed him. "We've copied your tape recordings and Legal is looking into all of this. We are also doing a voice match to prove it was Cleef and Sykes talking. Jack..." She turned her head. "Boyce Carter. I've got them looking for him, but no warrants started yet. Based on his conversation with Bogard we know he didn't pull the trigger, but he ordered the hit, and on his own damned son. I want you to get that bastard."

"I'll do my level best," Jack assured the new SAC.

Joven Cazalla sat, relaxed. This was not his first time in an interrogation room. The odds were pretty good that it would not be his last. The door opened.

"Mr. Cazalla. Thanks for waiting."

"Did I have a choice, Agent Medina?"

"You know who I am, do you? And him, what about him?' She thumbed to Jack.

"Detective Jack West. Yeah, I know you both; I make it my business to know my enemies."

Sophia opened the file. "You've an impressive rap sheet and friends in low places." She leaned back. "We have you dead to rights at a murder scene. Your fingerprints were found, and with your history, it's not looking real good for you. "

"What do you want, Agent Medina?"

"We want Omar."

"Good luck with that. Even I don't know where he is."

"You're not doing yourself any favors, Cazalla. " She paused and looked up at the ceiling, weighing her words. "What if you were offered a deal?"

"What? I tell you what I don't know and you'll let me go?" He smirked.

Sophia didn't speak; she stared at him, pushed away from the table, and stood.

"Detective West, let's leave Mr. Cazalla here to think about what he knows and what he will share. Then we'll come back, perhaps with an offer, maybe one he can't refuse."

Without a word, Jack got off his chair. He went out the door first, her following, and he glanced back as she relocked the door, leaving Joven Cazalla once again alone in the interrogation room.

At her desk, she plopped down and Jack took the chair at the corner.

"What deal, Sophia? We didn't discuss a deal. That was, pardon me for saying, a weak ass attempt at questioning."

"I've just started, Jack. Give me a break. Besides, you remember you told me Caden said they drank together, and he said Cazalla talked when he drank. He might have spilled some personal information we can use in our favor. Janet is making a call to Ward. She wants to find out what he might know that I might use as leverage."

"So getting Omar is all you want, is that it, Sophia? What about Stan Cleef, Theo Sykes, and Marcella Águlia? Or since these are DEA you gonna leave it to the FBI to clean that mess up?"

"Damn it, Jack, pull your jockey shorts out of your crack. We've got surveillance on Águlia. You know Sykes will be harder to find, but we *are* looking for him. What the fuck do you think we have Kasper doing? As far as Cleef, the dumb shit is in the building. He's clueless that we are onto him. Once he leaves, we have a detail following him."

"What, is there an air marshal on Marcella's trail? You think she wouldn't catch on to that? She's a smart woman."

"Oh, I wouldn't worry too much about who's watching her, Jack. The person we have tailing her is good. Better than Marcella ever thought she was. When the time is right, that damn turncoat will have some cuffs slapped on her. I can't wait to see her do the perp walk."

"So much for EOC, huh, Sophia?"

"What are you talking about?"

"Equal Opportunity Criminals."

She couldn't help it, she sputtered a laugh. "Oh yeah, that."

Jack's face got serious. "Look, Medina, I want to go after Carter, and me sitting here while you dance around with Cazalla is useless. Can you get me a copy of the taped conversation Bogard had with Carter?"

"Sure, but what use will it be? The recording is not admissible; Carter didn't know he was being recorded."

"Has your legal department considered the fact this was recorded in an office at a public place of business? Did anyone see the door opened or closed, did anyone question the other office personnel? Could they have overheard anything?"

Sophia's mouth opened and then shut. A crinkle formed between her brows, and she shook her head. "Jack, great catch. I hadn't given that any thought."

"Tell you what, Medina, I'm going after Carter. You do what you need to do to get Omar, or whatever you can to move that investigation forward. I'll help you nail Cleef and I hope Marcella's ass to the wall at Federal prison, but I want Carter for my triple homicide."

"And Sykes, Jack...aren't you in the least concerned about Kasper's safety?"

"Of course I am. What a thing to say. Jesus, Sophia. Let me tell you something about that kid, though. He's grown a set. When I met the kid, he was scared shitless of me, but not anymore. That pup has no problem telling me I drink too much, or telling me to fuck off. Plus, I found out he is a crackerjack marksman. His personnel files didn't tell me everything I needed to know, so I called his dad, retired Lieutenant Colonel Bergman, a few days before I met the kid. His old man worked with the Special Forces unit."

"Does he know you called?"

"Nah, it would embarrass him. His dad is very proud of the man his son has become. Growing up Kasper spent a lot of time with his dad's platoons. These were tough guys training in Special Forces. They were not just a positive influence on Bergman, they were great teachers. Shit, Sophia, if I was Sykes and knew this about Kasper, I'd be worried."

"So when you vetted him, you really did, back to when he was a toddler. Is that it?"

"Yes, I did, Sophia. I had to be sure I could trust him. And I hafta say the kid keeps a low profile on what he can really do, and he's smart."

"Well, if Sykes gets the drop on him, he could be dead. Theo Sykes is dangerous, Jack."

"Yeah, all of them are, and I am sure Kasper has grown some eyes in the back of his head. He has his own spidey senses. Look, Medina." Jack shifted his weight to see her face full-on. "I want to help you get your man, but since I've been given the green light to go after Carter, that's what I'm gonna do."

"Alright, Jack." She nodded thoughtfully. "I understand you need to close your case. You realize all of this will intersect, don't you? The HPD and the DEA will have a case together, and I know you want Carter for murder, but..."

"No buts, Sophia, I'm gonna nail him for a triple homicide, end of story." He stood straighter and crossed his arms.

"Maybe, Jack, I'm not sure. Don't you want to get the real gunman?"

He shrugged. "How about I get both?"

Jack butted in, "Carter might be useful to you and the DEA. I know how it goes, Agent Medina, and it sucks. You are gonna pull rank on me now, aren't you?"

Sophia rolled her chair back to look at him. It was just her and Jack in the office with three rows of cubicles, desks, chairs, and filing cabinets.

"Jack, we need Carter as a witness for the State; makes our job easier to convict people in our agency. We can put him in WTISEC. After that, he is on his own, so to speak. And he's not that smart. He'll think he got away with something. And my thoughts are he'll be back in the wrong company soon enough. I know you want to nail him because it was his son he allegedly called a hit on, but wouldn't you rather arrest the actual trigger man? "

He stayed silent, his eyes boring into hers.

"Jack, please help us nail Omar first and then slap cuffs on Stan Cleef and Marcella Águlia."

"And Sykes. What about him? Don't we wanna nail his ass to the wall too?"

"The reality is we'll have to worry about Sykes later. He is a helluva lot smarter than Cleef or Marcella. Stan's a dweeb. The man is in deep with bookies and if he was stupid enough to do this and stay there, then he is an idiot. Marcella is emotionally connected to Omar, so we can play on her sisterly feelings for him. We have plans in motion. But Sykes is different. He knows DEA and FBI protocol and how we work, so he'll stay one step ahead of us if he is still in the country. The FBI is casting a wide-net manhunt; however, I'm betting he's already left and in a non-extradition country laying on a beach with a drink in hand."

"On the FBI's Most Wanted List, what a claim to fame. Guess Bogard's murder will get no justice, even though he was scum."

"This is a clusterfuck. Jack, Caden said Theo is the man he called Old Motorcycle Boots. It was him he saw at the pawnshop that day with Walt Burch."

"Walt Burch's disappearance is probably a murder, another unloved case. Shit. We know Theo killed Bogard, and he isn't gonna answer for it. Makes me sick."

"Well, Jack, my plan is to get Cazalla to talk. Maybe he knows about Burch too. Espinar and Vega died at the hands of Omar, but if Joven turns, we will use him up. I also want to go at him alone."

"What? Why?"

"I feel...well, let's just say it's something I have to do, Jack, as a woman," she said and shook her head. "I know you are not a chauvinistic pig, but I have to do this my way. "

"How about I make a deal with you, Sophia?"

"I'm listening."

"I won't push this issue. You let me go after Carter. I need to get my case solved. If I can't hang him out to dry, I want the man who pulled the trigger on his orders. HPD needs to get closure for the murder of Robert Thompson, also for Jamere Carter and Lyell Taylor too, but especially for Thompson. His family deserves justice; Robert was just a kid. A boy who never gave his family worry and got caught up with the likes of Jamere Carter. The kid didn't have a rap sheet and he might have had a chance for a better life had he lived." Jack's goal was to put away the man responsible for their son's death, explaining just enough to ease their pain, if only a trifle.

"That's not a deal, Jack, that's a plan, one I am in total agreement with. What deal do you want?" She eyeballed him suspiciously.

"You make sure the DEA keeps me on the case until you get Cleef and Águlia. Don't push me out."

"Jack, we have no intention of pushing you out or taking you off the case. You'll be on this case for a while. There will be months of red tape, paperwork, and reports, so there's no deal to be made; it's already made and you are part of the team."

Jack backed up a step. "Good. Not sure how long it will take to find him. Who knows if he's running since Bogard's murder?"

"He might not know, if Cleef hasn't told him. And Theo doesn't care if Carter knows or not; he's out to save his own neck. This is news that has been kept under wraps. Everyone who was on scene was told to keep this quiet. The FBI ran some type of smoke screen with the local news."

"I'm gonna head over to Sea Star and do some canvassing about that day Bogard was there. I'll be cautious about what I say. Who knows, I might even run into Carter."

"If you do, text me, I'll get word to the SAC and we'll get agents out there to bring him in. Better us than you right now."

Jack pursed his lips and nodded. "It might be at that. Oh, one more thing."

"What, Jack?" She looked up.

"After this is over, and we have the time, how about dinner and drinks? We go as Jack and Sophia, not as Agent and Detective. You game?"

Her heartbeat sped up, but she remained calm outwardly. A dinner date, he was asking her on a date.

"Sounds good, as long as it isn't breakfast tacos and coffee, and I can leave my gun at home."

"Yeah, leave your gun at home, cuz I'm gonna bring you a sawed-off shotgun—*cha-chunk*!"

Jack left her, laughing and blushing. He smiled as he got in the elevator and went to the ground floor. He was still smiling when the elevator doors opened, releasing him into the lobby.

52

The phone was ringing off the hook while two couples in their late 60s stood at the front counter, suitcases and carry-on bags at their feet. The two ladies were standing in slouched downhearted stances, while one of the men huffed and puffed at the young woman behind the counter.

"Give me a minute, please," she said as she answered the phone, first one line then the other with "Sea Star Coaches, can you please hold?" Once the phones stopped their incessant ringing, she turned back to her four unhappy-looking customers.

Jack stepped back and stood to one side. He was waiting his turn, listening and observing.

The story was their bus had left twenty minutes early without them. They were not happy campers because another would not be ready to leave for two more hours and it was already booked, with no available seating. It was a back-and-forth of what could be done to appease these four people. They'd all traveled from Crockett, Texas, together to take a trip by tour bus to San Antonio. After a week there, they would head to Corpus Christi.

"The owner will be here within the next hour, and I'm sure he can arrange something to make everyone happy. Until then, we can put your luggage in a secured locker so you won't have to cart it around and it will be safe. There's a little cafe down the road. Why not go get a bite to eat? If you bring me your receipts, you will be reimbursed as part of our apology. It's the best I can do until the owner gets here." The woman's eyes beseeched them. The spokesperson for the foursome spoke up. "Okay, miss, we know it's not your fault, but we have to complain to someone, now don't we?"

"Yes, sir, I understand, I do. Now, if you will fill out this form, I'll get the locker keys so you can get your luggage squared away." Handing the man a clipboard and pen, she scurried off to get a key.

Forms filled in, she handed them the keys and directed them to the lockers.

"I've got your cell number, Mr. Gruber, and I know my boss. He'll make this right. None of you shall be disappointed."

The old man took hold of his rolling suitcase. "I'm sure it will work out, miss. Come on, Marybeth. Let's get our stuff locked up and go to that café. I'm hungry and my feet are killing me."

Mr. Gruber's wife got up and was followed by her friend Pauline, and Pauline's husband Buddy.

Jack watched them walk past the counter, through a side door. They headed down the hallway to lock up their belongings and left out the same door headed to the café down the road. He stepped up to the counter.

A hint of anxiety filled her voice, but she smiled. "May I help you?"

"You did a great job with those couples, my hat's off to you. Paying for them to eat at that café was a nice gesture. Is this a company policy for riders who miss the bus?"

A deep pent-up sigh rose from her lungs and she released it. "No, sir, it's not normal policy, but my boss is reasonable and will reimburse them. I know he will."

Jack's brows rose, but he made no comment. Boyce Carter was

not that sort of person. He knew this deep down. Poor girl will have to cover the bill herself, he was sure of it.

She shook herself out of her trance. "Besides, they weren't late. The bus left twenty minutes early. Oh, this is a mess, a fat mess. But it isn't your problem, sir. What can I help you with today? Plan a trip, perhaps a tour, or maybe you have a group outing you need to arrange?"

"No, ma'am, I'm not here to arrange a trip. The owner will be here soon. Is that Mr. Carter?"

A small laugh escaped her lips. "Boyce Carter, the owner? Well, he wished he were. But no, the owner is Hoyt Evans, and I'm his niece, Belinda Pinson. He's my mother's brother."

"And Mr. Carter's title is what, Business Manager?"

A frown creased the young woman's forehead. "First, who are you?" She stopped and her mouth formed an O. "You're with ICE, aren't you? Oh my God, I knew this would happen. I told Uncle Hoyt this would happen if he let them. I...uh, oh, I..." She stopped talking, knowing she'd said way too much.

"Ma'am, I assure you I'm not with ICE." Jack unclipped his badge and laid it on the counter. She looked down, and then her hand covered her mouth as she nodded.

"Are you the only one here?"

"Yes, sir," she answered, her voice low.

"When do the next buses arrive?"

"Tomorrow, late in the evening. The bus leaving in two hours is booked solid. Not an empty seat. And we have no place for these two couples to stay. Uncle Hoyt will do the right thing, though. I can count on him since he is back in town." She was still fretting over her latest dilemma.

"Where is Mr. Carter, do you know?"

She shook her head. "No, I don't. All I know is Uncle Hoyt is coming to the office, which is not normal. But Mr. Carter said he would be away on personal business." Then, under her breath, she mumbled, and Jack didn't quite catch it.

"Ma'am, I'm sorry. What did you say? I didn't catch that last part."

Again, she shrugged and gave him a slanted-eye look. "That if Carter were here, he'd not be nice."

"Nice, like how do you mean?"

"Like be nice to the old couples who just left. He'd tell them tough luck, get a room, and come back tomorrow."

"Oh, I see."

"I'm glad he's gone. I don't care for him or his buddies, but I have to earn a living. Besides, I've always enjoyed working with my Uncle Hoyt. You're the police; I'm sure whatever you want to talk to Mr. Carter about involves some of the funny business that goes on here. Am I right?"

Now he was getting somewhere. Any person who makes this kind of comment knows stuff, stuff that might help him, and this woman was a person he was very interested in questioning.

"Alright, Miss Pinson, we need to talk."

"Please, call me Belinda, and am I in trouble?"

"Are you willing to talk to me?"

"You make it sound like I should be afraid to talk to you. Should I?"

"No, you shouldn't, so let's cut to the chase. Are you aware your uncle is being extorted? And his tour bus company has been smuggling in meth. Sea Star Coaches has been using little old people, like those two couples who just left, as their cover. You mentioned ICE. What do you know about human trafficking?"

"I knew Uncle Hoyt was paying the Dragons money for their so-called protection. And he has been forced to let some men use his buses. I only found out about them smuggling people across the border a year ago. They said it's because these people want a better life. Anyway, that's the lie they told my uncle. Detective West, something happened after Mr. Carter's son was killed. You know about that, don't you? And not once have I heard that they've caught the killers either. Uncle Hoyt and I think it was the Dragons who killed Mr. Carter's son and those other two boys."

"Yes, I remember that. It was a triple homicide, but it is more than this, Miss Pinson. A lot more."

"Yes, sir, I know because there is other stuff I've overheard, but I've minded my business. I don't want my family hurt. And I don't wish to get into trouble either."

"Well, I am going to need to talk to both of you."

As if by magic, the bell over the door jangled. Hoyt Evans, a portly, slightly balding man walked in, looking a bit frazzled.

"Belinda, oh, sorry, didn't know you had a customer," Hoyt Evans said as the door behind him shut slowly, jingling the bell once more.

"Uncle Hoyt, this is Detective West from the Houston Police. He's, uh, well, maybe it's best you talk in private..." She cut her eyes over to Jack for confirmation.

Jack nodded, stepping toward the man with an outstretched hand. Hoyt Evans did the same.

"Yes, uh, Detective, we can, uh, step into my office." He hiked his pants up. Gesturing his head, he said, "First open doorway to the right down that hallway. Let me have a word with my niece about the four passengers who missed their bus. I will be right in."

"Thank you, Mr. Evans," Jack said. Then he headed to Hoyt Evans' office finding it a bit of a mess. Papers and files littered the desk, empty Pepsi cans, and a box of cheese crackers sat open at the corner. The trash can was full, and behind the desk were three metal file cabinets; three-ring notebooks, and message pads sat on the tops of two, and on the third cabinet sat two medium-sized banker's boxes, one atop the other.

Jack sat in the chair across from the desk. This chair had seen better days. The cloth on the arms was threadbare, the cushion had a cigarette burn and coffee stains, and was a faded light blue. He imagined Jerrell Bogard sitting in this chair, and across from him, Boyce Carter was sitting at the helm, acting as if he was a big shot. He smiled. The door to the office was missing. Someone had removed it from its hinges, and Jack wondered how long the office had been doorless. That would be one of the first questions for Mr. Evans; the second would be the number of employees. The third question, but not last, would be about customer foot traffic. No physical door to shut. There was not a door to block off the hallway from the front counter. Jack was sure whatever Hoyt Evans told him, Belinda, if she were listening, would hear every word.

In a busy office, the public could overhear or just walk in. It was a good place for an admissible recording, just like the parking garage in the Rubicon Building where Kasper recorded Cleef and Sykes. He re-scanned the top of the desk and smiled for the second time. A box of round toothpicks sat on top of the desk, next to the cup of pens and pencils—Boyce Carter's trademark. Jack always saw him with a toothpick. The small cylinder-shaped wooden stick hung out the corner of his mouth as he chewed on the end.

His interview with Hoyt Evans, then later with Belinda Pinson, was enlightening. Jack would get Vice to crack down on the gang extortion. The guy was being squeezed, and he'd bet so were several other businesses. When Boyce Carter sent him off for an extended vacation, this was the only time he was not afraid, and Carter had paid for his and his wife's trip on an extended cruise to Europe. At first, Evans had thought it was odd. However, the *other* people Carter worked for had deep pockets and it was their idea. It was also their idea that Carter take over Sea Star's management.

"Boyce said if I advanced him to Management it would be better for me," Mr. Evans expressed with a half laugh/grunt. "Yeah, better for my health as in they would not beat the holy hell outta me or worse. Detective, I have to tell you these guys scare the shit outta me. They wanted Belinda to leave, but that girl, well, she's a pistol, that one. She wasn't about to let them run her off. My niece out there, she's who ya should really talk to."

"Yes, sir, I will. I want you to do me a favor. No matter what, do not interact with these people. Act like nothing is going on and we haven't talked. It is safer for you this way, got it?"

Mr. Evans grimaced and nodded. "And after you talk with my niece out there, send her home, tell her I said so, will ya? I am scared for her, Detective. Anything happens to her and you won't have to worry about them shitass gang thugs doing me in, cuz my sister will kill me herself."

"No problem. I'll make sure she's safe. As hot as events are right now I don't expect Boyce Carter or his thugs or other associates will be coming around. Just please keep your eyes open to anything strange and call me, or 911, it don't matter, just stay safe."

Sea Star Coach Owner Hoyt Evans stood and walked around the desk, then offered Jack his hand. "I'm canceling all tours until further notice, Detective. Tomorrow's returning buses will be the last until this is cleared up. I'm gonna hafta pull money out of my pocket to get those four who got left behind taken care of. I'll get them set up with my competition. Never thought I'd say that, ever! But better they be safe and satisfied."

Jack agreed and was impressed Evans would pull money out of his own pocket. If those four old people knew what Hoyt Evans did for them, he would have lifetime customers.

WHAT A GOLD MINE. If they had let him work this case officially two years ago, he would have been able to investigate and could've spoken with Miss Pinson back then. The only plus side, two years in, and a lot had happened. And more information to use was better.

After his rather lengthy interview with Belinda Pinson, he sent her home to pack. He called Janet. He explained Miss Pinson would need to be in protective custody.

"Janet, make sure we put this young woman in better hands than y'all put Bogard in. I've given her a lot to think about in view of the information she's told me. And Janet, I talked to her about going into WITSEC. If she intends to be a witness for the state, leaving Houston for good will need to happen. The gangs here will see she gets punished, and these thugs' arms stretch all over Texas. That doesn't even include the cartel. "

"I'm on it, Jack. Text me her address and phone number, and I'll let her know someone will be there to fetch her. Once I get it set up, I'll text you who and when. Have you called Sophia yet?"

"No, not yet, wanted to get you on this ASAP. Next thing I need is an arrest warrant for Boyce Carter. We need to find that son of a bitch, and soon."

"Okay, I'm on that too. Have a few favors I can call in to push it through. I'll get it done today, not to worry. Anything else you need from me, Jack?" Janet needed to finish this call so she could start all the balls rolling.

"Two things. Once we have Carter in custody, and since Stan Cleef is not on the run, and I gotta say it, what a stupid prick. I want him pulled into the interrogation. Let's set this up at the DEA office after they pick Carter up. And second, what's the news on Sykes, any word?"

"It looks like he is in the wind, not a peep, not a sighting, nothing. Jack, I'm afraid he's already skipped town or the country."

"Kasper still on it?"

"Yes, he's been scrubbing camera footage at the airports, bus stations, even the railways. We have agents looking into Amtrak's cameras. There has also been an APB put out. Law enforcement has his face plastered with all travel venues and departure points. There is another problem."

"What's that?"

"If he is driving, we don't know what vehicle to put a BOLO on, which also means we have no plate number. Hell, as far as we know he's in Mexico or Canada right now."

Jack got really quiet, letting his inner intuition speak to him.

After a few long seconds passed, Janet said, "Jack, you still there?"

"Yeah, still here. Janet, Sykes hasn't left yet, or my gut says he hasn't."

“I have to disagree with you. Why would he stay when he knows we‘re onto him? Hell, if it were me, I’d have left three days ago.”

“Because he has unfinished business, and he won’t leave until he has completed it.”

“Oh yeah, you think so? And want would that be?”

“Kasper Bergman. That’s Theo Sykes’ unfinished business, Janet.”

53

Kasper was still in one piece, and no one had shot at him yet. He met up with Jack at Quinn's and they'd tossed back a few beers, trying to relax. It was difficult when the bad stuff was happening. Murderers on the loose, men who trafficked humans of both genders, gangs terrorizing their neighborhoods. Buying, selling, and pushing meth with the help of the cartel. Thugs killing on orders and no one knew how many more unthinkable actions. Dead DEA agents, agents on the run like Theo Sykes. Or stupid agents like Stan Cleef who had no clue they were onto him. And DEA Agent Marcella Águlia, a capo for the very cartel she had sworn to stop. What a joke.

"Your eyes are bloodshot, Kasper. Are you getting any sleep?" Jack asked.

"Uh-huh, with one eye open these days." Kasper drained his mug and held up a hand to get Grady's attention for another tall boy. "I know one thing, though. I'm sick of scrubbing camera footage. I've focused on the airport and have two agents helping me, but it's pointless. He isn't foolish. Sykes will keep his mug away from the cameras. I've been thinking about something."

"What's that?" Jack pushed his empty mug back.

"That Sykes is still in town. He has connections, shipping channels, railway, and with his lowlife friends he can get out of here, out of town or the country several ways. Some freightliner can let him stow away below and he'll be gone and we won't know it."

"Your point?"

"The guy has a cell phone, still uses technology, like his computer. When I found his hidden IP address, I tapped into some of his lesser-known names, and I am following this footprint. Just need to be cautious."

Jack leaned forward, his forearms resting on the table. "Could he know and be leading you on a wild goose chase?"

"Nah, or I wouldn't have this information to give you. Here..." He handed Jack a paper folded in half.

Jack unfolded the paper, read it twice, then shoved it into his pocket.

"Just like a mini soap opera, huh?"

"Yeah, Jack, ain't love grand?"

Two days later, the Criminal Apprehension Team (CAT) finally caught up with Boyce Carter. The jerk-off was found sitting at a local restaurant having dinner with his wife. After being arrested for the murder of his son, Mrs. Carter went ballistic. They had to subdue her and have uniformed officers brought in to take her home. Mrs. Boyce Carter would be a person Jack was also interested in talking with.

In the outer office of the interrogation rooms at the DEA building, Jack watched Boyce Carter. In interview room three, Carter sat upright, hands folded and laying on the table, not a worry in the world. A toothpick was waggling up and down between his teeth. He moved it to the other side of his mouth with his tongue. What was it about Boyce Carter and these damn toothpicks?

"Mr. Carter." Jack pulled out a chair.

"First, Detective, why am I here, and not at the police station? And second, Jamere's murder was now on two years ago. There ain't anything new I can tell you." Carter pulled the toothpick out of his mouth, broke it in two, and dropped it into the crinkled-up flat metal ashtray used for the occasional smoker. He stared at Jack.

"Okay, let's talk about something else then. Let's talk about Jerrell Bogard. Did you know he taped a conversation you had with him?"

Carter was silent.

Jack leaned back, relaxed. "At first, we thought we wouldn't be able to use the recording. It was taped in your office at Sea Star. Only that isn't your office, is it? "

Boyce Carter leaned away from the table. "I don't know anyone named Bogard. And yeah, I use that office at Sea Star from time to time. What's your point? It's not like it's against the law for me to be in the office of a place I manage. Is it?"

"Huh, well, Bogard—that would be Special Agent Jerrell Bogard of the DEA. He says he knows you. Why would he lie?"

Carter pulled out an individually wrapped toothpick from his front shirt pocket, slid the plastic off, and stuck the toothpick in his mouth. He rolled the plastic into a little ball between his thumb and forefinger, staring down as he did, before tossing it into the metal ashtray. Three or four long minutes passed. Jack sat, waiting on an answer.

"Oh yeah, that man. I remember him, he was complaining about a ticket he bought his elderly neighbor. The old man got sick. Mr. Bogard wanted a refund. "

Jack's face stayed stony; his eyes bore into Carter's, who was bold-face lying.

"I've got a copy of the tape, Carter; you want me to play it for you? It's a recording of you incriminating yourself on several deeds, all punishable by prison or worse." Jack held up a hand stopping him from spouting out more lies. "Let me tell you what we have, Mr. Carter. We have you telling Bogard you were speaking with Cleef—that would be DEA Agent Stan Cleef—about ordering a hit on another DEA agent named Clive Bebchuk, who is now dead. I'm sure you've seen the news." Again, Jack's palm rose to prevent him from speaking.

"Uh-uh, let me finish. You all but admitted to smuggling product using Sea Star Coaches as your cover. There was also a statement you made. You are in control of gang activity between Sunnyside and the Third and Fifth Ward. We have you stating you are a known associate of a high-level cartel member, one Joven Cazalla of the Villa Lobos Cartel." Jack paused, but only for a beat.

"Oh yeah, and my favorite part was what you said at the end of the recording. How it was your damn luck to call in a hit on the boys who were stealing product from that Irish fuck's store, and it was too bad one of those dumbass kids was your son, Jamere Carter. But hey, how did you put it, it was just business?" Jack watched the man's face.

Carter was emotionless. It was scary to believe this man was like the kid, Michael Myers, in the *Halloween* movie franchise, soulless without an ounce of emotion. Leaning back, Jack draped his arm over the back of his chair, waiting for a response.

The clock ticked, minutes went by, time was nothing to Jack. This was part of his job and he had nowhere else he needed to be.

"Let's say you have this tape, allegedly. It could have been me talking to someone, but here's the deal: no one informed me I was being recorded and even if I said all of this, you can't use it against me or in court. So I'm not admitting it was me, could be someone who sounded like me, or acting like they was me, just to cause me trouble. I mean, I was torn up. Someone killed my boy, was the only boy I had."

"Yeah, I saw how torn-up you were when we came to give you the death notice." Jack's lip curled up in a nasty way; this man was a real piece of shit. "I met a very nice young lady named Belinda Pinson at Sea Star a few days ago, and she and I had a nice chat. And the owner, Hoyt Evans, came in too. You know the door on his office is missing, and it sits at the end of a hallway next to the front counter, the same office you call your own?"

Carter shrugged, and Jack smiled.

"A very public area with people coming and going and with the door missing, anyone can hear everything that goes on in that office. Miss Pinson's heard plenty over the past two years. And Mr. Carter, it makes me fucking giddy as hell to tell you the recording *is* admissible."

A look crossed Boyce Carter's face—an evil, nasty expression. "Bogard is a liar; he would do anything to save his ass. He's in deep and wants to take me down too. Well, I ain't gonna let him take me with him." Carter pushed the chair back a hair so he could cross his arms, and he was still chewing on the toothpick.

"Don't matter to him any longer. The man's dead. It hasn't been in the news, not yet, but your pal, Theo Sykes, offed him. Do you figure you're next on his list of ends to tie up?"

Carter shrugged but didn't speak, his eyes narrowed in anger.

"Stand up, you douchebag." Jack turned to the camera at the top corner and nodded, which was the signal for the two armed officers to come into the room. "Boyce Carter, you are under arrest for the murder of Robert Thompson, Lyell Taylor, and your own son, Jamere Carter. You have the right to remain silent..." Jack continued his Miranda rights.

The hate in Carter's eyes ran deep. "You bastard, I didn't kill them. Jamere was my flesh and blood. How could I do that? You should be looking for the man who pulled the trigger. It wasn't me. If that tape is all you got, then you ain't got nuthin'. I'll be out on bail tomorrow."

Carter pulled the toothpick out of his mouth. He tossed it toward the metal ashtray and missed, so it rolled off the table.

"Maybe, then maybe not. I know you aren't gonna win Father of The Year, although you might get a vote or two if you give up the shooters. You get a few years shaved off your sentencing, or better yet, not get the needle."

The door opened, and two armed officers walked in. One went in behind Carter to cuff him, and the other stood by to assist in the event Carter became physical. Once cuffed, Jack got nose-to-nose with him; reaching inside the man's front shirt pocket, he fished out a handful of individually wrapped toothpicks.

"Can't have you taking any sharp objects into the jail with you, now can we, Boyce Edward Carter? Or should I just call you Bec?" He spelled it out, "As in B-e-c-k?"

That was enough to set the man off, and Boyce Carter, a man who'd appeared to be without a single emotion went ballistic, because being called Beck proved Jack West knew a hell of a lot more than he'd figured.

Jack took a single step backward, as the officers each took an arm confining Carter's movement. He stared at the coldhearted, calculated man. Three men dead because he gave the go-ahead with orders to kill. This could get him the needle, and even though Jack loathed the thought of another human dying, men like Boyce Carter and the dead Cyrus Shelton weren't human. They were monsters in Jack's book.

The door to the hallway opened and Stan Cleef walked in. To say he was in utter surprise at seeing two armed officers restraining a handcuffed Boyce Carter with Detective West standing by was an understatement. Stan's facial expression had Jack forcing down a laugh.

"Uh, Officers, Detective West, I didn't know anyone was back here. I'll leave you to it," he stammered, his gaze darting to Carter's face for a nanosecond before he took a step back.

"Agent Cleef, no, please stay. These officers are taking this man to be processed and I need a word, if you don't mind." Jack's voice was calm.

"Oh, well, sure, yeah, of course." Stan nodded and glanced back at Carter. Jack did not miss Carter's frown.

"There is a confidential matter I want to talk to you about. Meet me in room three. I have to make a quick call down to Processing, and then I'll be in." He watched as Stan walked toward room three, turned, and gave Jack the thumbs-up as the other officers waited.

Okay, well, crap, Stan thought, *just great*. If it had only been Jack standing there, he'd have ignored his request. But the other two officers had been eyeballing him, waiting for him to acknowledge Jack's request.

Once Stan was tucked away in room three, Jack gave them the nod to move Carter to Processing, thanking them for their help.

Cell phone in hand, Jack called Sophia.

"Medina," she answered.

"Sophia. It's Jack. I just arrested Carter for my triple homicide. They are taking him to be processed as we speak."

"You get what you needed?"

"Not yet, but I'm not done wheeling and dealing with him. We know he called in the hit, but if he gives us shooters, then maybe he can shorten his prison sentence, but no guarantee was given. Also, I've got Cleef in room three—"

"Are you nuts? You can't arrest him. We are—"

"...shutting up and listening, that's what we are."

Sophia snarked out a laugh. "Okay, okay, Jack, what's your plan?"

Jack explained Cleef had walked into Carter's being led out in cuffs.

"Sophia, all this info was on need-to-know. Carter's involvement has not been public knowledge and Janet told me back before I left for Mexico that Bebchuk and Cleef hadn't needed to know. As far as I am aware, before Bebchuk was blown to smithereens, neither him nor Cleef knew we were on to Carter. And since this news has still been undisclosed, I want to see if I can get him to incriminate himself, say something, and get it on tape."

"What do you want me to do?"

"I want you to come watch the interview from the monitoring room, and be there in case I need backup."

"Alright, I can be there in twenty. Do you think you can hem-haw around and not piss him off until I get there?"

"Yeah, I think so, Medina. I'll hit record on my way in. My phone will be set on vibrate, so text me two times in a row to let me know you are in the monitor room. Got it?"

"Yeah. I got it, text twice. See ya in twenty." Sophia disconnected. "That was Detective West, he said..." Sophia recapped their conversation for Deputy Director Remy Walsh.

Deep in thought, Stan's head snapped up when the door opened.

West took the chair near the door at the end, his back facing the closed door. Stan sat on the other side.

"Sorry, Stan, didn't mean to keep you waiting, you know, red tape."

"Yep, paperwork. It's always a pain in the ass. What do you want, Detective?" The skinny man pushed his seat back just enough to cross one leg over the other. His left arm draped over the back of the chair, causing his jacket to tug and pull, revealing his shoulder harness and sidearm. Jack gave it a split-second glance, thankful he'd unstrapped his Glock. Not because he wanted to shoot Agent Cleef, but then again, if he had to he would. Cleef was dirty, a disgrace to the agency, and repulsed Jack to the nth. One question all good cops had was why? Why go into law enforcement if you would not uphold the law? Stan was a horse-race junkie and all-around gambler and wasn't good at it. Deep in debt and too ignorant to get to Gambler's Anonymous. The man probably lived his life on the premise of, "I feel it," and "This is the big one, I'll be set for life." He was gonna be set for life alright, a new life in prison.

"First, I want to say how sorry I am about Bebchuk's murder. I can't imagine losing my partner much less knowing he was a target, and I could be the next victim."

"Yeah, it happens in our line of work. Bebchuk was a decent bloke," Stan Cleef heartlessly stated. He didn't give a fuck. Bebchuk was dead.

"You worried, Stan?"

"Me? Why should I be worried?"

"If you were working a case together and got too close, you think they'll be after you next?" Jack leaned back, relaxing his posture.

"West, what are you doing at the DEA building? Why are you not over at HPD?"

"I'm working with Agent Medina, tying up some loose ends. Back to my question. Aren't you nervous you could be next?"

Stan Cleef's eyes narrowed. There was something in Jack's tone which set him on edge.

"I'm smarter than Clive was, and got people watching my back." Stan looked at his watch and backup.

"People like Jerry Bogard. Is that who you mean?" Jack's phone vibrated in his pocket. Sophia was in the building.

"Maybe, but Bogard's been out of pocket a few days. Lila Beaumont said he'd be out for an extended period. And to tell you the truth, why they put her in charge as the acting SAC is beyond my comprehension. "

"She seems okay to me, "Jack commented, knowing Cleef was a chauvinistic pig.

"A woman in charge pisses me off."

"Oh, I don't know, Stan, women seem to be smarter than men, and they don't have the God complex like some men do."

"Whatever. Now, what do you need to talk to me about because I don't have time for all this Chatty Cathy shit?"

From the corner of his eye Jack saw the red light on the camera blink twice, and he knew Sophia was in the monitor room. It was time to open up on this scrawny skeleton-face man.

"How well do you know an agent named Theo Sykes?"

Stan's right hand came up to rub the back of his neck. His brows dipped in thought. "Hmm, Theo Sykes, guy's in Tech, ain't that right?"

Jack nodded with an "Uh-huh."

"I've seen him a few times with Bogard, but I don't know the guy. We've never talked. Why?" Cleef uncrossed his legs, sitting up a little straighter, and Jack watched his every move. Just looking at Stan he knew the man could react like a feral cat in a split second.

"No reason, except Kasper, a kid from HPD Tech, has been working with him. He said the guy's weird."

In the monitoring room, Sophia smiled. Once Kasper listened to the recording, he would be miffed that Jack was calling him a kid again.

"Oh yeah, well, don't know this Bergman either. Look, West, if all you wanna do is chitchat or gossip like an old biddy hen, get one of the gals from the secretary pool to gab with ya. I ain't got time."

Stan stood, and as he did, Jack scooted his chair back toward the door. "Have a seat, Stan. We're not finished yet."

"What the fuck? Who do you think you are, ordering me around, and in my office? You have some balls, West." Cleef took two steps toward the door, and Jack stood, blocking his way.

Five-foot-ten maybe, weighing about 145 pounds, Stan was a mere whip of a man who was no longer in the best physical shape. Jack was six-foot-one and 215-225 pounds, depending on how much fast food he'd had to live on in the past few weeks.

Stan stopped; his forehead wrinkled in a nasty way, and his lip curled up at one corner in a sneer.

"You wanna step aside, Detective, so I can leave?"

"What I want is for you to take a seat, Agent Cleef, because I'm not done with our talk." Jack stood his full height and squared off his shoulders. Outweighing Stan by at least seventy pounds, there was no way Stan could best him in a pushing contest, nor move him out of the doorway.

"What are you going to do next, hold me at gunpoint, West?" Stan backed up two steps, his eyes never leaving Jack's face.

Jack didn't bat an eye when he said, "Will I have to, Stan?"

A strained laugh gurgled up from Stan's throat and he took the remaining steps he needed to get back into his chair. He sat, his legs opened, both feet planted on the floor, and crossed his arms.

"Alright, Detective West, what the fuck is it you're after?"

"You, Stan. I am after you."

54

His eyes narrowed in question and he leaned an elbow on the table, eyeballing Jack as his brain did a rewind and fast-forward. Why would Jack say such a thing? There was nothing he'd done to throw up a red flag or point any fingers in his direction. Carter would have never mentioned his name. Theo would never rat him out, and neither would Bebchuk, unless he did it by séance. Bogard, now that asshole might have, but he hadn't talked to Bogard in several days, which, yeah, that was odd.

"Okay, I see. It's a cat-and-mouse game and I'm the unsuspecting mouse, is that it?"

"Nah, Stan, you're no mouse, you're a rat. And there's some bad news I'd like to tell you."

"Okay, Jack, what news? I'll bite." He sneered.

"Jerrell Bogard was murdered a few days ago."

"Is that so? Hard to believe, since I would have heard about it. He is my SAC, you know, and I do still work at the DEA. Not to mention I am a senior agent with higher clearance levels than most."

"Uh-huh. Well, he's dead, shot, double-tapped, execution style."

Stan's brows arched up, and he tried to hide his shock. "Who would've wanted Bogard dead, and why in the hell wasn't I informed?"

Jack heard the question but didn't answer. "You said you didn't know Kasper, the kid from HPD Tech."

"So, I don't know him. Is that a crime?"

"No, Stan, it's not a crime. It's a bold-faced lie, that's what it is. I never said his last name, and you said, let me quote, 'Don't know this Bergman either.' Funny, I never said the kid's last name, but you knew it, Cleef. How is that possible, you a mind reader?"

"You said his last name, I heard you say it, besides, it don't matter, we don't have a moderator listening in." He smirked.

"Yeah, your word against mine won't be too good of odds for me, the lowly homicide dick."

"West, you're a titty-baby, aren't you? I've heard tell you think you're hot shit."

He would not respond to Cleef's attempt to provoke him. Jack was well aware the story of his punching Captain Brooks was widespread amongst law enforcement and other agencies.

Sophia watched wondering where Jack was headed with all of this. Stan might be tired of their banter, but he'd said nothing to assist Jack in making a case against him.

"Stan, why don't you cut the bullshit. It's over and you know it. You saw Carter cuffed and headed out with his police escort. Man, that guy sang like the stool pigeon he is, trying to cover his own ass."

"What the hell are you implying, Jack, that I'm a crook or a killer?"

"Both."

Stan stood abruptly shoving his chair back, and so did Jack. They stood like teenage boys, facing off before the fight began.

"West, I'm leaving, and you're getting out of my way."

"I guess you can go. I got what I needed."

Stan Cleef's eyebrows dipped. "What is it you think you've got, Jack, cuz I can't see you got a damn thing?"

Still blocking the doorway, Jack's eyes cut up toward the corner of the room where the camera hung, and Stan's eyes followed.

"So, you got me on camera, that's it? Huh, well, I hate to tell you, it ain't enough. Good luck, Jack. Now get out of my way."

His eyes bore into Cleef's, but he did not move.

Agent Cleef stared back, hate filling his eyes. "I'm warning you, Jack, move or else."

"What are you gonna do, call Beck and have me blown up like you did Bebchuk? Or have the living hell beat out of me like McCready? Or, let's discuss Umberto Vega. He was another loose end. You and Theo needed Vega outta the way, but you used him first to kill Espinar. Then what was it you called Bogard, a whiney pussy who wasn't gonna cut it? Isn't that what you told Theo? Oh, and by the way, that same day, once you hit the stairwell, we got Theo Sykes saying that he was looking forward to blowing your fucking skeleton head off your boney-ass shoulders. "

In his mind's eye, he thought back to a conversation he'd had with Theo. All of this was said in that conversation, but how did Jack know? Theo? Nah.

"Not sure what game you're playing, West, but I don't appreciate all the insinuations. Now, move the fuck over and let me pass, or else."

Jack took a step over to let him pass, and just as Stan put one foot out the doorway, he said, "We got it all on tape, you talking to Sykes, and got Carter on tape talking to you. Don't hit me with the inadmissible bullshit either. You were in the parking garage of the Rubicon Building, a public area, and Carter was in the office at Sea Star Coaches, the one without a door, next to the sales counter, another very public area. So, Stan, we got you by the balls, your skinny little balls. "

"Unless you have a warrant for my arrest, move out of my way." Stan Cleef brushed by the detective, his arm whacking into him as he passed. Cleef pushed the door open and was face-to-face with Agent Medina.

"Medina," Stan said, sidestepping to pass her, and he kept walking.

Sophia turned toward Cleef. "Uh, hey, Stan, hold up, will you?"

Stopping, he inhaled and exhaled in aggravation. *Now what*, he thought as he turned around to face her.

Sophia Medina had him at gunpoint, and without thought he reached for his gun and then shook his head as he lowered his hand.

"What the fuck are you doing, Medina? Holster your piece and stop dicking around. You're gonna hurt someone."

"You know the drill, Stan. Two fingers, slowly. Then lay it on the floor and take four steps backward."

"Uh-uh, not until you tell me what in the hell is going on."

"You are under arrest for the murder of Clive Bebchuk, for starters. And there's a lot of other shit I'm gonna hit you with, and you won't be seeing the light of day for a long time, a very long time."

"I want my rep, and I want to talk to the director, now." Stan stood, planting his feet firmly, his arms dangling at his side.

Jack was on Sophia's right, his eyes bored into Cleef's.

"Your piece, Stan, now," she repeated herself, her gun aimed at him, hand steady.

He did as she asked, and with two fingers pulled his gun from the holster, then squatted and gently laid it on the floor. Stan rose slowly as his right hand moved underneath the left lapel of his jacket and Jack reacted quickly.

With his left shoulder, Jack shoved Sophia, and she stumbled, losing her balance and his momentum had him barreling forward toward Stan. Stan's hand came out from under his jacket, holding a small-caliber semiautomatic. Sophia fell to the floor on one knee, her left hand bracing her fall, her Sig Sauer still in her right hand waving in the air.

Jack closed in on Cleef just as Cleef's hand was clear of his jacket, brandishing his BUG (Backup Gun) a .380 ACP. Jack's left hand took hold of Cleef's right wrist, forcing it up and out, and with his right hand he punched the scrawny weasel in the breadbasket, which forced Stan to double over. Stan's left hand came around to smack Jack on the side of his face, but the detective's upper body weight was too much for Agent Cleef to bear. He lost his balance falling backward landing on his buttocks. Then he fell directly back, with Jack following, landing on top of him. West still had Cleef's right wrist in his grasp, and Cleef still had the gun in his fist. The sound of a gunshot resonated in the room. After the gun blast echo died down, the room was deathly quiet and time stopped.

As if someone hit the play button, Sophia was upright and called out, "Who's hit? Jack, are you hit?"

"No, and neither is Cleef." Jack had Cleef's right thumb, bending it backward in an awkward yet painful position and the agent yelped, letting go of the smaller pistol. Jack knocked it away, sending it sliding across the floor.

Jack got up then bent down, grabbing Stan by the lapels of his jacket hauling him upright, then spun him around, bringing his arms behind him. He took the cuffs from the back of his belt and slapped them on, clicking them shut tighter than normal.

"Shit, West, you're gonna cut off my circulation, you got these fucking cuffs too tight."

"Stow it, Cleef, you ass, you were gonna shoot us. Fair is fair." Jack tugged at Cleef's new jewelry.

"Where'd the shot land?" Sophia stood, looked around, and laughed.

"There is nothing fucking funny about this, Medina," Stan growled.

"Shut up, Stan. Jack, look over there." She gestured toward the bay of monitors. "In your attempt to murder us, you also killed a computer monitor. Now we have you on destruction of federal property too. And let me begin, you sack of shit, by telling you, you have the right to remain silent..."

Boyce Carter had been placed in County and in Holding for ten days while processing his official paperwork. His ties to the Dragons confirmed, his juvvie records which were sealed had to be legally acquired. This took time. Legal had voice forensics and speaker comparison professionals handle both audiotapes: Kasper Bergman's recording of Sykes and Cleef, and the deceased Jerrell Bogard's recording with Boyce Carter. There was also the recorded conversation between Bergman and Sykes that Jack had overheard in the parking garage. Three recordings, all of which involved major players: Theo Sykes, Stan Cleef, Boyce Carter, and one dead Jerrell Bogard. It wasn't looking very good for the ones who were still alive. Jack had worked endlessly on getting every scrap of evidence to convict Carter and the shooters to close up his triple homicide case, his main objective.

Bail Hearing for Boyce Edward Carter

"All rise," the bailiff called out. "Court is now in session, the Honorable Leland Elks presiding."

Judge Elks took his place at the bench and in a clear voice told everyone to be seated, as he shuffled through files on his massive desk. His eyeglasses sat purposely at the end of his short round nose as he thumbed through papers, until he come across whatever he was looking for.

Looking up, the Judge's head turned toward the prosecution's table, and he cleared his throat.

"Will the defendant, Boyce Edward Carter, please rise."

From a few rows back, Jack watched as Boyce Carter stood next to his attorney, a man known to represent some of the lowest degenerates of the twenty-first century, Defense Attorney Ted Ascherio, affectionately known to the opposing side as "Ted Asshole."

To save himself from the needle, Carter had given up the names of the shooters who gunned down Lyell Taylor, Robert Thompson, and his own son, Jamere Carter. The evidence was overwhelming. Once the investigation went full throttle, Jack had no idea how many puzzle pieces there were. Carter's involvement with organized crime went deep. His association to the Dragons led him to his friendship with Joven Cazalla, an ex Brown Cobra. This news was quite illuminating since no one had been privy to the fact Cazalla had been a Brown Cobra long ago. With this new information the puzzle pieces began fitting together to make more sense to Jack.

Carter faced a charge of murder-for-hire, as well as several charges of drug distribution and human trafficking. He wouldn't see daylight until he was dying, and that might be iffy. They say you see a bright light as you are dying, but Jack figured that was not what evil souls saw—what they saw had to be far less appealing.

Shaken out of his stupor of where evil dead men ended up, he heard the Judge asking Carter how he pled to the charge of murder, and Jack heard the man say, "Not guilty." He shook his head. Not guilty of pulling the damn trigger is what you mean, he thought.

"And the charge of conspiracy to commit murder, how do you plea?"

It was a very low answer, and the Judge had to ask him to repeat it.

"Guilty, Your Honor."

The courtroom was silent, but for only a split second.

The scream was bloodcurdling and ear-piercing and the chaos that broke loose unsuspected, as was the sound of gunfire in the courtroom. People dropped to the floor, diving for cover as the blasts rang out. One-two-three, then the fourth shot sounded before the shooter was subdued in a mass convergence on one woman, who was still screaming when they wrenched the gun from her hand. People stood in shock, Judge Elks' gavel banging the top of his desk, his voice ringing out, "Order in the court, I demand order in my court! Bailiff, call 911, get an ambulance. Officers, clear my courtroom. Now!" His deep authoritative voice had everyone scrambling. Jack watched as the attorneys for the defense and prosecution tried to revive Boyce Carter, who now lay on the floor of the courtroom, bleeding and dying. One shot had hit him at the base of his neck, and one in the shoulder before he crumpled. The other two shots flew past him, and luckily no one else had been hit. He watched as Carter's attorney looked up at Judge Elks, blood on his hands and on the front of his white dress shirt, shaking his head. Boyce Carter was dead.

"How in the hell did she get in my courtroom with a gun? I want some answers and I want them now! Call Security and get an investigation started immediately, I will not stand..." Judge Elks was ranting, and rightly so, he was furious something like this would happen but more incensed it had taken place in ***his*** courtroom!

The screaming stopped; the woman was in custody, her hands cuffed behind her, tears streaming down her face. Jack watched as they walked Evelyn Carter, Mrs. Boyce Edward Carter, out of the courtroom.

THE CHAOS HAD SETTLED, and although there was a lot to attend to, this was not on Jack's plate, so he headed outside. The shooters involved in his triple homicide were being hunted down. It might take a few weeks, but they would track these three men down and do everything in their power to see that they were prosecuted to the full extent of the law. There was a long way to go. It pissed him off Carter was dead, he wanted the man to rot in prison, but now his only hope was the man was now burning in hell. Sitting on a bench outside the courtroom, his head down in thought, someone took a seat beside him. Jack raised his head and looked over.

"Hi, Jack. "

"Sophia. Hi yourself. I didn't know you were here."

"Too bad I missed all the commotion. I just got there for Cleef's arraignment."

"Be sure to double-check Security."

Sophia shrugged her shoulders, shaking her head with a frown. "Nah, they've postponed all other hearings until they clear this up. The courthouse will be shut down for an investigation, so they'll move all hearings to next week, or to another location."

"Y'all got any new news on your case?"

"Sounds funny you calling it my case now, and not *our* case."

"Yeah, I know, but I need to get back to Homicide, I...well...I just need to, that's all."

Sophia nodded.

"We have eyes on Cazalla, he is back in Mexico."

"What about Marcella?" Right after Stan's takedown Jack headed back to HPD, so he was out of the loop.

"She was apprehended at the airport three days ago, and boy, was she surprised."

"I bet. I'm thinking she thought she was untouchable, right?"

"No, not that, I mean, yeah, she thought we weren't on to her, but this entire time one agent had been suspicious. They had gleaned more concrete evidence to add to what we'd found to solidify the arrest. "

"Janet never mentioned another undercover agent to me, did she to you?"

"No, I had no idea at all. Seems the Director gave her leeway to place agents in positions she deemed necessary, and it surprised the hell out of me."

"Well, who was it, anyone I know?" Jack thought back to Owen McCready aka DEA Special Agent Caden Ward; who else might have been under cover that he would not have suspected?"

"Would it flabbergast you to know it's Special Agent Jenny Martin?"

Jack's brow crinkled and a smile spread over his face.

"Flirty flight attendant Jenny?" He laughed outright, then explained her flirtatious behavior on his flight into Mexico the same day he met Marcella and Espinar.

"Yes, sir, the same. She's been on to Marcella for three years. Janet sent her on another assignment last week, but can't say where. Because of Marcella's close ties to Villa Lobos, she's worried about Jenny's safety, so her whereabouts will be top secret until further notice. "

"I suspect Caden Ward's situation is about the same, isn't it?"

Sophia nodded her answer, and they were both silent for a few minutes.

"Any news on Sykes? Sightings, chatter, anything?" Jack was worried Sykes might still be gunning for Kasper.

"Nothing. Not a single peep. Stan was grilled until I thought the man was gonna pass out, but he swears he hasn't heard from Sykes since before Bogard was killed. Marcella isn't talking, so she's no help. We told her we know about her and Sykes' affair, which she denies."

Jack's laugh was bitter. "Kasper stumbling onto their illicit emails isn't proof enough for her? It makes me sick they were using the young girls and boys they were trafficking in their torrid affair. They make me want to vomit."

"She is going to be charged with a lot of things, Jack, and sexual assault and indecency with minors is only an nth of what she will go to prison for. As for Theo Sykes, he'll be on the FBI's Most Wanted, and there is an out-and-out manhunt for him. He's smart, so he'll be harder to catch, I'm afraid."

"Kasper will be watching his back and more eager than ever to get into Quantico. Theo Sykes will be a thorn in his side until the guy is caught and thrown behind bars."

"I'm betting Theo Sykes won't show his face in the United States for a long time, so it shouldn't worry Kasper too much."

She was probably right, but Jack was still gonna warn the kid to keep eyes in the back of his head, advice which would serve him well as an FBI agent in the future.

Again they were silent, in their own thoughts, each wondering what was wrong with a person who did these types of things.

"Jack, I'm sorry your guy got killed. He got off easy, no lifelong jail term. But the shooters, once you get them, maybe they will get to wait in line for the needle, ya think?"

With a bob of his head Jack answered, "I hope so. At least I can explain this to Robert Thompson's family and give them closure on their son's senseless murder. It's too bad it won't be over for them until we have the shooters in custody."

"You'll get them, Jack, I know you will. You're a bulldog who never gives up." She placed her hand on top of his and smiled. "And I am thrilled to have had the chance to call you my partner." Slipping her hand under his, she held it and squeezed. "I'm gonna miss you, Jack."

He turned his head to see her. "Miss me, why, you going somewhere, Medina?"

She sighed as she entwined her fingers with his, and nodded. "Yeah, I'm being sent on special assignment and I'll be leaving in a few days."

"Where?"

"Can't disclose that information, Jack, sorry."

A chuckle gurgled up. "Yeah, I know, I'm need-to-know only, and now I don't need to know, right?"

Sophia grinned and shrugged. "Just like old times, huh?"

"When do you leave?" His thumb began caressing the top part of her hand in slow sensual movements, his eyes bore into hers.

Sophia's heart lurched, and she felt that certain desire flood her veins. Her head bent, watching his thumb caressing the back of her hand. "After Cleef's arraignment, I'll have a week to get things in order. I will be gone for six months, at least. After that, who knows? "

Removing his hand from her grasp, he lifted his arm placing it around her shoulder, and pulled her closer. He bent his head, his lips closer to her ears, his hot breath on her neck, and she shuddered in anticipation.

"Well, Sophia Medina, ex-DEA partner, and a woman who kissed the socks off me several times and stirred a desire in me I thought had died, I have a question for you."

Her voice cracked, stuck in her throat, her yearning for him bubbling like a volcano. "What, Jack?" Whatever the question was she knew her answer. She would not deny him, not even one night.

Jack whispered into Sophia's ear what she wanted to hear, and for the next week they would have each other. Neither one looked past that, for in their line of work one never knew how many days one had left to live. Living for the moment and in the moment was all they cared about—for now. Who knew what the future might hold?

EPILOGUE

Grady sat the pitcher of beer down, and two fresh, frosty mugs. "Put it on my tab. Jack can get the next one."

"Sure, kid."

Jack watched Kasper pour two mugs of beer, pick up his mug and raise it.

Jack's brow arched. "What we drinking to, kid?"

"Me."

"Okay." Jack clinked mugs with him. "Here's to you, kid, for whatever reason."

Both men took long, robust drinks.

"Why are we drinking to you? You get laid or what?"

"No, better. I've applied for and been accepted to Quantico. But, I've decided to stay two more years with HPD, and get some field work in with Homicide, Robbery and Cyber and Vice. I could go sooner but really want some of this experience first. "

"Well, whatdaya know. Hell, Kasper that's fantastic news. Good job." Jack lofted his beer, and they clanked mugs one more time.

"Yeah, I already discussed it with Art and Clarissa, and they'll work out a schedule so I can work in Tech and then they'll hire someone I can train to take my place as well as cover for me when I'm in other departments. "

"Two years, huh? It'll feel like forever, ya think?"

"Nah, Jack, it won't. Houston crime keeps us so busy; two years will fly."

Jack had to agree, Houston crime was relentless, it hardly let up for anyone to breathe.

Two Years Later...Back at Quinn's Pub

"I'M GONNA MISS YOU, you little nerd scaredy-cat." He winked and drained the rest of his beer.

"Ah, Jack, you say the sweetest things. I'm gonna miss you too, you drunken jackass."

It was quiet for all of two minutes before they busted up in laughter. Kasper rushed on about his new career move, and Jack began giving him advice.

After Quantico, Kasper had no idea where he'd go, but assured Jack they'd never lose touch.

"Be a lot of hard training and some other jackasses to watch out for while you're there. Don't let anyone stand in the way of what you want. Got me?"

"I won't. After working with you, Jack, I've sorta learned how to be a smart-ass, hard-ass, and jackass." He grinned and continued. "I've given it some thought and although I love the technical aspect of law enforcement, cybercrimes, wiretaps, and all that stuff, I'm thinking of moving on to another specialty."

"Oh, yeah, and what would that be?"

"Profiling, what'da think, Jack? You think I could be good at profiling?"

Jack thought about Kasper's skillset. The kid had a technical background. When he'd had his confrontation with Sykes in the parking garage, he'd kept a cool head and was funny to boot. He recalled how rattled Kasper had been in the beginning, flustered, and worried, then in no time flat, the young man admonished him for drinking too much and as time went on the kid got a mouth on him—a smart mouth—and Jack liked his moxie.

"Ya know, Bergman, I think you're gonna succeed at whatever you decide to do. So, yeah, I think you'd make one helluva profiler. But don't let that be all you do."

"What do you mean, have another field of expertise?"

Jack signaled Grady for another pitcher of beer, and he held up two fingers.

"Grady, another pair of frosty mugs, and add in two shots of your best whisky."

"Got it, Jack, be right with ya," the old pub owner called back.

"Yeah, kid, what I mean is, keep your technical side up to date. You're damn good at what you do with computers, so don't let that fall to the wayside...and..."

Grady Quinn set two shots of his best whiskey down and wiped his hands on an old bar towel. "You guys need more. Just holler." And like always, the old pub owner shuffled off to tend to his other bar patrons.

"Really, Jack, you back to double boilermakers?" Kasper eyed the drinks.

"No, and let me finish my sentence. And don't forget to have a life. Get a girl, even if you get one just for a while, geezers, Bergman, get laid every once in a while, do you some damn good."

Jack pushed a shot over to Kasper and an empty mug and poured them each a good head of cold beer.

They took the shot glasses, dropped them into their beer and downed the drinks, slamming the tankards on the table.

With a hearty laugh, Kasper saluted Jack with a "Hooah!"

They emptied the second pitcher and enjoyed some lively banter before they departed. Outside the front doors, Jack waved at Kasper and left the kid standing alone.

Kasper leaned against the old brick building, watching traffic pass by. Soon he'd be in Virginia, at Quantico, with a dozen other trainees. He'd miss Houston, but he was accustomed to moving about, growing up as an army brat. With his hands in his pockets, his head down, he walked to his car, wondering where his career as an FBI agent would take him. It would be interesting, this was a fact, and it would be dangerous. If Jack West had taught him anything, he taught him courage and to never give up.

Sitting in his car, he turned the key, revving the engine, and stuck it in reverse, looking over his shoulder. This little act made him aware of one thing, or one person to be exact. Theo Sykes. He was still out there, at large, and Kasper knew the man would be gunning for him. Sykes, a disgraced, murdering, now-on-the-run ex-DEA agent, would be a fugitive on the FBI's Ten Most Wanted.

Kasper Bergman, FBI Agent, would be watching over his shoulder and ready when Theo Sykes showed up again.

AUTHOR'S NOTE

Word-of-mouth is crucial for any author to succeed. If you enjoyed *Trust No One*, please leave a review online—anywhere you are able. Even if it's just a sentence or two; it would make all the difference and would be very much appreciated.

Thanks,
Deanna

ACKNOWLEDGMENTS

I want to thank the following people:

My husband and number one fan, Travis—thank you for your continued support and for making me power on in the face of writer's block and everything else that kept me from typing "The End."

To Sharon Jaeger, my beta reader, a woman whose input is of great value to this writer—and thank you for just being there for me, no matter what.

To the wonderful world of the Internet—and Internet researching—I know, Big Brother knows my search history, and given my novel's subject, well, need I say more?

To other writers and storytellers who have taught me all the many ways a story can be told—thank you for doing it first.

ABOUT THE AUTHOR

Trust No One is the fourth book in Deanna King's *Jack West Mystery* series. Deanna lives in Texas with her husband.